D1132358

AS THE ROAD
NARROWS

AS THE ROAD
NARROWS

JAMES ANHALT

 Lancaster
& Sterling

New York

As the Road Narrows is historical fiction. Although it was inspired by historical events, the work is the creation of the author's imagination. Names, businesses, characters, places, events, organizations, and incidents are used fictitiously and are not to be construed as real. Any resemblance to actual organizations, events, locales, or persons, living or dead, is entirely coincidental.

Cover design by RLD Robin Ludwig Design Inc
Illustrations by *Nadia*

Library of Congress Control Number: 2020912727

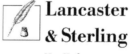 **Lancaster
& Sterling**
New York

Interior designed and formatted by

 **E.M.
TIPPETTS
BOOK DESIGNS**

For Nadia, my sunshine

*And for all the eclectic and wonderful people
I've met along the way,
you gave me the inspiration to write and to live
life to its fullest.*

*What lies behind us and what lies before us
are tiny matters compared to what lies within us.*
                                        -Henry Stanley Haskins

Chapter

1

As Jeremy Pipkins settled into his sun-lit breakfast room and unfolded the Sunday *Kansas City Sentinel*, his comfortable world unraveled as coffee splashed across the headline.

COP KILLED IN LITTLE ROCK

A Little Rock police officer was brutally murdered Saturday night. The blood-soaked body of Daniel Coyle was discovered in the parking garage of the Lancelot Inn.

Jeremy dropped the paper as the truth hit him. Dear God, he had killed a man. A cop. He was wanted for murder.

In the chaos of the raided party, a shadowy figure had loomed over Alicia. Jeremy had only hit him once. Not hard.

The vice-president of First Commerce Bank squirmed in his nineteenth-century club chair. When he regained his equanimity, he read the graphic account of the murder. The article also expounded on a detail that hardly seemed relevant—violent crime statistics comparing Little Rock with New York City.

Perspiration flooded down his starched oxford button-down. He needed to inform Alicia. Finding out from others, she'd overreact, give them both away. He must tell her the facts calmly, rationally. Shield her from inflammatory newsprint.

The article spilled onto page two, with a half-page photograph of the parking garage. More mundane statistics, a bit of rambling about the dissolution of the traditional family unit, declining morals as depicted on television, and a graph: church attendance versus murder rate from 1910 to the present. Since they had no facts on this incident, the extended commentary digressed to past horrifying murders.

Jeremy brushed wavy black hair from a pale forehead and attempted to gather his thoughts, to comprehend this latest event in a weekend of turmoil. It had started, quite innocently, with his frivolous wish for one spark of adventure before turning forty.

He stared at harsh black print on coffee-splattered paper.

This was no dream.

DETECTIVE AL HARWOOD pulled up in front of a three-bedroom ranch-style on the south side of Little Rock. Built in the '60s and already dated, it was like every other house in the subdivision—they all had the same floor plan, though the developer creatively put some garages on the right, some on the left. Danny's was on the left, with a camouflaged duck boat parked alongside. A cinderblock sat under the boat trailer tongue, secured to the trailer by a chain, a half-ass attempt to impede neighborhood crime. More weeds than grass, a dead tree next door, rentals had taken over this block. It was five years past time to move. Danny wasn't going to move, not now.

Harwood regretted that Danny had never moved up through the ranks, never got decent pay—too much of a hothead, always running his mouth.

A lever-action Daisy BB gun, its rear sight bent, lay on the concrete doorstep. Rust had begun to invade scratches on the barrel, and someone had crudely carved Danny Jr. into the stock. The detective kicked sideways, it disappeared into twigs and leaves where flowers should be.

After several knocks, a woman on the high side of thirty opened the door. Instantly, her face collapsed. Harwood's skinny frame on the doorstep at daybreak told the whole story, nothing needed but details.

"Sit down, Lois." A bony finger pointed to the couch. "Let's talk before the kids wake up."

She fought back tears. "How'd it happen, Al?"

"I don't want to talk about it. You sure don't want to hear it."

"Damn it, Al, tell me!"

"Attacked by a maniac. He was watching an elevator exit in the Lancelot Inn parking garage. I wasn't expecting trouble. A routine bust."

Harwood tried to stay calm, tried to keep the tone of his voice even. He'd done this before. Three, maybe four times, though never with a cop's wife, never about a close friend. His piercing steel-gray eyes turned toward the hallway that led to the bedrooms. Lois's mother lived nearby. After the news soaked in, he'd call her to look after the kids. No need to get child services involved. A police officer killing is a personal thing.

"Sally and Danny Junior," Lois murmured. "How do I tell the kids?"

"Your mother can help."

Help? Harwood didn't even know what that meant. How do you help tell kids they'll never see their father? How do you explain to a mother that she is now the head of the family, the sole breadwinner, mentor, disciplinarian? You got the whole goddamn job, lady.

"Who would do such a thing?"

"A heartless pervert." Harwood scratched the palm of his left hand.

"But why? Why was he guarding a hotel parking garage?"

"Simple vice raid. Didn't expect trouble. Just a bunch of deviants."

"Deviants?"

"It's my fault. I should've had at least two guys at every exit, but I didn't have the manpower, wasn't expecting trouble. Didn't know there were so damn many."

Lois struggled to hold back another wave of tears. "Did these people have guns?"

"Hell, no. All naked perverts." He jerked a pack of Lucky Strikes out of his shirt pocket. "No place to conceal a weapon."

"Then how could they kill Danny?"

"Bizarre MO. Fire extinguisher smashed his skull."

Harwood spit it out. Blunt. "There was a violent killer in the group." He jammed the smokes back in his pocket.

Lois sat on the worn-out couch in her worn-out bathrobe. Now a worn-out widow. Silent, stunned. Starting to realize that after the casserole parade, she'd be alone?

"He was supposed to be off this weekend." She fumbled in her robe for a tissue. "For the past month, Danny Jr.'s been looking forward to the fishing trip with his dad . . . with you and your son."

"Something came up. State attorney general's orders, statewide operation."

"He said you made him work."

"I offered him an optional shift, chance to pick up some extra money."

"Optional? Danny's life with you was never an option. He always did what you asked. Even becoming a cop."

"I didn't mean for him to think he didn't have a choice about last night. About anything."

"How about me, Al? What choice do I have now?"

She stared at the wall. He stared at the floor. A spider ran across the frayed carpet, hid under the couch. Harwood wanted to follow.

"Did you get him?" Her voice crackled.

"Not yet. Slipped away, but we have the names of everyone in that hotel last night, and surveillance video too."

"I pray that you find him. We owe that to Danny."

"Swear to God, I'll find him."

"He needs to pay for this, Al."

"The bastard will pay. After dealing with me, he'll look forward to sitting in old Sparky at Tucker Prison."

JEREMY PIPKINS GAZED out of the floor-to-ceiling glass window of his office suspended thirty stories above Kansas City. Watching people scurry purposefully in all directions, he wished he had a purpose, a sense of direction.

His recently re-furnished office was strictly Danish modern. The horizontal lines of a desk and credenza, made of straight grained wood, were punctuated by the vertical lines of a stainless-steel pole lamp and hat tree. No flowery patterns or bright-colored accents. No extraneous items to clutter the room or the mind. The walls and carpet could only be described as beige. One personal item stood alone, a sentinel on the desk. Two photos hinged together, framed by chrome, standing as a V. On the left his smiling wife Alicia, on the right his two children—Edward and Elizabeth.

When Jeremy's father had promoted him to vice president, he had thought sitting in this office might give him a fresh boost of enthusiasm; all it had done was add two unwanted inches to his waistline. The exhilaration had lasted less than a week, the job really hadn't changed; the cage was just more luxurious. Randolph G. Pipkins wanted his son to follow him as president, and Jeremy wasn't going to disappoint the old man, not now, not this late in the game. Hell, he had just turned forty, he could ride it out.

"Pardon me, sir."

He swiveled toward smiling Miss Shipley. "Yes."

"Your four o'clock appointment is here."

"Four?"

"Yes, Mr. Babcock."

"Oh, certainly, ask him to step in. Wait, Miss

Shipley. Did you get Babcock's application from Risk Management?"

"I just returned from there, they haven't received it. I thought you may have found it unsuitable for consideration."

"Not received it. What's the extension number down there?"

"Perhaps we should look around for a moment, Mr. Pipkins."

His secretary bent over a tidy stack of papers on the credenza, while Jeremy desperately searched his inbox.

"I believe this is it over here. It has your approval but nothing else."

"Damn." Handing over a plain manila envelope, Jeremy said, "Put it in here and rush this down, get them to push it through fast. On the way tell Babcock I was suddenly called away to advise the city planning commission. Ask him to come back at two o'clock tomorrow."

As she exited he wondered—*How does she get into those skirts?*

Jeremy took no pleasure in being the boss's only son. Top performance was always expected—no, demanded. The old man never cut him any slack. He had been at the bank more than ten years now. Started right after getting his MBA from Princeton. Alicia was a classmate, then girlfriend; a year after graduation they married. The Kansas City Commercial Bank was interesting, even fun at times, those first few years. And the money—no complaint there. Then came the inevitable promotions— after all, he was expected to follow his father's and his grandfather's path—president of the bank. Somehow this past year it had become all too dreary. Same people, same routine, same problems.

How had he not sent the Babcock file downstairs? After all the work in processing it. A six-million-dollar deal. One that he had brought in himself, not something his father had passed down. Everything checked out— good collateral, good financial history, good references. Babcock's displeasure at the delay would make its way to the old man for sure. Certainly, Miss Shipley could get risk management to move his paperwork to the top of the stack. Invaluable that girl—and her backside!

He had never wandered off the straight and narrow road, but Miss Shipley sure was a temptation.

Jeremy reached for the afternoon edition of the *Sentinel* that always arrived on his desk late in the afternoon. The headline caught his eye:

66 AMERICANS SEIZED AT U.S. EMBASSY IN IRAN

He thought about the peanut farmer from Georgia, Carter would undoubtedly handle this poorly. If only Reagan had gained the Republican nomination instead of lackluster Gerald Ford. Reagan would have certainly won the election and we wouldn't have these foreign relations problems and high gasoline prices. Three years ago, at the '76 Republican National Convention, right here in Kansas City at Kemper Arena, his father had fought unsuccessfully to put Reagan at the top of the ticket. Now we're stuck with a bleeding-heart Democrat.

The far right-hand newspaper column had a blurb about that overly ambitious politician in Arkansas.

ARKANSAS GOVERNOR TURNS LAND DEVELOPER
Apparently not content with his $35,000 salary,
the governor and his wife are involved in a real estate
scheme to sell vacation home sites in a development
called Whitewater Retreat.

Rumors of indiscretion with the ladies of Little Rock had circulated since his being elected last year. Now that liberal was displaying his greedy side with questionable real-estate deals. Unfortunately, today's turmoil at the bank overshadowed any politician's mayhem.

Then a smaller headline below the fold grabbed his attention.

MODERN TECHNOLOGY AIDS POLICE
In addition to the many perverted participants arrested
by the diligent Little Rock police force last night, elusive
deviants are being identified through hotel registration.

They'd never registered. Dodged that bullet. The Lancelot Inn had been fully booked so they'd stayed two blocks away at the Beauregard.

He scanned frantically, searching for facts. A terrifying one vaulted toward him.

Although some guests registered at the Lancelot Inn
under false names, police are scanning security video tape
recordings to identify all persons entering the hotel.

He reached for the gold pocket watch passed down from his grandfather, jammed the newspaper into his bulging hand-tooled leather briefcase and stormed past Miss Shipley to get to the elevators before the exodus at five o'clock. He needed to get home fast and discuss this with Alicia, over a well-shaken martini.

A

CCELERATING ONTO THE outbound expressway, Jeremy settled into the soft leather of his Cadillac and breathed deeply, savoring the new car smell. After crossing Brush Creek, fog settled over the stream of red taillights anxiously making their way to suburban retreats.

He stayed in the right-hand lane; traffic was heavy, visibility poor, his mind engaged.

What a day! Total disaster. He could understand Little Rock keeping this on the front page, but he thought the Kansas City paper would move on to some salacious local story. Alicia will definitely spin into a tirade. And that Babcock file, how could he have not sent it downstairs?

Red taillights lit up, tires screeched, he sensed the stench of hot rubber.

Brake pedal to the floor. Grip the wheel tightly. Go for the shoulder.

The heavy Cadillac left the ground, bounced down an embankment, slid into a ditch.

Macabre-minded commuters gawked through their windows while they flashed by ten feet above. Jeremy felt like a fool staring through the mud-splattered windshield of his Cadillac convertible, sitting motionless in a ditch. His white knuckles still gripping the wheel.

Damn it! Just my luck.

Until now the Caddy looked brand new. Safety crusader Ralph Nader had destroyed the great tradition of American convertibles. Jeremy had been forced to have one fabricated out of a two-door hardtop. The Le

Cabriolet luxury package cost a fortune. But he liked eyes on his Cadillac—top down, wind in his hair, power beneath his feet. Like sex—beauty, turbulence, unbridled fury, and danger.

Now the magnificent machine was sitting in a ditch.

He took stock. He didn't seem to be hurt, from what he could see, the car was all right, though there were probably some scratches and dings on the passenger side. The ditch was wide, with shallow sides. Could a tow truck even pull it out? The Caddy sat pretty level.

He stroked the steering wheel, admiring the space-age instrument cluster, feeling the leather seat beneath him. Ever since college, he'd driven practical cars—square, reliable, nondescript sedans. Buicks and Oldsmobiles, in staid, conservative colors. But with his fortieth birthday barreling in, he had indulged in a brand-new 1979, Cotillion white, red leather upholstered convertible whim.

He turned the key. The big V-8 rumbled to life. Without really thinking about it, he hit the gas. The engine roared, but the wheels spun helplessly in the muddy ditch.

He jammed it in reverse, hit the gas again, and shot backward two feet before the wheels spun. Back in first, punch the gas. The car lurched forward, threw mud ten feet, caught traction, and fishtailed along the bottom of the ditch. He let momentum build, then cut the wheel to the left.

The two-ton Caddy hit the shoulder like a whale breaching the surface.

JEREMY TOOK THE next off-ramp and pulled over. The tingling in his hands eased off, the adrenaline subsided. Another close call. Bad timing after the ill-fated event in Little Rock, endless hassles at the bank. The merry-go-round. Hard to jump off when it's spinning so fast. The prestige of being vice president at his father's bank had faded. Or had it ever existed? Tired of counting piles of superfluous money. Tired of falling short of his father's expectations. Just plain tired. But time for change. Finance didn't suit him—the chaotic oscillations, insipid number crunching, hectic negotiations, questionable practices.

Why had he gone to that ridiculous party? Why had he paid any attention to that client's exaggerated story during a three-martini lunch? Why had he talked Alicia into that escapade with the plea of, "One spark of adventure before turning forty"? That gathering had proved more explicit and more bacchanalian than the vicarious quest he'd expected. After a couple of drinks, he'd wandered off into a room full of guys having conversations about fast cars and fast football, not fast women. Feeling out of place in the midst of constant macho banter and anxious to leave, he had searched for Alicia. Finally, in a loft room, he'd found her, on a king-size bed, naked, with another woman, surrounded by spectators.

Suddenly a rampant stampede had ensued, with the police bursting in and arresting people. Fortunately—unfortunately as it turned out—Alicia found her dress and they escaped through a rear door into an elevator to the underground parking garage.

Where life had changed forever. A figure in the shadows had grabbed Alicia; in the dim light Jeremy had grabbed something to fend off the attacker. A fire extinguisher. They'd run back to the Beauregard, packed, and raced through the night to Kansas City.

He'd had no idea that he'd bludgeoned a cop. A sentry guarding the exit. He had a plausible excuse, though not one to expose to the light of day, not one to reveal to coworkers or friends. Certainly not his father.

Enough lamenting the past. He threw the Caddy into drive and burned rubber the length of the ramp. Time to take action. Time to work out a plan with Alicia. Time for a drink.

"NOW THE POLICE have video tapes from the hotel lobby!"

"We were never in the lobby." Jeremy embraced his wife's curvaceous body. "Remember, we came in through the parking garage?"

"A fragment of luck in our favor." Alicia recoiled. Golden-hair swished across flawless tanned shoulders. "We actually murdered a policeman!"

He raised a chunky finger to his lips. This conversation was certainly not appropriate for the children, eight-year-old Elizabeth, and fifteen-year-old Edward. "No, we didn't. It was an accident. And you weren't even involved. An innocent bystander."

"Co-conspirator, they'll say."

"They won't say anything. No one knows we were there."

"This is your fault! Your entire fault. 'Let's go to this party,' you said. 'A bit risqué—but all professional people—teachers and nurses and maybe a banker or two. Do something impulsive before you turn forty!

Experiment with other lifestyles! Put some excitement in our lives.'"

"I don't believe I misrepresented the event."

"Certainly not! The excitement part was remarkably accurate."

"I conducted myself in a respectable manner. Although you became somewhat carried away."

"You're the one who suggested experimenting."

T HE DINNER CONVERSATION was terse, with Alicia limiting her comments to, "Pass the potatoes." She cleaned up in the kitchen while Elizabeth finished her homework. Then the girls took a dip in the lap pool. Elizabeth tried hard to match her mother's long, graceful stokes in the water and perfectly balanced warrior pose on the yoga mat.

The boys spent the evening in the basement gym practicing putting.

"Your grip is perfect. Now try placing your feet closer together." Jeremy took pride in his son's golf skills. In fact, he envisioned the day that Edward would beat him by a few strokes. Every Saturday they played a round at the Mission Hills Country Club, which bordered their home.

Edward moved his feet a couple of inches. "I feel off-balance."

"Turn slightly so that your addressing the ball at exactly ninety degrees."

"Your turning this into a trig exam."

"Since you mention it, how is the trigonometry going?"

"Squeaked past Friday's exam. Don't worry, Dad, I won't let math keep me out of your alma mater."

A FTER AN EVENING of avoiding each other, a truce evolved in the library.

"Damn it! This is driving me insane." At 10 p.m. Alicia was fidgeting on the settee. "We need to know more."

Jeremy hesitated, turned toward his wife, and a tuft of black hair dropped onto his forehead. He unfastened the top button of his mauve Mission Hills Country Club golf shirt and slipped lower into the plush leather chair. He was no longer the linebacker from his Princeton days, but his shoulders never slouched forward. He walked over to the wall-long bookshelves, located the appropriate slot, and replaced *Discourses on Livy*. He'd reread it out of fascination with Machiavelli's thoughts on morality and religion.

Then curiosity won out. He flipped on Channel 3 news. The Kansas City stations seldom carried Arkansas news—nothing interesting ever happened in the neighboring state. But if this was a slow news day, they may have a short blurb.

"Police Officer Murdered in Little Rock." He leapt three feet closer to the TV. The anchor read the intro in short, staccato bursts, spitting out words. "Details are sketchy. The violent murder occurred during a raid on an orgy at the Lancelot Inn in Little Rock."

A face Jeremy hadn't seen before filled the television screen. An unflattering mug shot—deep, sunken eyes—a lost, bewildered look, staring into bright lights.

The authoritative voice of the anchor boomed over video of the same woman in handcuffs hobbling to jail.

"A schoolteacher from Pine Bluff is identified as the ringleader. The luxury hotel suite registered in her name has been cordoned off as the forensic team's investigation continues."

A square-jawed man in a wrinkled suit popped-up on the screen. Sergeant Alvin Harwood was saying, "She's an exhibitionist, experienced at enticing innocent women to do things that they would not otherwise do. Our undercover informant described her as a deviant bisexual dominatrix."

Jeremy stared at the television with his mouth half open. Alicia murmured softly. She had a blank expression, as though she were concealing some secret behind that glacial façade.

"A RE YOU TRYING to become a television star?" State Attorney General Carlan Walker shouted into the phone.

"The reporter jammed a mike in my face," Harwood said. "Got to say something."

"No, you don't. And what's this bisexual dominatrix bullshit?"

"That's what your inside guy told us."

"Hell, that's not even a crime."

"It ought to be."

"Not unless she snuffs a guy. Or a woman."

"Sorry, did I grab the spotlight?" Harwood sounded far more sarcastic than he intended, but he didn't give a damn. Danny had died because of Walker's ego.

"Just catch the bad guy, Harwood. I'll keep the public apprised."

The click on the phone as Walker hung up sounded

like the trigger of a revolver being cocked. Harwood stood squarely in the AG's firing line.

He gripped the arms of his chair. If only he'd walked out of the office on time last Friday. Never picked up the phone and gotten sucked into this mess by the ambitious attorney general. Because of that call he'd missed his son's basketball game, preseason match, but still important to be there. Too much harassment from above to transform the PD's image in the community—be polite, show a presence in troubled neighborhoods. At that moment, all he'd cared about was spending the weekend with his best pal Danny—fishing for bass on Greers Ferry Lake, two guys and their sons. No wife with a list of complaints beginning with the screen door that sagged on its hinges. No screwball assistant DA with a degree in criminology trying to make brownie points with statistical analysis to pinpoint high-crime parts of the city.

But he'd taken one last call. "Harwood." He remembered answering abruptly.

"Sergeant Harwood, this is State Attorney General Carlan Walker, do you have a minute to speak?"

"Yes, sir."

"I discussed your record with the chief last night during dinner, particularly the quick-witted resolution of that convenience store murder last month. Quite impressive. You seem ambitious, a man on the way up."

He had immediately sat at attention and reached out to slam his door shut. "I try."

"I've found that trying pays off."

"There's not much room at the top, competition for lieutenant is rough."

"I hear you. Knowing the right people often makes a difference."

Harwood scratched his hand with his right index finger. The severed tendon itched whenever he thought about it. And he thought about it often.

"I'm aware of serious criminal activities which are about to occur in Little Rock. Perhaps you could be of assistance."

"Do you want me to investigate?"

"No, I've got a man on the inside. Just make the bust."

A newsworthy bust. That got him in good with the brass. "Hell, yes. When?"

"Saturday. Late."

"No problem, I'll have two officers standing by."

"I need you there, personally. This has to be handled correctly—it will be a high-profile case."

"Isn't it strictly a city matter?"

"This is statewide. May cross the borders."

"Borders. What borders?"

"Listen! We have a governor that is up for reelection next year. A very liberal governor. A governor whose wife is speaking at the U of A in Fayetteville on Saturday. A governor who may be looking for a playground on Saturday night."

"Saturday is a problem for—"

"The chief implied you were ambitious. I thought you'd be eager to have your name on this."

"Where?" He checked his watch. "What time?" If he had left then, he'd have arrived just in time to see Tony checking the center-court seats, looking for his father in the usual place.

"Just pick out twelve dependable men," Walker said.

"Twelve?"

"This is important. The media may just show up. Even if our star guest doesn't make an appearance, I want to assure the citizens of Arkansas that the moral foundation of this entire state is firmly protected."

Harwood considered Walker a typical attorney—more than half politician, comfortable moving people around like pawns. Since becoming AG, Walker's political ambition had grown along with his arrogance. One loudmouth on the radio even speculated that Walker had his eye on the governor's office. But Harwood had ambitions of his own—he needed a lieutenant's pay to get Tony into the best possible college. College kids were the ones getting the promotions these days, leaving old timers like him behind. The game had changed. His son needed to be one of the winners.

"I need a time and place to put it together."

"Saturday night, Lancelot Inn. Something called the PJ Masquerade. I'll be in touch with the details."

Harwood had glared at the calendar tacked to the wall, grabbed a black marker, and scrawled an X through Saturday and another through Sunday. Easy enough. The hard part: telling Tony. But first, break the bad news to Danny—he'd understand, a bit of positive spin would smooth it all over. He had dialed his oldest friend, his friend even before he was on the force.

"Danny, me boy, we can't go fishing this weekend. So how'd you like to earn some overtime?"

Now the phone was jangling, echoing off the walls of his dull green box of an office, jarring Harwood into the present. He ignored the phone, modeling what he should have done last Friday. He tapped the pack on one side, tipped out a Lucky, flipped his Zippo, and took a deep drag. Time to quit whining about the past and act. He stared at those two large black marks scrawled on the calendar. Two days that he and Danny had not enjoyed fishing. Followed by hundreds of days that would not be enjoyed by Danny Coyle.

Careful What You Ask For
Alicia Pipkins

Chapter
2

"I've been up all night. Thinking about the local paper still exploiting that Little Rock story." Jeremy slammed his coffee cup on the counter.

"You need to get hold of yourself. We both do. "Alicia mopped up the spill. "Take a day to recuperate. Steady our nerves."

In about twenty minutes they would send the children out the door to catch the school bus. Alicia had already notified the principal that she would not be able to teach her second-grade class at Independence Elementary

School. Jeremy tried to think of a reason to avoid the office today. He would need to call his father with a substantial excuse. Randolph G. Pipkins, the president of First Commerce Bank took all absences seriously.

Alicia stood up, flipped on the TV, and turned the sound down low.

"Do you know these people?" The announcer sounded as though he expected an immediate reply. Behind him, a different black-and-white picture popped up every five seconds. "Call your local authorities. They are wanted for questioning in the murder of a police officer at the Lancelot Inn in Little Rock. Other security recorders in the area may be used as the search broadens."

Jeremy recognized two of the blurry images frozen on the screen, avid Razorback fans obsessed more with football than scantily clad ladies.

"The party was BYOB!" he shouted, then put his hand over his mouth.

"What are—oh, my God. That doddering liquor store with the peculiar name and bars on the windows. The place we stopped at while walking to the Lancelot Inn."

"Saints and Sinners—Intoxicants for Every Occasion. Remember, no one was behind the counter when we walked in? When the clerk appeared, he apologized. He'd been changing the surveillance tapes in the back room."

"That frightful man with a wart on his nose telling us about the recent robbery, boasted that next time he would blow the head off any intruder. That camera above the counter must have caught both of us. Jesus Christ, Jeremy, what if the police find that recording?"

"I know. A couple in the area, buying liquor at the time of the party."

"You've got to do something—if my parents ever

found out—the school—they wouldn't put our pictures on TV, would they?"

"Calm down, darling. I'll get that tape."

"But how?"

T HE EXPRESSWAY HEADING south out of Kansas City narrowed down to Highway 71 as it headed toward the Arkansas state line. Jeremy planned to stay on this two-lane road all the way to Alma, Arkansas, then pick up I-40 to Little Rock.

After maneuvering through the bottlenecks at Bentonville and Fayetteville, the traffic thinned. He checked his grandfather's gold pocket watch. Hit the gas. The Caddy blew past West Fork. A ray of hope blazed through the windshield. Now craggy oak trees and clapboard houses with rickety porches dotted the picturesque Ozark hillsides. Higher into the mountains the curves sharpened. The road narrowed. The shoulder disappeared. Air currents from the semi up ahead swept low hanging tree limbs out of the way with a thunderous roar.

As the truck up front slowed on a steep hill, Jeremy swerved into the left lane, floored it. The fuel-injected V-8 did not hesitate. Back in his lane, he noted the gas gauge.

Around a sharp corner a huge pecan tree sported a weathered red-and-white sign: CORN HUSK DOLLS. Elizabeth, she would find those dolls fascinating. Why hadn't he brought her here? Why hadn't he taken the family to the Ozarks?

He recalled making this trip with his parents on a vacation many years ago. Patchwork quilts waved from ropes strung between trees for out-of-state tourists who wanted something more than store-bought bedcovers. Wood-slat baskets sat under shaky, tin-roofed fruit stands overflowing with green apples, turnips, fresh-picked green beans.

Jeremy envisioned living on a hillside or in a quaint village like Mountainburg—a change from his high finance world. But how long would it take to die of boredom watching the grass grow?

He started counting dead armadillos squashed on the road.

A few hours with no radio reception and no one to talk to except Jeremy Pipkins. It wasn't just a miserable day that had brought him here. It was the same thing that had him driving the Caddy out of a ditch. Midlife crisis was almost a cliché. At Princeton he had thought of himself as a full-bodied linebacker, now he felt like a hollow body at the back of the line. A man hits an age where mortality is looking him in the face, and he panics, tries to recapture his wild youth. Thing is, Jeremy never had a wild youth to recapture. He was just getting old enough to get a little wild the first time around.

Banking had never interested him. Being the only son, he had no choice but to follow in his father's footsteps. His children were maturing, well on their way to independence. They would have choices.

The shiny bright spot: a sixteen-year marriage holding strong, though waning slightly toward colorless routine.

By the time he hit Interstate 40 with its stream of red taillights, he was struck with the sensation of following the herd. A desperate steer in the stun line, halfway through life on the road to slaughter, eager for a chance to escape into the fast lane.

Or was he a fool for bartering a secure life for one spark of adventure?

L ATE MONDAY AFTERNOON, downtown Little Rock was active and open for business. Jeremy soon discovered that finding a good place to park was a challenge. Private lots made it hard to leave in a hurry, and you had to deal with a parking attendant. The fewer people who saw him, the better.

On the third pass, he located the perfect spot—close, but not too close. On East Fourth, a one-way street headed toward the interstate on-ramp. No chance of tangled-up traffic, no chance of a wrong turn. And it had an alley in front of it—easy to pull out in a hurry.

The busy section of the business district ended a block away with second-hand stores and pawnshops. Seedy was not a problem. Picturesque was not his objective.

He grabbed a handful of quarters and filled the meter. Parking tickets left paper trails.

God, he was already thinking like a criminal. One last thing and he'd be out of this chaos.

" G IFTS FOR BUSINESS associates," Jeremy placed a bottle of Macallan Cask Strength on the linoleum countertop at the Saints and Sinners. "We're gathering at the Beauregard Hotel this evening. I need to make a fine gesture." Impressing the clerk would obtain his trust. The cashier, however, appeared stone-faced, like he'd heard every bizarre story a hundred times before.

"Clever name for this establishment, any idea of its origin?" Jeremy was establishing rapport.

"Smart-ass priest over at St. Mary's. We supply a half-gallon jug of Mogen David for communion every week." The reply was disturbingly monotone.

"This has enough of a lingering pepper finish to entice a bourbon drinker into the world of single malt scotch."

"Yeah." The clerk shrugged without looking up from a front-page blaring something about the governor and the McDougal's real estate dealings. At least Saturday's fiasco hadn't made the headline today.

Jeremy scrutinized the high-end scotch bottles. With a subtle nod of approval, he culled out an eighteen-year-old Laphroaig. "Heavier and smoky, distilled around Islay." He examined another.

The daytime clerk didn't have the physique of the Saturday night hired hand—that deranged bodybuilder had bragged about keeping a 9 mm Sig Sauer under the counter. "Could sever a head from the body," he'd blared. Today's deadpan flunky still made Jeremy uneasy. But who would not trust a distinguished businessman in a sharply pressed suit? He'd added a stage prop to impede recognition—a realistic mustache from last year's Halloween party. The drawn-out performance gave him time to build up his nerve.

Four bottles of the finest stood like Scotsmen defending the Highlands. Reaching for his billfold, Jeremy grimaced. "This is quite an embarrassment. Um . . . may I use the gentlemen's room? The doctors have just diagnosed prostate cancer, I'm losing control."

"Uh, toilet's not for customers. Kind of a mess."

Jeremy stared into the clerk's eyes, placing him into a compromising position.

"Through there, then left." The clerk pointed to the storeroom doorway.

Scanning the dark, cramped storeroom gave his eyes time to adjust, while trying to erase the vision of a 9 mm weapon. Does a hollow-point bullet tumble around ripping up spinal cords the way the night clerk had boasted? Is that gun kept under the counter during the day shift? What was he doing here instead of relaxing on the patio with Alicia, discussing the day's routine over a martini? What delusions had made him think he could play James Bond?

Is that a murmur of voices out in the liquor store? Or is it just the constant gurgling of the toilet?

Across from the toilet, on a shelf crowded with Old Crow, was the video recorder. On the shelf below, neatly labeled cassettes organized by the day of the month and a letter system. No time to analyze the system. He stuffed all of Saturday's cassettes into his coat pockets and turned to leave.

The clerk filled the narrow doorway.

Jeremy tipped his head and thrust his right shoulder forward, fired up as though he were back on the line at Princeton. He spotted a rear door, faked to the right, then broke out to the left. He reached back, pushed over a stack of liquor boxes behind him. The clerk stumbled. Turning the knob with his right hand and forcing the door open with his left shoulder, Jeremy charged into the alley.

The alarm tripped. A deafening klaxon.

JEREMY FOLLOWED THE memorized route—down four blocks, over two. No clerk on his tail—the booze on the shelves was worth more than a few Beta tapes.

Careful planning paid off—he'd be safe at home in a

few hours if some wannabe hero didn't take after a guy running through downtown. A white guy in a nice suit. People would assume he was late for an appointment.

Faint, yet distinct, the alarm kept on clanging.

It looked like the block with LUCKY DAY PAWN across the street. But the parking spot just before the alley now belonged to a Chevrolet pickup.

He ran to the corner. This was Fourth. He looked back one block; no one parked there this late in the day. Frantically he ran one block toward the interstate. No Cadillac Le Cabriolet in this direction either.

His Cotillion-white convertible was gone—another crime added to the statistics of Little Rock. He ran into the nearest alley as red flashing lights flew by.

Life had come around full circle.

Was he chasing his tail?

"HARWOOD." AL HARWOOD flopped into his chair and grabbed the phone in one single motion. A long day of interrogating suspects hadn't revealed one damn clue—tight-lipped bastards. Running around naked, and nobody knows nobody.

"Just got a call from a patrolman responding to a liquor store alarm downtown," said the dispatcher, words crammed close together.

"I'm too goddamn busy with the Coyle case to be bothered with some liquor store heist." Harwood started to slam the phone down.

"The thief ran off with surveillance recordings."

"Who gives a shit?"

"Saints and Sinners. Half block from the Lancelot Inn."

Harwood surged to his feet. "Block all the streets heading out of downtown. ID everyone crossing the bridges. Even the outbound interstate."

Harwood dropped the phone and ran out the door.

His man!

*You'll Never Get to Heaven
if You're Afraid of Heights*
Randolph G. Pipkins

Chapter

3

Jeremy looked up at the high embankment of the interstate, a man on foot would attract attention. Walking along the road that passed underneath the busy thoroughfare, he saw decaying buildings on the far side. Like so many cities, the elevated expressway had become a divider, locking some in, locking the unfortunate out. This didn't look like a safe way to get out of Little Rock, but he didn't see a better one.

The road had more potholes than asphalt and thoroughly petered out in front of a boarded-up red brick building. Squinting, he read a faded sign over the door:

Choctaw, Oklahoma & Gulf Railroad. Rusted rail lines in front of the building ran out onto an arched bridge spanning the river. He followed the forgotten steel trail toward a majestic bridge with four sections anchored by enormous concrete pilings. The first arched section spanned marshland and a narrow channel of water. In the fading light he could make out a tall tower on each end of the second section. The next two sections had arches just like the first.

Cautiously, he stepped onto the first section. Hopped from railroad tie to railroad tie. Maneuvered through the maze of ironwork lit by a crescent moon. Looking toward downtown, he could make out three other bridges crossing the river. Red lights flashed on each one. Definitely police looking for him. Had they found a correlation between the incident in the parking garage and the theft of a few Beta cassettes? Had he initiated an intensive manhunt?

The truth hit him like a blow to the stomach. Of course. Bending over. Facing black water far below. Teetering in limbo between passing out and vomiting. He reached out and grabbed onto hard metal. But it wasn't stable. It wavered like him.

A LICIA STAYED IN her bedroom all day. Hour after hour, she paced back and forth, flipped on the TV, turned it off, turned it back on again.

Channel 3 led with the story for the umpteenth time. "A sobbing Janie Franklin was led into the county courthouse by sheriff's deputies. The state district attorney was quoted as saying, 'They laugh in the face of our laws and God, but when they are caught, the tears start to flow.' Although Mrs. Franklin has excelled in her teaching career, there are allegations that she may have induced students as young as ten into the homosexual lifestyle. These accusations have not been confirmed. Pine Bluff school board officials continue to investigate."

Highly mixed emotions swept over Alicia as she thought about Janie Franklin. She was nothing like the person described on TV. They'd only been together for an hour, yet that was enough time to understand and connect with a person as sincere and candid as Janie.

At first glance we seem so different, that's an illusion, we both want the same thing, family, friends, a satisfying career. And of course, love and affection, in whatever form that may take.

She began to feel some responsibility for this fiasco. Promised herself that the minute this disaster faded, she would be more understanding about Jeremy's troubles at the bank, help him alleviate worries about getting old.

Alicia kept staring at the babbling TV, wanting the barrage to cease, but afraid of missing some facts amongst the distortions.

"The following press conference was held by Arkansas State District Attorney Carlan Walker this afternoon," the Channel 3 anchor said as a prerecorded news clip popped up on the screen.

"We are still piecing together this bizarre tale," Walker said. "Sadly, it's impossible to prosecute these deviants on charges of immoral behavior because irresponsible court decisions allow perversion. This must change!" The DA's fist hit his desktop like a preacher thumping the pulpit with a leather-bound Bible. "All participants will be charged with prostitution. Each couple paid twenty dollars to attend. They claim that this did not even cover the full cost of the hotel suite, but their poor business sense is no excuse. A fee for sex was charged—it is prostitution. Additionally, marijuana was found in the hotel suite—controlled substance charges are pending."

A frantic knock on the bedroom door announced more disturbing news.

"Mom . . . There are some men at the front door."

JEREMY'S STOMACH RUMBLED louder than the distant sirens. He stood up straight. Wiped pasty vomit onto his sleeve. Clenched the thick chain stretched across the bridge—a yellow sign wired to it said DANGER. There were no railroad tracks in front of him. No bridge at all. He looked up. The entire second section of the elevated bridge loomed overhead, left at the top of its run years ago so that barges could pass.

He spotted a ladder. Steel rungs crudely welded to the outside of the tower led to the rail tracks above. Without thinking, he started climbing. Compared to police raiding the party, plowing his Caddy into a ditch, and triggering a burglar alarm—this was a cinch.

In less than two minutes he proudly reached the top of the ladder. Pride immediately turned into humiliation— the elevated tracks were still six feet away. It looked like Rube Goldberg had personally designed this disaster. Even when he stretched as far as possible, the end of the rail line was a full foot away.

Momentum was the obvious solution. Newton's first law of motion: An object in motion stays in motion— unless acted upon by an unbalanced force. All he needed to do is keep that unbalanced force thing under control.

Clutching the top rung with his right hand, he threw

his body into an oscillating motion, rhythmically shifting his weight to increase the momentum. With a leap of faith, at the top of the arc, he flew those extra few inches. Grasped the rail line.

Swinging onto the elevated tracks, he felt the video cassettes stuffed into his pockets dig in. The only link placing him close to the scene of the . . . crime. Dropping the cassettes one at a time, he watched them descend and disappear into the water. When he released the last one, a strong gust of wind caught it, lifted it slightly. His bulging eyes saw the black plastic box flutter away like the erratic flight of a butterfly, not sure which way to go.

Surely, the wind couldn't carry it into the marshland— or worse onto dry land.

He began stepping from tie to tie across the elevated rail line; it was no time to let his imagination get carried away by unpredictable river winds. He recalled hearing about gephyrophobia in Psychology 101, the fear of crossing bridges. Was he afflicted with that ridiculous phobia? Holding tight onto a girder. Stopping to catch his breath. Looking down made things worse. But he could not resist. An object swept past in the water—a log, a plank of wood, a body? Amazing how fast it went by in the seemingly still black water. If he fell from here, what town would his body be floating past at daybreak?

He cautiously descended a ladder on the far side of the second section. Like returning to the ground after retrieving a ball from a rain gutter, coming down was much harder.

The third section of bridge took no time. Confidence returned. Just put one foot in front of the other.

One section to go, then—

His heart stopped. His world stopped. Nothing but

water ahead. The rails . . . gone. A massive steel arch looming overhead was all that remained of the last section.

Turn back, give up, jump in? He refused the obvious options. Red lights flashed even brighter on the other bridges—this was the only way out of Little Rock that got him closer to home. This was no place for careful planners. For those that hedged every bet. No place for cowards.

He bet the house. Started crawling up the arched girder. Inching along on all fours. Using the rivets as rungs. Working with cards sadistically dealt.

Reaching the top of the fifty-foot arch turned out to be easier than predicted. But like the ladder, coming down posed a problem. If he kept going headfirst, he'd be disoriented in a matter of seconds. He felt like a cat up a tree.

At the top of the arc, on hands and knees, Jeremy slowly started turning around so that he could descend feet first. Halfway around, he felt a turbulent burst of wind. Every muscle tensed. Manicured fingernails dug into layers of rust. Rivets ground into black-and-blue kneecaps. Sheer determination kept him on the curved beam. For an eternity, he held still. Head bowed. Body hunched. Waiting for the hurricane-sized blast to subside. All the while thinking of the carefree flight of the Beta cassette—fluttering down toward the river—or worse, into the muddy riverbank.

The descent down the arch was not as bad as he had feared. It was far worse.

Arms spread. Fingers gripping the edges. Slipping rivet by rivet. Ratcheting down. Tearing the knees out of his gray pin-stripe suit. The angle rapidly increasing.

Limbs numb. Staring at steel inches away. Slipping a fraction. Slipping an inch. Falling free.

Down onto the far end of the railroad tracks.

The ten-foot fall jarred him but left him essentially undamaged. Sprawled on the corroding rail line. Struggling to regain his senses. Rebuilding his resolve.

Before the children woke up in the morning, he would make it back to Alicia.

SOLID GROUND UNDER his feet. No black water racing under railroad ties. Energized by a surge of tenacity, Jeremy sought a way to get out of Arkansas fast.

He stumbled along a road next to a concrete flood wall on the North Little Rock side of the river. Across the road, makeshift shelters leaned against a drab warehouse. Deplorable looking piles of rusty metal and canvas. The sort of thing drug addicts and lazy bums throw together. Derelicts who stand around convenience store gas pumps with their hand out instead of looking for work.

Do they actually expect or merit anything better? Ever since we backed down and handed Vietnam to the communists, recruits who couldn't hack it added to this troublesome blight. He moved into the shadows on the far side of the road to avoid the mumbling sounds and vacant stares. Yet he couldn't resist looking over his shoulder for a last stolen snapshot of the blank faces aimed at him, realizing that only a tattered narrow road separated him from those tired and shopworn figures. Stiffening his spine, walking taller, he recognized the one thing in his favor—hope.

The temperature dropped. An evening mist drifted off

the river. The glow of a massive neon sign poked through the humid haze, JETTER'S PIT STOP.

Semitrucks were lined up in three precise rows as their masters ate dinner, downed coffee, and popped a couple of NoDoz. I-30 and I-40 intersected a few miles north—from there they could head in any direction.

Walking fast, looking straight forward, Jeremy attempted to look inconspicuous in a torn and crumpled Brooks Brothers suit. Surprisingly, he made it to the restroom without a single snide remark. After cleaning up, he passed through the café on his way to hang out at the diesel pumps in hope of hitching a ride north. Several truckers were huddled around a TV watching the 10 p.m. news. Anxious to get home, he didn't slow down until a familiar face flashed onto the screen.

Alicia! In handcuffs!

"Startling news in the murder of highly respected police officer Daniel Coyle developed just one hour ago. The Action 12 News Team just obtained these facsimile photographs from our sister station in Kansas City. Alicia Pipkins, a second-grade elementary teacher, has just been arrested. There is an arrest warrant out for her husband Jeremy Pipkins, vice president of the First Commerce Bank of Kansas City. The two suspects were traced to the scene of the vicious murder through a key for a luxurious suite at the Beauregard Hotel which police found near a service exit to the parking garage. Allegedly, the couple had intended to spread their perverse activities throughout downtown Little Rock, until they were intercepted by heroic Police Officer Coyle."

Damn! That's what happened to the key.

"Those guys at parties like that are just flat weird," one trucker said.

"Yep, who would stick it to a woman what's all perverted like that," another replied.

"Why not just go to that little place down old Highway 59 a piece, put down your twenty-dollar bill, and have a good time?"

"Darn right. Just you and a woman, nobody watching."

"Fine women there, honest, no rushing you."

"It's a long haul from Tupelo, don't want no rushing."

"Bastard takes off and leaves that little old wife to get the blame."

"And he killed a cop."

"Smashed his skull fifteen times with a hatchet, I heard."

Jeremy dashed out of the café before the jury staring at the TV had him strung up by his balls with a rope.

As the door swung closed, he heard, "Golly, that guy on TV. I just saw a bum what looked like that in the john."

Night air hit him as he tried to clear his head. He wasn't sure what had shaken him the most—news reports of his wife being escorted out of the house by police, the attorney general shouting about fallen women, the police closing in, or the truckers from hell searching frantically for someone beneath them on the morality scale.

He ran across the concrete expanse, dodging eighteen-wheelers as they jockeyed for positions at the diesel pumps. On the edge. In darkness. Knee-deep in brush. Sounds beat his eardrums—diesel engines idling, defective fluorescent lights in the pump canopies buzzing, the constant sound of rubber against concrete on the interstate.

Was it time to stop this charade? Explain what really happened. Consenting adults. An accident. Not a crime. A shadowy figure attacked my wife. He didn't yell police.

Mistaken identity. In the wrong place. At the wrong time.

Pessimism slipped in. The attorney general seemed more intent on advancing his career than finding a cop killer. The media were swarming in a feeding frenzy. The police wanted revenge. They'd throw the book at him. Lawyers more interested in boosting their prestige than serving justice would grandstand, pick him apart. He couldn't go down that road.

He may have become a criminal, but he wasn't a quitter.

He had to leave there immediately—the cops would know his location when that trucker who had recognized him got to a phone. Half the guys in this truck stop knew what he looked like.

He spotted a trucker climbing into his cab. Maybe he hadn't seen the news. "Are you going north?"

"Not supposed to pick up nobody. But you sure look like you need a break," said the skinny road warrior, whose face had not seen a razor in days. "Headed west to Alma, then I turn north—up Highway 71 to Wal-Mart headquarters in Bentonville."

"That would help immensely." Perfect—halfway home. Out of the dragnet.

The trucker sped through the mountains of northwest Arkansas with no stops for coffee. Constantly jabbering about getting back to his family. A sentiment Jeremy silently shared.

The sympathetic teamster dropped him off at the corner of West Central and Highway 71. Downtown Bentonville, Arkansas. Was this Wal-Mart headquarters?

Not much here—no city maze with a smokescreen.

This didn't look like a great place to hide.

Chapter
4

A bright new Holiday Inn sign lit up the highway. Realizing that he looked like someone in distress, Jeremy thought up a story about his car running out of gas and slipping into a ditch while walking to town. This late at night, there would probably be only one desk clerk, and hopefully no one else around to ask questions or nosy onlookers whispering about unsavory vagrants. A quick, simple check-in, if the desk clerk hadn't watched TV.

The motel lobby looked like the hundred others he'd been in—a green potted plant near an aluminum framed window, a green Holiday Inn logo on one wall, and of course, a wholesome-looking desk clerk. Except this desk clerk was in a conversation with someone in a dark, poorly tailored suit. Could be a cop asking questions. A plain-looking black sedan was parked under the canopy out front. But how could the police have followed him here? Was this cat-and-mouse game making him paranoid? Suddenly a thought hit him: the police could track his location through a credit card charge. He didn't have much cash, but he couldn't afford to leave a trail. Turning abruptly, he left.

No people on the sidewalk. No cars in the street. Alone. Standing on a dark street corner. In a strange town. In the middle of the night. With nowhere to go.

He trudged off through a residential neighborhood for no reason other than an urge to keep moving. Houses with yards and garages seemed more reassuring than cinder-block buildings lining a deserted highway. Besides, a patrolman would stop and question someone meandering amongst businesses in the dark. This wasn't the big city. People didn't walk around late at night.

One winding street, lined with tall elm trees and well-established homes, possessed a familiar air of affluence that distinguished it from the others halfway down the block. A dog began to bark in a backyard. That got another one going. Then another. This did not feel at all familiar. He turned back and aimlessly plodded into a mundane subdivision. Abruptly a fur-matted mongrel showed up out of nowhere. More likely a stray than a fence-jumping guard dog. Right now, Jeremy was the stray, an interloper in this long-legged mutt's territory. He backed off slowly. Not looking away. Yet not looking it straight in the eye.

The confrontation was a short one, but he didn't slip away feeling as though he had prevailed.

Aｌｉｃｉａ ｗａｉｔｅｄ ａｓ long as possible. Unable to hold it any longer, she squatted warily. Attempting to minimize contact with the cold stainless-steel toilet. She relieved herself hurriedly before anyone passed her concrete cage.

No books. No TV. And perhaps no sanity. Instinctively she knew their psychological strategy—make her feel isolated, alone, helpless. Alicia had her own strategy—money and intelligence. She hadn't said a word without counsel present. Although in here, law enforcement held the dominant position; the courts had not declared concrete and steel, cruel and unusual.

The questions went on for what seemed to be hours. One detective, then another, the same questions rephrased. She never replied before receiving a nod from her attorney.

"Did your husband lose his temper often?"

"No, never."

"How often did he hit you?"

"He did not."

"If upset, would he lash out with his fist or tend to strike with an object?"

"Neither. He never descended to violent behavior."

She had not done anything wrong except panic and run. Did the police really think their primitive tactics could intimidate a mother of two, a second-grade schoolteacher? She wasn't some pampered trophy wife. She had a career, an income of her own, and had been thinking for herself for her entire marriage.

No, she would be fine. It was Jeremy who troubled her. Poor, indecisive, meandering, Jeremy.

She had the shame. He had the murder.

JEREMY SPED UP. Walking fast. Almost jogging. Attempting to come up with a brilliant solution. The neighborhoods became newer; tract houses lined up like soldiers. Three blocks by four blocks on one side of the road. Two blocks by five on the other. Plots of suburban development surrounded by fields of soybeans. Being a commercial banker, he knew that commodity markets fluctuated considerably, as did the weather. And Wal-Mart was growing faster than soybeans. One lump sum from a developer seemed a better choice these days.

At the corner of a bean field, he saw a small wooden structure all on its own. No door or window on the street side. He ventured around back in search of shelter, away from people and dogs.

A bolt jammed in a hasp secured two flimsy doors that met in the middle. Cautiously lifting the bolt, he braced himself. Rusty hinges announced his arrival. He peered inside. Saw nothing. Heard a squeak. Then a skitter. It didn't sound big. But as a precaution he stood behind one door and flung the other wide open.

The shed housed only one thing, a small vehicle of sorts, dark green with the letters John Deere in bright yellow. A cross between a riding lawnmower and a farm tractor, by his city-guy guess. It did not appear as though this agricultural implement would mind company for what little remained of the night. The previous occupants apparently had their own exit.

Pulling the door closed shut out the wind and the world. The world as he'd known it. The road had narrowed. Options had dwindled to a ten-by-ten shed. But enough self-pity, what option did Alicia have? A dull gray image of her appeared on the wall of the shed. Time to accept responsibility. He had dumped this disaster on Alicia, he would make it disappear.

He paced back and forth trying to think it out. Trying to develop a plan. Like the tiger he'd seen as a child at the Kansas City Zoo. Pacing back and forth in a cage only three times the length of its body. Five steps in one direction. Five steps in the other. Repeated over and over. Looking for a way out that did not exist.

Sleeping on a concrete slab turned into a challenge, particularly while small critters drifted in and out. Jeremy drifted in and out also. In and out of sleep . . . He recalled Alicia waiting for him outside the Princeton locker room, just after the homecoming game in their junior year. He hadn't actually been put into the game, but when he came out of the locker room . . . Well, Alicia acted as though he had scored the winning touchdown. After a pizza at Poncho's and several beers, that's when they did it. Both late bloomers. But that night everything changed. It wasn't so much the sex, it was the bonding, A nineteen-year bond, a bond broken last Saturday. A bond broken by murder.

H ARWOOD SAT AT the counter of Jetter's Pit Stop, tossing back his third cup, hoping that caffeine would shake some facts loose. Pipkins had vanished—in a strange city, bristling with roadblocks, without a car— his Cadillac had already shown up at the impound lot, worse for wear after a joy ride.

A big shot banker. Leather-soled wingtips. Business suit. Just evaporated. In fact, evaded a two-state alert.

A trucker reported seeing a likely suspect at this truck stop. "Jet black hair. Torn suit. Bruised forehead." That all fit. After recognizing Pipkins on TV, the trucker had searched for the beat-up guy. No luck.

Every sheriff's department and highway patrol in northwest Arkansas and western Missouri were checking with waitresses, clerks, and the men who cleaned restrooms. All night long they hit every truck stop, rest area, and gas station between here and Kansas City. Twenty-four-hour surveillance had already been set up on Pipkins's house and the bank where he worked. All the routine stuff.

But Pipkins was not a professional criminal. He would not think like a criminal. That made it harder to calculate his next move.

Would he head west? I-40 could get a person cross country fast. In three hours, he could be in Oklahoma. Seven hours would put him in Texas. By tomorrow he could be sitting on Santa Monica Beach, watching girls in bikinis. But probably not, that shyster has too much family and money in this part of the country.

East? Desk jockey like him wouldn't find much camouflage in Tennessee.

South wasn't much of an option. Hardscrabble hillsides, dusty cotton fields, then Louisiana swamp. No places for a city boy to hide.

To Harwood, north seemed most likely. Retreat to the safety of home. High-class guy like Pipkins would seek out an urban environment. The family money could tuck him away in a cozy condo.

Then again, panic and fear may have set in; a scared rabbit like him could be holed up in some beer joint right here in North Little Rock. Tomorrow morning the frightened fugitive might show up shivering on a street corner.

What corner? What direction?

Unless . . .

He signaled to the waitress who had been working behind the counter last night. "Mrs. Ellis, can you—"

"Ms. Ellis."

"Ms. Ellis." Had that woman's lib crap made it to North Little Rock? "Could you describe last night? The people in the restaurant, bits of conversation, odd comments, any trivial detail about the activity, unusual interaction between customers. Anything and everything."

"Not a usual night. The truckers crowded round the TV. They all had ideas about who done it. Course, all the weird sex talk riled them up."

"Everyone knew about the murder in Little Rock?"

"Oh, yeah. And they all had something to say."

Harwood stuck out his cup for a refill, then flopped into the large, empty corner booth, underneath the sign that said Reserved for Three or more Truckers.

Retreat to the safety of home, down the rabbit hole? A likely plan. Unless everyone in the states of Arkansas and Missouri knows where home is. So Pipkins panics. Hops onto the first truck he can find.

Which still could have taken him anywhere.

Harwood looked out at the lot. Big rigs pulled up to three diesel islands. One after the other. There were eight trucks out there now. Five of them looked like first cousins, white with blue letters.

All five had Wal-Mart plastered on the side.

Harwood decided to play the odds.

7-ELEVEN SERVED BREAKFAST all day—Danish wrapped in cellophane, coffee in a paper cup. While scrutinizing the shelves and keeping one eye on the freckled clerk, who was staring at a TV through thick, black-rimmed glasses, Jeremy helped himself to lunch: a package of Twinkies slid into his pocket. He needed to conserve cash. He had been labeled a criminal. May as well learn the trade.

He attempted to remain inconspicuous while pouring three packets of nourishing sugar into his coffee and wrestling with the cellophane wrapper on the morning entrée.

"This is further proof of how the morality of this state has declined precipitously under the present liberal influence in state government." This declaration blared from the clerk's black-and-white TV. A serious looking man with slicked-down hair was staring straight into the camera, speaking as though he had been given spiritual insight directly from God. "I'm going to clean up this state, get rid of the filth, make our cities churchgoing communities again."

"Sounds like the attorney general wants to be governor," the clerk said to no one in particular, although Jeremy was the only one there.

And he was leaving, as soon as possible.

Chapter
5

Three vital hours wasted at the Wal-Mart Transportation Headquarters in Bentonville. Harwood knew that businesses big and small acted the same. All smiles and "We want to help in any way we can." The bottom line—their bottom line—was no negative press, "One of our employees would never aid a criminal, even unwittingly. They are not allowed to pick up hitchhikers." He'd gotten variations on that theme from three different executives at progressively higher levels of authority, before finally obtaining the phone numbers of thirty-seven truckers that had passed through North Little Rock last night.

On the seventh call he hit pay dirt; the trucker reluctantly admitted having picked up a shaggy-looking black-haired guy in North Little Rock and dropping him off in Bentonville.

Rummage around Bentonville. A hunch. A longshot. Police investigation meant poking around. Asking questions, Flashing a picture. Following credit-card transactions.

Everyone had to eat something. Sleep some place. Travel somehow. Those activities involved contact with people. That's how criminals got caught.

Harwood started driving around. Checking out places to get food. Inconspicuous motels to bed down for the night.

D ETERMINED NOT TO spend another night pacing back and forth with his new friend John Deere, Jeremy widened the search for a cheap motel that he could negotiate for a small amount of cash. No questions asked.

One block off 71, on a street that look tired, a hand-painted sign said Bountiful Blessings Mission. Faded paint on the store front barely managed to declare the previous occupant of the building as Harley's Grain and Feed. Loitering on the broken sidewalk was a cluster of derelicts in shredded shirt sleeves sharing smokes and complaints about the weather, the government, the poor hand they'd been dealt.

Jeremy walked slow. They wore better clothes.

"If you're fixing to eat, better hurry up and get signed in," said one down-and-out who acted like a self-appointed alpha male.

Sheepishly, he stepped inside of one of those places his father referred to as "Hell of a lot better than those bums deserve." A bearded, bespectacled man greeted him with piercing eyes. Cheerful, yet weary. He had the appearance of a person three steps away from being one of his own homeless flock.

"Welcome, brother. I'm Reverend Goodell."

"Evening," Jeremy kept his eyes lowered. "I was wondering if you have space for—"

"Don't be shy, all are welcome here. Our mission is to spread the word of the Lord and give the veterans of the jungles of Vietnam and the streets of America a warm place to sleep."

"Very gracious."

"Join the line, a volunteer will register you. We eat at six. Prayer meeting at seven."

Jeremy joined the line and kept an eye on the routine. Everyone removed their caps and pulled up their shirttails while turning all the way around, and raised their pants legs to expose the top of their socks. Apparently, an inspection for hidden weapons and bottles.

"This guy's got pupils larger than a squirrel's nuts," a volunteer said with a sneer about a man in the front of the line.

"Rupert," Reverend Goodell raced toward the offender, "You've disappointed the Lord, and I ain't none too happy either. You can have your supper brought out to you. We won't have no drunks sleeping here."

Disappointed, the wino with bulging eyeballs silently departed. Jeremy cringed. He hoped that his eyeballs would pass the gatekeeper's scrutiny. One by one, they filed along. Finally, it was his turn.

"Name?"

Jeremy had been checking his back. Looking around. Not paying attention to the questions the man in front had answered.

"Je, Je, Jasper. Jasper Jones." Jeremy had no idea

where he got that name from. He had to come up with something quick, he could no longer be Jeremy Pipkins.

"Jones." The volunteer squinted and waved him past.

The Bountiful Blessings Mission evidently did not allow backpacks inside. Another volunteer stood in the doorway of a closet and attached tags with a string to belongings as the men checked them in. Jasper—he may as well get used to the new name in case someone called him by it. Jasper did not have as much as a backpack, a cardboard box, or even a paper bag from Safeway. It took a while to file past this closet door, as every second or third guy had a special request, or even a demand.

"Don't put my pack on the top shelf, might fall, there's a thermos in there."

"Careful with my stuff, don't put it by the door now, you hear? Somebody might come by and snatch it right up."

"Henry, you know I keep this door locked after check-in," the volunteer in the closet replied.

"Never know, somebody could swoop it up when you not looking."

Jasper turned to the man behind him. "Some of these people are rather particular when given a free place to sleep."

"If you were lucky and had a house, like I did once, and somebody came in and plopped their feet on the coffee table, you'd raise a fuss. Well that's how it is with us. All we own is these old packs. We're mighty particular how they is treated."

Dinner tasted good, better than lunch, though it wasn't hard to top Twinkies and Pepsi. More than that, to his dismay, he felt part of the group, one of the homeless. Reverend Goodell even picked out some secondhand clothing from a room that the Bentonville Missionary Baptist Church kept stocked through semiannual clothing drives. And he looked better in the castoffs than in his battered Brooks Brothers suit.

Surprisingly, the dinner conversation amused and informed "Jasper." No probing questions like Why are you here? No judgmental attitudes. Just everyday talk, folks passing the time while enjoying a meal. The level of education and astute observation impressed him. Some of these drifters had just fallen on hard times and were resolved to get back in the game. Others seemed to have given up. An articulate street person called Darrel, who looked forty but may have been closer to thirty, sat across the table from Jasper. They discussed current events like Jimmy Carter recently commuting the prison sentence of Patty Hearst. Darrell agreed with the president because Hearst had been locked in a closet and sexually abused by the Symbionese Liberation Army. Jasper did not agree. Hearst had actually joined the SLA, a bunch of multiracial militant revolutionaries. Besides, Stockholm Syndrome was nothing more than a liberal excuse for cooperating with kidnappers.

"Is Bentonville really the headquarters for Wal-Mart?" Jasper asked.

"Sure is," Darryl said. "Wal-Mart started here, the first one is just down the road."

"Amazing that such a profitable firm is based in this small town."

"Yeah. Sam Walton lives six blocks away."

"Now there's an entrepreneur who knows how to run a business."

"They didn't think much of that bugger at the place where my brother worked," said another well-spoken man sitting next to Darrel. "He worked on the production line making shoes—decent job, everybody knew everybody, owner lived right there in Fort Smith. Then Wal-Mart placed big orders, they expanded fast, that's when things changed."

"That sounds like a good arrangement," Jasper said. "Growth is essential to business."

"Didn't turn out that way. Wal-Mart became a really big customer, got bossy, that little company couldn't say no. Last year Wal-Mart bought them out. The big shots got rich, but the guys on the line aren't happy working for a humongous corporation. Somebody suffers when they advertise them low prices."

"Well . . . they are good at distribution and marketing." He should have let it go, but this out-of-work transient didn't comprehend the overall business environment.

"That is one way of looking at it," Darrel said.

Jasper was about to pick up the argument, but he decided to back off, not bring further attention to himself.

"Everybody loves Wal-Mart," Darrel added. "It's cheap. But one day it'll eat the heart and soul right out of this country."

Following the prayer meeting—which he actually found less boring than sermons at the First Presbyterian Church—a lively discussion about Jimmy Carter trusting the Russians ensued, while some men, like Jasper, kept to themselves and read books. There was one smoke break outside at nine. Reverend Goodell didn't approve of drinking and he barely tolerated smoking. Twenty-two foam pads were lined up in two rows on the concrete floor. Lights went out at ten sharp. The indigents on both sides of Jasper were intimately knowledgeable about every aspect of the American penal system. He didn't really want to know about it, but he couldn't resist listening.

"You know in federal prisons there's no parole and you don't get no time off for good behavior. You do the whole thing."

"You sure?"

"If they give you five, you're in for five. You do the time, think about what you done wrong, talk to Jesus and come out a true disciple."

"Never been there. Never done no state time either. Just city and county."

"I been in jail here once. They respect you pretty darn good."

"Yeah, they're okay. Stay away from North Little Rock, those jailers are mean sons-of-bitches."

"I heard that."

"And the prisoners aren't any better."

"Ain't nothin compared to what my brother-in-law said about state prison. He had a cellmate that got his nuts blowed clean off by that Tucker Telephone gadget."

"I got to go check on my stuff, man. Don't want nobody messing with my stuff."

The hobo on the other side turned toward Jasper. "Don't go closing both eyes, some bastard goes around here at night and puts little slits in your fingertips."

Rhythmic snores would have put him to sleep if it weren't for the sudden hacking and coughing from every direction. Flat on his back, staring at a dingy metal ceiling, one thing became clear—working at that damn bank was not what he wanted to do with the second half of his life, the half that he hoped he still had to live. And live is what he wanted to do, not just survive in a whirlpool of money, constantly swirling, schmoozing clients, consistently failing to meet to his father's expectations.

He vividly recalled his father's tormenting blast last Monday as he burst into the conference room. Late. Ten insipid robots had turned toward the door, all senior management—gray pinstripes, sitting bolt upright, pen in hand, ready to note any wisdom Randolph G. Pipkins decided to impart. Monday morning massacre, week after week.

"Jeremy. Tardy again," his father had bellowed.

"Sorry. Traffic was horrendous on Mission Road," he replied.

"It is always horrendous."

"It was extraordinary this morning."

"A situation easily rectified by leaving ten minutes earlier."

The robots stared at their yellow legal pads as if some imperative message were about to appear.

"Roberts, pick up where you left off."

"That's it, sir. Armour and Company will finance their new meat-packing expansion with us, a twenty-year commitment."

"Excellent, Roberts. Especially since we are experiencing a yield-curve inversion," his father continued. "Now Jeremy, for the month just ended, where are our total deposits?"

"Down just slightly, sir." It was his turn in the barrel.

"Down just slightly, sir. What the hell does that mean?"

"It is the first month in nine years that deposits have not escalated. But I do not think it is a trend, just an aberration."

"This is a bank, Jeremy. The dollar is our unit of

measurement. Exactly what is the size of this aberration?"

"Four hundred and thirty thousand, sir."

"Why?"

"Things are a little tight out there right now. Prices have been rising, inflation is currently 13.29 percent, while the unemployment rate is 6.1 percent and heading higher. The Arabs are getting all the blame because of high oil prices, but we may be doing this to ourselves. The Fed has it all wrong. People just do not have as much to put away for a rainy day."

"There are people out there with jobs. There are people out there with money. Get them to put it in our bank!"

The robots flashed a grin.

"But money market mutual funds are offering higher rates, it's hard to compete."

"Excuses. We can't loan out money to industry leaders like Armour if money is not coming in. If left up to you, we'd be waltzing off the gang plank like the savings and loan associations. You never seem to grasp the essentials of finance, Jeremy."

Another round of hacking and coughing followed by muted curses jarred Jasper back into his new reality. He began to appreciate the advantages of sharing a room with John Deere.

But this was just a temporary setback.

Or was it?

HARWOOD DRAINED HIS third cup of coffee in the Holiday Inn lobby. Yesterday's search of Bentonville's motels and restaurants had turned up nothing. After breakfast, he had called home to tell Judy that he would be in Kansas City for the next two days. She had a question about a stopped-up drain, and Tony wanted to brag about a trigonometry problem that he had just worked out.

Every guy walking out the door carried a bulging briefcase and had a confident smile plastered on his face. Not a woman in the place. Not one hair over the ear. Not a scuffed shoe in sight. La-di-da salesmen headed for Wal-Mart to promote their wares.

A clerk he hadn't seen before took over the front desk. Harwood walked up and flashed Pipkins's photo. Made the obligatory inquiry. Just for the record. Pipkins probably knew he would stick out here. No charges had shown up on his credit card. Unless he had planned all this and carried a briefcase full of cash, he wouldn't splurge here when cheap motels lined the highway.

"Yeah, he was in here." The desk clerk didn't hesitate. "He looks a lot better in that picture, but I remember the face."

Harwood felt his adrenaline kick up a notch. "You sure?"

"We're trained to remember our customers. We get a lot of repeat business."

"Do you remember what room he stayed in? Did he pay cash?"

"Didn't stay here. Late last night, really lasher, he walked in, watched me check in another guest. When I looked up, he was gone."

Pipkins had hung around Bentonville. The area had grown rapidly but it still had a rural culture; folks would remember a stranger. If Pipkins tried to stay the night, he'd have left a trail somewhere. And Harwood had the nose of an old-school bloodhound cop. Everyone makes contact with someone. Everyone must eat. Everyone must sleep. Ask enough questions, eventually you'll hear the right answer.

Time to change the plan. Stick around a few hours. Recheck the motels, cafés, fast-food joints, then move down the food chain to grocery and convenience stores. Work one side of the highway. Then back up the other.

"This guy in the photo may have looked tired and shabby. Dark black hair. Slick-talking city guy. Not from around here."

"Get lots of strangers passing through on the way to Springfield. Don't pay much attention." Most were not at all helpful. That was expected. Just keep asking.

And then: "A guy like that came through yesterday. Maybe the day before."

"Anything unusual about his behavior?"

"Kind of jumpy. And shook when he counted the money."

"He paid in cash?"

"Yep, a lot of it. Filled up a GMC with dual rear tires pulling a horse trailer."

"Horse trailer?"

"Said his stallion had a date up near Joplin."

Harwood turned abruptly. This longshot had misfired too many times.

E VERYONE HAD TO clear out of the mission by nine in the morning. His roommates dispersed quickly, leaving Jasper alone on the street. "Look for a job," Reverend Goodell had said. Right now, staying out of jail was Jasper's primary challenge. Get a job? With no resume. No work history. No references, no Social Security number—not one he would dare use.

How was Alicia coping? Self-survival had dominated his thoughts for three days now. She was probably struggling as much as he was. Maybe more. Police interrogation, a jail cell, intrusive reporters, caring for Edward and Elizabeth, and worst of all, incessant diatribes from his father. Alicia was strong-willed, but could she hold up to that relentless barrage? He wanted to call her—that would be like buying a rope and hanging himself. That would not help her. Or would it?

Here he was, walking the streets. Looking over his shoulder. Unable to help the person he loved most in this world.

Keep moving. Don't make eye contact. He was thankful to Reverend Goodell for the hot meal and clothes. They were out of style by at least a decade, but they did the job. For lack of anything else to do, he started to explore Bentonville, Arkansas. Overwhelmed by a compulsion to understand how he got there kept him constantly moving. Pacing up and down streets, oblivious of his surroundings. Trying to piece it together. What had gone wrong? What fatal mistake had he made?

And Jasper Jones—where had that come from? Comic books? A Saturday morning TV adventure?

But he couldn't be Jeremy anymore. And Jasper Jones was as good an identity as any. He said it aloud a few times to get accustomed to the sound.

Time. He needed time for things to cool down. The police would move on to other cases. Real cases. With real criminals. With intent—no accidental mishaps. The AG, who was out for blood, would get elected to whatever he wanted to get elected to. The police couldn't afford to watch Alicia forever. If he could work out a way to last a few weeks, he might find a way out of this.

Jasper slipped inside of a laundromat to escape the intensifying sun, found a chair against the far wall, stared at a bank of dryers energetically tumbling clothes, and pretended to be waiting. A homeless person enrolled in on-the-job training. Learning to live on the street.

A young mom with a clothesbasket under one arm and a toddler under the other abandoned her newspaper and left, opening the door with her backside. Jasper grabbed the paper before some housewife beat him to it.

MURDER SUSPECT QUESTIONED

He read the crumpled front page for the third time. More depressing news.

Police continue to hold Alicia Pipkins, a teacher at Independence Elementary School, in the Kansas City jail. She is being questioned about her involvement in the murder of Little Rock police officer Daniel Coyle. Her husband is the subject of a six-state manhunt.

Squinting under the flickering florescent light, he attempted to make sense of this bizarre revelation. *My father must be doing something about this. Surely, he can get her released. If he's not too pissed off or humiliated.*

A SIGN ON THE highway caught his eye, it simply said OLD ROY'S USED STUFF and PAWNSHOP—best prices in town.

Jasper peered through the window; shotguns and

deer rifles lined every wall. One .30-06 bolt-action with a scope appeared brand new, and a 12-gauge double-barrel Remington looked just like the model 1889 he hoped to inherit, an antique that required hand-loaded black powder shells. He recalled his grandfather saying, "Boy, never use more than three drams of black powder. Too much or pack it too tight, and that old shotgun will you blow your head off." A glass case glittered with pistols, watches, and old-fashioned brooches.

He felt a lump just below his waistband—the pocket watch he carried everywhere except on the golf course. He pulled it out and extended the gold link chain that had secured it to his belt loop for the past twenty years. His grandfather, Alfred B. Pipkins, founder of the First Commerce Bank, had given it to Jasper on the day he'd graduated from high school. The distinguished man had become feeble, he could not wind it, and he no longer cared to measure his remaining time. The solid gold Elgin timepiece had been a Christmas present from Alfred's wife. Jasper stuck his thumbnail into the thin ridge surrounding the case, pried open the hinged back cover, and read the engraved inscription.

MP to AP
XMAS 1927

Not very romantic, Jasper thought, but typical of two stern people who had always loved one another.

Grasping the stem between his thumb and forefinger, he fully wound the main spring and watched the second hand tick off each moment as it had done his entire adult life.

"It's been in my family since 1927," Jasper said.

Old Roy held the watch for what seemed like five minutes, then he pulled out an eyepiece and closely examined the finely etched face. "Eight bucks." The pawnbroker placed it on the glass countertop and pushed it back toward Jasper as though he wasn't expecting a deal.

"It's solid gold."

"Shucks, why didn't you say so? Chicken farmers come in here all the time asking for solid gold. They won't settle for that chrome-plated Jap junk."

"How much will you give me then?"

"Eight bucks."

"I need more than that." Jeremy looked around for support that was not there.

The pawnbroker lowered his eyebrows, put a thumb and forefinger on the tip of his chin, as if he wanted to help this down-on-his-luck vagrant, but profit margins were thin.

"Now that ring you got on, that looks genuine. I'll give another eight bucks for it."

TWO SQUANDERED DAYS. How could Pipkins disappear in this hick town? Black hair. Brown horn-rimmed glasses. Five foot ten. 184 pounds. Chubby face. Around here, a pansy like that should draw more attention than a topless go-go girl at the First Baptist Church.

With the help of the local Barney Fifes, Harwood had checked all means of transportation, all motels, all law enforcement for surrounding towns in all directions. Detectives had been watching Greyhound bus stops and truck stops in the county. Nothing.

Down a ragged side street, tramps loitered in front of some kind of a mission. Worth a shot, then get the hell out of here.

"Hi, guys."

A nod from one wino. A grunt from another. The other five looked away.

"Don't worry, I'm not from around here. Got no beef with you guys. Just trying to find someone. His family is worried." Harwood stuck the photo into each face, one at a time, studying the reaction. It didn't take long on the street to develop a deadpan expression that got used on the cops regardless of what they wanted to know. Seven times, a shake of the head that said, "Never saw that guy."

Harwood didn't bother with a departing salutation. He pivoted, ignored the OPEN AT 5 sign, and walked through the mission door.

"Not open yet, brother," said the back of a man whose beard stuck out on the sides.

"Police, Little Rock. Just a few questions if you can spare a moment, sir," Harwood said, using the politest voice he could manage.

"There is no drinking or nonsense takes place here, just a meal and a prayer."

"I'm certain of that, sir. This involves an out-of-town visitor. His family is concerned. He may be confused, a stroke or an accident. Maybe amnesia. Perhaps you can help." Harwood held out the photo.

"That might be a guy who spent last night here. He looks sort of fancy in that picture."

"A prominent family. Genuinely concerned."

The bearded man studied the photo. "Yeah, that's him. Sure of it."

Bingo.

SEVENTEEN DOLLARS AND forty-three cents. Jeremy, or Jasper as he now called himself, never thought he would be counting pennies. Tonight he would find an old motel well past its prime and get a solid night's sleep. Something with a soft bed and no threat of cut fingers in the night.

However, first things first, and the first thing he wanted was a drink. Jasper began to look for a watering hole. Every imaginable business lined Highway 71—gas stations, insurance agents, motels, furniture stores, supermarkets—but he had yet to see a cocktail lounge or even a beer joint.

Although the pocket watch his grandfather had given him was now on display at the pawnshop, his internal clock said that cocktail hour had arrived.

He returned to the convenience store to inquire about the cheapest happy-hour hangout. The same freckle-faced clerk was standing behind the counter. Shiny black hair dangled across his forehead, partially covering thick, black-rimmed glasses that magnified wide-open eyes. Eyes that seemed to hope for something new and exciting just around the corner. How did he manage that optimism from behind the cash register in a 7-Eleven, in a place called Bentonville?

"Hey, your hair is almost as black as mine," the clerk exclaimed.

"Yeah, almost." He didn't think it was anywhere close, but Jasper wasn't looking for an argument. "Where can I get a drink around here?"

"The Slurpees are on sale. Only forty-nine cents."

"Not what I had in mind." Jasper glanced toward the wall. At least this place still had a timepiece. "It's 5:15."

"We have three assorted flavors of Gatorade, including the new fruit punch."

Abruptly pivoting around put him inches away from a strawberry-blonde china doll. A full inch taller than he was, not skinny, and definitely well-proportioned. He looked down at faded blue-jean shorts, cut off and frayed in a stylish, provocative manner. Her wrinkle-free shirt was whiter than her flawless complexion.

Knockout gorgeous.

"Dry county." She sounded like a Yankee imitating a southern belle. "Drive thirty miles north or go thirsty."

"Prohibition has come and gone."

"Not here. What's your name?"

"Jer-Jasper—Jasper Jones." Again, he was not ready for it, he should have been, but he wasn't.

"That's cool. Most of the folks where I work are from someplace else, they pick out a name they really like."

"But it's really my name. My parents picked it out."

"Sure." She tossed her head to one side. "Jasper sounds really adventuresome. That'd fit right in at Marble Mine Village."

"What do they call you?"

"Ginger Feliciano." She took a step closer. Casually ran the back of her hand along his forearm.

He took half a step back. Ginger seemed friendly. A bit too friendly, but surely prostitutes did not consider Highway 71 lucrative territory. At the moment, she seemed to be the safest way of finding out about the area—easy to talk to, but not a nosy local who would try to figure out why he was hanging around this rural hill country.

"Pretty name," he said. "Is that Marble Mine place far from here?"

"Across the state line, near Branson, Missouri. You are new to here. Marble Mine Village is famous in this part of the country."

"Yeah, just passing through. What's it famous for?"

"Hokey carnival rides and a fake frontier village."

"You don't seem like a carnival ride kind of lady, what took you there?"

"It's an out-of-the-way place where people mind their own business."

"Must be, I've never heard of it."

"Caters to hicks from the hill country. Come on up and find out for yourself. Just follow me."

"Don't have a car. Well, not at the moment," Jasper said. "In fact, I don't have much of anything right now."

"You look safe enough, I'll give you a lift. There's a backroad shortcut that will have us there in a of couple hours."

"That would be asking a lot."

"I've got a six pack and a half-pound of baloney in the fridge," Ginger said. "There's a few jobs open at the village. Don't pay much, but you can get by."

"I don't really have experience in the amusement park business."

"Believe me, the standards aren't high. You can spend a night or two at my place."

"Well . . ." He stroked his chin while thinking it over. No car, poorly dressed, surely she realized that he didn't have much money and wouldn't try to rob him. Yet she didn't come off as a kindhearted Samaritan in the habit of picking up strays. However, after spending one night in a tool shed and another in a homeless shelter, it was tempting. "That is a generous offer."

"You ought a go to Marble Mine Village." The freckle-faced clerk couldn't shut up any longer. "They got a really cool cave."

Without even realizing it, the quest sucked Jasper in. He never really analyzed all the implications—never actually made a decision. Just got in Ginger's battered Datsun. With all the fuss the media was making, going to Kansas City right now was probably not a clever idea, and this place sounded like a good bolt-hole. Curiosity got the best of him. What the heck was Marble Mine Village?

Besides, he might find a job.

Harwood spent the evening in the back room at Bountiful Blessings Mission. Waiting. That's what cops do.

By 7 p.m. drifters and con artists had filled the place, everyone had stuffed themselves on biscuits and bowls of brown liquid with floating clumps of something. Only the regulars showed up at the flophouse that night. Had one of the seven deadpan vagrants outside warned Pipkins? Had he made it to Kansas City by now? Plotting a route to St. Louis? Chicago? Toronto?

Goddamn options were endless. He had no choice. He needed to widen the search.

Harwood declined an invitation to the prayer meeting and slipped out the door. Out on the street, deciding which way to go, he spotted the splintered fragment of a baseball bat on the curb. He knew that in a neighborhood like this, it hadn't experienced the thrill of a home run. Baseball had never thrilled him, not since that summer night between fourth and fifth grade. The night he had run into the house with blood running down his face, onto the kitchen floor.

His old man's words still hung in the air. "Hope the other punk looks worse than you, kid."

"There was six of them!" he had yelled. "We were just hanging out in the alley, down by Old Lady Prichard's burning trash barrel."

"So, what caused the ruckus?"

"They started calling me names like shrimp and skinny wiener. Then Danny Bierbauer hit me."

"That your excuse for slithering away?"

"They're all bigger than me."

"You must of done some stupid thing to piss them off!"

"I didn't do nothing."

"That's your problem, kid. You did nothing."

"You're a cop." He wiped blood on his shirt sleeve. "Arrest em."

His old man had shoved his baseball bat into his hand and pushed him out the door.

Rubbing the torn tendon on the palm of his hand, staring at a left index finger that hadn't moved since that night in the alley, Harwood recalled that that was when his attitude had changed forever. But enough whining about the past, that was the last time he'd lost a confrontation, and he sure wasn't going to lose to a chubby, over-sexed banker.

A quick stop for gas and caffeine, then get the hell out of this town, drive straight through to Kansas City. Tomorrow he would spend hour after hour sifting through this so-called respectable banker's life. Talking to the wife, relatives, business associates, acquaintances, and yet-undiscovered deviants. He'd find that loyal someone from Pipkins's past, an old college friend, a relative with a cabin in the woods. Somewhere he could go to ground.

As he grabbed for the door handle on his way into the 7-Eleven, a kid with goofy black plastic glasses sprang through the doorway.

"Oops." The clumsy teenager didn't even slow down. "Sorry, mister."

Tired and bleary-eyed, Harwood staggered back one step and watched the freckle-faced yokel jump into a pickup.

A middle-aged woman squinted suspiciously from behind the convenience store counter. She looked like the observant type; hopefully, she had her head screwed on straight. "Just a minute while I set up my till, just got on duty."

Harwood waited. Impatient. But he waited.

"Have you seen this guy?" He threw down the picture of Pipkins and five bucks for gas.

"No. Been working here three years and two months. Never seen a guy like that."

Laissez-faire

Ginger Feliciano

Chapter
6

To Ginger, the Arrow Point Motel seemed strangely like home—home being Brooklyn. People crowded together, minding their own business, sharing as little or as much as they cared to over a beer on the front steps.

When the Corps of Engineers closed the spillway in 1958, water had backed up around a rocky ridge near the dam, forming a four-mile-long peninsula known as Arrow Point. A block-long, single-story motel had opened two weeks before Table Rock Lake began to fill. The ambitious owner wanted to be ahead of the pack. The motel never had a sign; the Arrow Point General Store located across the street acted as the office. Quickly constructed of white clapboard with screen porches, it looked like a low profile, suburban version of a southern plantation. For the first three years, the Arrow Point General Store and Motel had a reputation for being the best place to stay out on the point, mostly because it was the only place.

Over time the lake became popular with vacationing families and retirees—powerful ski boats, fast bass fishing boats, pontoon boats with roofs and gas grill barbecues, all buzzing back and forth. Developers with big dreams teamed up with investors and contractors. They built motels and restaurants, then full-featured resorts, then luxury condos. The humble Arrow Point General Store and Motel survived—barely—catering to eleven residents (at the moment) who paid by the month. All eleven had a definite opinion regarding the overgrown vines, prolific creepers attached to the screens, and something that looked like poison ivy growing in front of the place. Some called it seclusion, some considered it encroachment, others cursed as they broke off branches while struggling with groceries.

Ginger worked at the Marble Mine Village amusement park four miles down the road. Marble Mine, an extensive series of tunnels and caverns, had been an actual mine in the 1800s. When the mine gave out in 1888, the owners decided to make their money with subterranean tours. The tours continued on a small scale until Frederick Fosdick had purchased the mine and surrounding property in 1950. Gradually, the cavern tours became less significant within the sprawling amusement park called Marble Mine Village. With the aid of deep-pocket associates in Chicago, a wilderness village evolved, replicas of pioneer buildings, rides for the children, mountain music, restaurants, and gift shops. Plenty of gift shops.

Ginger's job suited her well. Embellished with a beautiful dress and a parasol, she wandered around with a smile. That was it, that was all Ginger needed to do to make people feel happy. That's the way her life had always been, and she played the role well. Now halfway through her first season, she had become somewhat bored. After a sudden departure from New York for reasons she never chose to disclose, this Ozark rest stop was a chance to recover, catch her breath before hitting the West Coast. Her experience on the live stage would be useful in California. She had been in a couple of Neil Simon things, one played for seven months. She even did some Shakespeare during her senior year in high school. Staying out of the spotlight and saving money were goals enough for the next year or two.

And this Jasper person might be interesting company. Intelligent, down and out, and likely to be suitably grateful.

"Shower's in there." Ginger pointed to the bathroom. "I'll make a sandwich while you clean up."

JASPER SLIPPED INTO the bathroom and reached in the shower for the hot water tap . . . The knob was missing. He tried the cold water. Stuck. Stepping inside, careful not to slip, he grasped the handle with both hands and took a deep breath. A few drops struggled out of the calcite-laden showerhead. He twisted harder, the handle wobbled, the pipe within the wall groaned. Icy water gushed from around the handle and blasted his stomach.

Making the best of it, he tipped his head to wash his

hair as a familiar voice chimed in his head. *Don't forget to wash behind your ears, Jeremy.* Alicia often said that, teasing, as though he were a young boy. She'd sneak up, open the shower door, always with the same melodic tone. *Don't forget to wash behind your ears, Jeremy.* Sometimes she was naked. Sometimes she joined him. Sometimes—

"Hey, don't use up all the cold water," Ginger barked. Also teasing, although her tone was less melodic. She stuck her arm in the shower, holding a Wilkinson. "This is for shaving my legs, but I guess it'll work on your face."

The bathroom fit right in with Room 127, his new home away from home. The living area set a new standard for Spartan—a faded red couch, a TV that looked like it might work, and a lamp with a thick leather glove beside it, which Ginger advised wearing when turning the lamp on or off. The dining area had a small round table adorned by cut glass salt-and-pepper shakers, possibly pilfered from a roadside diner, and one chrome-legged chair with split vinyl padding. A lumpy bed in an alcove had a powder-blue velvet headboard flanked by nightstands with missing drawers.

Awkwardly, out of necessity, they settled in. Both needed something—something essential—food, shelter, clothing, a reason to exist.

To Sergeant Al Harwood, who took up one-fourth of a huge leather chair, Kansas City looked intimidating from thirty stories up. He knew the chair's purpose: make those who waited for Randolph G. Pipkins feel small and insignificant.

Harwood had looked forward to interviewing the wife

first thing in the morning. In an interrogation room. With a tape recorder and a staff prepared to type a confession at a moment's notice. His boss, Lieutenant Elliot Heckler, trashed that plan in a terse 7 a.m. phone call. Randolph Pipkins must possess enough clout to demand a meeting in his office before Alicia Pipkins made a statement. Rich bastards always played hardball. He braced for a swarm of lawyers, on hand to carefully filter each word.

One hour and ten minutes later, a secretary ushered Harwood into Randolph Pipkins's office with a brusque "Follow me." Harwood complied with a poker face. He'd been left waiting to give his nerve a chance to erode. But he'd pulled the same stunt on too many suspects to fall for that kind of crap.

Behind a massive mahogany desk, Randolph G. Pipkins, president of the First Commerce Bank, sat erect and motionless as though posing for a portrait in the National Gallery. Harwood scanned the room—no pictures. Brown walls and carpet. Pedestrian furniture. In a gray pinstripe suit, perfectly pressed white shirt, red tie—bold red, no stripe—Randolph Pipkins was the only distraction in the room.

Pipkins stared. Didn't offer a handshake. "I take it you're the man sent over to sort out this . . . disastrous debacle."

"I'm Sergeant Al Harwood. Little Rock Police Department. Yes. And we refer to it as murder."

"A murder is what you may have in Little Rock. I refer to the fallacious and defamatory accusations toward my son."

"We have reason to believe he was at the scene."

"What plausible reason?"

"A short distance from the murder site, we found a

key to a room at the nearby Beauregard Hotel. Your son and his wife were registered as guests in that room."

"A short distance from . . . nearby . . . It all sounds rather vague. Hotel keys are lost by the thousands, duplicates are made."

"He attempted to make a reservation at the Lancelot Inn. They were fully booked and recommended the Beauregard."

"That would seem to indicate that he did not stay at the hotel where this incident occurred."

"The fact is—"

"The fact is your police department has falsely accused my son of being a sexual deviant and murderer. My attorneys are contemplating litigation."

"Tell them to feel free. We haven't accused your son of anything. The media has done that. We only want to speak with him."

"I'm sure he could readily explain this."

"If so, then why did he run?"

"More unsubstantiated accusations."

"A liquor store clerk, a truck driver, a hotel receptionist, and a reverend at a homeless mission have all positively identified him. Are you saying he's on vacation?"

"Don't be absurd."

"If you were to help us speak with your son, we could clear this up in a minute."

"I'll do all I can. Although like you, I have no knowledge of this situation."

"When was the last time you saw your son?"

"Friday."

"Did he discuss his plans for the weekend?"

"He mentioned the possibility of a brief visit to Lake Eufaula."

At last. New information. "Eufaula? What did he plan to do there?"

"Like I said, he mentioned the possibility of visiting there with Alicia."

"Sounds like he changed his plans."

"Have you checked?"

Harwood paused for a moment. How could he have checked on something he didn't know about?

That was all Randolph needed to regain control of the conversation. "My daughter-in-law, why have you arrested her for murder?"

"We haven't. Who told you—"

"The mother of two young children does not seem a likely suspect. A person of her stature certainly would not participate in the purported activities at that hotel."

"She's not formally charged with any crime. Yet. We're just holding her for questioning."

"Is that what you do to everyone you question?"

"When they refuse to talk to us, yes. After all, her husband has fled."

"She will speak with you this afternoon. With our attorney present."

"That's a lot of precaution for an innocent person."

"Enough misunderstanding and distortion has occurred."

"Hopefully, she won't distort the facts too much."

"Hopefully, your investigation will discover some competence and start to hunt for actual criminals."

"Well, we'll see, won't we?" Harwood stood. "Don't get up, I'll show myself out."

A FTER BEING PROCESSED for release, as they called it, Alicia waited alone in a gray office. Barbara Sullivan, her friend from school, had agreed to pick her up and save her the disgrace with the family, at least for today. She was grateful to Jeremy's father for his legal help, but she had no illusions of him being a sympathetic ear when they finally met.

She had said extraordinarily little and admitted to nothing under the advice of astute and well-paid attorneys. The police had encouraged her to talk-and-walk, but she listened to the lawyers and held out. And true to their word, she was being released without charges today.

Loud voices echoed from an office down the hall. She listened intently while waiting for Barbara.

"You can hold her five more hours! You knew I was coming!"

"Already processed. My orders are release her now."

"An hour ago, her father-in-law said I could talk to her with a lawyer present this afternoon."

"She has an army of lawyers about to escort her home."

"She probably witnessed a murder! The murder of a police officer! A friend of mine!"

"Your DA never pressed charges."

"I never interviewed her!"

"You sure took your time getting here."

"You can hold her for seventy-two hours. There are five more hours left on the clock."

"She's not going anywhere. Your DA files charges, we'll pick her up." The voice got softer. "Look, we're talking about a very prominent family."

A uniformed officer stepped into the dreary room and

silently motioned Alicia down the hall. As she passed one of the offices, a bony-faced man, head tipped down to light a cigarette, cast his eyes upward directly at her.

She had never, in her life, seen so much raw hatred. And it was directed at her.

H ARWOOD BACKED OFF the wife to keep from tripping over lawyers. Still, he'd dangle the bait, Pipkins would crawl back to the wife soon. Kansas City PD had agreed to keep up the surveillance on Pipkins's house, but they balked at keeping a watch on his father. Randolph G. Pipkins pulled the strings, and those puppets danced.

If he couldn't talk to that rich bitch now, he'd check around the places where the supposedly respectable Mr. and Mrs. Pipkins worked. Maybe someone would provide insight into these people. How they lived. Offhand comments they made. Where they went when they weren't working. Know your prey. Best advice his grandfather, the old elk hunter, had ever given him.

He hurried back to the First Commerce Bank for a talk with whoever scheduled Pipkins's appointments, filed his papers, took his phone messages. He needed to talk to that woman before Randolph thought of spreading his influence in her direction.

Secretaries knew more than people realized, even their bosses. Especially their bosses. As they silently hovered around, powerful executives soon forgot they were anything more than animated office machines. Day by day they absorbed tidbits of information. Clandestine rendezvous. Undisclosed bank accounts. Intimate knowledge not available to spouses and family.

Waiting for Miss Shipley to return from her errands,

he peered into Pipkins's inner office, attempting to understand this complex fugitive. The furniture looked plain but expensive. An organized desk—paper, pen, phone, obligatory photo of the wife and kids—the essentials of business. Neat, except for a tall stack of documents rising from the IN tray. The office of the classic company man. Of course, company men often have secret lives.

"May I help you?"

Harwood turned and was confronted by a beauty-queen blonde—speaking of secret lives. Five-foot-nine in remarkably high heels. Well-tailored, above the knee dress. Provocative for a professional setting. Easy to imagine this centerfold and straitlaced Pipkins making a mess of a neat office after hours.

Formal introductions, then a quick move to gain her cooperation. "Everyone is concerned about Mr. Pipkins. I'm hoping we can locate him soon and sort this all out."

"The papers say he killed a policeman." Miss Shipley sounded upset.

"That's . . . the media's opinion. We need to talk to him. He may have seen something. May have a clue to what really happened."

"I certainly don't know where he is."

"Of course not. But tell me about last week. Did he act differently? Do anything out of the ordinary?"

"Not really. He was a bit upset about the Babcock loan, but I smoothed that out the next morning."

"Were there any altercations?"

"Mr. Pipkins, fighting? No, never."

"How about this Babcock, did he have a grudge?"

"Definitely not with Mr. Pipkins, he got his loan really fast."

"What about the ladies around here. Did he ever . . . take advantage of his position?"

"Gosh, no. He was always a perfect gentleman."

Well, she was loyal to the boss. As long as the paychecks kept coming. Or other benefits she may be receiving. Broads that beautiful never bothered to type faster than ten words a minute. "Did he speak with anyone about plans for the weekend?"

"He had arranged for someone to look after the children."

"What plans did he have?"

"Mr. Pipkins did not discuss his personal plans with me."

No, of course he didn't. He was a perfect gentleman. "Well, thank you for your time."

"Pleased to help. I hope you find him. He couldn't possibly have committed a murder. He just isn't capable."

Isn't capable! He slammed a fifteen-pound fire extinguisher into Danny's head. Pipkins is a damn good actor, or this sex-bunny blonde is hiding more than his location.

JER—JASPER, IT WAS Jasper now—nervously followed Ginger as she breezed past the front desk with a smile and a nod. He peered into an accounting office with four desks piled high with stacks of paper, many poised to fall on the floor. Behind each desk a gray-haired lady looked up, saw Ginger, and immediately got back to work.

Without knocking, Ginger marched into an office with a brass name plate that said FREDRICK FOSDICK. An overweight, fiftyish looking man, wearing an out-of-date vest and wide tie, greeted her with an even wider smile.

Ginger had simply explained that every Friday afternoon, she helped around the office. A rather extravagant-looking office. Genuine oak-paneled walls, definitely not plywood laminate. A chandelier and wall sconces with red velvet lampshades warmly lit an overstuffed couch. The deep carpet with red-and-black tones seemed dark for an office. Overall, it reminded Jasper of a brothel—not that he'd had any experience there. He snatched a glimpse of an adjoining full-featured bathroom—au nouvelle French, complete with pull-chain toilet, claw-foot tub, and a turn-of-the-century bidet. The desk looked hand carved, with intricate patterns suggestive of Louis XIV. Not the sort of thing you would expect in the Ozark Mountains of Missouri.

"Miss Feliciano tells me you're looking for employment," said Frederick Fosdick, general manager, and part owner of Marble Mine Village.

"Yes, sir."

"Tell me about yourself."

Jasper took a deep breath. No work experience that he could admit to. No Social Security number that he could submit. He knew that many details made a lie sound believable. He had contrived what he hoped was a convincing story.

"Well, my name is Jasper Jones, and I must admit that I am a recovering alcoholic from a deeply religious family in Yazoo City, Mississippi. My family has abandoned me, and right now I'm looking for a second chance, a chance to repent and set my life straight. I never got a Social Security card because I've always lived on and helped manage the family cotton plantation. When I started drinking, my family disowned me because I got drunk and drove into a lamppost on Main Street in broad daylight while much of the town, including Reverend Elroy Billy and his wife, were watching. Oh, they pulled my driver's license. I want to rejoin the Baptist Church once I have earned a little money and become a respectable part of the community again." Jasper gasped for breath.

Fosdick shook his head as best he could—an extremely thick neck held it firmly in place. Ginger hid a smirk with her hand.

"What can you do? Besides guzzle whiskey."

"I'm rather good with numbers. I can do a bit of accounting."

"How about carpentry, blacksmithing, leather work, wood carving? Stuff like that."

"No, sorry."

"He's a real fast learner, Freddie—er, Mr. Fosdick," Ginger piped in.

Mr. Fosdick glanced toward Ginger, frowned, then turned back to Jasper. "Any specific skills at all?"

"Golf, I have a six handicap." Jasper was trying hard to find some common ground with the rotund man. Then realized this guy could never get around a golf course—he instantly backed up and tried again. "Photography, I've taken some fairly good pictures. Even know my way around the darkroom."

"Really? I think I've got something for you."

"It's a hobby. I don't have any professional references."

"None needed. Meet me at the Marble Mine entrance at four. Now, Miss Feliciano and I have some business to go over." Fosdick glanced at Ginger, then at papers on his desk.

Jasper Jones had been dismissed. And employed.

L IVELY MUSIC SATURATED the humid air in a grassy tree-shaded area near the main entrance. On an elevated stage, three singers in long skirts sang Country and Gospel, "Rocky Top Tennessee" followed by "Softly and Tenderly Jesus is Calling." They set the mood—have fun with the family, learn about frontier life, and spend some money while you're at it.

Jasper acted like a kid set free on the playground. Two whole hours of free time before meeting with Fosdick. Close observation revealed that Marble Mine Village was an astute business venture. Something for the entire middle-class family, a mix of frontier crafts and amusements for children. Unique and fascinating if you were eight years old. Ginger wasn't far off the mark when she called it hokey.

Wilderness Road, the main drag in Marble Mine Village, provided a glimpse of Ozark life in the 1800s. Some buildings looked authentic, although after asking he learned they were moved in from surrounding locations. The rest of the buildings were replicas with supposedly accurate details. The Wilderness Church had a steeple, though it had no bell—a sign stated that cast-iron objects of that size seldom made their way to outposts like this. Jasper stuck his head in the door, a bright-eyed young man dressed like a frontier preacher stood at the pulpit. A half dozen tourists reverently listened.

"Many devout Christians consider this a real church because every Saturday at one o'clock we have a genuine preacher. Couples come from as far away as Fayetteville and Joplin to exchange wedding vows at the famous Wilderness Church in Marble Mine Village."

The nearby Old Trail School had a similar peaked roof with a tin stovepipe chimney instead of a steeple.

He recognized McGuffey's Homestead from Ginger's description. She had told him that she crocheted and sold blankets from a vintage rocking chair in the quaint cabin. A large oval-shaped galvanized tub hung on the porch along with a cast-iron teakettle to heat the water for bathing. Quacking and bleating from a nearby squat building announced a barnyard that served as a petting zoo. Several signs warned against petting ducks and pigs, but baby goats and sheep were allowed close to the children. One lamb jumped at the chance to snatch an ice cream cone from a toddler.

Two men labored diligently in the woodworking shop. An old-fashioned mechanical device helped sand, buff, and chisel intricate doodads from wood—walking sticks, wall plaques, salt-and-pepper shakers—frontier necessities that wheedled hard-earned money from tourists. Storefront after storefront. Demonstration after demonstration. All selling something—candles, yarn, iron whatnots, woven and crocheted goods, hand-crafted leather, frontier soap, Aunt Mildred's jellies and jams.

A realistic-looking concrete tree towered over a playground. Children were climbing up inside the trunk and teetering along an overhead walkway suspended by cables. Twenty feet in the air, a childhood treetop adventure.

Elizabeth and Edward would have had fun here when they were younger. Somehow, there were always things to do at the bank, the years had passed too fast. You just don't get a second shot at some things.

A small steam train circled the park, providing an overview and a chance to get off your feet for a while. He passed on that opportunity—an awfully long line for a ten-minute sit-down.

The Flooded Mine ride seemed popular, judging from the line strung out in front. He heard children's screams from the tunnel, along with that of a grandmother.

Of course, there were plenty of opportunities to eat—hot dogs, fried chicken, an ice cream parlor, a coffee shop for old folks, a fudge shop with two-inch thick chunks of chocolaty goo and lollipops big enough to elevate your blood sugar for an hour or two.

At 3:50 he ducked under a four-foot-high opening in a plywood wall painted to resemble a cave entrance. A clever fabrication apparently designed to test a person's ability to maneuver through Marble Mine. Standing up straight, hands behind his back, a young man, obviously a college student dressed up in an official looking dark-green shirt, stood guard at the cave entrance. The shiny metal nametag over his left shirt pocket said, CALEB. Jasper declared himself a potential tour photographer, waiting for Mr. Fosdick.

"Great!" Caleb smiled, a bit too enthusiastically. "Ramus didn't show up this morning. There were harsh words with Fosdick yesterday. Doubt he'll be back."

Ginger certainly got on well with Fosdick. Jasper had his suspicions.

"I'm about to start the last tour. You can listen in if you like while you wait for Fat Dick . . . Mr. Fosdick."

Caleb hadn't told him where to stand, so he took his place behind a low fence that was meant to herd visitors toward the entrance. It made him feel more like an employee.

Caleb clapped his hands to get the small crowd's attention, took their tickets, then jumped up on a milk crate.

"Before we descend into the depths of the largest

room in this cave, the Big Bat Belfry, I'll tell you how Marble Mine got its name. In 1869 Henry T. Blow, a mining geologist, searched southwest Missouri for lead. He came up with the idea of looking below ground in these natural caverns to determine what minerals were present in the area. While exploring with a kerosene lamp, he discovered several pits. In a deep cavernous space, he dropped a rock into a dark pit to determine its depth by counting off the seconds, while listening for the clink of stone on stone. No sound. He tried it again. Still no reply. Then again, and again. Not once did he have the opportunity to apply his mathematical skill and calculate the depth. So, he thereby declared it a bottomless pit. His faint lamp made it difficult to identify rare or desirable minerals. Although he did conclude that much of the caverns contained white marble, a valuable material then and now. On reaching the surface, he christened the caverns Marble Mine.

"In later years, further exploration revealed that Henry T. Blow heard no sound because of bat poo. Thousands of bats, over hundreds of years, had deposited piles of guano twenty-five-feet deep at the bottom of those pits. Curiously, the guano, useful as a fertilizer, was more valuable than the marble. If he had had a stronger lamp, these caverns might now be known as Poo Mine."

After waiting for the obligatory laughter, Caleb motioned toward the steel stairway that led down into the Big Bat Belfry.

With a clatter, Mr. Fosdick burst in, huffing and puffing, with an old wooden tripod slung over one shoulder and a leather-cased Pentax hanging from the other. The visitors stood back as though he might explode, which looked like a possible outcome. Sweat poured off him, his face glowed bright pink; he looked like a lobster just pulled out of the pot.

Time to start showing that he could do the job. Jasper reached for the tripod, kicked open the legs, leveled it out in an expert manner. He thought Mr. Fosdick might request a demonstration, but Fosdick's only interest was letting someone else lug that gear around.

"That's where you . . . line them up," he said between pants. "Forty people . . . four rows . . . short kids in the first row . . . on the ground . . . spread the rest out . . . on the concrete risers. Get them all to smile without the kids looking dopey. Take two pictures . . . be sure. Unload the film . . . run it over to that girl . . . at the mine exit. She'll develop it . . . have the pictures ready . . . by the time the tour is over. You get thirty-five cents . . . every one they buy."

"Is that all, sir?"

"No. You return the cable car . . . to the bottom of the tunnel. Leave it there . . . ready for the next tour."

Jasper had meant—Was thirty-five cents all he got? "How do I get back out of the tunnel?"

But Fosdick was gone. For someone so overweight and obviously out of shape, he moved surprisingly fast.

Chapter

7

Harwood nodded and cast a brief smile toward Barbara Sullivan. Of all Alicia's co-workers, she was the one most likely to have useful information. She was the one who had picked up the wife after she'd been cut loose. But no one wanted to be involved in this scandal. He'd had to lean on the principal of Independence Elementary School to even get an introduction to Ms. Sullivan.

The Sullivan woman stayed seated at her desk. "How can I possibly help?" she asked, with a half-ass attempt at returning the smile.

"Perhaps a little background information?" Harwood got down on her level. Jammed himself into a third grader's desk. "I know this must be embarrassing and awkward for you."

"Why? I've done nothing wrong."

"Of course not. How long have you known Mrs. Pipkins?"

"Five years. Since she began teaching here."

"Had you been a close friend all that time?"

"Still am. She was alive as of yesterday afternoon."

Harwood panned the rows of desks. "It must be quite a challenge looking after so many youngsters."

"We are all trained professionals here."

"Did Mr. and Mrs. Pipkins go away for the weekend often?"

"Actually, last week was the first time I know of."

"So you did know about last weekend?"

"Only after the fact, detective. We mostly talk about playground discipline and school board bureaucracy."

And yet, Pipkins's wife had turned to her when she was in trouble. Their friendship had to go deeper than that. Still, it said something that this co-worker was shielding them. If she believed they lived a secret swinging life, she wouldn't be so protective. "Did Mrs. Pipkins seem to be having trouble at home lately?"

"Not that I heard. Look, Detective, if you want dirt you've come to the wrong place. As far as I know, Alicia and Jeremy lived a quiet, peaceful life together. Their biggest domestic problem was a stray golf ball in the back yard. I don't believe she did what the papers say. And I certainly don't believe he killed someone. They are good parents. They love each other very much."

There it was again. The ideal couple. And yet he could place Pipkins and his wife at the scene—or near enough, despite what the old man said. Pipkins was the one who had stolen the tapes. His car had shown up in Little Rock. He was ID'd at the truck stop. And Pipkins had run.

So, what was going on here? How had the perfect couple managed to kill a cop?

Or worse, kill a cop and get away with it.

A LICIA CLIMBED INTO the high bed all alone. The sheets felt crisp and clean. Then they didn't. Her blistering body instantly turned them moist and dirty.

She jumped down and began to pace, her back and forth ritual perfected during incarceration in a bleak concrete cell.

The moment she had stepped out of the police station, the media had mobbed her. Reluctantly following her attorney's advice, she had made a statement, a declaration of innocence, and a plea to Jeremy. As he had phrased it, a distraught wife imploring her husband to explain the unfortunate mishap.

She had presented her statement quite effectively, she thought. Then came the barrage of questions. Blurted out. Hostile cannon fire.

"Did he do it?"

"Have you been in contact with your husband?"

She'd been warned to ignore these verbal assaults, to immediately start walking with her head held up. And she almost made it.

Suddenly a sniper's shot rang out. "Have you participated in sex parties often?"

"No! I certainly have not," Alicia shouted.

Two lawyers had grabbed her arms. Quickly shuttled her away.

Now, she kept a careful watch on the driveway. As soon as the evening paper arrived, she scurried out and grabbed it to shield the headlines from the children's eyes. The front page proved worse than she feared.

WIFE DENIES BEING SEX PARTY REGULAR

That was when she stopped feeling clean.

Today there would certainly be news of some sort, Jeremy pulling into the driveway, or at least a phone call. No—not when he realized that he was the major news topic in two states, perhaps the whole country. Certainly, he'd turn himself in. She stayed near the phone. If a call came, it would be the police saying that he was safely in custody.

She took a deep breath and turned on the TV, resolved to endure the icy stare of well-lit news anchors wearing makeup. They would cast aspersions on Jeremy and her, but they might have some news. Raising her head slightly, wet eyes glaring through red gaps, disdain took hold. Their exaggerations. Their accusations. Their lies. The party she had gone to seemed mundane in comparison.

"Police continue to search for a white Cadillac convertible. Pipkins's car is a new special edition Le Cabriolet. Cadillac reported making only one hundred of this luxury vehicle last year. Chrome Le Cabriolet letters on the side easily identify this rare version. If you see a car similar to the one on your screen, call your local police."

She stared, dumfounded. The Little Rock Police had already informed her they had Jeremy's car in their impound lot. Had these people even bothered to check their stories?

"With a price tag of over thirty thousand dollars, Pipkins is believed to be the only person in the entire state of Missouri to purchase one of these flamboyant vehicles. Reportedly, the family flagrantly displayed—"

Alicia's pastel-blue high heel slammed into the screen. The TV picture contracted to a single white line. The sound buzzed with static.

AL HARWOOD GAZED out an eighth story window of the once grand Alistair Plaza Hotel in downtown Kansas City. He'd eaten supper in the hotel café—the formal dining room had closed for good five years ago. Businessmen now preferred to spend the night along the expressways, out in the suburbs. The food wasn't bad if you liked meatloaf or chopped liver with onions. The curved mahogany counter where Harwood had sat retained its 1920s elegance. A staff older than the hotel didn't bother to fill up the three huge chrome urns anymore; an eight-cup Mr. Coffee sufficed. It wouldn't be long before this place became another boarded-up landmark or a parking lot.

Today had not gone as planned. That prick Randolph G. Pipkins had thwarted his strategic, early-morning meeting with the wife. He had no beef with her—her husband was the one who had swung on Danny. At least now she was out on the loose where hubby could get to her and make a fatal mistake.

That secretary with the well-rounded ass stuffed in a slinky dress had provided no useful information. There must be more going on than a professional relationship. Clothes and a hairdo like that didn't come cheap. Good thing Little Rock PD didn't provide that sort of temptation.

The schoolteacher outright denied cooperation.

She must know the Pipkins family secrets. Why? Why protect them? Did she join in their games? A cozy little threesome?

He switched off the TV. Yanked on the tab of a third can of Miller. Damn news—same crap they ran in Little Rock. He went over every event again. In sequence. Not simply reacting to the latest bizarre revelation. Rationally, this case wasn't about sex, morality, or even a good cop's death—it was about Carlin Walker's political ambition. Walker was feeding the press. Keeping the frenzy going. And by agitating Pipkins Sr., he was hampering the investigation.

Time to get back to the home turf. Kansas City PD seemed more interested in not offending Randolph Pipkins than catching the man who'd killed a police officer. The devious codger had kept him away from Pipkins's wife. Backing down on that one had taken a lot of control—if only he could have pressed her in an interrogation room. No use harassing her now. Pipkins would turn up in a day or two—exhausted, starving, and desperate. A pampered pussy like him, the perfect gentleman with a thirty-grand car, couldn't survive on his own. Before long, the façade of innocence his wife had erected would crumble. That would be the time to gain her confidence and discover the path to Pipkins.

He pulled the cellophane tab and tore open a new pack of Luckys. Same brand that Danny smoked. Hell, they'd shared their first smoke together. He'd dared Danny to snatch a pack from behind the counter, while Old Man Snyder was slipping a box of Kotex into a plain brown paper bag for a neighborhood lady. Danny had never been shy about taking on the dirty side of a childhood adventure. In fact, that attitude had carried on until last

Saturday night. Until the moment his head splattered open.

Harwood flicked the wheel on his Zippo with the same wrist action he and Danny had used from day one. He took a deep drag. Started muttering to himself while thinking back to that pivotal night in his career. First year on the force, when he and Danny were rookies, fresh out of the academy.

"A miserable summer night, humidity had us stuck to the seat of the squad car. When the call blared out of the car radio it sounded routine—another Saturday night domestic dispute. Tempers rise when the weather is dismal. When we pulled up, glass shattered, it sounded like chaos. A good-sized object flew out through a window. A gun shot rang out. Someone ran out and took off between the houses. We burst though the wide-open front door. Cleon Colfax, a punk I immediately recognized, stood over a woman lying on the floor. Large chest wound. Blood gushing. Colfax wiping a gun with his shirt tail. He dropped the gun. Threw up his hands with a smirk. Danny kept a bead on him. I pulled out my cuffs. Realized this guy would walk. No prints on the gun. Some flunky took off in a hurry. Not Colfax's first time to make the front page. This would be high profile. My opportunity for recognition. A chance to get on the promotion ladder. Holding the gun by sticking a pen up the barrel, I pressed Colfax's prints on the handle.

"Problem was, the broad didn't die. All that blood and she pulls through. Starts blabbing to a fancy-ass lawyer about how I put the prints on the gun. Stupid bitch covers for the boyfriend. Says the goon that took off in a hurry pulled the trigger. That's when Danny saved my ass. Said the bitch was lying to protect her darling

Romeo. Out of love or fear—probably both. I came out a hero. Could've been different. Could've ended my law enforcement career before it got started. That's the kind of guy Danny was. The kind of guy he'd always been. Watching my back. Pulling my dick out of the ringer."

The cigarette stub burned down to his fingers. Harwood reached out for the ashtray. Saw the sign out the window and realized that he was here all alone, at the Alistair Plaza in goddamn Kansas City.

He picked up the phone. Talking to Judy always calmed him. After only one ring he heard, "Hi, sweetie." She must've been waiting by the phone.

"It's good to hear the voice of someone I can trust."

"What's the matter, Al?"

"I really tried to give Mrs. Pipkins a chance to tell me her side of the story. Clarify how she wound up at the party, explain how their hotel key wound up behind the parking garage and why they were staying at the Beauregard Hotel. Everybody's holding back something. Money buys a lot of loyalty."

"But it doesn't buy friendship."

"It can take it away. These people took Danny."

"When you get home, I will show you some real friendship. Are you driving back tonight or early in the morning?"

"Need to stay here over the weekend. Nose around. People with money agitate folks. Somebody will want to even the score and expose the Pipkins family secrets."

"I really need your help setting up tables at the church jumble sale tomorrow afternoon."

"It'll have to wait till next weekend. Can't let this case run cold."

"The church is not going to reschedule because you're too busy."

"This case is far more important than—"

"Yeah, I've heard that too many times. Talk to Tony now, he's got some news about a basketball game."

"Put him on."

A big game missed last night. And there would be another tomorrow. No way could he get there in time.

A FTER A WEEKEND of disappointing dead ends, Harwood sped through the Little Rock squad room on Monday morning. No one said a word. All he heard was his firm rubber heels pounding the floor like storm troopers in a black-and-white movie. He kept his eyes straight ahead; he knew the looks the other officers would be giving him: all somber on the surface, disguising the grudges they held inside. Hard to keep friends while bucking for lieutenant.

They probably looked at his handling of this case as a crazed obsession for revenge. Maybe they were right. But they lost a colleague, while he had lost his best friend.

During his weeklong absence, the world had not stopped spinning; a backlog of cases waited on his desk. Poking out of the clutter, the eight-by-ten of Judy with Tony and Sally was slightly askew. With a nod to his family, he reached out and adjusted the angle of the photo. He stared at Tony, five foot nine now and only fifteen. That kid had a basketball future.

Two wasted days in a hick town, and three more in Kansas City wrangling with Old Man Pipkins. The clock was ticking, Quick results were crucial. Close in before Pipkins caught his breath. Before he found a safe harbor.

Being outsmarted by a horny banker from Kansas City and stonewalled by the father made him the number one topic of discussion in the department today—emasculating pity over his failure crowded out everything else, even the Razorbacks' stellar Saturday performance. Leaning back, he lit up a Lucky Strike. Last one in the pack, he needed to pick up a carton. The machine down the hall only had filtered smokes in crush-proof boxes. What kind a guy would walk around with one of those in his pocket?

The wife was the link. Pipkins's weak spot. But . . . maybe this guy didn't give a shit about his wife. Some men didn't. But if he did show up and there was a handgun in the house, she was probably so pissed she would finish off that oversexed weasel. That would round this case out nicely, although he'd be robbed of the satisfaction of pulling the trigger.

Right now, Pipkins was on the run. Hadn't used a credit card. Obviously hadn't planned this well. Or at all. He'd call the wife, beg for forgiveness and money.

Harwood flipped through the Rolodex. Like all successful businesses, police work relied on contacts. He found a card and dialed.

"Hey Louie, did I disturb the FBI's morning tea?"

"Al, are you out of bed this early in the morning?" FBI agent Louis Fisk fired back.

"Got a tough case going. Up against big money in Kansas City."

"Sorry about Coyle. Know you guys were close."

"That's why this case is important. I need a wiretap across state lines. I know you feds can get that gear into action fast."

"Sometimes. Since congress passed Title III, it's not easy."

"What's the hitch? I need this, Louie. Whenever you guys wanted a snitch in Little Rock, I came up with a name."

"I'm on your side here. A federal judge will need to sign a warrant. I can probably get that quick if you show probable cause. But it's only good for thirty days."

"That should be long enough."

"Sure, but here's the real curve Title III throws. The police can only listen for two minutes. If the conversation is not pertinent to the case, you must quit listening for thirty seconds, then you can listen for one minute, then off again for thirty seconds and so on." Louie paused to catch his breath. "And by you, I mean LRPD. This is labor intensive. The local taxpayers foot the bill."

"Jesus Christ! We have to sit there with a stopwatch?"

"It gets worse. The bad guys have caught on. They discuss the weather for two minutes, then spend the next thirty seconds talking dirty."

"No problem with my guy. He's not a pro, just a rich banker's bastard." Harwood scratched the palm of his hand. "Can we do a trace at the same time?"

"Sure, but if he's out of state, forget that one-minute bullshit you see on TV. It will take Ma Bell twenty minutes to do a complete trace, but they can get it down to the city in less time."

"It's my best shot. Let's get the wheels rolling."

Chapter

8

Using Jeremy's key, Alicia took the executive elevator that only stopped on the thirtieth floor. Randolph had declined to meet her for lunch at the Mission Hills Country Club, saying that it might not be appropriate at this time. That meant Randolph had declared it inappropriate, and it was not open for discussion.

It took all the courage she could gather to agree to meet in his office. She had only entered Randolph's royal court once and then had sought refuge in Jeremy's shadow.

Riding up in the elevator gave her one last chance to scan the list she had compiled last evening. It was a given that Randolph's time was valuable and could not be wasted.

Stick with the topic. Steer the conversation toward

helping Jeremy. Make him answer all the questions.

His secretary appeared out of nowhere the moment the elevator doors spread. Alicia buttoned her navy-blue blazer while trying to keep up. Before gaining her poise, she found herself seated in front of Randolph's massive desk. The dark wood made it look like a courtroom. Her father-in-law's scowl made it feel like Judgment Day.

"Were there any of those journalists hanging around below?" Randolph did not blink. Did not glance away. "Those television reporters can be particularly obnoxious."

"No . . . no one, Randolph. And how are you today?"

"I will be much better when this public relations disaster is behind me."

"I certainly hope that you are better soon . . . Randolph." She was aware that she kept saying his name, trying to humanize him. She must rein herself in.

"It seems as though there is never any good news in the paper these days," he said. "Someone was shot on the street just below last night. A black kid of course, undoubtedly robbed for money from a drug transaction or a prostitute's receipts. Although the paper did not see fit to print that detail."

"Jeremy is our biggest problem right now." Alicia sat up even straighter.

"Jeremy has always been a problem. There was always something a bit different about him. Somehow, he never fit in here at the bank, at college, even in grade school. Always wanted to be a rebel, but he was never particularly good at it."

"Have you heard from him?"

"No. He's the only person I know of who hasn't tried to tell me something. Or elicit information."

"Have the lawyers developed a plan?"

"Plan? What plan do you anticipate?"

"A defense for Jeremy. A strategy to support his innocence."

"Worthy defense counsel do not openly discuss strategic planning." Randolph leaned forward. "What were you doing at that hotel?"

Here it comes. Stay composed, voice steady. Firm, but not aggressive. "We! We were just taking a day off from the burdens of making a living and raising a family."

"From all reports, that was not all you took off."

"You've said yourself—reports cannot be trusted. Can you offer any information? Any support?"

"Jeremy will do that . . . when he decides to come back from vacation."

"Maybe he wouldn't have felt such a need for a vacation if you hadn't pushed him so hard." Alicia withdrew a tissue. "Pressed him into a job for which he had little aptitude. A job he hated but did in order to please you."

"Nonsense. He was given every opportunity and never truly took advantage of any of them. In grade school he once, and only once, complained about his name, said it made him seem like a sissy. I instantly set him straight. In Kansas City the name Pipkins means something. It opens doors. His great-great-grandfather, Jeremy R Pipkins, distinguished himself as a financier of the steel industry in Derbyshire, England during the last phase of the Industrial Revolution. He should have looked upon that name with pride, not as a source of schoolyard taunts."

"Schoolchildren do not care who their great-great-grandparents were. Perhaps if you had been more understanding?"

"What is there to understand? The boy has simply never been aggressive enough. He could never comprehend that successful businessmen focus on grand goals; followers worry about the consequences." Randolph gripped the edge of his desk with both hands and lowered his voice. "He played collegiate football, marginally, made the varsity team, but sat on the bench. I went to the games anyway."

So this was all about protecting the precious Pipkins name. What else had she expected? Why was she even here?

She began to understand why Jeremy might want to run away from home. Wherever he was, she hoped he was all right.

"GET SMART! RANDY Smart," the baritone voice bellowed from the TV. "Tonight our exclusive Randy Smart investigative report profiles the decline of a deviant man. Randy looks at the seamier side of the headlines, the forces that disintegrate American life, undermine our social mores, and persuade our children to do things we never imagined. He uncovers the true story behind the sex party and murder in downtown Little Rock. Janie Franklin, a first-grade schoolteacher. . ."

Alicia endured several minutes of mudslinging before turning the volume down during the commercial break. Granted, Janie Franklin was unconventional. But the more Alicia reflected, the more she realized Janie was not a bad person. Her passion may have been unnatural, but she'd expressed it in a considerate manner. And, damn it, what business did the world have to judge what they'd done? She certainly felt better about Janie than about the self-righteous voyeurs, satiating their lust while watching what masqueraded as Action 3 NEWS.

She couldn't resist turning the sound up when Randy returned.

"The ringleader of the sexual deviants arrested at a downtown Little Rock hotel two weeks ago has been fired. The Pine Bluff School Board declared that the first-grade teacher would pose a threat to the morals of that community's youth."

So the sensationalist news reporting had made it to Pine Bluff and cost Janie her job. She felt sorry for the full-figured brunette that she had met briefly. She was a sincere, caring person.

Alicia turned off the set, moved to the window seat and stared out at black nothingness. No husband to talk to, two children to care for, two in-laws driving her nuts. What next?

A fly buzzed behind her then mysteriously disappeared—its third pass. Every time she lined up two or three facts and attempted a minor decision, the fly made another attack. It must have come in during the day and was now seeking refuge for the night. One fly in her entire two-story Mission Hills colonial prison, and it chose to join the greater metropolitan community in attacking her.

The fly returned to the window, provokingly walked across the slick surface. Alicia rolled up a newspaper. Approached slowly from behind. Stealthily gaining ground. Got into position. Raised her arm back.

Crash.

The china figurine that had daintily held a parasol, the family heirloom handed down to Alicia on her wedding day, lay in pieces on the floor. The ever-vigilant fly returned to its roost.

She kept an eye on the door and listened for the phone, almost by habit, now. Jeremy had to contact her soon. They would work it all out. He was a meticulous planner; he would know what to do, explain what had really happened. He probably had a room full of lawyers plotting a strategy.

Why hadn't the media even mentioned Janie Franklin's husband? Was he comfortable with what Janie did? He'd been at the party, too, so maybe they were comfortable with each other. Was he supporting her now that the entire world was against her? Did she have family nearby? Or did she feel all alone too?

Alicia picked up the phone and dialed directory service. "Pine Bluff, Arkansas, please."

Chapter

9

Ginger peered under the sheet. "You have trouble standing at attention, soldier?"

"A bit self-conscious, I guess," Jasper said.

"I'd have thought you'd gotten over that in high school."

"Maybe after we know each other better, I'll—"

"Maybe?"

Jasper couldn't come up with anything else to say. He was just holding on, holding on to anything that wasn't intent on destroying him. She didn't ask questions such as: Where are you from? Have you been married? Do you have children? He appreciated that, and he didn't ask questions either.

In the small space they got along reasonably well, two shipwrecked survivors stranded together, vastly different people with one common goal—survive and wait for a chance to escape their own demons. He just didn't feel comfortable with her. Particularly here in bed. After everything he'd been through, he didn't really want to share a bed with anyone but Alicia.

At times Ginger exhibited spurts of kindness, taking him in, getting him a job—he could never have done that on his own. He owed her. The days were all right, but at night, in these close quarters, there was no air, no light, no peace. At least the toilet had a door, although Ginger never bothered to close it.

This is just temporary, he tried to convince himself. A chance to regain my strength, both body and mind. I'll work out a way to put my family back together. Alicia will back me. I'll come up with something.

Ginger seemed to like it out here at the quiet end of Arrow Point. She certainly was friendly when mingling with the tourists at Marble Mine Village. And a bit more than friendly with Fosdick. But underneath the friendliness, she kept to herself. Like she had her own past, one she'd prefer to keep hidden. It definitely felt creepy.

But then, who was he to complain?

JASPER LOWERED HIMSELF into the water, three feet deep, cold, and black. He sloshed forward into the dark void pierced by a faint yellow glow up ahead. The splatter of water against the hard wall of the tunnel sounded like a waterfall in that concrete raceway. The water felt frigid through the heavy rubber waders he'd found in the maintenance shed.

Something bumped into his foot. A fierce shiver shot up his leg, surged through his spine. Could there be water moccasins in this black water?

Around the first curve, a grotesque scene lit by one dim lantern depicted the horrors of a mine flooded with water. Water rushed in as two prison convicts futilely struggled with a hand pump, an ancient jerry-built affair with large steel handles opposed to each other, like a hand-operated railcar in silent movies. No matter their crimes and lack of remorse, did they deserve this tragic finale?

A ridiculous hoax, of course, a one-of-a-kind Ozark Mountain fabrication. Fosdick had insisted that Jasper stay late to repair flooded cell number three. His instructions had been brief and emphatic. "The cable attached to a convict's arm, so that he can feed a chunk of wood into the buzz saw, has busted loose from the elliptical pulley wheel contraption. Bolt it back together."

Jasper would have preferred something more detailed. How do you bolt back together a busted contraption?

Fosdick made Jasper realize something he'd never noticed before—he had been a good boss. In his department at the First Commerce Bank, he had never made unreasonable demands or harsh comments. People seemed to like working for him. Then Jasper remembered Miss Shipley, his secretary. When his father would go on one of his tirades and harass him, had he taken it out on her? When the children made him late in the morning, had he marched past Miss Shipley, not even glanced at her, just uttered a terse, "Coffee ready yet?"

He moved on, slowly, both hands full of what tools

he could gather from the tool shed. What size bolts held contraptions together?

He had told Ginger not to wait, not that she would have. So, he would walk four miles to the motel unless he got lucky and one of the locals came by. But not many people headed out to the Point late in the evening.

At last, flooded cell number three—the defective buzz-saw spectacle. A convict stood at a large bench, feeding lumber into a fully exposed, three-foot tall, whirling circular saw blade. A lantern directly above cast shards of light off the saw blade's teeth as it viciously spun. A wooden crate labeled EXPLOSIVE sat precariously next to the buzz saw. As a safety precaution, a red water bucket with bold white letters that said FIRE waited nearby. Wooden boxes labeled DANGER and DYNAMITE lay recklessly scattered around. Inexplicitly, someone had labeled one large black metal can BUTTER. A large brass bell attached to the wall apparently served as a warning in time of impending disaster.

Time to ring the bell.

Jasper dragged himself up out of the water and into the scene, carefully skirting the buzz saw. He spotted a thin steel cable, coiled and dangling overhead. Higher yet hung the elliptical pulley, concealed behind a WARNING sign. He looked around for boxes he could stack up to reach the dangling cable.

Clank—steel against steel. Waves began to churn in the tunnel. Jasper ducked behind the convict, staying far away from the buzz saw—that thing looked like it could rip your arm off. Was this a trap? Was Fosdick part of a plot? Jealous because he lived with Ginger? Had the cops set an ambush?

The buzz saw buzzed. The convict froze—the cable

was broken. Jasper froze—his whole life was broken.

Peering from behind the protection of the sturdy convict, Jasper witnessed a large metal ore car floating by, followed by a loud clank. Then another ore car. This one contained a shadowy figure. The intruder strained to raise a large object, then bounded onto the scene.

"Thought you might need help. Ginger said you were here working late." Caleb stepped into the lantern light, holding a complete mechanic's tool kit in a metal case. "Didn't Fosdick show you how to turn on the ride and float in on an ore car?"

"No, he's big on demands and short on explanations. At least with me."

"He's that way with everyone. And by now he's figured out that you live with his favorite employee."

Tall, wiry Caleb stood on sturdy Jasper's shoulders, threaded the cable over the elliptical pulley contraption and fastened the end loop with a U-bolt.

"Oops, just a minute." Caleb began undoing something. "I almost saddled a dead horse."

They tested the convict; his arm worked great. Then gathered the tools and prepared to leave.

"What did you mean about saddling a dead horse?"

"You should place the molded saddle portion of a U-bolt against the loadbearing side of the cable loop. The prongs of the saddle protect the twisted wire strands and create less abrasion. When you saddle a dead horse, the saddle is on the dead, nonloadbearing side of the cable. Not critical in this application, but a good rule to follow."

"Where did you learn that?"

"Guying fence. Growing up on a farm, you learn to do everything."

"Working in a bank—err, an office environment, a

person doesn't get a lot of mechanical experience."

They rode out in an ore car. Jasper imagined himself as a tourist. Edward would be thrilled with this ride, Elizabeth would scream, and Alicia would put her hands over her eyes.

At times Caleb had seemed a bit odd, out of touch with the modern world. But now Jasper saw him in a different light, as a friend. Near the end of the ride, the canary placed in a cage to warn of disaster hung motionless. Upside down. Jasper felt like that canary, sent in amongst convicts to test his resolve.

JASPER HARDLY SLEPT that night. Visions of Tucker Prison flashed through his mind. Flooded mine convicts wore black-and-white stripes. The crank spun round and round. Propelled by a hand tattooed with Christ on the cross. A lightning bolt flared from a penis. Men chained together attacked the earth with long-handled picks. They carved out a grave. Cast in a disjointed comrade. Waves flooded in.

He woke up, soaked in sweat.

He rolled over toward Ginger. His head slid off his pillow. Into that neutral valley between his pillow and hers. At the top of his temple, a sharp jab. Cold. Rigid. He reached out. Took hold. It fit into his hand. Perfect. Too perfect.

He had never seen one up close, but there was no mistaking the distinctive shape—Smith & Wesson snub-nose revolver. Every detective novel had one—easy to conceal, accurate enough at close range.

Ginger stirred. Shook the sleep from her eyes. Grabbed it out of his hand. Fast and sure.

Her wide-open eyes and shiny white teeth lit the room. She grinned like a possum. "Girl's got to protect herself these days."

"Do you really think that's necessary?"

"Now, won't you sleep better knowing I'm here to look after you?"

He smiled and nodded. Beginning to think he'd never sleep again.

Chapter

10

Harwood slammed the phone down. Good thing the department didn't have money for a modern phone system. That cheap Jap plastic would've busted. He'd just received unwelcome news: the warrant for a tap on Pipkins's home phone had just lapsed and Lieutenant Elliott Heckler refused to ask a judge to renew it. Too expensive. What bullshit. It had only been a month. These things took patience. Eventually Pipkins would call home. He would get lonely. Call for sympathy. Whine about how rough it was to stay ahead of the cops. Ask for money. A Western Union transfer. Or maybe he was stupid enough to dream up a cash handoff in a coffee shop.

Time to put the backup plan into motion. The higher-ups would not be getting their bureaucratic hands dirty on this. A wiretap was the best way to crack this case—damn near the only way to crack it. Pipkins would invariably mention clues leading to his location.

Wiretaps were expensive—Keeping a technician available twenty-four hours a day was pricy. Then you had to constantly deal with those clowns at the phone company.

Money seemed to be the only thing that Heckler cared about anymore. The tight promotion policy made everyone afraid to piss off the brass. Hopes of a career move had generated a cover-your-ass attitude all up and down the line. Loyalty and respect for other officers took second place these days.

But what choice did he have? If he didn't follow the rules, the evidence couldn't be used in court. Some high-priced lawyer would get the bastard off on a technicality.

To hell with the rules. Randolph G. Pipkins didn't play by the rules. He manipulated the Kansas City PD.

No need to divulge how Pipkins is located. There is enough circumstantial evidence for a conviction. Time to make another visit to Kansas City.

A L HARWOOD STOOD on tiptoes behind shouting parents. He'd arrived with only two minutes and twenty-three seconds left in the game. Tony handed off to—damn. Russellville intercepted. Number Thirty-Nine took a shot. Russellville led by sixteen now. He could barely see his son looking toward the center-court seats. Parents filled all the good seats; for the first time this season Harwood was not one of them.

The Pipkins case had screwed up his life again. Cincinnati PD had a suspect in custody that fit the profile—late thirties, no ID, no visible means of support, picked up for flashing teenage girls outside of a school event, kiddie porn found in his motel room. After three phone calls, they faxed a mug shot. Guy turns out to be Filipino.

Assholes. No wonder crime rates were soaring in Cincinnati.

He shouted and waved his arms to let Tony know he'd arrived. His son seemed to pay more attention to center-court seating than to who had the ball.

"We have a foul. Bradshaw, number forty-nine, is replacing Harwood."

Tony on the bench—one minute and nine seconds left on the clock.

He threw his weight against the panic bar on the gymnasium door. Rushed outside. Lit up a smoke. The tip of the flame scorched the end of his cigarette. He vowed to put an end to this Pipkins case.

Then put his life back together.

HARWOOD JUGGLED BOXES, cables, and a new roll of duct tape on the narrow walkway to the back door. The slower-than-usual pace brought on a depressing realization—the lawn had turned yellow. He fumbled with the doorknob, loose and ready to fall off—he kept forgetting to bring a Phillips screwdriver from the garage. Another damn thing he needed to fix.

Gadgets and tools covered the kitchen table. He strained to understand handwritten notes from the tech-geek at a questionable private-security firm. Carefully ripping off a strip of duct tape, he secured the voice-activation contraption to the small audiocassette recorder. When connected to a phone line, the handmade gizmo purportedly started the recorder when someone was speaking. The nerd had assured him that one cassette tape would last a month.

The equipment and clandestine advice had cost a month's wages, but he counted on it being as effective as a wiretap. Forget tracing the call, everyone hung up within a minute or two. The private-security expert thought a fancy place like Pipkins's would have a utility distribution point in the garage, maybe even a separate room for that kind of stuff.

He'd have to wait until next Saturday and put this plot into action on his personal time now that Heckler had caved to financial constraints. And this plan certainly did not comply with PD guidelines. These recordings would not produce admissible evidence, but he was no longer concerned with that. All he needed to do was get his hands on Pipkins.

"You know Tony has ball practice this afternoon." Judy marched straight to the coffee pot.

"You take him." He noticed she hadn't gotten dressed yet. Lately it seemed like she couldn't be bothered. "I got work to do."

"Is that the tape recorder that Tony wants?"

"No, this is department equipment."

"That's a RadioShack box."

"Heckler's cutting corners on everything."

"More work on a weekend. How about a day off? Time with Tony and me."

"I have to figure out how this stuff works."

"You haven't been home on a Saturday for weeks. And I've lost count of the days you've been in Kansas City. What the hell's driving you, revenge for Danny Coyle or your hurt ego about not solving this case?"

"Just working on a case, like all the others."

"The others didn't drag on like this. The others didn't keep you out of town for days at a time. The others actually left something for me and the kids."

He tore open a box of cassette tapes. The crinkling of cellophane reverberated off the kitchen walls.

No sense tearing jagged wounds open farther. Judy had a point, but she'd cool down when this was all over. He'd make it up to her. She often complained about being a cop's wife, but it was a hell of a lot easier than being a cop.

She was both right and wrong. It wasn't about Danny so much anymore, but it wasn't just his ego. It was his career. His reputation had suffered more damage when that goddamn banker had slipped past him again. The smirks would vanish, and the whispers would cease when that pervert pleaded for mercy. But first he would need to find Pipkins, figuring out how this stuff worked might be the easy part.

How was he going to put this device into action?

I N THE MORNING, Judy backed off and dragged Sally to church, with the promise of putting in a good word for Al. Early Sunday was always Al's quiet time, although he could have heard birds chirping in the backyard if he had bothered to listen. He used this time to think things over, analyze the past week. What went right? What got screwed up? What hood got off on a technicality? Lenient judges hadn't been a problem in Little Rock, but now a woman judge in the Pulaski County Juvenile Court believed fifteen-year-old punks from Roosevelt and Bond were actually children. Hard to see them as kids when you met the victims of their crimes.

Everything seemed to be a big problem lately, magnified somehow. Maybe Judy was right. Had this case taken over his life? What if Pipkins was the hapless midlife crisis he seemed to be? His wife and kids seemed like good people. Could he be that different?

He just needed to talk to that son-of-a-bitch. Think this out. Danny was a hothead at times. Had he overreacted? Had he provoked Pipkins?

A rustling cereal box broke the silence. Tony was up earlier than usual. In typical teenage fashion, he slouched around the house, not boisterously announcing his comings and goings as he had in previous years. But he and his son still got along well, talked about basketball and school every week. They planned Tony's college future and fishing trips. Although there hadn't been a fishing trip this year—the time spent in Kansas City had axed their weeklong float trip down the Buffalo River.

"Take your breakfast over to the table while I get more coffee."

Tony shuffled along, balancing a large bowl of cereal—half a box of corn flakes sloshed in what was left of the milk. He was wearing a ripped T-shirt, pajama bottoms, and one athletic sock. Harwood didn't even try to figure that out. Tony had never been an early morning person.

"What's up this morning?" Harwood looked directly at his son, gave his full attention. "You don't usually surface until nine."

"Don't know."

"Things okay at school?"

"Yeah."

"You sure?"

"Yeah. But . . . but my game's off."

"What's the problem? That shoulder bruise healed all right?"

"Shoulder's okay."

Harwood looked down at his favorite cup, rotated it slightly to avoid the chips on the rim. Judy had bought it for him on their trip to New Orleans, back before they had kids.

He'd interrogated gang members who were chattier than his son at the moment; something had changed, but he didn't know how hard he should press Tony. The kid needed space. Or maybe he needed help. He took a long sip of coffee. Took time to think. Talking to Tony was becoming more difficult. Moody, self-conscious. Typical teenager?

"So, what's not okay?"

"My offense is good, but I can't land a shot."

"You just need a little practice. We'll work on it this morning."

"Nah, I'm hot in practice. It's the games. I screw up during the games."

"Sorry I missed last Tuesday."

"It's okay. You didn't miss much."

"I'll be there this week. Promise."

He tried to remember what it was like as a teenager. When all you had to worry about was school, sports, and girls. The only thing he could remember was—it wasn't easy. Being a jock helped, the guys on the team were a ready-made social group. Talk usually involved the latest basketball hero or rumors that this week's opposing team were a bunch of dorks. Girls were a frustrating mystery, but he figured all teenage boys went through that. Could Tony have girl problems? Or problems for lack of them? He hardly seemed interested, though that was probably an act. Had he reached the age when jerking off wasn't enough?

This wasn't stuff he wanted to talk about with his own kid.

Being a cop made it hard to put himself in Tony's place. Many of the teenagers he came across were fathers before they reached twenty. How does a cop relate to his son's ordinary problems when he works with teenage burglars and dope dealers every day?

"PLEASE GET THE door, Edward," Alicia said, while slowly stirring a pot of spaghetti, "it's probably the dry cleaner."

She made a home-cooked dinner most nights, especially on Saturday when she had more time; it was her way of trying to keep the family together. What was left of it.

Edward ran back to the kitchen. "It's a policeman, Mom. In a suit. Some kind of detective."

The man stepped into the foyer without an invitation. "Good afternoon, ma'am, I'm Sergeant Alvin Harwood from Little Rock." Harwood politely held out his badge. "Perhaps you may be able to help me, may I come in?"

"You already are in." His shoes had a spit shine. He wore a neatly pressed suit. A firm jaw made him look tough, although given his short, slender stature Alicia thought that scrawny might be a better description.

"The young man's action implied that I should follow him."

"Do you have a warrant?" A nod toward the stairway sent Edward to his room.

"No, but—"

"I have nothing to say without my attorney present."

"And I have absolutely no questions for you, ma'am. I just want to close this case."

"Well, close it."

His eye contact would not let go. "Just need your cooperation for a minute. So far we've avoided involving you as an accomplice."

"If you were going to prosecute me, you would have done so already."

"The DA wanted to put you in prison for ten years. My boss talked him out of it, he didn't think it would be fair if you couldn't raise your own children."

He had a soft voice and seemed . . . meek. Although Alicia suspected a cunning creature dwelt under the surface. She reluctantly invited him to sit down at the kitchen table. She did not offer coffee.

"We're about to close this case," Harwood said. "The DA asked me to take care of a couple of details."

Alicia wasn't sure what to make of this. Could it really be over? "And Jeremy?"

"No news there. We are no longer actively pursuing your husband."

"Then why are you here?"

"Well, as you know, we do still think your husband killed Detective Coyle," Harwood said. "But we're coming to see it as unintentional—an accident in the heat of the moment."

Alicia concentrated on controlling her face. Her lawyers had told her to not even admit she'd been there. And she didn't trust this Harwood.

"If your husband does show up, my boss can get him out of prison in eighteen months with good behavior.

He has a personal relationship with the parole board. Minimum-security detention, it's like a hotel."

"This still doesn't tell me why you're here."

"We can only afford to stay on a case for so long. I've tried to close this twice, but my boss is a stickler for details."

"What details?

Harwood scratched the palm of his left hand with his right index finger. "We need to confirm that he's not hiding in the house."

"That's preposterous."

"Believe me, I know. I think my boss got his job through the Peter Principle—he kept being promoted until he reached a prominent level of incompetence, then they didn't promote him anymore."

Alicia laughed. Jeremy would understand this man's logic.

"Just a quick look around," Harwood said. "Then I can sign off on it and have this all behind us."

"If that's all it takes."

"Good. Let's start in the garage."

HARWOOD GLANCED ACROSS the garage. His eyes locked onto a sleek sedan. "Sharp-looking Jag. What year?"

"Well, I can't quite recall."

He acted as though he were about to reenter the house. Suddenly opened the outside walk-through door. Looked both ways. Locked it. Then quickly unlocked it while blocking her view.

"'74, I think," Alicia paused for a moment, "Jeremy gave it to me as a birthday gift."

He would return in half an hour and slip through that door while the family ate dinner, before they set the burglar alarm for the night. After connecting the recording equipment across the phone line, he would bypass the alarm mechanism for the garage side door—that would allow him access when returning each month to change out the audio cassettes. At the end of this escapade he would promptly remove the recording equipment and the door bypass wiring. No one need know how he'd located Pipkins. This kind of operation required patience; a trait criminals lacked. Eventually Pipkins would call, he was sure of it.

The rest of the sweep went quick. Until the last room, at the far end of the mansion, the son's room. Harwood had all kinds of questions for Edward, what year in school, his favorite sports. Sometimes he played the good cop. Building trust could be useful.

He felt somewhat guilty, barging into this family's home, taking advantage of a woman struggling with two children. But not guilty enough to keep him from bringing justice to the man who'd carelessly taken Danny's life.

When he left, Harwood assured Mrs. Pipkins that it had finally ended.

He knew her problems had only started.

A LICIA HAD PLENTY of time to think—more than she wanted, especially during long weekend nights. Even reading evaded her.

She had grown up in a world of books. Her dad had taught high school history and her mom taught English just down the hall. Grandpa had been a school principal for the brief time that she knew him. He had died young, a sudden heart attack at fifty-five. So, she'd become a teacher, had never considered any other career. And it suited her fine.

With boys, her choices had been less obvious. Late to the party some might say. Tomboy, late bloomer, bookworm—her mother's excuses.

"A pretty girl, a senior this year, you think she would've broken three or four hearts by now," Aunt Jessie had said, trying to turn it into a joke.

Alicia felt that her mother had really wanted to say, "What's wrong with you, young lady? Think you're too smart for those boys?" Truth was, she hadn't known and hadn't cared why she never played the dating game. She'd just never given it much thought.

Of course, there had been high school prom—Waterloo waiting for participants. Opposing armies picking sides, eager to go down in history—even Napoleon wasn't smart enough to stay out of some battles. Why was everyone so intent on that challenge? Wally Bohrer had been the first to ask, and she jumped at the chance. She probably could've done better, but she definitely could've done worse.

Mom was so excited. "I think yellow is in, yes, I'm sure it is. We'll need to book Bernadette now; everyone will be getting their hair done that day."

Were things different when Mom was young? Or had she forgotten? On the surface, it seemed a reason to dress up, be important for a night, keep the tuxedo rentals in business. A young lady's coming out. To guys it was a license to get drunk and get laid—or at least say that they did.

Wally accomplished the first, no problem there. Although she would have bet he was somewhat embarrassed returning that rented tux, encrusted with recycled peach-flavored vodka and pizza. He wasn't successful on goal number two. She submitted perhaps a bit too soon, letting his hand slip into her bodice. That spurred him on way too much.

She grabbed his wrist. "It's really late. But it's really been fun." She never knew what story Wally told. A girl was either labeled a real nympho, who dropped her panties on cue, or so goddamn frigid you couldn't thaw her legs apart with a blowtorch. It seemed a no-win game, but she didn't care. In the fall, she was off to college.

College had been a far different scene. No Wally, no mother, no interfering aunts. Lots of books, campus protests, women's issues to argue. And one cute professor with a goatee and tweeds who was interested in more than political discussions over bagels and hibiscus tea.

Then along came Jeremy. Kind of shy, real polite, just the slightest bit chubby, a little like her—sort of cute and really smart. They got along great, right from the start. Still would if he were still here.

But what had happened with Janie Franklin . . .

She had a lot of thinking to do.

JASPER WANDERED THE park in a daze; the morning had been spent in a yelling match with Ginger. Rick, the motel manager, had come to the rescue by offering to upgrade them to the Arrow Point Motel deluxe two-bedroom suite for only ten dollars more a month. It wasn't really much of a bargain since Jasper was relegated to the bedroom with a leaky roof. But the moldy smell was worth it, he now had his very own room.

Time to quit rehashing his present dilemma. He

began envisioning a family vacation—Alicia on his arm, Edward and Elizabeth tugging this way and that. Wanting to climb the old concrete tree and stagger across the swinging bridge, fearful of riding in an ore car through the flooded mine, interested in hearing a history lesson at the Old Trail School.

The Old Trail School amused grade-school children with its pretty schoolteacher, her hair in a bun. Visitors of all ages sat at the desks and learned about frontier education. Reading, arithmetic, geography—basic cognitive skills for future store clerks, miners, and farmers.

Jasper wondered if he had ever fit comfortably into a desk that small. His grade school, Kansas City Prep, educated tomorrow's leaders. The Old Trail School did have one superior attribute—cute as a button Miss Barnes.

At ten thirty, one thirty, and three thirty, Miss Barnes presented a history lesson. Her desk sat in one corner with a large American flag just behind it. She had a brass bell with a red maple handle on top of her desk; it announced the start of the school day and the end of recess. On the chalkboard, she had written a quote from Francis Bacon, wisdom regarding the varying quality of books. Stern Abraham Lincoln hung above the blackboard; his framed photograph nailed to the hand-hewn logs. Next to him, George Washington looked uncomfortable, probably those false teeth. The formidable pair reminded Jasper of his grandparents. A cast-iron stove sat in another corner, its blackened tin pipe disappearing into the ceiling. In winter, students would feed in logs and empty the ashes. Kerosene lamps hung on all four walls, supplementing light that came through the windows on dull winter days. On one side wall hung photographs of Confederate heroes, General Robert E Lee, and President Jefferson Davis.

"Hi," Miss Barnes said as he wandered into the schoolhouse. "I've seen you coming and going, you must work here somewhere."

"I'm the mine tour photographer." Jasper pointed to the floor. "Spend most of my time down there."

"It's nice to see that you've surfaced this morning. I'm Julie Barnes."

"Jasper Jones. You seem like a real schoolteacher."

"Not really. My father is the minister of the Mount Olive Tabernacle in Branson. I teach Sunday school and Bible class on Wednesday night."

"Then you are a real teacher." Jasper felt clumsy. He hadn't been in polite company for a while, his idle chatter skills were a bit rusty.

"We're having a social at the church hall on Saturday. Just an informal get-together. If you can come up out of the ground for a while, please stop by."

"Saturday. Well . . . sorry, can't make it. Thanks, though."

"Maybe some other time."

"Yes, maybe some other time."

He wanted to go. Meet other people. But he had no car, and he could hardly show up with Ginger—she wasn't church social material. Besides, fending off Ginger took all of his fortitude. And meeting more people would increase the risk of unintentionally giving away information. Clues. He didn't think the police had given up.

Chapter

11

D idn't look like a Schlage lock. Definitely not as easy to pick as a chintzy Kwikset. Harwood squinted while pointing a miniature penlight at the side door of Mrs. Pipkins's garage. His left hand slid a tension wrench into the keyway, damn hard to do with a severed tendon that had locked up his index finger. A deep lock. High-end commercial grade. Probably had eight key pins instead of only five. His right hand inserted a pick tool until he felt the first key pin. While raising that pin with the pick, a slight pressure on the tension wrench kept it in place. Then he pushed the pick further into the keyway and felt for the second pin. Raised it and advanced to the third. The lock tightened up. Probably raised the second pin too far. Withdrawing the pick and jiggling the tension wrench reset the pins. Using a smaller pick got him as far as the fifth pin. It seemed stiff, couldn't raise it high enough. Damn it. Pull the tools out, apply a spray lubricant, start over again. Headlights flashed from down the hill at the bottom of the driveway. He jumped behind a large holly bush. Didn't move until the car was in the garage and the door closed.

This was getting too risky. He'd only ever picked three or four locks, when he'd needed a quick look around without reasonable cause for a warrant. And he'd never come across a lock this complex.

There was another way of getting into that garage. It would mean coming back tomorrow and being very persuasive.

HARWOOD CHECKED INTO a mom-and-pop motel on the south edge of Kansas City. Cheap—expenses were adding up. Paid with cash. No one but Judy knew he was in Kansas City. He intended to keep it that way. At least the place had an in-room phone.

"Hi, honey. Sorry to call so late. Lot of traffic."

"Where are you? Thought you'd be home by now."

"Still in Kansas City. New development. Need to check it out tomorrow."

"Yeah, we've had our own developments here. That piece of junk Plymouth stalled again. In the middle of an intersection!"

He held the phone to his ear by tipping his head toward his left shoulder. Fumbled for a cigarette. Tried to come up with a reply that would calm Judy down. She continually complained about that two-door Duster. It was almost a classic. Needed to keep it running until Tony finished college.

"Did you get it started okay?"

"No. You weren't there when I needed you. I asked you to help me get ready for Mother's birthday party tomorrow. You weren't there, Al. You never are anymore."

"I'll finish up here first thing in the morning. Get to the party before she blows out the candles."

"Don't bother."

The loud click and dial tone told him he'd lost that battle. This war had to end. That banker wouldn't evade him much longer. Just one mistake is all it would take.

ALICIA HAD FORCED herself to dress up this morning. She had even purchased a new dress that was stylish yet conservative enough for the First Presbyterian Church. She added a touch that she seldom did, a large-brimmed hat with a satin bow on one side. Its fawn velvet complemented her complexion. She slipped on a pair of chestnut-brown Italian high heels. The ones Jeremy had splurged on, the ones that he said put her on the same level as a young Lauren Bacall. For the first time in a long time, she thought she looked pretty.

She impatiently waited for the children at the garage door. "Edward, you cannot wear those shoes to church."

"Why not?"

"They're white. They're tennis shoes. Your grandfather would have a fit."

Alicia found getting the children ready for church—or maintaining any semblance of normal life—proved harder each week. Edward and Elizabeth were prone to rebellion in their own ways. And, for that matter, so was she.

It was times like this that she missed him most. Jeremy knew how to get through to Edward. How to cajole him. How to be a mentor. When to be his best friend. When to play tough.

Time to draw on her own inner strength, as she had done all her life. Soon after the wedding, Jeremy's father had mapped out a life for her—a place on the ladies organizing committee for the Presbyterian church's annual fête—a behind-the-scenes position coordinating the mayor's annual prayer breakfast. She would have nothing to do with any of it, and told Randolph so, then accepted a teaching position for the fall term.

"Elizabeth, come down immediately, we'll be late!"

"I can't find my blue hair ribbon."

Alicia tossed the car keys on the counter, poured another cup of coffee, and flopped into a kitchen chair.

"Mr. and Mrs. Randolph G. Pipkins will not be pleased," Alicia said. Then under her breath, "Tough shit."

Minutes later the doorbell rang.

"That cop is back," Edward said. "The skinny one with the pointy nose."

Alicia nearly dropped her coffee cup. She sent Edward to his room without telling him to say, "police officer."

Well, she would give that detective a piece of her mind. Although he might have news. But why hadn't he just called?

"Mrs. Pipkins, I wasn't expecting such fashionable dress."

"I wasn't expecting a police detective. It's Sunday. Religious people dress up for church."

"I certainly understand that. Most Sundays I'd be with the wife and children at the First Baptist Church. But new facts have emerged. My boss, Lieutenant Heckler, wants this cleared up as soon as possible. He is being pressured to close this case and move on. Just a moment of your time. I have some photographs, you may recognize him, he may be the man who misled your husband. He may actually be the killer."

"Jeremy was set up?"

"A definite possibility." The detective tipped his head down and looked up, as though looking over imaginary bifocals.

"Come in." She found it hard to believe that this doleful-looking man had a family.

The detective quickly spread out several surveillance pictures. Fiddled with his ring. A simple wedding band. Turned it around one way, then the other. For no reason. Apparently a nervous habit.

"Listen," he said. "While you study these, would you mind if I use the restroom?"

He headed toward the bathroom in the back of the house before Alicia could direct him to the guest bath just around the corner.

Alicia sat alone on the couch scrutinizing the stack of photos. Could there be more to this than she'd realized? Was Jeremy a pawn in some nefarious scheme? The detective was a smooth talker, but underneath he was nervous. Wound tight. Like an animal on the prowl.

What was his real agenda?

SLIPPING INTO THE garage and swapping the tape went fast. Finding the keys that he remembered hanging on a hook in the kitchen took a minute. He spotted them on the kitchen counter next to her purse. The husband's a fugitive and she's all prettied up and headed for church. Yeah, say a prayer for Danny, lady.

Harwood pressed both sides of the two house keys into clay molds. Slipped the molds back into his suit coat pocket. Returned to the living room and jumped into a spiel before she could ask questions.

"I see you have a math student in the family." Harwood nodded toward an open textbook on the coffee table. "My son took geometry last year. Now that he's on to trig, I'm not much help. The kid knows more about angles than I'll ever figure out."

"I don't know that Edward will go on to trigonometry. His interests lie more in the arts."

Mrs. Pipkins did not recognize the man in the photos. No surprise. They were old surveillance snapshots of a sleazeball who pimped UALR college girls to traveling salesmen.

Harwood apologized for the inconvenience, mentioned that it was the last lead, the case would be closed in a day or two, then quickly departed.

Sitting in his car, he carefully removed the molds from his coat pocket and placed them in the glove box. Tomorrow he would have keys made from the molds. His plan depended on one of those keys fitting the walk-in garage door. Hopefully, the tape he had just retrieved would give up a clue to hubby's location. Then he would slip in and pull all of the recording equipment. If not, he would return next month and swap cassettes again.

Eventually Pipkins would contact the wife.

J ASPER WAITED PATIENTLY by the exit of Marble Mine Village. Ginger always took her time leaving. Fridays were the worst—after her weekly visit with Fosdick, she seemed to like hanging around talking to the women in the accounting office. Ginger did everything at her own pace. But she had a car, and he wasn't about to walk back to the motel. Jasper made effective use of the wait, cheerfully greeting other employees—fewer of them now that fall semester had started at college.

"How did you do at McGuffey's Homestead?" he asked when Ginger finally arrived.

"Not many people today."

"We only ran five mine tours, no families, just retired people. They don't buy pictures."

"Only two more days to go."

"Are they going to close for the season?"

"Monday."

"Everyone's been asking. Are you sure? They haven't posted a notice."

"Trust me. Monday."

"Does any of the park stay open?"

"Hell, no, Freddie's already packed for Florida."

Jasper knew it would close soon, tried to ignore it. He'd become good at that lately. After the escape from Little Rock, he'd felt like a deer in the headlights, afraid to move in any direction. Confidence in some sort of a future was only beginning to seem possible.

"Better start looking for work," Ginger said.

"Got any ideas?"

"Waiting tables and acting are all that I know. And the performing arts are really limited here."

"I've never acted or waited tables."

"You're not a bad cook, when you get off your butt."

"Not professionally, I couldn't."

"Do you really think you got to be a professional around here?"

A DAY OFF AT last. Jasper had worked every day, an energetic attempt to fill his coffer. He would spend the coming week putting Marble Mine Village in mothballs to preserve it for next season. What would happen after that worried him. Ginger had already started to look for winter employment. She tolerated his presence while he paid half the rent and cooked all the meals. A pragmatic arrangement, no room for benevolence.

From the deck behind Buster's Café, on the very tip of Arrow Point, he looked out at Table Rock Lake. On this high spit of land that jutted out into the broadest bend of the reservoir, he couldn't see the far shore.

The world he'd left behind—Alicia, the children, the bank—seemed like another continent. Had the banished misfit Pilgrims sat on Plymouth Rock thinking of their homeland and friends left behind? Stranded in a strange land. With strange inhabitants. Wondering if they would ever see home again. Had that prompted Thanksgiving? The cool weather made him to think of the holidays ahead—memorable dates approached—Thanksgiving, Christmas, New Year's, and the last day he'd seen Alicia. What kind of an anniversary would that be, for either of them?

He started walking down the trail that ran along the ridge. Thinking about his homeland. Was Edward doing okay in school? Did Elizabeth need braces? He felt as though Alicia were beside him. They had never taken hikes in the woods, and they should have. But they had shared a lot of quiet times like this, when they spoke, intimately, without saying a word.

"It's hard to imagine all this water came from a modest stream up in the mountains," he said.

She replied affirmatively without making a sound.

He kept going along the trail that clung to the cliff side. The late-day sun sparkled on the tips of waves. A northwest breeze molded a light chop on the lake. Distant boats became even smaller, perhaps fishermen heading out to try their luck at night. The whine of their motors had faded to nothing.

He sensed her presence. Appreciated her more than he ever imagined possible.

I appreciate you too—he was sure she had just said it.

ALICIA TOOK IN the pretentious happy hour scene at Tiffany's Cocktail Lounge. Groups of two and three ladies, free from the bonds of marriage but seemingly eager to repeat past mistakes, perched on stools around high tables, displaying the merchandise—pouf hairdos, bright red lipstick, plunging necklines, and the widest, whitest smiles they could manage.

Barbara had bragged that this watering hole now ranked as the hottest spot in Kansas City to meet eligible men. Alicia stayed supportive and did not say that they probably weren't eligible for anything outside of the bedroom. And even then, they probably disappointed. Why else would they wind up here?

"How are the kids holding up?" Barbara searched for a distraction while waiting for a nibble—eye contact from a stranger or a smile cast over a shoulder from up at the bar.

"Edward's adapting, he's a tough kid. Has a couple of friends he plays golf with, open-minded kids that are tolerant of others. They often walk to the driving range near the clubhouse."

"How about Elizabeth?"

"She's . . . a different story. Extremely sensitive, doesn't really understand what the girls in her class are teasing her about. Little bitches, neither do they."

"One thing is for sure, whatever life throws at your kids, they'll come out on top. They're survivors." With her mouth closed, Barbara tied a knot in the stem of a cocktail cherry, a mysterious trick she had learned at a frat house in college.

"How about you?" Alicia asked. "Any news from the home front?"

"The home front is hunky-dory, as long as the asshole formally known as my husband stays away."

Alicia scanned the retreads propping up the bar. Bell-bottom pants, mutton-chop sideburns, polyester leisure suits, belts that had run out of notches. She refused to buy a ticket in this loser's lottery.

"You work at Hardaway, Masters, & Dunn, don't you?"

Alicia looked up at the six-foot-two hulk leaning over the table in a black suit, black turtleneck, and enough cologne to incapacitate a medium-size rhinoceros. She smiled. "No."

That threw Casanova off balance. "I know I've seen you somewhere."

"Maybe we've met professionally? I'm a parole officer."

Barbara raised her hand to hide a snicker.

The lounge lizard didn't even notice the dig. "The Vapors Rendezvous on Prospect Avenue, that's where I've seen you."

"No. Definitely not me."

Alicia usually disliked being rude, but with this jerk she kind of enjoyed it. She wouldn't even be in this meat market if it weren't for Barbara, her recently divorced friend who needed support while she dreamed that the right guy would soon wander into her life.

And Alicia wished her good luck with that.

THE LAST THING Alicia had expected was a call from Janie Franklin. Her mind raced back to the party and the tragedy that followed. It wasn't the memory that shocked her. It was how different she was now, the way her life had evolved in new directions during the past three months.

Yes, Alicia had called Janie weeks ago, to find out how she was doing. Janie had told Alicia about losing her position as a first-grade teacher. The only job she had been able to find was serving breakfast at a truck stop while enduring rude comments from long-haul drivers. Her husband had left for some small town in Maine or Massachusetts, somewhere back East. Within minutes, a rapport developed as the chatter intensified. Of course, she had told Janie to call if she ever needed a friend.

And now, here she was, on the phone, telling how her house had finally sold. She'd barely broken even, but she'd kept her good credit rating. Everything she wanted to keep, including her nine-year-old daughter, fit into a station wagon. In two days, Janie would start the long drive to her parents in Seattle and suggested a stopover in Kansas City.

Alicia's first houseguest in over a year. She had to check on the guest room. Make sure there were plenty of towels. Ensure everything looked neat. Janie and her daughter would spend the night.

How did this happen?

Don't want no flames licking the meat
Harpo

Harpo's
Hog Pen

Hickory
Smoked
Pig

NO-DRINKING-ON-OUTSIDE-THAT-THE-LAW
YOU-CAN-BE-ARRESTED-BY-POLICE

Chapter

12

"**I** have entered the exciting world of serving food to our hungry bourgeois community." Jasper stood in the motel room doorway, hands on his hips.

"You got a job?" Ginger peered over her ragged Vogue magazine.

"Sure did, although it's not with a major player in the food service industry."

"Absolutely amazing. I suppose you think I'll drive you all the way to Branson every day."

"It's just down the road. Harpo's Hog Pen."

Ginger instantly flipped from cynic to laughing so hard she rolled off the couch.

138

"Hey," he protested, "I don't laugh about your job at the Waffle House."

"That waitress gig is a way to make quick money, a temporary diversion, until I save enough to get out of this Bible-thumping hell hole."

"Well Harpo's actually serves outstanding food. I've already had a free sample."

"Is your gut queasy yet?"

"Happy as a clam. Harpo's is immensely popular with the early evening diners around here."

"Yeah, the happy hour, beer and a burger crowd."

"We specialize in barbecue, not burgers, thank you—and I bet the tips are good."

"We? Are you on the fucking board of directors already? I've seen that place and cringed every time I've driven by. The windows are filthy and the parking lot is full of pickup trucks sporting gun racks and hay bales."

"Yes, and lots of trucks means lots of tips. And we do have an extensive menu."

"And what might that be, besides barbecue and Budweiser?"

"Here, I brought one home so that I could familiarize myself with it. The 'Pig Sandwich' is the most popular entrée." It had started as a light-hearted jest, exaggerating his new job as though it were a distinguished career opportunity. He missed the animated banter, the exaggerations he enacted to amuse Alicia.

"A three-page foldout, I am impressed—and this plastic laminate will protect against the corrosive effects of Harpo's barbecue sauce."

"I believe that Waffle House also laminates their menus."

Ginger resumed her intense laughter. "I don't

believe this tagline—Slow Cooked Pig, even better than Grandma's."

"Aggressive advertising. It's the American way." Pretending he had landed an executive position had been a game. Now he just wanted to berate the pretentious bitch.

Ginger took another swipe. "Perhaps Harpo hired a Madison Avenue marketing firm to spruce up his image."

"Sounds like good business sense to me."

"Someone with good business sense would've put those resources into propping up the building."

Beyond Ginger's negative attitude and chatter about saving money, something did not make sense, she was holding something back. Why not move on now? She could bankroll more cash just about anywhere else. He knew why he was staying in this out-of-the-way place, but why was Ginger hanging around? Was she also hiding something?

JASPER PULLED INTO the parking lot ten minutes early; he didn't chance being late on his first day of work. Although parking lot seemed like an exaggeration—dirt potholes surrounded Harpo's Hog Pen.

He parked in the back between two mud puddles, hoping that an intoxicated fisherman wouldn't open his pickup door and carelessly put a conspicuously un-rusted dent in Ginger's Datsun. Driving a car seemed awkward—it'd been months since he had gotten behind the wheel. Ginger had conned him into driving her car to Branson for an oil change while she enjoyed a bottle of wine and a Harlequin paperback. Jasper had started to tell her that he didn't have a driver's license, not one that he dared show. But the right words escaped him, and then the drive to Branson turned into an adolescent adventure. A bored teenager cut loose for the first time, burning rubber in second gear, feeling the G-force on every sharp curve.

Well, as much as a Datsun B210 would allow.

Jasper paraded into Harpo's and paused to let his eyes adjust. Glass globes dangling from cloth-covered wires strained to give off a dim yellow light. Unvarnished floor planks loosely held by large shiny nails were scattered with last night's peanut shells. Above the bar, grand, out-of-place paintings portrayed Wild West scenes.

"Hi, Harpo."

"Well, if it ain't that assistant chef and headwaiter what actually showed up." Harpo stood behind the bar next to a sign that read If You're Drinking to Forget—Pay Me Now.

"Let's roast some pork." Jasper played good-humored restaurateur—residual joyride adrenaline was still flowing.

"Slow down, young fella, I don't cut no corners. If you fixin to learn about being a pit master, c'mon out back. I'll show you how to keep a fire going without scorching the meat."

"What's a pit master?"

"You about to find out."

Harpo could not have weighed over one hundred pounds. A two-inch wide belt was cinched tighter than necessary, leaving a foot of unused leather dangling in the air. Dusty flat-toed boots looked as though they had never seen a can of Shinola. Nothing matched—dark-green pants, a red-and-black checked shirt that probably started life as flannel, and a light-blue T-shirt. His scrawny face had an odd, chiseled look. And warm, moist eyes didn't fit the rest of his hardscrabble body—those eyes reminded Jasper of his grandmother.

Harpo slipped on leather gloves and dragged a sheet of rusty metal across the ground.

Jasper peered down through smoke into a hole lined with bricks. "I didn't know you actually cooked in the ground."

"It's pit barbecue, like my people did. Don't know how white folks got the guts to call it pit barbecue when they cook it in a metal contraption."

"Did your family barbecue when you were young?"

"We lived in a tenant house on a cotton farm. When Mister Clyde butchered hogs, he give us one. Didn't have no cooler, so we smoked it and added spices to make it last."

"Where are the ribs?"

"The pigs are resting comfortably in the cooler."

"Want me to get them?"

"Now, you just take your time. I keeps the bricks hot all night with oak logs. In the morning, I chucks in hickory."

"Looks like it could use a couple more logs now."

"Naw, can't use too much wood. It's called a smoker for a reason." Harpo dipped his fingertips in a bucket and flicked water on a log that was threatening to flare up. "When the hickory's burned down to coals, we'll invite the pigs out. Don't want no flames licking the meat."

"Hickory is a hardwood. Why not use it all the time?"

"I cuts oak from around here. Hickory cost good money."

Harpo slipped the metal sheet back over the pit and invited Jasper to split logs for tomorrow's fire. A half hour later, his aching arms swept the floor in front of the bar while Harpo reloaded the cooler with beer.

"Time to dress the pigs," Harpo announced without preamble. He lined up the ribs on a long wooden table in the middle of the kitchen. His eyes moved slowly from left to right, studying each slab. Instantly, white slivers flew off each rib as he slashed fat away, creating jagged meaty edges. Then in one smooth motion, he flipped every rib over, bone side up.

"Yank the clear sheet of skin right off." Harpo slipped his thumbnail under the thin membrane and ripped it off in one piece.

Jasper struggled to get hold of the skinny film. "This slippery stuff probably doesn't taste good."

"Don't know about that, but it keeps the smoke flavors from going into the meat." Harpo patiently waited while Jasper kept fumbling. "Take that knife an work up an edge, then just give it a jerk, like pulling off a bandage."

After Jasper tugged fragments of membrane from each rib, Harpo gave them a coat of yellow mustard.

"Do you want the ribs to taste like mustard?" Jasper said.

"Won't none of that linger after the cooking. It gives the spices something to stick to."

Jasper watched Harpo dump powders from dented coffee cans; he smelled garlic, paprika, chili, pepper.

Harpo reached into a bag labeled Domino and sprinkled white granules. Jasper couldn't help from asking, "Why are you putting white sugar in there?"

"Gives a nice saucy finish, like caramel. Brown sugar don't do that."

"What's that brown syrup?"

"Molasses. Makes it all clump together."

After stirring the bowl with a wooden spoon, Harpo gently massaged each rib with the dry rub.

Jasper loaded the ribs into a large bucket and hauled them out back. Then Harpo slid back the metal cover and lowered in a rib-rack fashioned from angle iron and rebar.

Jasper watched as Harpo fussed over dozens of details. He moved one slab of meat from one side of the smoker to the other with long, cast-iron tongs—flipped one sizzling chunk of meat end over end—then examined each piece, scooting some forward, pushing some back. Did that tedious routine make a difference? All they wanted to do was sell pork with beans and slaw for $2.99 a plate. Getting a Michelin star was not part of the game plan.

Finally, Harpo slid the metal cover over the pit and pulled out an old pocket watch. Jasper looked away—it was a cheap, chrome-plated version of the one that he had left behind in Old Roy's pawnshop.

"How long before we check to see how they're doing?"

"We ain't checking. Don't want no heat getting out. Wait two hours, and I'll show you what's next."

Jasper settled down and took mental notes of the countless tasks needed before the doors opened for business. His most amazing discovery was Harpo's patience with a lengthy list of what must have seemed like stupid questions. Harpo seemed to take pride in passing on his secrets. Defending the job to Ginger had been a reflex, but he could actually come out of here with some marketable skills.

Precisely two hours later, they were back at the pit. Harpo wrapped each slab in yesterday's black and greasy aluminum foil, as though he were covering a newborn with a flannel blanket.

"Do you ever serve barbecued beef?"

"I ain't no crazy-ass Texan."

Not quite an hour had passed when Harpo declared it was time for the last stage of the process. He pulled off the foil and basted each rack with a thick brown sauce.

"How will we know when they're cooked?"

"Grab a rack of ribs an pull. When the meat slides off the bone real easy, they're done."

Throughout the evening, Jasper pulled ribs out of the smoker and waited on tables, a task Harpo's wife Hattie had enjoyed until she passed away three years ago. Harpo had managed to get by until this year when old age had attacked with vengeance. Now working behind the bar took all his energy.

About a quarter past ten, when business slowed down, Jasper acted on an impulsive urge to know the fascinating man's story. "How did you wind up here?"

"I was young and restless. Headed west for some excitement, never got farther than this."

"Was it difficult to get started, for a . . . a—"

"A nigger boy? Colored folks weren't looked on kindly in Stone County when I showed up here."

"Were there many others? Other black people you could hang around with?"

"Fact is, I might've been the only one. Some called me Uncle Tom, guess cause I worked for that white guy."

"What white guy?"

"Guy what owned this place. I never knew him by nothing but Sir."

"You didn't know his name?"

"Long funny name. Papageorgaon I think. From Poland or Ireland, or some such strange land."

"What did you do for him?"

"I washed dishes and cleaned up. He didn't care much for me at first. I was young, didn't pay good attention. Later on things changed. He let me start doing some cooking. One day he got burnt bad on the hand, and I pulled out the family recipe for barbecue. I been cooking ever since."

"Where is he now?"

"Long dead."

"How did you acquire this property?"

"He dropped dead behind the bar one day. Heart attack, they said. There weren't nobody else, so I just kept on cooking."

"Do you own this place? Did you get title to the property?"

"Never seen no papers. Don't know how to read, anyhow."

"Have you paid the taxes?"

"I can read numbers. When bills come, I pays them."

"If it's been long enough, you may be able to get a quit-claim deed."

"What would I do with that?"

It seemed as if Harpo had paid his dues and earned the respect that weekend fisherman and local farmers showed him. Jasper doubted that local church ladies ever stepped in here, although one decently dressed customer took a pulled pork sandwich home to his wife.

A rowdy group at the humongous table ordered their third round—apparently a seven-pound, nine-ounce largemouth bass called for a celebration. It had been weighed, photographed, and documented—could be a record for this season. Jasper's fascination with southern Missouri's peculiar attitudes and customs lured him into listening in on the conversation.

"Where'd the go-kart out back come from?"

"Might of escaped from Marble Mine Village."

"Took me a look, nameplate says Datsun."

"That's a Jap car. My dad fought them buggers in the Philippines, said they was a vicious swarm of hornets, never would surrender, just holed up in caves and let you roast 'em alive."

"Bunch o' piddly-ass foreigners, making piddly-ass cars."

"Louie Hawkins over at the Ford place in Springfield said them cars was death traps. Have a fender bender and they crumple right up, trap you inside, then the tank blows."

Jasper faded into the storeroom. Every few minutes he checked on the smoker and watched for vandals near Ginger's defenseless foreign vehicle.

Chapter
13

The door opened, and Alicia's world changed.

She made a quick mental snapshot of a composed Janie Franklin. Cascading brown hair. Twinkling eyes. Strong cheekbones. Pink lipstick emphasizing a pleasant smile. A unique shade of eye shadow complementing a perfect complexion.

Like an awkward teenager, Alicia stood there stuck between *Hi* and *Please come in.* Then the dam broke. "Hi. Come in. It's so good to see you. This must be your daughter."

"Sure is. Phoebe, say hello to Mrs. Pipkins."

Janie looked around a moment, then picked out the couch and motioned Phoebe to join her. They both perched on the edge of their seats, as if they were in a museum.

Alicia suddenly recalled that they had been living

on a truck-stop waitress's salary. "Let me get Edward and Elizabeth." She savored the chance to fall back and reorganize. "Won't be a moment."

Alicia prided herself on her skill in the social graces, but today, in front of the children, she didn't know where to start. Janie broke the ice and began with a fictitious anecdote that she had concocted on the phone with Alicia—a cover story for the kids about how they had met years ago as college students. "What ever happened to that cute professor you were with when we met at that peace rally in St. Louis?"

"Oh, him? I last saw him two years after college, at a homecoming game. Probably retired by now."

"We go . . . went to one or two U of A games every season."

"We haven't gone back to Princeton for a Tigers' game since Edward was born."

Janie gave Edward a warm smile. "Do you play any sports?"

"Uh . . . golf."

"My mom plays golf." Phoebe said. "Her handicap is eight."

Edward perked up. "You have an eight handicap?"

"Not now. Haven't played for a while."

"Probably wouldn't take much practice to get back there."

"Bet you do well yourself. Looks like you've got enough upper body strength to drive two hundred yards."

"Two-twenty-five on a good day."

"I'd call that an excellent day."

The conversation flowed freely. Alicia's anxiety faded. Janie's melodic voice was pleasing, and she pronounced each word clearly, not a tinge of Arkansas drawl. Alicia noticed the impeccable sentence structure and a vocabulary as wide as her own.

The permed hair topped with a wiglet seemed to amaze Elizabeth. Large swaying earrings sparkled with every animated movement.

Janie's figure was more athletic than Alicia remembered. She suddenly blushed at what she remembered. It'd been brief. Dimly lit. How could she possibly know so many details?

Lemonade and strawberry shortcake in the sunroom should have been simple. But as everyone pulled back a chair, Alicia realized she had set one too many places. This was the first time she had entertained since Jeremy disappeared. An embarrassing faux pas that emphasized that someone was missing. Alicia poured the first glass too fast, and it overshot onto Janie's shortcake.

Relax. It's just lemonade and strawberry shortcake with friends.

"What grade are you in, Edward?" Janie said as she refilled his lemonade. It sounded so casual.

"Actually, we don't have grades like regular schools. You just move up in each subject as fast as you can."

"Sounds quite innovative."

"Kind of a college prep sort of school."

Janie leaned towards Elizabeth with a nod of approval. "Pink sneakers and hair ribbons, you look like a creative girl."

"Yeah. She creates a lot of noise." Big brother couldn't resist the jab. Alicia gave him a tap on his shin.

"My school's fun. Not full of drips like Edward's."

So much for impressing our houseguests. But that thought passed quickly. Janie's perfect-pitch laugh put a smile on everyone's face. Pretentiousness just seemed futile around this congenial woman from the middle of Arkansas.

"What's your favorite subject, Phoebe?" Alicia mimicked Janie's infectious smile.

"Math and music. I like them both about equally."

"You sure have a wide range of interests."

"Mom says I should try out a lot of things. A broad horizon, she calls it."

"Sounds like good advice."

Alicia had foreseen a disheveled woman, overwhelmed by misfortune. Instead, here sat this polished, self-assured person, lighting up her sunroom. She had always been reluctant to invite guests into her home, and during the past months, there had been none. Only Barbara had stopped by. No other friends called, and Alicia did not encourage them.

And now, a whirlwind of energy had blown into her life.

Alicia cleared up in the kitchen while Janie and Edward spent an hour discussing the advantages of Edward's new graphite-shaft driver. Elizabeth and Phoebe disappeared in the playroom to discuss girl stuff.

Alicia drew a deep breath and gazed out at Janie demonstrating a golf swing to Edward. Her stance looked strong and accomplished. She addressed the ball with her legs slightly spread, hips in line with the shot, buttocks tucked in.

Her narrow waist, full hips, and fertile look took center stage.

Janie's daughter wanted the same things as hers—the latest sneakers, good grades in school. And some attention, although when they got it, they went all quiet and looked away.

This entire day . . . It almost seemed normal.

And yet, what she knew about Janie . . . well . . . her friends would have said that normal was not a factual depiction.

Late in the afternoon, at the small table in a corner of the sunroom, Janie poured a second round of lemonade that Alicia had spiked with Jack Daniels. Edward went back to his schoolwork. The girls chattered in the two-story playhouse on the far side of the backyard. The sun dropped lower, and the trees wavered as a breeze swept in from the golf course.

"I can tell your kids do well in school." Something in Janie's voice said that she really meant it.

"Edward does pretty well but struggles with math. Sometimes I worry that he spends too much time on homework and not enough making friends. Elizabeth is smart as a whip, but a social butterfly." Alicia appreciated the chance to talk about her children—it had been too long. "How about Phoebe? She's certainly well spoken."

"She loves school, always straight As. But, where we come from, math whiz is an unwelcome label for a girl."

"She seems resilient enough to handle it."

"I'm glad we're moving on. Getting sidetracked by a football jock is a hazard for a young girl in Pine Bluff."

"Football can be a hazard here, too. Fortunately, my kids haven't shown much interest. Jeremy's the football nut."

Suddenly it got quiet.

"Didn't mean to open up that can of worms," Janie said.

"You didn't, I did. Somehow it's still hard not to drift back there."

"Are you getting on okay?"

"Sure. I have a rich and powerful father-in-law looking after me for the grandkids' sake. It's you I worry about. Losing your job. Your husband abandoning you."

Janie slid her hand along the edge of the table, in Alicia's direction. "Let's just kick back for now and not worry about each other."

FIVE DAYS LATER, while sweeping the floor, Jasper noticed Harpo in a corner thumbing through an old Western book he kept behind the bar. Jasper knew that Harpo couldn't read, he just gazed at the many illustrations.

"You seem fascinated by the old West."

"You can learn a lot about folks from books. Hattie used to read this one to me. People thinks that old Judge Parker was nothing but mean. Fact is, he didn't agree with hanging. Some even said he cried after sentencing the first four men to the gallows."

"That is a revelation."

"I guess a person can get used to anything if he puts his mind to it."

Jasper realized that Harpo wore the same clothes every day. Only one thing changed—when it got hot in the kitchen, he rolled up his sleeves. Could Harpo possibly have another identical set of clothes, or did he wash the same set each night? His clothes were always spotlessly clean in the morning, but never ironed.

Jasper gazed up at one of the five old paintings that hung above the bar. The one in the middle fascinated him the most. Four black horses raced through sagebrush pulling a large stagecoach. The frantic driver swung a whip. Red storm clouds swirled down from the mountains. A winged angel hovered over a shadowy figure while grasping a billowing banner emblazoned with the proclamation: SE PIENSA QUE HAY ES MAL—ESPERA HASTA VE MAÑANA.

"That painting over the bar looks like a period piece from the 1850s. Is it a family heirloom?"

"Garage sale in Branson. Just thought it looked nice."

Jasper thought that Harpo might have lucked into a bargain but decided not to draw attention to it. He couldn't risk some art dealer from Kansas City nosing around.

"It's Wednesday," Harpo said, "time to make up a bean batch."

"Bean batch? How do we do that?"

"I goes out back and tends the smoker. You drag a couple of cases of beans from the storeroom. And dumps twenty cans into that pot. Heat them up. Then you calls me, and we work some magic."

Jasper lugged a cardboard carton into the kitchen, slit it open and pulled out a can. Baked beans, a generic brand he had never heard of. Looked like Harpo picked up the cheapest thing he could get his hands on.

Jasper fumbled for five minutes with what he thought must be the most rudimentary can opening device known to man. The hand-held metal gadget had a curved blade and a flat metal section. He pressed hard and wiggled the pointed end through the can lid, then jacked the device up and down, producing a wicked looking ragged edge around the rim.

"Thought you'd have done finished by now." Harpo shook his head. "You're only halfway around the first can."

"An axe would be quicker. Don't you have a real can opener?"

Harpo stabbed the appliance into a fresh can, after three seconds of rapid wrist action the lid flew off. Harpo walked away.

Jasper eventually got the hang of it; all twenty cans made it into the pot. They were ready for magic. Harpo lined up jugs, jars, and dusty bottles. Jasper had a pad and pencil ready for this one. Dark viscous fluids and partially congealed syrups gurgled into the pot. When Jasper asked how much, the answer was always, "Keep pouring until it tastes right."

Harpo zealously tossed in chopped onions, cubes of pork, and chunks of fat. Finally, he reached in a box and pulled out a handful of brown-and-yellowish stubble. It looked like something Jasper's college roommate hid under his dorm room bed. Some clumps appeared to be dried grass. Others looked like pieces of leaves and twigs.

"Where did that come from?" Jasper was loaded with questions.

"Stuff I grow out back."

"Where'd you learn to cook?"

"My old man taught me some. He cooked for a place in Clarksdale before he left."

"Where'd he go?"

"Same place most black men goes."

"Is this his recipe?"

"Some. He worked in a dry rib joint where they rub on the spices. I start with that, an' then turn 'em into wet ribs."

"Why are they called wet ribs?"

"All that goo on your fingers and still you got to ask?"

THREE WEEKS ON the job, and Jasper knew when to pull a rack of ribs out of the smoker, how much sauce and slaw made a pulled pork sandwich something you'd dream about, and when to bus a table without making the regulars feel rushed. Harpo had looked tired all day and suddenly decided to leave early. Being Saturday, the Hog Pen stayed open until the late-night crowd called it quits. Couples out for a beer, fishermen off the leash for the weekend, and a few barflies often hung around until midnight. Jasper had never worked behind the bar, but he didn't say anything to Harpo. The poor guy didn't look good.

Around eight o'clock things got busy, Jasper rapidly flipped the caps from frosty bottles. Foam spurted from the neck as he slid them to the yokel who shouted the loudest.

"Corona with lime and a red beer." A hand with bright red nails waved a two-dollar bill.

He had noticed the two attractive women when they'd promenaded in and jumped up on barstools. They wore colorful western shirts fastened with pearl snaps, dangling earrings, and broad country smiles. The tight jeans on the one with flaming red hair drew his eyes. A firm thigh, a rhinestone rose on the rear pocket, a calf accentuated by tightly stretched denim—boldly anchored in snakeskin boots.

"Sorry, all we have left is Coors, Bud, and Miller." Jasper placed both hands on the bar and leaned forward. Sweet perfume overcame the smell of beer and shelled peanuts.

"Make it Coors," said the dark-haired cowgirl.

"I'm kind of new at this. What—"

"Yeah, we noticed," she said.

"What's a red beer?"

"That's a ladies drink," the pretty redhead said. "Since hard liquor ain't allowed in this county."

"Dump two ounces of tomato juice in a Budweiser," the dark-haired cowgirl said.

Jasper fumbled around for a flashlight—the electric wiring had never made it to the storeroom. He knew he had seen a couple of cans of tomato juice up on the top shelf. Holding the light in one hand, he could barely feel one big can while standing on tiptoe. He inched the can forward and tried to wrap his thumb around it. A thirty-two ounce can of Safeway's house-brand tomato juice fell on his forehead. He ran back to the bar, searched for a clean glass, punched two holes in the lid with the pointed end of the can opener, and poured what he hoped was two ounces. Tipping the glass slightly, he added Budweiser slowly so that it didn't foam.

"Pretty good." The redhead licked her lips slowly. "What's your name?"

"I'm Jasper. Jasper Jones."

"I'm Susie," said the young lady with glistening red hair. "This here's Anita,"

"You got a big lump on your head," Anita said.

Not something he really wanted to talk about at the moment. "Sounds as though you're regulars."

"Sometimes we come in on Saturday." Susie smiled. "When I can get a sitter."

Jasper looked along the bar to see if anyone needed a beer. Things had slowed down, so he popped the top off a Coors for himself. The cold beer felt good going down; it had been a long time. He wondered if Susie had an elderly friend watching the kids, or if she relied on a neighborhood teenager.

"Look at that Henrietta Hawkins over there." Anita tipped her head toward the far end of the bar. "Prancing around like a rodeo queen with titties the size of quart jam jars."

"Thinks she's hot shit cause her daddy's richer than a preacher on Sunday morning."

Jasper ventured a comment. "She does look like a flirt."

"I got no respect for a woman that don't leave with the guy what brung her," Susie said.

"She tries to steal another feller from me, and I'll throw that cat in a creek." Anita drained what was left of her Coors.

Jasper hoped this squabble didn't go any farther. He knew the trick to getting ribs crispy on the edges and juicy in the middle. He even knew how to make a red beer, now. But he hadn't been trained on how to break up a catfight.

When folks started to leave, Jasper shut down the kitchen. Put the beans and slaw in the refrigerator. Wrapped up the bread. Downed one more beer, while cleaning up the stove and keeping an eye on the bar.

With only a handful of customers left, he mixed a red beer and opened a Coors. "Thought you ladies might be ready for another. On the house."

"Why, thank you." Susie smiled and cocked her head slightly.

"Thanks." Anita kept folding her beverage napkin into precise geometric patterns.

"What kind of work do you do, Susie?"

"Checker. Over at Piggly Wiggly in Branson."

"I guess you meet a lot of interesting people."

"It pays the bills. Been there five years, worked my way up to the dayshift."

"Is it hard to get on days?"

"Sure is. What with raising three kids on my own, it's good to be home most nights to make sure they do homework and such."

"Three. How old?"

"Becky, she's almost twelve now. Missy's ten, in the fifth grade and really smart. And Cassie—well real name's Cassandra, but nobody calls her that—she's my baby even though she just turned eight."

"Eight, same age as . . . a friend of mine's kids."

"Oh, yeah. You got any kids?"

"Not that I'm aware of. Has your twelve-year-old started to think like a teenager yet?"

"Getting big for her britches."

"That's it. Boys are even worse . . . I hear."

"Sometimes I think it would be nice to have a boy. But that pony's come and gone."

"Some things pass you by. You can't get them back."

"With some things, you'd be better off if they had passed you by." Susie took a big gulp of red beer. "I'm making sure Becky don't make my mistakes."

Like a largemouth bass in Table Rock Lake, something shiny caught Anita's eye and she swam off toward a bumpkin in a white Stetson.

Once you got past her country ways, Susie seemed like any other divorced woman he'd known back in Kansas City. Barbara, Miss Shipley—they all fought the same battle, struggling with jobs, kids, and ex-husbands.

He supposed Alicia was dealing with all that now. Jasper mixed another red beer and opened a bottle for himself. "Did you grow up around here, Susie?"

"Naw, we lived in Tennessee when I was little."

"Oh, what city?"

"I wouldn't like to say, you'd laugh."

"Certainly not, come on, tell me."

"Frog Jump. Frog Jump, Tennessee."

He didn't laugh, but it wasn't easy. "Did you like it there?"

"Sure did, we had a little farm, with animals and all."

"You like animals?"

"Yup—pigs, chickens, even had a cow once. Gave them all names, they were my pets, til it was time to butcher them. That was hard."

"I bet. Why did you move?"

"You can't really live off a little old farm. Dad had a job at the munitions plant over in McKenzie, but when they lost the government contract, Dad lost his job, and we lost the farm."

"Oh, that's tough."

"Yeah, the bank nailed a sign on the door, and here I am."

Jasper looked around and realized that Anita had wandered out with the white Stetson. And everyone else had left too.

"You got a long drive home?" Susie showed her coy, country-girl smile again.

"Just a short walk down the road."

"How about I hang around til you lock up and give you a ride?"

"Oh, it's not far."

"No sense walking down the highway in the dark."

Jasper got in Susie's hard-ridden Mustang GT. He tossed an arithmetic book onto the back seat and shuffled a couple of empty Coke cans aside with his foot as he settled into the torn vinyl seat.

"Sorry, it's kind of messy, always shuttling kids around."

"That's quite all right, I understand, busy schedule."

Susie turned and touched his cheek with the back of her fingertips. "You're a really nice guy."

She floored it. The old pony had guts. Gravel flew. The tires squealed. The muscle car spun wildly onto Arrow Point Road.

Two minutes later Susie pulled into the Arrow Point Motel. The rumble of the Mustang's dual exhaust died.

"Thanks for the ride." He reached for the door handle.

Susie replied with a wet kiss. Her breasts pressed against him.

Decision time. All over again. Could he invite Susie into his bedroom? Hell, it was his business what he did in there. Ginger never asked permission for her extracurricular activities.

But life was convoluted enough. Relationships led to questions. Save money. Make a new life. Time to quit making bad decisions.

"Looks like my roommate's still up." He opened the car door.

"You got a roommate?"

"I do. It's complicated." It was all he needed to say.

Chapter
14

Jasper had spent the past five months learning the restaurant business. It'd grabbed hold of him. Given him something to live for. For the first time in his life he was working at something that really enthused him. Of course his aspirations grew far larger than Harpo's Hog Pen, but he figured that all restaurants worked the same. Be friendly to customers, provide an atmosphere your clientele appreciates, serve the best possible food at prices your patrons are willing to pay. And most difficult of all—find honest, reliable help.

Jasper reckoned that within a few more months he could refine his skills and work out a business proposal, complete with an action plan and a timeline. Of course, to handle a higher volume he'd need a modern smoker. Hired help wouldn't kneel over an in-ground pit like a Catholic praying for a miracle from a long-dead saint. Samuel the blacksmith would know how to make a smoker out of a fifty-five-gallon steel drum. A motorized rack would cut down on the labor while ensuring uniform cooking. He started sketching a drawing with the dimensions required to hold sixteen slabs. Using charcoal instead of hickory logs would cut costs, with a few hickory chips thrown in, so he could still say "Hickory Smoked." Only three obstacles stood in his way—financing, getting his family back together, and staying out of prison.

Harpo hadn't been feeling well again, the cold spring winds had gone to his chest. Jasper insisted on coming in early to fire up the smoker while Harpo slept in. There'd been an argument, but after a round of coughing, Harpo gave in.

Harpo arrived around three, with a sack of cut-rate white bread over his shoulder.

Jasper was annoyed that Harpo hadn't taken the entire day off. "You fuss about everything else, why do you always buy cheapo bread?"

"Don't want the bread stealing zing from the pig."

Jasper thought Harpo would inundate him with questions about how many customers had shown up for lunch. Not a word. Did Harpo have that much confidence in him?

"Besides getting you started with cooking, did your dad teach you the business side of running a restaurant?" Jasper said.

"Naw, he never handled much money. But I had me a real job once, working for wages."

"Where was that?"

"Where I growed up, in Mississippi. Learned mostly about what not to do."

"That can be important. What'd they teach you?"

"Wasn't ever allowed to serve no white person, but if we ever came across one, we had to say Mister or Miss, even if they was two years old. Had to talk soft and slow, never look them in the eye."

"They could force you to do that?"

"You could lose what little work there was. My brother didn't listen good, talked to a white woman on her own, out on the town square. White guy just come up and knocked two of his teeth out. Right there on the spot. We never did have no money for new ones."

"I . . . I hadn't realized things were so bad."

"Oh, yeah, back when my folks weren't allowed into the department store on the square. Had our own little room, round back on the 'black street.' That's where I worked, in a little room with a counter. I'd go up the back stairs and fetch shoes or shirts from the storeroom, whatever they wanted. Made lots of trips."

Jasper knew black folks didn't have it easy. Like the black guy and his son who had the sandwich place across the street from the bank in Kansas City. But what could a person really do about it? He decided to change the subject.

"How come Rick sells hard stuff at the Arrow Point Store and you're limited to beer?" Jasper wanted to learn as much as he could about the restaurant business. It seemed to him that the profit margin on cocktails would be higher than beer.

"Grandfather Cause. That's what I heard."

"You mean Grandfather Clause."

"No Grandfather Cause. It's cause the guy what owns that store has a grandfather that knows the sheriff."

The restaurant business had one thing in common with banking—you need to know the right people.

"Do you have any relatives?" Jasper could barely stand on his own two feet. He sure didn't want to be Harpo's only crutch. "People you can call if you get real sick?"

"None I knows of. There was just me and Hattie. We never could manage to make no young ones."

"I'm sorry. You've done well so far, having lost your wife, and not having a relative to rely on. What's your secret?"

"Life ain't that hard, boy, just four steps my papa taught me, master those and you sail right through."

"Just what are those steps, Harpo?"

"You born, you eat, you shit, you die. Plain and easy—don't go making life harder than need be."

Jasper tried to remember words of wisdom his own father had passed on to the next generation, namely him. Give Negros an inch and they take a mile was one that came to mind. He wondered how things were going at the bank. What would his father think of him working for a black man?

Or that he was happier working for that black man than he ever was at his father's lily-white bank?

"A FRAID I CAN'T keep you on no more." Harpo's voice sounded unusually soft. "Some crackerjacks done opened a fancy new place out on the highway."

"Has that new place at the junction affected your bottom line that much?"

"Big shots out of Kansas City. Bankers with big bucks. Don't know no more about barbecue than a bobcat knows about baking biscuits."

"That's terrible. You've been here for years."

"Sticking around a long time don't mean people has to keep coming back. What stumps me most is—if their food is so good, why do they have them coupons in the paper? Why do they have to give folks two dollars off just to get them to eat it?"

Jasper headed out to the porch and started sweeping as he always did before customers started to arrive. A burst of energy went into each stroke, pent-up tension. Big shots. Big bucks. Financed by bankers who double-checked their ledgers, ensuring financial stability, a good return on investment. He swept harder.

"I didn't mean for you to commence sweeping," Harpo said. "Got no money to pay you."

"That doesn't mean that a friend can't help a friend. Besides—learning how to cook and listening to you complain is better than a paycheck."

Jasper kept busy, tried to keep his spirits up. Harpo would need encouragement. He wondered how well corporate motivational strategy worked at a rib joint.

"That's not much of a fire," Jasper said as he peered into the smoker.

Harpo shrugged. "It'll do."

"You won't cook many ribs with that. Let me add a couple of hickory logs."

"Hickory's gone. Using nothing but scrub oak."

"Hickory adds flavor."

"Not many folks ordering a full rack these days. Just pulled pork and a dab of beans."

Jasper retreated to the stump at the edge of the field out back. Harpo had never made much money. Didn't need to. Didn't want to. Just wanted to cook pork, spicy beans, with fresh slaw on the side. The big franchises on the highway siphoned off just enough of the lucrative tourist trade, cabin owners, and fishermen to make life rough. It appeared people had less appreciation for authentic local culture and a greater desire to get a free piece of factory-baked pie.

That was it—remind people of what they were missing. Advertise.

"DROP ME OFF here." Jasper pointed to the stop sign at Maddux and Sycamore in Branson. "I'll walk on back to the motel."

Jasper had ordered five hundred flyers from the Holy Book Print Shop and Soda Fountain. It had meant literally digging into the meager savings he had buried behind the motel. He would distribute them along the twelve-mile hike to Arrow Point.

Ginger hit the brakes harder than necessary. "Can't believe that idiot Harpo's spending money to advertise."

"I believe this might be just the kick he needs to keep things going."

"The lazy bastard needs a kick. If he had any ambition, he'd be the one walking up and down the highway."

"He's getting on. And with the arthritis, he needs help."

"Well, if he's stupid enough to pay you . . ."

Jasper didn't mention that he wasn't getting paid.

He slipped his flyers under the wiper blades of cars parked in front of the cafés, ice cream parlors, and churches on Maddux Street. After turning onto Highway 76, he moved quickly through the Promised Land Motel parking lot. There weren't many tourists in April, but this was just a practice run. By next month, he'd be slapping these handouts on dozens of cars. For now, maybe a few adventuresome travelers would take the time to experience local culture on Arrow Point Road.

He slapped flyers on the cars at Presley's Mountain Music Theater. Went up and down both rows at the God and Country Grocery and Gas. He handed one to a farm boy spraying mud off a pickup at the Big Splash Carwash. And of course, he put one on every windshield at that fancy new franchise—Bozo's Barbie Q.

Jasper sped down Arrow Point Road, hoping to get to the marina before dark. He wanted to talk to the dock operator before he left for the day, get him to keep a stack of flyers on the counter, maybe even make a recommendation when asked. Jasper got the dockhand to make room for the flyers, but he sensed a lack of enthusiasm for making a recommendation.

He got to the Arrow Point General Store just after dark.

Jasper put on his friendly salesman smile. "How's it going, Rick?"

"It's going," Rick said, also wearing a friendly smile. It was well past five, and Rick was well into a bottle of rum and a package of pretzels.

"Got some great news. Harpo's advertising, and he's selected you as the primary point of distribution on Arrow Point."

"Wow. That's the best news all day."

"Exciting, isn't it?"

"Hey man—when do I start?"

"Immediately."

Jasper handed over a flyer, and Rick carefully studied each line of the advertisement.

HARPO'S HOG PEN

```
Featuring the famous PIG and PICKLE
A smoky pulled pork sandwich with slaw
            under the bun,
      Harpo's spiced-up beans,
   and a jumbo spear of dill pickle.
         Top quality pork
        The finest ingredients


We can't afford to give you two bucks off
  All we can do is smoke the best pork
              you ever ate
       Real friendly folks with
          real pit Bar-B-Que
```

HARPO'S HOG PEN

```
         Arrow Point Road
Look for the distinctive building
  and smoke pouring out of the pit
```

"Very impressive." Rick read it again, careful not to miss an important detail. "I'll have to try it sometime."

"You've been there fifty times. It's the shack down the road."

"What? Seriously?"

Jasper only hoped that tomorrow Rick would remember why that stack of papers sat on the counter. He made a mental note to come in every day or two to give Rick a refresher marketing course.

J ASPER GOT THE news from Ginger; Marble Mine Village would reopen for the new season in two weeks. Fosdick wanted him to start getting the park ready. Immediately. Typical Fosdick.

Jasper sure needed the money, but it would be hard telling Harpo he couldn't come around every day. He decided to play up the positive by talking about all the tourists who would soon flood in.

"That Presley's Mountain Music Show in Branson is becoming popular," he said. "Have you ever thought of expanding?"

"Those folks sure are welcome to come on over." Harpo chucked another log in the smoker. "I'm not moving there."

"No—open a second restaurant, get someone to manage it for you. Maybe a country cooking theme— breakfasts, lunches, early-bird dinners before the fiddle show starts at Presley's."

"You got gumption, young fella. Me and Hattie saved what we could over the years. I'll put up some money, you can pay me back outa the profits. Take my recipe and open a place—it's all on you."

Jasper's dream—something to hold onto, a restaurant to work in and a family to come home to. An anchor in what had become a turbulent world. It wasn't much, but he'd saved the tax-free income from taking mine-tour photos, making repairs around Marble Mine Village, and the tips from working at Harpo's. All securely stashed away in a Folgers can, two feet underground behind the motel.

Who was he kidding? He'd have to find a way to buy a fake ID, which wouldn't be cheap, and still have enough to start up a restaurant?

But if Alicia sold the house and joined him . . .

For the first time in more than eight months, he felt he might have a future. He'd become a respectable restaurateur. At the speed Branson was expanding, he needed to move fast and get in on the ground floor.

"It's on hold for now. Just heard that I start back at Marble Mine tomorrow."

"You're a smart fella. One day you'll do a lot better."

"Right now, I can't think of anything better than working here. I'll come in and help you on Friday and Saturday nights."

"If all those tourists show up, I might even pay you."

Harpo put a hand on Jasper's shoulder. It sure felt good.

Chapter

15

Jasper scowled at the aluminum and glass box anchored to the sidewalk in downtown Branson. The phone booth looked like a coffin. Could be his gateway to a new life . . . or the afterlife, if he stepped in and called Alicia. A call that would lay out an intricate blueprint for their future.

Climbing out of Ginger's borrowed Datsun, he pulled the raincoat he'd borrowed from Caleb up around his neck and glanced at the watch he'd borrowed from Harpo. Surrounded by a borrowed world, he swore he'd carve out his own world. Right here, in the scraggly-oak hills with winding dirt roads. Along with Christian believers and the unbelievable Marble Mine menagerie. The question was, would he do it alone?

A north wind drove down the White River valley. Dark storm clouds turned the gray evening black. The rain intensified. A stream raced down the gutter and gurgled into a sewer. One thing was sure, no one would venture into this maelstrom and witness his clandestine rendezvous.

His sponge of tangled hair had soaked up rain during four soggy treks up and down Maddux Street. The downpour cleared his mind. Unlocked fresh visions. Hammered dreams into reality. It was time to reclaim his life.

Time to move forward. Right now. No reason to wait any longer. Resolute Jasper Jones tramped toward the glass box.

Digging into a wet pocket and extracting quarters a few at a time, he lined them up like toy soldiers on the small metal shelf, four to a stack. He had absolutely no idea of what a long-distance call cost. Two weeks' worth of beer money stood in columns—that was how he measured the essentials of life these days.

A quarter dropped into the slot. A mechanical clunk echoed in the glass cage. The next coin slipped away. Fell and rolled out of sight . . .

The phone dangled on a coiled cord. A dial tone echoed off glass. Rage clashed with logic. Was this an opportunity to restart his life or another step down the road to disaster?

He retrieved the quarter from the coin return. Picked up the one next to his foot. Realigned his stacks of soldiers. Could contacting Alicia provide a trail for the police? It had been a long time. Surely more vicious crimes had ascended to the top of the list. Before he could change his mind, he dropped several coins in the slot and dialed the number.

Finally, a firm plan. Financed by assets Alicia could liquidate.

He sure didn't want to take money from Harpo. And the money he'd earned without help from his father amounted to a pittance, but at last he felt as though he was contributing to a new career, a new identity, a new life with Alicia.

But the children, that would be harder.

He didn't need to plot this all alone, Alicia would help.

"Hello. This is Alicia."

"Hi, it's me."

"Jeremy!"

"Are you okay?"

A pause. Then, "Please come home."

He shuddered like a child caught with his hand in the cookie jar. "I can't do that."

"Where are you?"

"I can't say right now."

Without warning, lightning attacked the steeple of the Holy Fire Spa and Tabernacle, causing the phone booth to violently rattle.

"Can't what? What's that noise?"

"Oh, just thunder. Are the kids okay?"

An even longer pause. He should ask the real question—had the police forgotten about him? The TV stations had talked about it every day, then once a week, then once a month, now the crime of the century did not rate a mention. But he realized, he wanted to know about the kids more.

"They need you. They . . . they need a father!"

Was she stalling? Would the police make her do that?

"Listen, darling, they wouldn't get a father if I went to prison. I have a plan to bring us back together. Sell the house, withdraw our savings. You and the children will love it here."

"Become a fugitive? Turn the children into accomplices?"

"I know of a place where we could run a small restaurant, near a beautiful lake in tree-covered hills, and there's a school nearby. It will keep us out of the spotlight."

"I don't want to live in the dark."

Long, long seconds passed.

"It would be a wonderful place for the children to grow up."

"You're the one who needs to grow up, Jeremy."

"I have. I've learned a great deal these past months."

"Just what have you learned?"

"That things are often not what they appear to be. Impetuous fools can mistake limestone for marble." Jasper trying to be witty, like back in college.

"Who gives a damn about that—come home!"

"Listen, Alicia, I miss you and the kids more than you can know. But I can't risk coming back. I have a plan, and it will work."

"You need more than a plan. Your father has power and influence. I've gone over this thoroughly with him. Give yourself up, and he'll have you out in two or three years."

"Two or three years! For killing a cop? I've read the papers."

"They exaggerate. Involuntary manslaughter does not sell newspapers. Even the police told me you'd be out in eighteen months with good behavior."

"You've been talking to the police?"

"Do you honestly believe I can avoid it?"

Jasper looked at the watch. He had talked longer than intended.

"I'll think it over. I'll call in two days."

"Think it over! You ruin our lives, call months later, and say, 'Oh, you and the children run off and hide with me in some storybook land.'"

"It's an enchanting land where you and the children—"

"Your father wants to help you. The police want to help. We can put things back together the way they were."

"I don't want things the way they were."

Click.

Jasper stared at the receiver, trying to sort out where the conversation had gone wrong. He began to realize just how far he'd come from the life he had lived—the bank, the big house, the predetermined life. He wanted none of it now. But he still wanted Alicia. And the kids . . .

But apparently, he couldn't have them without the life he'd left behind. And he didn't think he could do that.

He opened the phone booth door and stood face-to-face with a burly man. A man he had never seen before. Raindrops dripped from the stranger's hat brim. Lurching to the right, Jasper jumped onto the balls of his feet and ran faster than he had since college football. Expecting to feel the impact of being tackled. Rounding a corner. Attempting to put a building between him and the hulk with menacing eyes. As if that would make him safe. Like putting your head in the sand—if you can't see it, it can't hurt you.

Dodging around another corner. Gasping for breath on a steep incline. Taking refuge in a dark corner. Restoring his breath and his courage. Ten minutes of water-logged sprinting left him senseless.

Lively clarinet sounds drifted from a beer joint with a

neon sign that said Rusty Beaver. Pete Fountain played on the jukebox. "Do you know what it means to miss New Orleans?"

He knew what it meant to miss his wife, his children. But on the phone, Alicia had sounded older, like any other middle-aged woman. Deep, monotone, clipped. The rhythmic rise and fall of the bubbly college girl had somehow gone flat during his absence. Or had it disappeared years ago, and he just hadn't noticed?

No one had followed. He circled the block and looked back toward the phone booth. The mysterious man was talking on the phone. Some random person waiting to make a call. Were months of running and hiding taking their toll? Had it become official? Was he certifiably paranoid?

He took a deep breath.

Or was he feeling more alive than he'd ever felt in his life? He was Jasper Jones. Living the adventure. And part of him was really enjoying it.

HARWOOD DRAINED THE last of his lukewarm coffee. Glanced down the hall. And stuck his nose back in the *Arkansas Gazette*. He checked the paper every day. Some scrap of knowledge might give him an edge on securing that promotion. This morning he muddled through Section C, killing time until all the detectives were out on the street—didn't want to risk anyone hearing the Pipkins woman's phone recordings. Some fluff piece on page 9 portrayed Branson, Missouri as the up-and-coming playground for senior citizens with RVs. Nashville country singers were replacing mountain fiddle music. Nearby Marble Mine Village was already well established with families as the Disneyland of the Ozarks, the article claimed. Harwood had been dragged there as a kid, but he doubted people still bothered with that cornball crap.

On the second Saturday night of each month, he'd been driving to Kansas City and swapping out the audio cassette tapes in Pipkins's garage. Eight months and only two conversations related to Danny's murder. Pipkins's wife had called the Franklin woman, the schoolteacher who had booked the party hotel room. They chattered forever. Bitching about work, kids, media lies and hard-hearted cops. That kind of bullshit. But no mention of husbands. Then, a couple months later that broad calls back. She's giving up and leaving Pine Bluff, going to stop at the Pipkins house on her way to family in Seattle. The two of them getting together. He'd like to be there for that rendezvous.

But not one damn clue about Pipkins's location. Time to call it quits. Sometimes you just have to admit you went down the wrong road. On Saturday night he'd pulled the cassette recorder on Pipkins's phone line. Apart from her unorthodox sexual tendencies, the wife seemed decent. Just another mom on her own. Trying to get by.

Finally, the squad room cleared out. He took the cassette deck out of his desk drawer and listened to endless talk about third graders from that schoolteacher named Barbara. A request for a plumber. More talk about school kids. A question about homework. Then a man's voice.

Pipkins?

Harwood sat up. Grabbed a pen. Cocked his ear toward the speaker.

The line sizzled and crackled. A poor long-distance

connection? The constant splattering noise could be rain on glass—nearby window or maybe a phone booth. An inquiry about the kids. A plan to meet. To run away together. She didn't sound pleased. Then a booming noise. Harwood hit rewind. Carefully transcribed every word.

"Oh, just thunder. Are the kids okay?"

Harwood shuffled through the Gazette. The national weather map showed fair and mild conditions throughout the entire country . . . except for a narrow band of thunderstorms in the southwestern corner of Missouri.

One thing had constantly nagged Harwood. How had Pipkins escaped from Bentonville? He'd had no transportation out of there. Harwood tapped on the table. Counted off the options—no car, no plane, no bus, no support system. Friends and family were keeping their distance. So maybe he didn't go far. An unpredictable bastard. And clever. Had to be, to keep his head above water at that fancy-ass bank run by his father. The kind of guy who used any trick to keep from paying his dues. Harwood knew he had to think like Pipkins. Not like an average family man, not like a petty criminal—like a shifty son of a bitch.

All major city police departments had been contacted, and recontacted, especially in the east. Pipkins was an eastern kind of a guy, went to Princeton. Yet nothing could be taken for granted. People who wanted to disappear went to big cities. Small-town folks were curious, asked too many questions. Could a prominent white-collar banker like Pipkins survive in the rural hills of Missouri?

Harwood saw the world through slits, narrow squinting eyes that tightly controlled how much of the world he let in. His world had always consisted of facts.

But now emotion was clouding his view. That made this case hard to solve.

For the first time in his career, he added up losses instead of scoring wins. Pipkins had managed to elude him. Judy had threatened to leave him. The promotion to lieutenant was slipping farther away.

It would take money to put Tony in a top-notch college.

Harwood looked out the window into an alley, as though the answer to his questions waited out there. Was he wasting his time?

Scratching the palm of his hand, vowing to quit letting his injured ego affect his judgment. Grabbing a fresh notepad, he wrote down each fact of the case in chronological order. Starting from the beginning. Reanalyzing each step from a new angle. Had he missed something? He must have.

The tape recording—he went back to his notes.

"Run a small restaurant. A beautiful lake in tree-covered hills." Could be anywhere in the country.

"Things are often not what they appear to be. Impetuous fools can mistake limestone for marble." Was it some cryptic message? The wife didn't seem to buy it. Harwood yanked the Gazette out of the trashcan. Scrambled through the wrinkled pages for Section C. "Marble Mine Village was already well established with families."

An annoying tap on the doorframe resounded through his office. Harwood's mouth twitched.

A skinny detective with an east Tennessee twang poked his head in. "Briefing in two minutes. New case just came in."

"Yeah, hang on. I'll be there."

New case. How could they solve the old ones when new ones continually poured in? The department had cut off funds for the phone tap, they sure as hell wouldn't send investigators across the state line to Missouri. And the Mayberry cops in that hill country won't come up with anything.

Harwood arrived late for the briefing, with a plan to search southwest Missouri evolving in his head. Only one perplexing detail remained, how to keep Judy from complaining about him being out of town on his own time again.

Of course. Time for a family vacation.

Chapter
16

Harwood waited in a line that zigzagged back and
forth to conceal its true length of two hundred
yards. Children pumped up on a fast breakfast
of Sugar Pops jumped and chattered. They'd bounced
out of bed at six that morning, raring to start the frontier
adventure. Parents halfheartedly reined in their kids,
trying to conserve the energy they would need to survive
the day. They'd hurried out with only one cup of coffee
in order to get through as many Marble Mine Village
attractions as possible before the full force of the summer
sun hit.

"What the hell's the difference between the Family
Fun Wilderness Package and the Frontier Experience
Pass?" People stared. So what if he sounded like a hard-
ass cop in an interrogation room on TV?

"Be mindful of your language, this is a family park."

Judy Harwood placed a finger to her lips. "The Family Fun Wilderness Package includes the Marble Mine Tour."

"Do we really need to see a mine?"

"Of course, the kids have been looking forward to it. It's their summer vacation, let's have fun."

Fishing with Tony was fun. Standing in line at a corny theme park was not, but it kept Judy at bay, and he owed the kids some kind of getaway. Not a bad trade-off, zip through the park today and get down to serious business tomorrow—bars, motels, homeless shelters. If there was such a thing as a homeless shelter in this hillbilly haven.

JASPER LEANED AGAINST a workbench that had aged to dark indigo from years of oil spills and black iron bars. Before his underground shift, he often watched Samuel stoke the furnace to the temperature required to turn small metal rods into square nails. In pioneer days this simple job gave young apprentices a chance to hone their smithy skills. These days, red-hot coals, and the collision of metal-on-metal amazed freckle-faced boys as they watched Samuel flatten glowing bars with heavy strokes of his hammer. Reddish-orange coke in the furnace, rising smoke, glistening sweat, the clash of a hammer, a baritone voice describing the transformation of coal to coke and iron to steel—strictly a man's world.

"Jasper, I been searching high and low for you at the mine." Fosdick spread the words out one by one as he caught his breath.

"The mine doesn't open for half an hour."

"The smithy doesn't need your gawking."

"Yes, sir."

"I hear you been showing interest in the mine-tour spiel."

"I've listened to Caleb's talk."

"Yeah, but can you rattle off the whole nine yards at the right time?"

"Sure, it's not that hard."

"Everything is hard."

Jasper started to question Fosdick's logic, and quickly decided to stay under the radar.

"Business is picking up. People are in line too long for the cave instead of buying snacks and doohickeys these wilderness clodhoppers make." Fosdick jerked his head to the right as an indignant gesture toward the makeshift wilderness craft buildings. Samuel seemed oblivious and was getting on with his chores, but a stiffening of his shoulders gave him away.

"We've been busy." Jasper seemed glad of the work.

"We need to start the tours earlier and run them later. Caleb's already complaining about not getting a lunch break. Guy's not bright enough to walk through a mine and munch on a sandwich at the same time."

"He does need to talk while—"

"Yeah, here's what we do. You do the one o'clock tour, while he loafs around."

"Who'll take the pictures when the two o'clock tour starts? Caleb hasn't been trained on loading the film and framing the camera."

"Rush your one o'clock tour, take the Cable Train back down, hop through the mine and snap the picture."

"But—"

"Caleb's bright enough to herd them into four rows by himself."

"But—"

"Just run through the mine and click." Fosdick pivoted and disappeared.

Jasper now understood Fosdick's wisdom. Everything is hard.

A L HARWOOD SHOOK his head. The crowd seemed oblivious of the heat and humidity—one hundred wide-eyed faces mesmerized by the Happy Heaven Trio, a matching set of inflated bosoms and flared skirts singing gospel in three-part harmony. They looked like sisters, the same person in three assorted sizes—large, extra-large, and one size bigger than that. Harwood thought they were unconvincingly happy—who could be thrilled about working here? Clothed in almost patriotic attire, one wore a red dress, one wore a blue dress, but the rebel in the group was sporting white and chartreuse. They glanced toward one another with wet puppy-dog eyes as they crooned, "Hallelujah, we're raring to go."

Harwood couldn't help but think of a Super-8 film confiscated in a Little Rock raid, then passed around the station house—Lesbian Lovers Gone Wild.

"It's not really country-western—just a bunch of squeaky fiddles instead of guitars."

Fifteen-year-old Tony tapped his left foot, while five-year-old Sally sang along two words behind. Judy beamed happily with an arm around each as they swayed to the tune.

"Now they're singing church music, in the middle of the day, at a park." Harwood came to an undeniable conclusion about the hill country of Missouri—the gene pool had devolved into a murky swamp.

"It's gospel music. You'd know if you attended church with us."

"Sunday's my only day off. I want peace and quiet, not a bunch of chipmunks squawking and preachers thumping Bibles."

"A good thump with a Bible might do you some good."

"This sounds like something coming out of a jigaboo church." Harwood waited for a caustic retort from his wife. The music wailed. Fiddles screeched. Harwood turned. Judy and the children were gone, he had been talking to his wife but not looking at her.

Where in the hell did they go?

JASPER RUSHED TOWARD the employees' entrance to the mine. With luck, Caleb would be there early with a few handy pointers on conducting the tour. The crowd marched along Wilderness Ridge—grandparents craning their necks, kids begging to climb up to the tree house, mothers gravitating toward the weavers, while magnetism drew fathers toward the sinewy leather workshop or the heat and clang of the smithy. Jasper had acclimated to this obstacle course—don't try to fight it, jump with the flow. It was like sailing at Nantucket—catch the downwind when you can, and tack upstream as needed. Near the top of the hill Jasper heard the ten thirty show: "Hallelujah. I said, Jesus, please—you're not one to tease." The country and gospel show put all but a few in a festive mood. He waved to his three friends on the stage as he strode by. The ladies returned the gesture with a nod of their heads.

"Pardon me, sir." A frustrated woman attempted to smile. She grasped the hands of a boy and a girl, with head tipped down while eyes glared upward; she seemed to have fled an unpleasant dilemma. "Crochet? How do we get to the crocheting demonstration?"

"That way, turn left at the Wilderness Church, then look for McGuffey's Homestead." Jasper pointed toward the ridge. "There's a sign."

As they walked away, he wondered how Alicia was doing. Was anyone helping? Pointing the way?

AL HARWOOD FINALLY caught up with his family on the front porch of a shack that had a sign out front with the doubtful alias: McGuffey's Homestead. Judy explained that they were waiting for a demonstration of frontier homemaker skills.

Harwood mimicked the crowd as they watched a good-looking woman with a bright-yellow dye job stroll past Buckshot Barney's in Powder Keg Gulch. A silk parasol shielded her ghost-like complexion; the blistering sun lit it up like a halo, creating the illusion of an angelic pioneer lady. The virgin-white sunshade had fancy flowers and lace edges in three shades of pink. In the 1800s, a swanky gizmo like that would've come all the way from Paris. There's only one way a frontier woman could get that kind of money.

He had to admit this long-legged gal knew how to get a guy's attention. Somehow, she had managed to find a pink daisy for her hair that complemented the rouge on her cheeks. Her hair precisely matched the maple shaft on the parasol. Wavy curls flowed over her shoulders and flared into ringlets on her bright-purple bodice. She made quite a picture—he bet hundreds were taken, as tourists memorialized their glimpse of prairie elegance so they could brag about their hillbilly vacation. Below her long dress, cowgirl boots peeked out, bright purple and pink blotches on soft tan leather. He wondered if this hot babe would sashay into his family photo album—he could hear Judy exclaim, "She was a wonderful example of a brave frontier woman."

She didn't seem to be in a hurry as she waltzed along, directing tourists towards restrooms, smiling at children, smiling broader at fathers—she had that part of her role nailed down. The crowd on the porch buzzed louder as she got closer and it was obvious that she would be the one to demonstrate how to crochet a blanket. She coyly introduced herself as Ginger Feliciano and claimed to inhabit the chink-sealed cabin constructed from hand-hewn logs. The audience whirred with enthusiasm as they filed into the cabin, eager to discover how a God-fearing family survived on the frontier by making essential household items like blankets.

Grabbing a partially finished blanket, she jabbed it with crochet needles, made interesting comments, and gestured at the cabin's fine features at just the right moment. "Notice the blue gingham curtains."

Obviously, she had stage experience—with the skill and finesse of a magician, a blanket was born, colorful crocheted squares finely stitched together. Harwood thought that part of her shtick needed some refinement—she seemed to find household crafts harder to master than flirting. This classy chick looked out of place here; something was wrong with this picture.

"And many of these fine early American blankets are available for purchase."

Ah, here it is. The sales pitch.

"Right here in McGuffey's Homestead, in several patterns and colors to match the decor of modern American homes. Like yours."

Chapter
17

As Jasper prepared to lead his first tour down the long series of stairways to the bottom of the Big Bat Belfry, he turned to Caleb for last-minute advice.

"Don't worry," Caleb said. "These folks don't know the details. No one will notice if you forget something or get a date wrong. But a word of caution, you may have what is known in the tour guide business as a troublesome group."

"What makes you think that?"

"The tall, skinny one with the notebook and reading glasses hanging from her neck is definitely a schoolteacher."

"Why's that a problem?"

"They're never content with enjoying a colorful story

and a laugh at the punch line. There's always a question, and they keep on until they get a specific answer."

"How do you handle them?"

"Make something up. Act like you know what you're talking about. And add some minute detail, something she couldn't possibly know."

He'd dealt with customers like that at the bank. "I can manage her."

"The know-it-all Confederate history buff may not be so easy."

"Which one is he?"

"The souvenir T-shirt from Shiloh, and gray flattop cap."

"How do you deal with a guy like that?"

"You'll do just fine." Caleb waved as he headed to Freddie's Frontier Fried Chicken for a lunch snack. "Oh, don't let anyone hit their head on a low-hanging stalactite."

Getting the entire group to the bottom of the Big Bat Belfry proved a challenge. There were children who suddenly realized they had grabbed the wrong hand in the dark, a grandmother unsure if her heart would last for the whole tour, and the talkers—well, talkers are talkers wherever, more interested in being sure everyone knows the details of Mammoth or Carlsbad rather than seeing what's here in front of them.

"In the late 1800s they started giving candle-lit tours using rickety old ladders." Jasper's voice resonated.

The safety-conscious teacher leaned forward. "Wasn't that dangerous?"

"Absolutely, ma'am. They slid down the muddy slopes above you. Today, your convenience and safety are ensured by steel stairways and electric lighting." In twenty short minutes, he had become quite the promoter. Maybe today wouldn't be a disaster after all.

"BUT THAT YELLOW-AND-BLUE quilt would have looked nice in our bedroom," Judy said.

"You can get the same thing for half price at Wal-Mart." Harwood pointed at the sign on a rustic plank-board building, Mountain Man Leather. "That place just might have something worth taking home."

He tramped in with Tony close behind. They breathed deep; the room had the scent all men fall in love with, the sharp pungent odor of animal hides.

"Dad—look at the Bowie knife with the leather sheath." Tony pressed his nose against the glass countertop.

"Well, you're a teenager now." Harwood felt a jab in his side. Not a good time to press the issue with Judy; he moved down the counter. Tony had never demonstrated a tough-trooper attitude, too much influence from his mother. When this Pipkins thing was over, he'd spend more time with his son, man stuff. Next deer season, the hell with Judy, none of that .22 rifle squirrel hunting, get the boy a .30-06 bolt-action. And crossbow season, they'd get in on that action.

"Do you make any holsters for a concealed Colt .38 Detective Special?" Harwood believed in the tried and proven, especially with firearms—two-inch barrel, fixed sight, and a hammer block safety to prevent accidental discharge if dropped.

"Concealed?" the clerk said.

"Under a suit coat, if you don't want to advertise you're carrying a pistol." Harwood touched his side. It felt strange without the Colt pressed against him.

"No . . . Frontiersmen were proud to display their revolvers."

"Yeah."

"Got some great belts, hand tooled."

Harwood and family had already moved on.

WHEN THEY REACHED the ledge at the Temple of Doom, Jasper recalled Caleb's warning: "Don't let tourists lean on the handrail, it's not secure. Fosdick won't have it repaired until the end of the season, doesn't want to shut down the cave for a whole day."

"This chasm is hundreds of feet deep and way down there, at the very bottom, is a twenty-five-foot pile of bat guano," Jasper repeated Caleb's fable in an ominous voice. "The sound of a splat won't even reach up here. A long fall with such a soft landing won't kill you. A putrid smell will surround you, as you smother in blindness— before the devil knows you're dead."

Jasper took a deep breath.

"Mining for bat poo never occurred this far into the cave. It was too hard to remove from this deep crater, even though guano was selling for seven hundred dollars a ton. A lot of money in the late 1800s." His confident voice carried across the Temple of Doom.

The teacher slipped on her glasses. "Why was it worth so much?"

"It was processed and used in the manufacture of gunpowder. Also, its high nitrogen content made it a favorite with farmers. And the Army turned it into saltpeter to deter randy troops."

"Did the military really do that?"

"Only the losing armies." The guy with the gray

flat-topped cap finally found an opening. "There is substantiated documentation to show that Union General Franz Sigel tried to keep his degenerate German immigrant troops under control with saltpeter. This proved to be a counterproductive strategy, and he was forced to retreat from Bentonville. Low testosterone took the fight out of those Yankees."

Jasper knew it was time to call a truce. It reminded him of his grandfather's fervent belief that the battle over the rights of states hadn't ended at Appomattox. "The miners shoveled and hauled for four and a half years. Finally, the bats were pooped out."

Everyone laughed; Jasper had regained control of his contingent. "Improved lighting revealed that the cave consisted of limestone, not marble. The miners left, and the bats kept on doing what bats do."

"A CCORDING TO THE map, if we follow Wilderness Road up the hill it will lead to the Marble Mine." Judy pivoted so that the map was lined up with the route they needed to take.

Harwood threw up his hands. "We don't have to see everything."

"C'mon, Alvin, it will be cool in the cave. If we hurry, we'll make the two o'clock tour."

Al Hardwood tried to slow down, get ahold of himself, quit taking it out on Judy, let the kids have some fun, some fragment of vacation before heading back to school. Was this Pipkins case taking over his life? Shading his judgment? After all, maybe that Kansas City banker was just a frustrated middle-aged guy who got in over his head. The only way to know was to get him in custody, let

Pipkins tell his story, line up all the pieces and determine what really had happened. Danny never displayed finesse when dealing with suspects, yet why the hell had Pipkins shattered his skull?

"HERE WE ARE at the Pastel Pond," Jasper said, proud of his accomplishments on this first tour. No scrapes or bruises. No questions that he couldn't answer. No cardiac failures. He had successfully transported them from the Big Bat Belfry, past Satan's Sentries, and down through the Whirling Whiplash. There had been only one incident. After leaving the Temple of Doom, the schoolteacher slipped in the Mud Tunnel while asking her ninth question instead of watching her step.

"Near the Pastel Pond you can see a few green ferns and moss with a light-pastel glow. They're not native to the cave but began life here as spores carried on air currents. They're only able to grow due to the electric lighting. Speaking of light . . ."

Now came the most dramatic part of the tour. "Move in close to me, by this huge rock." He motioned them toward a three-foot high chunk of dolomite, with matches and a candle on top. He lit a single candle, then brushed one hand against a concealed light switch on the backside of the rock. The lights snapped off, leaving a dim, eerie, candle-lit pool.

"This is what early cave explorers saw. When tourists visited the cave in the early 1900s, five dollars got them transportation from Branson via horse drawn wagon on the old 'Nobody Knows How Old Trail,' two meals, a night's lodging, the use of the ladders, and one candle like this." At that point, he dramatically tilted his head downward as if portraying a villain on Broadway. "Should your candle go out, this would be your world."

He blew out the candle. After a momentary gasp, there was dead silence all around him. Three long seconds later, he flipped the light switch on. Now all eyes were open as wide as Jasper's.

Caleb had told him, "Play this like Macbeth and ye shall reap big tips."

They moved on to the steep incline between the Pastel Pond and the Crystal Cable Car Tunnel. "As we climb through this narrow passage," he said, "watch your head. The first rock protrusion hanging down from the ceiling is called Noddle Knocker for a reason. A few feet later, the second is the Rock with One Hundred Names—only three of them are suitable for a family tour such as this."

After negotiating the rocks with only a few minor bumps, they walked a short distance to the entrance of the Crystal Cable Car Tunnel. Jasper pointed toward the tunnel. Translucent calcite formations, lit by hidden lights, glowed in brilliant shades of red, orange, and pink.

"Varying amounts of iron within the rock produce this vibrant array of color." He had regained his stride, noting architectural facts and historical dates with an authoritative voice that made each one sound significant.

"Now we'll begin the last leg of our tour. An amazingly strong steel cable will safely pull our railcars through the tunnel, then out, up the mountainside, to the gift shop, where you may purchase a photo of our entire tour group."

And the tour group did look amazed, although, understandably, somewhat concerned.

The funicular railway consisted of three steel cages with diamond-patterned mesh instead of glass windows.

It looked contrived, put together here on location by the blacksmith on Wilderness Road, though it had actually been ordered from a railroad-car manufacturer in Baltimore.

Jasper realized that he'd let the tour run longer than usual. He rushed everyone into the three incline cable cars, turned on the powerful electric motor, and released the safety brake. The cars jerked into motion. At the top, the tourists quickly departed, anxious to get out of the steel cages clinging to the hillside by one rusty cable.

Jasper took the cable cars back down and rushed through the caverns, way behind schedule. Maybe Caleb would forego the pictures and start the two o'clock tour on time.

No, he wouldn't do that, they made too much off the photos. Fosdick would have a fit.

HARWOOD LOOKED FROM one rock wall to the other. He felt penned in, confined underground, while waiting for the two o'clock Marble Mine tour to start.

"Hello, my name is Caleb." The tall kid dressed in a dark green uniform with a brass nametag looked like a Junior Park Ranger. He talked slow and looked around as if he were waiting for adult supervision. "I'll be your guide on this tour."

Caleb? Harwood wondered if this was going to turn into a subterranean Bible tour.

"With temperatures between fifty-four and sixty degrees Fahrenheit, your tour will be pleasant and comfortable. First, I'll ask everyone to line up here on these three steps for a group photo, which will be developed and printed and ready for purchase as you exit the cave, just fifty minutes from now."

Harwood tried to decide if Caleb was Amish or Jewish. It sure wasn't a regular American name.

"Now everyone move close together, no tall people on the highest riser, please. Don't want to chop off any heads."

The group jockeyed for a suitable position. The women straightened their halter-tops and checked the children for blotches of chocolate ice cream. The men sucked in their beer bellies and checked their flies.

"Our Marble Mine photographer will be here any second." Caleb motioned. "Sir, you on the right with your arms folded, please move in closer."

A clatter rang out and everyone turned toward the steel steps.

"Here he is. The Marble Mine photographer." Caleb swung his arm around and pointed as though a celebrity had popped up on stage. The photographer climbed the last step and staggered into the light. A gasp had to do for hello as he rapidly set up the tripod and mounted the camera. Then he raised his right hand to show that he was ready.

"Everyone smile," he said, still panting. "Even you on the right, this won't hurt a bit."

Everyone laughed as he snapped it. Everyone—except Harwood, the guy on the right.

Their eyes locked. They both froze.

Holy shit . . . It's Pipkins!

Chapter
18

Jasper took the stairs two at a time, the dull clunk of his pursuer's feet maybe ten steps behind. He knew the pattern of the stairway, back and forth, a landing every forty steps—twenty the way he was leaping down them. The last few months had whipped him into shape, but this second run through the cavern was sucking up all his energy. His ten-step lead started to slip.

At the floor of the Big Bat Belfry he gasped for breath. "I didn't mean to do it!" he yelled.

"That's no goddamn excuse," said a voice, echoing back.

He could hear the cop wheezing; with luck, sitting behind a desk or in a squad car had put him out of condition.

"You're a dead man, Pipkins." Harwood's voice

carried throughout the Big Bat Belfry. "Kill a cop and you die."

The two-second echo made Jasper run faster.

Racing past Satan's Sentries, he quickly calculated his advantage in the dangerous maze of passages, dead ends, low clearances, and slippery slopes. His eyes were accustomed to the dim cave conditions and he knew the way—sort of—when he had time to think.

He couldn't risk looking back, slowing down even a fraction would surrender his slim lead.

The cop's noxious breath pulsed against the back of his neck.

Run. Run. Follow the lights.

Run and hope that cop gives out.

Fear morphed into terror. Dark stalagmites stood guard like surreal policeman. He slipped. Smacked into a protrusion on the right. Slammed against the left wall. Fell to one knee. His left hand grasped a stalactite.

The cop's words ricocheted off the stone sentinels. "Those convicts on the Flooded Mine ride have it easy compared to Tucker Prison."

A fresh shot of adrenaline spurred Jasper. Footsteps thundered behind him. Giant feet. Pounding feet. A relentless cadence on hard stone.

The instinct for survival demanded immediate action. He veered off to the right, into Phantom Canyon and ducked behind a stalagmite. His adversary sped past, racing toward a dead end. This deceptive divergence from the tour route went nowhere.

He silently hugged the stalagmite. It's that cop . . . The detective on the TV news . . . Harwood.

Water dripped from overhead. One drop every second. A torturous metronome. A deafening sound, reverberating throughout his subterranean prison.

A mind-boggling, mute interlude later, heading back toward the main route, moving as quietly as possible, he slipped while entering the Whirling Whiplash, a cantankerous, convoluted, corkscrew-shaped passage. A helical hell. His shoes scraped. He stopped. Looked back. Saw a shadow advancing. Started running. Progress slowed inside the Whirling Whiplash, the toughest stretch to negotiate. Sharp angular rocks jutted out from unexpected directions. His ability to maneuver the twisting contortions increased his lead by a few seconds as he sprung out of the spiral formation.

Starting out onto the narrow ledge in the Temple of Doom, Jasper kept to the balls of his feet as the shape of the ledge constantly changed. Elbows bent. Hands ready to protect his upper body and head.

He strained to lengthen his stride. Monstrous footsteps pounded behind him—Tucker—Tucker—Tucker.

His old football coach's command rang in his ear, *Get the lead out, Pipkins. Stretch your legs out farther. He's gaining on you.*

The footsteps' rhythmic pattern changed. There were two pursuers now. The additional drumbeat sounded softer. Less distinct. Off in the distance but getting louder.

Caleb? More cops? A tourist deputized to join the posse?

A pain on the right jaw. Vision blurred.

He'd smashed into a sharp rock protrusion. The world spun out of control. His arm swung out and grabbed a thin cold cylinder—the handrail.

He caught his balance.

Suddenly the cop was on him. Face to face. An inch

away. Jasper's spine pressed into the handrail. He saw eyes bursting with vengeance. Smelled hot, rancid breath.

"It will look like an accident." The cop spat words in his face. "They won't even notice the marks from my fist after you've tumbled end over end into that hell hole!"

Jasper recalled Caleb's words: *A twenty-five-foot pile of bat guano at the bottom—a putrid smell will surround you as you smother in blindness.*

The cop pressed harder. Slammed him backward. The railing screeched. One anchor tore loose. The handrail gave way by two inches.

The cop leapt back from the ledge. Jasper jumped to one side. Grabbed a vertical support.

The second pursuer lunged at him—thinner and lighter, but just as fierce. Jasper recoiled. Grabbed the second assailant. Rammed him against the handrail.

It ripped free. The second pursuer held on to one section of railing. Dangling over the precipice.

The cop sprang toward the ledge. "Tony!"

Small hands squeaked as they slipped down the dangling pipe railing. Until no handrail remained.

One high-pitched scream—a decaying echo.

Then nothing. No sound. Not even a splat.

Viciously. Silently. Suffocating in bat shit.

Jasper tried to move. He wanted to move. He just fucking couldn't.

The cop from Little Rock lay on the rock ledge. Head dangling over the edge. Shouting into black nothingness.

Jasper tried to think, come up with a plan. If only one man crawled out of this hole in the ground, he'd do everything possible to make sure he was the one.

One last chance hit him—the Pastel Pond!

"You're a goddamn dead man." The cop was standing.

Instinctively, Jasper turned, ran. A burst of hope took over.

Only the Mud Tunnel separated him from his goal. Rather than rock, the floor was slimy mud—actually decomposed bat poop. His confidence grew. He had a chance.

Behind him, the cop slipped and sloshed. He didn't know the trick—run like a duck, point your toes out at forty degrees.

A greenish glow lit the way, the Pastel Pond. Jasper sped up. Both feet gave way. His face slammed into the mud.

He clawed into the mud, a stubborn attempt to get up. A hand grasped one ankle. He kicked hard. Gained freedom for a moment.

On his feet. Scrambling. Just inches away, the massive rock in the center.

Strong arms clamped down around Jasper's shoulders. Tackled from behind. Instinctively, as if stretching out to receive a pass. His fingers hit the light switch.

Instant darkness.

Now Jasper had the advantage. He knew the field. And he had a flashlight in one pocket. He scrambled free. Around the rock, three yards downfield, dodge left, avoid the water hazard. He turned on his flashlight, held it close to his chest, and blocked the light with his body as though faking a lateral pass.

Thundering through the narrow passage toward the Crystal Cable Car Tunnel, he kept his head low. Extremely low. He heard his pursuer. Right on his heels. Inches away.

He ducked.

There was a wet smack behind him as his pursuer found the Noddle Knocker.

Jasper ran to the Crystal Cable Car Tunnel entrance. Jumped into the lead incline railcar. Flipped a large switch to activate the motor. Pushed the long brake handle forward.

The chain of cable cars lurched upward.

The incline railcars climbed up the tracks through the Crystal Cable Car Tunnel, out into the afternoon sun, and headed up the mountain.

Alone in a steel cage, fear took hold. Fear for his life. Then guilt. The guilt of being responsible for the loss of a second life. Someone young.

A sickening thought hit him. Who was Tony?

DAZED, HARWOOD FOLLOWED the incline train track up the steep hill as fast as he could. By the time he reached the top, he had somewhat recovered. He raced down Wilderness Road in search of a security guard. Not a damn one in sight. He spotted a teenage girl selling cotton candy in a small booth.

"Help! Someone pushed my son over a ledge in the mine."

"You may want to report that to—"

"I need the fucking paramedics."

"The First Aid Station, it's right behind McGuffey's Homestead."

Harwood ran in the direction the girl had pointed. Most people saw him coming and dodged out of the way. Those that didn't tumbled like bowling pins.

"Don't have what you might call a para . . . medic, but I hear they got one in Branson," said the retired bookkeeper from Joplin dressed in a crisp white uniform with a nametag proclaiming her to be NURSE PRESTON. "I'll call Mr. Fosdick."

"Make it fast! My son is down there!"

Frederick Fosdick showed up in a surprisingly brief time, although it took a minute to restore his blood oxygen to a level that allowed him to speak. "What's this about pushing?"

"One of your employees pushed my son over a ledge in the mine." Harwood jammed his badge in Fosdick's face. "Get a rescue crew, now. We need ropes, battery lanterns, a stretcher."

"Where did this happen?"

"Toward the end of the mine tour, at the ledge with a flimsy rail."

"I'm afraid those pits are bottomless."

"Cave tour bullshit! Move!"

"Get some strong men," Fosdick yelled at two groundskeepers who had just arrived. "Take all the equipment this gentleman wants to the cable cars." Then he headed for the office to call his lawyer.

Chapter
19

Jasper stood at the top of the concrete tree, an enormous, surprisingly realistic-looking oak. Laughing children giggled while climbing the spiral staircase within it, then ventured across an unstable swinging bridge to play in a tree house. From the top of the tree, Jasper watched for Ginger.

Minutes later, he saw the cop with his jaw jutting outward, his arm around a sobbing woman, with a young girl struggling to keep up. Pushing their way through the mass of tourists, they trooped toward the mine.

His family. It was as bad as he feared. Tony must be the cop's son.

Where the heck was Ginger? He needed her help to escape this fantasy hell.

HARWOOD AND SIX sturdy men with no rope-climbing skills lay on the ledge and followed the harsh light of a lantern as it scanned the deep pit. Its beam hardly pierced the darkness. No way to get down there, not now, not with these carnies and meagre equipment.

Everyone, except Harwood, agreed that no one could survive such a fall. The oldest of the crew declared that no one had ever gone that deep into the cave. One said it was seven hundred feet straight down. Another claimed some electronic gadget had measured a thousand.

Harwood ignored their bullshit, refused to give up, even though there was nothing to see.

No broken body. No teenage basketball star.

No Tony.

JASPER DROPPED INTO step beside Ginger, head low, not looking around. Blending into a crowd had become second nature to him. "Did you have to stay late?"

"Just chatting with the new preacher at Wilderness Church. Kind of cute, not really a preacher, you know." Ginger smirked, delighted with the titillating challenge of leading a preacher astray.

"I'm kind of in a hurry today."

"What's the rush?"

"I'm leaving. It's time to move on."

"WHY SEE . . . the manager?" Judy managed a few words in between sobs. "Just call the local police."

Harwood rushed her along. Was he the only one who understood the urgency of what was happening?

"To make sure a real rescue team has been alerted. Plus, these local cops don't know a damn thing about a murder investigation. Got to act fast before Pipkins has time to make a move."

A secretary looked up as they opened the door labeled Administrative Office. She told them that Mr. Fosdick was terribly busy this afternoon. He flashed his badge. She would see if Mr. Fosdick could spare a few minutes.

"Now!"

Suddenly, Judy burst into tears. "You're working, aren't you? This whole family outing is a scam." She retreated into a corner. "You're here after Pipkins."

Harwood ran past the receptionist and burst into the fat bastard's office.

Fosdick looked up, squarely at Harwood. "Are my men taking care of the situation?"

"Those hayseeds are useless, and you know it!" Harwood grabbed the phone and dialed 911.

"I've already inquired, there are no subterranean rescue services in Branson," Fosdick meekly interjected.

"EMS, rescue services in Springfield," Harwood barked into the phone, "make it fast, we have a fall victim in Marble Mine!

"I'm a police officer. A fifteen-year-old boy has been pushed off a cliff inside Marble Mine, near Branson. Dispatch a rescue team immediately.

"Don't give me some shit about your usual service area. This is attempted murder. The publicity will be statewide. Don't force me to say that you refused to help my son.

"Be sure that team includes someone with rappelling skills and equipment. Someone with know-how in controlled descent on sheer rock faces. They'll need a thousand feet a rope, harnesses, carabiners, a belay device, and a stretcher."

He slammed the phone down. "Shut up and listen," he said, then jammed his badge in Fosdick's face. "I need the name, address, Social Security number—everything you've got on that mine-tour photographer."

"Little Rock Police? A bit out of your jurisdiction. We have a capable security team."

"My son fell through the broken railing in your sham of a mine."

"I'll have my secretary check the personnel files."

"Now, you shyster!" Hardwood grabbed Fosdick by the shirt, threw him against the wall. Fosdick's eyes bulged, his face turned deep purple, his mouth dropped open, a muttered word dribbled out, a wet stream of drool slid down his jaw. "You're more interested in suppressing bad publicity than rescuing my son!"

Speechless, Fosdick ran out with a trail of blood gushing from his nose.

Harwood grabbed papers off the desk, scanned rapidly, tossed them aside. An Ozark Insurance Limited Liability Policy fell apart as it flew in the air. Judy cowered on the couch and hugged Sally.

Three long minutes later, Fosdick returned from his secretary's desk with an answer.

"The photographer for the Marble Mine tours. . ." Mr. Fosdick seemed to have regained his composure. "I'm afraid he is not an employee."

"He's in your mine taking pictures. Don't you fucking pay him?"

"A freelancer. Gets thirty-five cents for each photo people buy. Cash deal at the end of the day."

"You mean off the books, no taxes."

"No, an independent contractor. We collect the sales tax. We report our share of the profits. It's up to him to pay his own taxes."

"You must have some goddamn record on the guy. Where does he live? Phone number?"

"Not really, just an informal gentleman's agreement. He shuffled in here, said he could take pictures, did a decent job, knew how to schmooze the proud mothers."

"How do you know he's really a photographer?"

"He made the dumb kids that come through here look good. That's what the job is about."

"What's his name?"

"Jones, I believe. Talk to the mine-tour supervisor."

H ARWOOD KNEW IT would take the rescue team at least two hours to get there. Time he would spend getting his hands on Pipkins. He ran back to the mine entrance—speed made the difference. Get to the friends and coworkers fast, before they realize the guy is in trouble. Before they have time to make up a story. That goofy tour guide at the mine would give up information.

"Hey, Caleb." Harwood held out his badge as though he were sharing photos of a family vacation. "Guess you've heard about the accident."

"You know, I warned them about that railing."

"At the moment I'm interested in your photographer friend. I believe his name is Jones?"

"Yeah, Jasper. How can I help?"

"Just need some information. You know where he lives?"

"No idea. He shows up every morning before I get here. Don't know where he comes from."

"Phone number? Friends? You must know something about him." Harwood tried to make it sound as though there were some deficiency in Caleb's personality if he did not know details about someone he worked with.

A soot-covered train engineer poked his head through the door. "You still here?"

"Just closing up," Caleb said.

"I'm looking for the photographer." Harwood butted in. "Do you know him?"

"Jasper Jones," the engineer said. "Nice guy."

"Where does he live?"

"No idea. Don't know him that well."

"Somebody must know this guy."

"Ginger does," the engineer said. "He rides to work with her every day."

"Ginger—does she work here?"

"Sure. Pretty girl, walks around with an umbrella."

Harwood marched off.

"SO, YOU'RE TAKING off." Ginger paced back and forth then abruptly stopped and placed her hands on her hips. "Sticking me with the rent."

"Come with me," Jasper said. "We'll stick Rick for the rent."

"It's tourist season. We're making good money." She flopped on the couch. "I'll take a walk in the fall."

"Suit yourself. I'm going now."

"The hell you are. Paying full rent won't leave me enough for a start in California."

"Sorry. Can't stay."

"And just how are you planning to leave?"

"I thought you might drop me off at the Branson bus depot."

"Kiss my—"

Bang. Bang. Bang. The motel door shook. Not the kind of knock you hear when a neighbor comes by wanting to borrow sugar.

Jasper braced himself. Not even his eyes moved.

Ginger laughed. He hated that laugh. He wanted to lash out. Primal instinct for self-preservation kept him in check.

Ginger jumped off the couch. Headed for the door. "Let's see who's eager to visit."

Jasper headed for the bedroom. Ginger's bedroom. Off-limits—but the rulebook had just swirled down the drain, like used toilet paper.

Barely audible voices filtered into the bedroom. Coarse. Filled with curses—both hers and the man's.

"What do you want?"

The man's words were unclear, but the tone exposed his intent. Violence. Aggression.

Jasper held Ginger's revolver up close, near his face. Checked it—all cylinders full, hammer half-cocked.

Still arguing. The same bitter sound. No one seemed to be gaining the advantage on this verbal battleground. Could she be demanding a warrant? Telling the cop her roommate wasn't here? Probably not, she wasn't that loyal.

Heavy noises. Shuffling. A lamp crashing. The brazen visitor had entered.

He pulled back the hammer—fully cocked.

Feet spread. Arms extended. Sweat poured onto his eyelids. Stung. Vision blurred. Everyone thought he was a murderer. Was he about to prove it to himself?

212

Total silence.

The doorknob turned. The latch clicked. Old hinges screeched.

"What the hell are you doing?" Ginger reached out, grabbed her Smith & Wesson by the barrel and swung it away from her.

"Where's Harwood?" The only words he could manage.

"Who's Harwood? That was fucking Fosdick."

"Fosdick? Why?"

"Accused me of stealing his money. And he says because of you some cop's kid fell through a railing and he might be sued. I've had enough. I'm getting out of here, too."

Jasper packed rapidly—shave kit, underwear, a couple of shirts and he was ready to go. Everything he owned fit in a backpack.

Ginger had problems, Ginger always had problems, but Ginger had the car.

"I don't have a suitcase." she whined. "Lent it to someone."

"Doesn't matter. Just throw your junk in the car trunk."

"You should never lend stuff to nobody." Ginger seemed more intent on ensuring that she would remember her lesson regarding generosity than on getting out of town fast.

Jasper thought she seemed . . . disconnected. She didn't realize Harwood could show up any minute. He wasn't going to explain it—not all of it. He needed to think up a quick story.

"Look, Fosdick's mad at me too. Blames me for not

fixing the railing." He grabbed a pile of her clothes. "We need to move fast."

"I don't want my makeup all jumbled up."

"I'm sure you'll be able to keep it nice and tidy in a jail cell."

That got her moving.

HARWOOD BANGED ON the Administrative Office door, twisted the doorknob, rammed his shoulder against it. Only secure door in the whole damn place. Judy looked on, trembling, and silent. She'd been numb for the last hour. He ran to the main gate; a few stragglers shuffled out, looking broke and exhausted.

At the main gate, he yelled at the lone Marble Mine Village employee overseeing the exodus. "Who's in charge of this zoo when Fosdick's not here?"

"Ah . . ."

Without waiting for some half-baked answer, he frantically ran off searching for an employee over twenty, an authoritative adult. On Wilderness Road, a gray-haired man with a large ring of keys shuffled along, looking for stragglers and securing frontier buildings. "You. Do you know Ginger?"

"Really pretty girl," said the man with the keys. "Fancy clothes, you know, like in magazines."

"What else can you remember about her?"

"Real nice smile, lots of white teeth. No chips or fillings."

"That's all you noticed—her teeth?"

"Wouldn't be Christian to go staring elsewhere."

Jesus Christ. Was this Fosdick's capable security team? Harwood jogged away.

He changed tactics, put on a happy face, raced off to the parking lots and began quizzing the teenagers directing traffic. Anyone who looked like they worked there and would remember personal details about a pretty woman.

"Hi, do you guys happen to know Ginger?" Harwood asked two lanky bumpkins working in parking lot E.

"Kind of," said the one with a mop of straight hair parted down the middle.

"Where does she live?"

"Well, I really never talked to her."

Harwood believed him. "What make of car does she drive?" He thought that was the kind of thing they would know.

"Some kind of foreign thing—I think."

"Yeah, it's German or maybe one of those Jap cars."

"What color?" Harwood said.

"It's green,"

"Or it could be gray. Hard to tell, real old and faded."

"What state on her license plate?"

"Not Missouri or Arkansas."

"Or even Oklahoma."

He could see these kids wanted to help, it made them feel important, but he doubted they could count past ten with their shoes on. "What color were the plates?"

"Color? Don't know."

"Weren't nothing like from around here."

Harwood abruptly turned around without saying thank you. He had solved cases with less. All he needed to do was drive around, check the parking lots of cheap apartments and residential motels, keep an eye out for a small faded foreign car with out-of-state plates driven by a pretty girl with nice teeth.

But far more urgent was that rescue team from Springfield arriving any minute, skilled medics with decent equipment. Tony's last chance.

A Maserati is Safe When Locked in the Garage
But That's Not What a Maserati is Built For
Jack Crane

Chapter
20

"I HOPE THIS RATTLE trap makes it to New Mexico." Ginger held the wheel tight.

Jasper noticed a severe wobbling. The front end had to be way out of alignment. "I thought you wanted to go to California."

"I do, but New Mexico is on the way. I want to see my best friend ever."

"I guess no one will look for us there."

"We can catch 65 in Branson, head south to I-40, hang a right and, bam, we're in New Mexico."

Jasper held a flashlight to the US map spread on his knees. South into Arkansas, not a good plan. On the other hand, telling Ginger what to do would be difficult.

"What part of New Mexico?" He needed to word this carefully. "Big place."

"Near Taos."

"Oh, that's way up north. Years ago, Dad and I drove to the Platoro Valley in Colorado, just north of Taos. Hunted elk there."

"Like I say, I-40, zip, we're there."

"Not really. Lot of truck traffic on 40."

"Do you have any idea what you're talking about?"

"Of course. We can take 65 North out of Branson, then pick up Highway 160 across Kansas. It will take us all the way to southern Colorado, then drop right down to Taos."

Ginger didn't say yes or no, just held the juddering wheel tight.

JASPER JAMMED THE gas hose in the Datsun's fill pipe and got busy scraping a month's worth of bugs off the windshield. Then, playing the happy vacationing couple, they sauntered inside the 24-hour convenience store.

"How do we get to 65?" Jasper said.

"Follow the road that way," the clerk pointed with his right hand, "it tees into 65. You folks headed north or south?"

"South," Jasper replied.

"No, we're going north." Ginger slapped her hands on her hips.

"I'm sure we decided on south, darling." Jasper said south distinctly, almost mouthing the words, hoping she'd get it.

Ginger leaned in close to the clerk, almost touching his head. "North."

Jasper waited until they were on US 65, heading north out of Branson. "Are you really that stupid? The police are going to check all the gas stations, looking for an old beat-up Datsun, asking which way it went. And you just told them."

"You don't like how I do; you can get out and walk."

Jasper settled in and started to sulk. The entire world was conspiring against him. Especially Ginger, she had jumped the fence and taken the opposing side, insisted on going north for no other reason than being confrontational. She enjoyed rattling his cage. The reality of the situation sank in, the practical side, the banker's view. The dream of owning a restaurant was now a nightmare. His real future was fugitive from justice, unable to get credit, a pathetic prospect whose business plan was a farce.

JUST OVER THE Missouri-Kansas border, Ginger started yawning and decided to nap instead of wrestling with the Datsun's shaky front end. Jasper took control of the unstable vehicle; for the moment he also had control of unstable and unconscious Ginger, but he did not have control of his unstable life.

He shifted his weight in the pint-size bucket seat. With knees jammed against the dashboard, it felt tight, hemmed in, a tin can on wheels, filled with the stench of Ginger's cigarette smoke and cheap perfume.

He tried to imagine a better life. One where he did have control. A prosperous life. Instead of bouncing across Kansas in a beat-up Datsun, he'd race up the Pacific Coast Highway in a high-class vehicle, something agile, with power. A stylish European two-door Mercedes or even a Porsche. No—a sexy Italian machine, A sleek silver Maserati, with black leather interior. Cruise the hills of San Francisco with Alicia, then head to Napa to check out the vineyards.

Abruptly, a Welcome to Coffeeville, Kansas sign whizzed by while the speedometer wavered well above sixty. Jasper instantly let up and attempted to stay two miles under the limit. Couldn't risk a ticket.

The sudden change of speed aroused his obstinate passenger.

"It would've been a whole lot faster to take I-40 straight across Oklahoma and the Texas Panhandle to New Mexico," Ginger said.

"It wouldn't be fast if we were sitting in a police station."

"We swiped ten grand from a third-rate amusement park. That isn't going to warrant an APB across four states."

"Wait, wait, wait! Ten grand? We?"

"Aren't we full of questions today?"

"You stole ten thousand dollars?"

"Not all at once. A little here. A little there."

"Oh, well, that makes it okay."

"Fosdick just wants me gone so that his wife doesn't find out about our Friday afternoon romps in his playroom."

Jasper swallowed a comment about payment for services rendered. Not wise to agitate her, she's already irrational.

THE GREEN TREES of Missouri had faded into rolling grasslands as they bobbled across Kansas. Many miles later, the hills flattened out into arid land plotted in endless rectangular fields, embedded with green circle patterns crafted by irrigation sprinklers. A monotonous checkerboard, occasionally broken by lost muddy rivers, frustratedly seeking a path to the ocean.

Jasper finally broke the silence. "We need to change our names. Let's do it now and get used to calling each other something else."

"I like my name just fine. You do whatever the hell you want, Jasper Jones."

"No. From now on, I'm Jack. Jack Crane."

"All I did was petty theft. That railing deal with the cop's kid is your problem, you paranoid son of a bitch."

JASPER—JACK—DIDN'T CARE FOR the turquoise-and-pink clapboard shack with a beach scene painted on one side. But the only other buildings at this nameless crossroad were a faded motel and an old-fashioned gas station with no hotdogs on rollers under a heat lamp or even cellophane-wrapped donuts. Jack's opinion didn't count for much. If you were hungry near this wide spot in the road, you ate at the Sunset Diner.

Everyone within fifty miles of this speck on the map seemed to be hungry. A parking lot bounded by plastic palm trees was full of heavy-duty pickups and one faded slab-sided Lincoln from a previous era. Yes—that's right, plastic palm trees, and a large, ragged banner stretched between two phone poles made the outrageous claim, Volleyball Tournament Tomorrow. Would tomorrow ever arrive in this corner of Kansas?

Discretion in this gaudy restaurant might be a challenge.

Inside it smelled of animal fat and onions sizzling on a black iron grill, hairspray, barnyard boots, fragments of hay poking from checked flannel shirts, Right Guard, cattle, breath mints, fresh paint, and tobacco. The odor of hard work and hard luck mingled with promise and romance.

Despite the beach motif outside, the inside was classic 1950s roadside diner. It looked as though a flamboyant new owner had renovated the outside, then given up on the project. Vinyl booths lined one wall. A yellow Formica counter ran along the other. A glass case displayed pies topped with four-inch high meringue. The waitress reminded him of a Harvey Girl he'd seen in an old black-and-white photo at an art exhibit.

Jack headed straight for the only empty booth, without looking around and drawing attention.

"Let's go squeeze in at the counter." Ginger cocked her head toward the farmers balanced on chrome swivel stools. "It would be nice to chat with the locals."

"We need to eat fast and get some rest. We've got a lot of miles to cover tomorrow. Need to stay alert."

"Alert for what? Nothing to see here but clumps of grass and scraggly-ass cows."

"And the Highway Patrol. We can't leave a trail of breadcrumbs. Save the chit-chat until we get to Taos."

"Screw you. And I don't mean that literally."

Ginger ordered black coffee. Jack opted for water, he wanted to get a good night's sleep. They both decided on a Sunset Burger that promised to be the biggest and best west of Kansas City. By the look of the other patrons hanging over the edge of the counter stools, he felt confident that they would deliver on big.

Jack tried to avoid eye contact with the humongous

farm boy staring at him from the next booth. Baby-faced, heavyset, he didn't sit straight—his torso aimed straight up toward twelve o'clock noon, while his head leaned counterclockwise somewhere between ten and ten thirty. A burger, the Sunset Cheeseburger, five inches thick counting the tomato and onions, slipped from the farm boy's hands, bounced twice on the floor, then rolled to a standstill. Completely intact, barely damaged by the impact. No one else in the place seemed to notice, so Jack played the same game and intently studied the menu even though he had already ordered.

While Jack waited for his opportunity to attack a Sunset Burger, he looked over the crowded diner. Studied one or two people at a time. Subtly, so that no one would notice. If the police could find him hundreds of feet underground, they could find him anywhere.

After downing a glass of water, Jack could no longer ignore the urge to head for the restroom. As soon as he pushed through the door, he found himself inches away from the baby-faced farm boy with the runaway burger. He stepped back against the towel dispenser.

"Can you help me?" The farm boy held up a large index finger with a contact lens balanced on the tip.

Startled, Jack turned and rushed back to the booth.

He restlessly tapped one foot and kept one eye on the men's room door. Eventually baby-face emerged, his large finger still held in the air, with no glint from a contact sitting on top. Then he realized, the person was mentally challenged—maybe Mongoloid, or just a bit slow.

There was a lot of misfortune in this world. Who do you help? When do you look the other way? He felt bad and tried to explain it to Ginger.

"Eat up and get out." She grabbed the last of his fries. "We got our own problems."

JACK DIDN'T GET much sleep at the faded motel by the wide spot in the road, although Ginger looked well rested the next morning. He went into the gas station to pay cash while she waited at the pump. Then he ran across the road to the Sunset Diner for coffee and six Danish to go. The towns were far apart out here. Besides, the fewer the stops, the fainter the trail.

On the way out, the headline in a *Kansas City Sentinel* vending machine caught his eye.

MARBLE MINE MURDER

He bent down to read the small text underneath.

The deranged banker who killed a Little Rock police officer last year has struck again. This time he viciously tossed a 15-year-old boy into a bottomless cavern. Tony Harwood, the mild-mannered son of Sergeant Alvin Harwood, was following his father through a cave at a tourist village in the Missouri Ozarks . . .

Jack jumped into the Datsun without buying the paper. Definitely didn't want Ginger reading those distorted details. He wasn't sure where she drew the line on moral transgressions, or if she even drew lines. But he didn't want to bet that she'd tolerate travelling with a child killer.

Chapter
21

Taos consisted of one long highway with a dozen dirt roads jutting out at odd angles.

"Look at that walking jewelry store." Jack slowed down to check out a long-bearded character in an oil-cloth coat that hung down to pointed-toe cowboy boots. "Crumpled western hats loaded with silver and turquoise seem to be all the rage this season."

"We're not in Kansas anymore, Dodo," Ginger said.

"I believe the dog's name was Toto."

"Yeah, and I bet you also believe in the Wicked Witch of the West."

Smirking, he nodded in agreement. *Proof is sitting right here.*

At a Y in the road, they pulled in to Allsup's Grocery and Gas on the edge of an enigmatic cemetery—mounds of crusty gray dirt pierced with weathered wood crosses and plastic flowers. Jack filled up while Ginger asked about White Rabbit Farm.

"There's an Indian on the road to Taos Pueblo that's got a bunch of rabbits," said the clerk in Allsup's.

"Never heard of it," said a mother balancing a child on one arm and a gallon of milk and a jar of jelly on the other.

"Sounds like that commune place out on Conejo Mesa," said a cowboy wearing a black Stetson as he put gas in a pickup with two goats in the back. "Follow the highway north, take a left at Arroyo Hondo."

A mile north the motels and Mexican restaurants disappeared. So did everything else. To Jasper—Jack—it looked flatter than Kansas. Open. Vast. Definitely spectacular. He could see forever—mile after mile of sagebrush lit by bright sunshine. A flat table with sharp, jagged edges, canyons cut by raging rivers. But who could survive here on top of the world?

"Kind of pretty in its own way," Jack said.

"Yeah." Ginger glanced out the window for a moment. "If you don't like grass or trees."

Eight miles farther north, at the top of a steep downhill grade, the endless empty was broken by an official looking sign: Entering the Arroyo Hondo Land Grant.

"Who granted it to whom?" Jack said. "And when?"

"And who the hell wanted it?" Ginger said.

The highway dipped into a valley with huge cottonwood trees along a creek. Halfway down the hill, a hand-painted sign on a bare wood shack with bars on the windows said RITA'S BAR. It looked as though it'd been out of business for years, but there was a dust-covered jeep out back that looked like it might have a few months of life left in it.

Immediately past the creek, they turned at the arrow pointing to Arroyo Hondo. The town consisted of a single block lined with a dozen adobe houses which looked abandoned. Not one single car, flower, dog, or person. A brown, lifeless world. Every house had a flat roof and dirty windows with lace curtains, the kind of curtains Jack remembered in Grandma Pipkins's house. They went one block and stopped at the corner of Camino de Placitas and East Vigil Road.

"Is that it?" Jack said. "Two streets."

"Why even bother to give them names?" Ginger's sugary southern accent had totally disappeared, replaced by a nasally Brooklyn inflection.

He turned and crossed a small wooden bridge with a bent sign that said Rio Hondo. Jack thought it looked more like a creek than a river. The road curved around, headed back to the highway, and ended up at Rita's bar. At least the bar had a vague sign of life. A hand-painted sign tacked to the door said OPEN, yet it was locked. Jack warily knocked while Ginger touched up her nails in the Datsun.

"Bueno Dios, Señor. Come in." The melodic voice rose at the end of the sentence.

One bare forty-watt light bulb barely penetrated the dusty air. Jack's eyes strained to take it all in. A fat gray cat dozed on the plywood bar top. Old photographs hung at awkward angles on unpainted plank-board walls. Cobwebs connected every bottle and antique trinket on the shelves against one wall. And behind the bar, in a faded sundress that may have once been yellow, the oldest woman he had ever seen was ready for business.

"Do you speak any English?" he said.

"Si. You like cerveza fría?"

"Sure, Rita."

"I not Rita. She lazy. Not dependable. I her mother."

"What's your name?"

"Itzel Montaño. My father builds bar. I live here ninety-four years."

The old woman shuffled from behind the bar and opened a small refrigerator that rattled and hummed on top of a pool table.

"Got any Coors?"

One at a time, she took five bottles from the refrigerator and held them three inches in front of her face, then shakily pried the cap from a bottle of Budweiser. "Forty-five cents, exact. No change."

Jack handed over two quarters, which Itzel examined closely, relying on fingertips rather than eyes. She looked up suspiciously, felt the coins again, then smiled when she realized that she'd just received a tip. She opened a ragged notebook, bent over, and entered the sale into her ledger.

"You know how to get to the White Rabbit Farm?"

"Huh. Crazy people! Not many left."

Jack jumped as the cat leapt from the bar onto the pool table. "How do I get there?"

"Is easy, Señor. Down hill to town, go left where Elfego Sanchez used to live. After the yellow sign that say Road Narrows, do not turn around, the sand, it is loose."

"What's the name of the road?"

"No name, no much road, maybe you see tire tracks."

A FTER TAKING A left turn where Jack guessed Elfego Sanchez once lived, they bounced along a dirt track for three-quarters of a mile until being confronted by a fork in the road. Jack hit the brakes, dug in his pocket, pulled out a quarter and called, "Heads right, tails left." Impulsive, no logic, guided by chance. He smiled—Life is changing.

That left turn soon crumbled, definitely the road less traveled. Jack could hear the old Datsun drag across rocky outcrops—the transmission, the oil pan, something was scraping. Not a single sign of life, and Jack's confidence in taking chances started to wane. Two torturous miles later, he gave in to pragmatic reasoning, and looked for a place to turn around without sinking up to the axels in loose sand.

Excitedly, Ginger jabbed her indignant finger at a blue oval sign full of bullet holes that advertised Eggs for Sale.

"Turn here. Marcy said they were in the egg business."

"Who the heck comes out here shopping for eggs?"

"Who cares? She also said this place was in the sticks, but this is fucking crazy."

That last turn to the left had them heading toward the river, where a young woman sat on a low concrete bridge, her feet dangling in the water as she strummed a guitar. Jack pulled over and hesitated; this wild goose chase got stranger with every twist in the road. Ginger jumped out, so he followed. The skinny woman walked toward them. At a distance, her brown skirt looked like deerskin, but then he realized it was loose woven cotton. Her brown suede boots were loose fitting and crumpled. A bandana covered her forehead, nothing flashy, a shade of light tan that matched her healthy complexion.

"Hi, I'm Molly." Her broad smile barely fit on her face.

"Ginger." The clipped monotone reply hung in the air.

Both women stared at him.

"Uh . . . Jack Crane. Nice to meet you."

She actually seemed more like a girl than a woman, with long hair drooping over an oval face which didn't wear glasses, but somehow looked like it should.

Ginger got right down to business. "We're looking for Marcy Blue."

"Sorry, you missed her. Left six months ago. Almost everyone's gone now."

With the sun threatening to disappear behind the Sangre de Cristo Mountains and only vague remnants of road between them and civilization, Ginger jumped at Molly's gracious offer of supper and a place to sleep. Jack began to list the advantages of leaving immediately. But Molly had already squeezed into the back seat with her guitar.

The road climbed a steep hill, curved right, and ran along a falling-down wall made of exposed mud bricks which seemed to be melting. The abandoned compound with broken corrals and a bunkhouse may have once been a ranch. Now they were on top of a mesa. In the distance, he could see a canyon with massive black cubes of exposed rock stacked hundreds of feet high.

By the time they got to what was supposedly White Rabbit Farm, Jack thought that the Road Narrows sign was an understatement. As for the name of this place, a rabbit couldn't possibly live here, and calling the half-dozen makeshift mud buildings surrounded by dirt and cactus a farm was an outright lie.

The buildings had flat roofs and walls of hand-molded

red clay. Round logs stuck out of the top of the walls, probably some sort of roof brace. The only substantial building had a rounded section sticking out of the middle of the roof, making it look like a medieval sandcastle. A struggling green plot in the middle of a clearing had probably once been a much larger cultivated field. On the far side of the field, he could make out two triangular structures that appeared to be the pole frameworks of teepees. Lonely and lost, the set of a spaghetti western, abandoned for a decade or two.

THE SMALL KITCHEN, or cook house as they called it, looked far different on the inside—it was actually warm and cozy. Jack studied the wood-burning cook stove. He'd never seen one. The only window had a curtain made from a Led Zeppelin T-shirt. There were two straight-back wood chairs at either end of a well-made table with bench seats long enough to crowd four people on each side.

"Homey." Jack knew a compliment could never hurt.

"Sometimes in the summer, we cooked for fifty people in this cook house." Molly's note of pride told him the light-yellow walls and turquoise trim were her inspiration.

Ginger plopped into one of the chairs. "How'd you stuff fifty people in here?"

Molly grabbed a dented Rayovac flashlight and hopped toward a four-inch-thick side door. A carefully crafted slot in the door allowed a wooden bolt to slide into the doorjamb. A simple and sturdy latch. Someone who knew what they were doing spent a lot of time on that mechanism.

"We call this the drumming room." Molly swung the door open and aimed the flashlight through the opening. "Stick your head in, but don't take anything in there you're not willing to part with."

"What's the problem?"

"Not enough people here to maintain things. The adobe walls weren't coated with a fresh top layer of mud every year, water seeped in, and the vigas rotted."

"Vigas?"

Molly aimed the light at the ceiling. "Those big, long roof supports."

"Who came up with the weird floorplan?" For once Ginger was the conformist.

"Native Americans. It's called a Zia, the sun symbol. The circle with four rays pointing out represent the four seasons, the four compass directions, the four times of each day, and the four stages of life"

"Looks like an octagon to me."

"Use your imagination."

Jack stood up for the room. "This structure is rather elaborate. In fact, it's somewhat aesthetically pleasing. I thought you people would be more inclined toward Russian architecture."

"Russian architecture?"

"Typical communist stuff. Austere. Gray rectangular concrete slabs."

"It is quite possible to construct simple and functional structures that are also visually soothing and blend into the landscape, rather than those glitzy offensive structures in bourgeois suburbia."

"Home construction feeds the economy and . . ." His voice trailed off, time to shut up.

Molly explained that the founding members had

designed the room for twenty-five people but fifty could squeeze in. They had sunk it three feet below ground in deference to Native American Churches, or Kivas, which are underground. Elders from the Taos Pueblo helped work it all out.

"It's my night to cook, but we can't eat until that damn Zipper gets back with some firewood."

Jack wondered who or what a Zipper was but didn't ask. "What's for supper?"

Molly dragged a gunnysack of potatoes out of the closet. "You peel while I wash the broccoli." She looked at Jack.

"I'm not a potato-peeling type of person."

"Around here you peel or go hungry."

"I've worked in a restaurant kitchen, but—"

"Everything after butt is a pile of poo. If you've worked in a kitchen, you've peeled spuds. We already have two bums here who think they're above it all. Do not need another."

"Culinary art and food preparation are two distinctly separate disciplines." Jack took the high road—she was a bit cocky, and he was still pissed about spending the night out here. He didn't mention that Harpo left the skins on his French fries. He recalled Harpo saying *That's where the good Lord hid them vitamins.* The Sunset burger was the last decent meal, so he started peeling.

"Well, Chef, do your culinary skills include feeding hogs? Ralph and Charlotte and all their little piglets will love the way you prepared those potato skins." Molly handed him the galvanized pail full of food scraps and the old chrome flashlight. "Pig pen's fifty yards to the right. Bon appétit."

As he turned toward the door, a strange-looking

character walked in with an armload of wood. He wore a peacenik's tie-dyed T-shirt, but his large owl eyes behind wire-rimmed glasses made him look more like a Harvard professor.

"This dude stopped by for supper." Molly nodded toward Jack.

"A night and a meal. That's it." He planted his feet and spread his shoulders. "Not a whole lot of food on hand. We're in the process of shutting this place down."

"The grouch in the doorway is called Zipper," Molly said.

"Jack . . . Crane." Jack wasn't sure if Zipper was a first or last name, or if it mattered. He didn't extend his hand. He doubted hippies had adopted that custom from the establishment.

Zipper stepped aside and pointed toward the dark outside. "Watch out for rattlers."

"Rattlesnakes?"

"No, we have a lot of babies here. Yes, rattlesnakes."

"What do you do if you see one?"

"There are various recommended courses of action. Three Hail Marys is as good as any."

"He's blowing smoke up your tailpipe." Molly shook her head. "Not many large snakes at seven thousand feet above sea level."

He scanned the sagebrush looking for pigs and looking out for snakes with the feeble flashlight. Bossy little bitch. But he was hungry, what choice did he have?

Jack's first encounter with pigs was not as bad as he'd feared, just dump the bucket over the fence and they were friends for life. When he got back, the distinct odor of boiling broccoli filled the cook house. Pots and pans constantly clanked as the skinny girl called Molly prepared supper. Ginger had gone off somewhere to freshen up for dinner.

Zipper motioned Jack to sit at the table and said, with that stupid grin men reveal to each other, "Has Ginger been your old lady for a long time?"

"She's never been my lady, not in that way. Traveling companions, that's all."

"She's bitchin', got legs that go on forever." Zipper slapped his knee, his voice rose, the pitch sharpened. "She could wrap those legs around a guy, strangle him to death, and he wouldn't even complain."

"I guess."

"So, you don't mind if I jump her bones?"

"Good luck, and God bless."

"Of course, the thing that makes a woman look really beautiful is some good weed."

Jack decided to play along, for something to do. "Is Molly your girl?"

"She thinks she's too good for the guys up here."

"Oh? Are there a lot of guys here?"

"Me and Habeeb. When he's coherent. So maybe she's got a point."

"Habeeb?"

"Habeeb. Mechanic, scientist, jelly brain, Dr. Timothy Leary disciple, and a Grace Slick groupie."

"Sounds . . . well rounded."

"When he's not out to lunch."

"I guess you were glad to see another woman pop up here."

"I've already got my hands full." Zipper held out two cupped hands with the palms facing upward.

Jack had lost interest in the conversation almost as soon as it started. He nodded noncommittally.

"Cinnamon's an airhead, but she can brighten up your day. Rosemary's a brick house. Got meat on her bones in all the right places, but she can have a cow. Don't piss her off, man."

Jack directed his attention toward Molly as she boiled water in a coffee pot on the wood stove. When it started to bubble, she tossed in a handful of coffee.

"You need to run that through a filter," he said.

"A little chilly water will make it settle." She added a cup of water.

The door opened and the tiny eating area quickly filled up. A pleasant, fair-haired woman introduced herself as Rosemary Meadow and gave him a warm hug. A tall, slender reddish-blonde curtsied in a quirky way and announced that she was Cinnamon Stick. A man who looked like he had forty hard years behind him sat down and mumbled, "Habeeb." Then Ginger returned and asked forgiveness for showing up with blotchy makeup, due to the lack of running water and the unflattering light of a kerosene lamp. No apology for not helping out.

Molly served up the food and everyone dug in.

Jack picked at the edges before deciding to eat—broccoli, beans, and boiled potatoes with salt. Nothing else. He had to wonder if Zipper's abrupt comment about not having much food and shutting this place down had been an apology for such a simple meal or a complaint about more hungry mouths to feed. "Why are you leaving?" he asked.

"The owner wants this land back. Why, I don't know. Some nonsense about Earthships."

"And they call us potheads and dreamers," Habeeb mumbled.

"Earthships, that sounds exciting," Ginger said.

"Where do they come from?"

"It's a kind of large house," Rosemary said, "mostly underground, environmentally sound and comfortable. I've heard that some are even luxurious."

Jack didn't plan to stay long enough to care about Earthships or anything else in this isolated outpost.

The door crashed open, Jack lurched as though he were about to dive under the table, and everyone stared and then laughed as two pint-sized hippies bounded in.

"You seem a bit jumpy," Zipper said.

"Yeah, Jumpin' Jack." Habeeb managed to chuckle. "Just like the Stones song, 'Jumpin' Jack Flash.'"

"These are my girls," Cinnamon said. "Tiger Lily is eight and Pumpkin Patch is almost six."

Both bobbed and twirled as though a deep offstage voice had just congratulated them on a brilliant performance.

Everyone except Jack had plenty to say. He wasn't eager to make new acquaintances. He didn't want to leave any impression that these delusional potheads and quirky pixies would remember. His only interest was getting out of there as soon as possible.

"Ginger, there's a spare bed in the room that I share with Molly," Rosemary said. "Cinnamon and her girls have their own room."

"We share everything," Molly added. "We call it tribalism, like the Indians. But we're not brought together by ethnic origin. We gathered as an alternative to greed, materialism, and war."

"It works for us," Rosemary said. "Although the mainstream claims that communal life is impossible, that sharing everything you've got is against the laws of nature."

"More like against the laws of capitalist greed," Molly said.

"Which derive from the puritanical dogma: 'Work hard and benefit from the fruits of your labor.'" Rosemary sounded like a preacher. "During the Industrial Revolution this was extrapolated to mean benefit from the fruits of your neighbor. In other words, build lots of sweatshops."

He realized he was in one of those few remaining pockets where hippiedom still reigned. He could understand a few stragglers from the fold, who were just interested in pot and coasting through life. But these people were trying to live by a social and economic theory not only to the far left of Randolph G. Pipkins; it was left of Bob Dylan. He tried to picture Zipper at the First Commerce Bank, nine o'clock on a Monday morning, seated at the big conference room table, debating the virtues of communal wealth sharing. By contrast, the potato skin joust with the smart-mouth skinny girl seemed trivial.

Low profile or not, Jack couldn't resist a question. "Speaking of economics, do you farm here or work in Taos?"

"We're a self-sufficient agrarian community, escaping the greed of soulless cities." Rosemary rattled off her litany. "Grow only what we need, don't deplete natural resources, and share amongst ourselves."

"A community can't survive on just a bean field."

"We make real stuff with our hands, heads, and hearts."

"Did you make these forks? Or manufacture the glass in those windows?"

"We buy essential items." Obviously, Zipper had put up with Jack long enough.

"So where does the money come from?"

"A bit here, a bit there," Zipper said. "At one time we had two trust-fund babies."

The talk of money caught Ginger's attention, predictably. "Trust-fund babies?"

"Inheritances from wealthy relatives," Molly said. "A bit doled out every month."

Another chink in their armor, one of many flaws he saw in their utopian plan. But he decided to let it go. He couldn't get into a discussion like this without subtly revealing facts about himself, facts that might aid the police. Besides, this group certainly wouldn't appreciate the opinion of a commercial banker.

Well, he was only there for one night. Tired after the long drive, angry with Ginger for being a thief, surrounded by radical communists, he just wanted to get some sleep and get to California.

"What's your last name, Cinnamon? I didn't quite catch it." Ginger had lost interest in those trust-fund babies who had decided to spend their money on better things than beans and broccoli.

Jack shrank back and tried not to throw something at her. Why ask about last names? Then they ask yours. The simpler it is, the less people remember.

"First name's Cinnamon Stick, but they call me Cinnamon for short. Don't have a last name—kind of like Sinatra or Elvis. One name gets the job done."

He looked back at his plate. What he wouldn't give for a plate of Harpo's slow-roasted pork. A polite inquiry about protein got him a long response about the protein content of beans. He made a mental note not to bring that up again.

Later, Jack sat at the table alone, digesting the broccoli and protein-laden beans as best he could. The skinny girl with the headband, tonight's cook and dietary nutrition specialist, apparently pulled kitchen patrol as well.

"Can you give me a hand?" Molly held out a towel. "Dry the dishes and stack them on the shelves while I wash up."

"I'm not good at domestic chores." He stared out the window at a pitch-black sky filled with thousands of pinpoint stars.

"Crikey. Do you like to eat?"

"Sure, if it's not beans, potatoes, and broccoli."

"If you want to participate in tomorrow's beans, potatoes, and spinach, start drying tonight." She tossed the towel in his direction.

"We'll be on the road first thing in the morning."

"Grab the towel. I'll cook up a nice hot breakfast to get you off to a good start."

It was too early to retreat to his room, so he grabbed the towel.

Chapter

22

Sleep did not come easy. What the skinny girl had called coffee churned in his stomach. And the broccoli bubbled to the surface every half hour. Molly seemed to work hard in the cook house, but there was only so much you could do with what she had.

The army surplus cot with an olive-drab canvas stretched tightly over a wooden frame provided slightly more comfort than sleeping on the floor. Molly had bothered to bring him an itchy old blanket and a pillowcase. Stuffing the pillowcase with his Levi's and a couple of shirts got his head off the canvas. After an hour or two, it turned strangely cool. There was a tiny potbelly stove but no wood or matches. How did these people survive in the winter?

At 2 a.m., just as he started to doze, a pack of coyotes circled around the so-called farm. It reminded him of Saturday matinees a long time ago, Indian tactics, whoop and holler to unnerve your enemy before the attack. There were probably only four or so on the edge of the compound, but it sounded like twenty of them on the doorstep.

At some point in the night, Jack sensed movement in the room. He checked the door, there was no lock. Just how wily were these coyotes and hippies?

By 5 a.m., predawn light was filtering into the barren room. Last night Molly had explained that the reincarnated bed sheet nailed above the window was spending its second life as a curtain. He pushed the so-called curtain aside. There was just enough light to see the outdoor toilet.

When he opened the door on the outhouse, his mouth fell open. The skinny girl smiled and said, "Morning."

He sped back to the room and waited by the window. She hadn't seemed the least bit embarrassed. Just sat there wearing nothing but a smile and a T-shirt. There probably wasn't a single door lock—or bra—on the entire . . . farm.

After waiting his turn, he wished he had just gone behind a tree. The outhouse was full of flies, and last week's *Taos News* served as toilet paper. Then he remembered that the only tree in sight wouldn't provide much privacy with its three-inch trunk.

By now, he was surprisingly hungry. If Ginger insisted on taking an hour to curl her hair and apply the perfect shade of eye shadow, he would swallow his pride and accept the skinny girl's offer of a hot breakfast. It was hard to screw up pancakes. Maybe she'd drench them in hot maple syrup.

As JACK WALKED past the groveling pigs, he hoped that Ginger was at the wheel, ready to go. Behind the tool shed, an old pickup and a Volkswagen Microbus patiently waited.

The beat-up Datsun was gone!

He ran toward the cook house. Fast as he could. Fireball sun in his eyes. Gasping. Trying to suck oxygen out of thin mountain air.

His left foot hit a hole and he pitched forward. As the commune dwindled, prairie dogs were reclaiming their land.

The fifty-yard sprint turned into a hobble. Steadying himself against the doorframe, taking a deep breath, he shoved the cook house door open. "Has Ginger gone into town?"

"Don't know where she went." Molly shrugged. "Heard her leave in the night."

"You didn't try to stop her?"

"It wasn't my turn to look after your girlfriend."

"She's not my girlfriend!"

"Kind of sounds like she's your girl enemy right now."

Rosemary arrived next and began to set the table, followed by Cinnamon and her two active daughters. As they sat down, Zipper and Habeeb silently showed up.

What else could he do? He sat down to breakfast.

Jack sullenly picked at his food. No pancakes and hot maple syrup, but fortunately fried eggs provided the protein instead of beans. Thank God for small favors. Bacon would've been nice, but Jack feared that if he mentioned that, the skinny girl would hand him a knife and order him to discuss the matter with Ralph or Charlotte or one of their piglets.

"Your friend sleeping late?" Naturally, Zipper showed an interest in Ginger.

"No, she took off in the night." Molly sounded almost sympathetic.

Zipper had planned to go into Taos to find a market for the pigs. He readily offered to drop Jack at the bus stop in time to catch the 11:15 to Albuquerque. From there he could transfer to wherever he wanted to go.

P ACKING WAS NOT a long procedure. Pull the Levi's and shirts out of the pillowcase and screw the cap on the toothpaste. Jack reached to the bottom of his backpack— he wanted to pay for the bus fare without exposing his total net worth of 649 dollars. He fished around for the small brown paper bag.

He yanked out two T-shirts and a spare pair of jockey shorts. Probed around. Tipped the pack upside down. Three pairs of socks and a broken comb. No paper bag.

Damn Ginger!

"You ready?" Zipper's head poked through the door.

"My money's gone."

"You're sure having a bad day."

Jack stared at some invisible object, somewhere in space. He had a vague sense that his life had been spiraling downhill ever since he decided to have that once-in-a-lifetime fling on his birthday. And now here he was, broke, homeless, and wanted by the police, hiding out with misfits who didn't believe in money.

"Tell you what," Zipper said, "I'll drop you at the Western Union office in Taos and spring for a phone call to your relatives."

Zipper seemed unusually cooperative. Probably

anxious to get rid of annoying burdens, like pigs and unexpected hungry visitors. "Don't have any relatives. Can you lend me bus fare?"

"You may not have noticed. This is a farm, not a bank."

"I'll mail it back to you when I find a job."

"Afraid not. We're all leaving here soon. Who knows what direction I'll head?"

Even the pit where he'd ended up was evaporating. Jesus.

JACK'S ENTIRE WORLD emerged as a bleak silhouette; the sun's low angle formed an eerie outline. A monotone landscape with distant mountains in three shades of gray. Spindly cholla cactus and sage dotted the dreary foreground.

He remembered those days just after college. Days filled with nothing but future. Alicia, career at the bank, starting a family—nothing but upside.

He took inventory of the sideshow he was now forced to inhabit. Two men—Zipper and Habeeb, society's outcasts and probably drug users. Three women—Molly, Rosemary, and Cinnamon—communist sympathizers, who might actually look pretty after an introduction to hot running water and a tube of lipstick. Tiger Lily and Pumpkin Patch—cute and precocious, were they destined to become professional communal gardeners?

Which one of these oddballs could he ride out of here with, without being arrested for drug-induced anarchy or burning a draft card in public? Careful inquiry is what it would take. Evaluate each resident of this asylum, then with luck and God's grace he would get out of here.

He followed a meandering path to the edge of the compound. It looked like the kind of trail coyotes would use while keeping humans awake. It led to a red-and-blue wood bench shaded by a scraggly tree filled with tiny green olives. A good place to work out his problem. Like the canary in the flooded mine ride, he felt as though he was hanging upside down in a cage.

"Sounds like you're making some tough decisions."

He sat upright. Molly was standing beside him. Where had she come from?

"I didn't realize I was thinking so loud."

She sat down next to him. "Telepathic communication. It's rare when people get this clear of a connection."

"Really?" Jack saw light in the distance. It blinked three times. "Someone's flashing their headlights, over on that hill."

"It's just Zipper coming back from town."

"What's the flashing about?"

"It's our signal. Zipper still uses it out of habit. When this place buzzed, drunken Chicanos would sometimes sneak in to make trouble."

"Not such a friendly neighborhood after all."

"We don't get reamed anymore."

"Things are looking up."

"So, why the hurry to leave?"

"Never said I was in a hurry."

"You were thinking it." She tapped her temple and smiled like a schoolgirl. "Trying to think of a way to get out of here."

"Not what I thought a commune would be like."

"Remember, we're the dregs. The movement's played out. The war's over—until the next one. The others have moved on—went mainstream, got jobs, picket fences, and mortgages."

"Well, like the rest of you, I need to move on."

"I thought an adventurer like you would enjoy the freedom out here."

"Like my dad said, 'Freedom is great, but it comes with a lot of responsibility.'"

"It depends on how much stuff you're dragging around."

"Sounds like something you picked up at Woodstock. Freedom just means you got nothing left to lose."

"It's easy to become a slave to your possessions. Or even commitments you're not willing to part with."

He thought of his Cadillac Le Cabriolet. "I guess stuff can weigh you down."

"Then, why worry about leaving? Things will work out."

"I don't think Zipper likes me hanging around."

"Zipper doesn't trust you. If fact he doesn't trust anyone over thirty, including me."

"You don't look anywhere near thirty."

"Thirty-one. These days I don't even trust myself."

"Wow, you look a lot younger."

"That's what not eating dead cows will do for you, old man."

He smiled at that. "I still think Zipper would be happy if I left sooner rather than later."

"Zipper will never be happy. He's too smart."

"Can't wait to hear your theory on that."

"Like all intelligent people, he's read a lot. Knows something about everything. Been to one of the best colleges."

"You sound like you've been to some good schools yourself. And you seem pretty smart."

"I'm not smart, I'm wise. Like you."

"Won't argue that, I'd probably lose. But that still doesn't explain why Zipper's mad at the world."

"He analyzes every damn detail of every damn thing in his life. Noodles it to death until there's nothing left but facts and figures stripped of all hope. Transactional relationships with every drop of emotion wrung out."

"And you really think you and I are wiser than that? And happier?"

"At least we're working on it. You can't fix what you don't know is broke."

Jack didn't think of her as beautiful, though if pressed for an opinion he would have responded with something like *Kind of cute, in a natural way.* "How about you, what's the future?"

"Still trying to work out which way to go." She looked at the distant mountains, as though each peak might be a viable option.

"Which way to go?"

"Haven't you ever had trouble trying to decide what to make of your life?"

"Those decisions were always made for me."

"How convenient. So who'd you piss off to get sent here, to the end of the road?"

The question was too big for a bantering answer. "I guess, in a way that's kind of what happened."

"Don't kid yourself. We make our own decisions. Even letting someone else decide for you, that's a decision."

Jack quit talking. This was new. She was new. Surprisingly clever. But way too sarcastic.

Chapter
23

Al Harwood stood in the doorway with his chin jutting out. "You think walking away will make things better?"

Judy returned his stare. "If you'd walked away, Tony would be alive."

"Now you're blaming it on me?"

"You couldn't even take your children on a vacation. Give them your undivided attention."

He slammed his fist on the doorframe. "It's not my goddamn fault that maniac killed Tony!"

"It's your fault this family's torn apart! All you care about is revenge. You're obsessed with Pipkins."

"So, you're pulling your support? Just like the department. They won't spend another nickel on the case, so I have to work it on my time."

"It's not in their jurisdiction."

"Danny's murder sure as hell is."

"Pipkins is long gone. You can't chase all over the country on your own."

"Is that the way it's going to be?" Harwood scratched back and forth on his left palm. "On my own."

"I have had it with your policeman's honor. Taking responsibility for every injustice. Evil people kill good guys like Danny. You're not responsible for every bad thing that happens."

"More of your Psychology 101 babble."

She shook her head. "We're leaving. Sally and me. I've had enough of playing the cop's wife on steroids. Spending weekends alone. Wondering when someone will knock on the door—like you did with Danny Coyle's widow."

The door closed. They were gone.

Al Harwood knew only one way to solve his family's problems. Find that fucking banker.

BY THE THIRD day, the sun's rays seemed to bore through his skin by ten in the morning. Jack was trying to collect his thoughts, not an easy task.

Yesterday the low humidity had felt good, relief from clothes that continually stuck to his body, the only good thing this place had going for it. But today that had turned into a nightmare. His nose dried up; his skin started to itch. In all of recorded history, had it ever rained here?

He slipped into the cook house in search of a snack. He wasn't expecting brownies or even a package of Twinkies. Anything would do, as long as it wasn't beans or broccoli. The forced diet was doing him good, but he hadn't had a treat in days. He hoped to sneak at least a spoonful of peanut butter or better yet, jelly.

"Hey, dude, what's up?" Instantly Zipper was in his face.

"Just checking . . ." Jack wasn't about to admit that he'd been trying to sneak food. "Just checking our stock of potatoes, seeing if it was time to dig some more."

"Potatoes! That reminds me of a dude who once lived at the Hog Farm over near Peñasco. He moved out here with Wavy Gravy and some chicks from the coast. The guy needed a favor. Problem was he already owed me—"

"Hey." Jack had no idea what he was talking about. Maybe Molly's warning about Zipper's tirades were valid. "How'd you get that scar on your forehead?"

"The fuzz. They tried to bust up a protest with what they called batons. Felt more like baseball bats, but we didn't give up any ground."

"Yeah, at times they did overreact."

"How'd you get out of spraying villages with napalm? Spend some time in Canada?"

"Student deferment." Jack didn't mention the advantage of having a father with influence on the draft board.

Zipper's lack of regard for personal space began to annoy him. He stepped back six inches.

Zipper immediately closed the gap. "Got your eye on Molly?"

"Not really." Jack tried to look away. Hard to do at that distance.

"When she's not looking, you grab an eyeful. I've seen."

"So? She's cute."

"Kittens are cute. She's a tiger. Not worth the trouble, man."

Zipper was seeming less and less like a hippie. Too abrasive and chiseled. He didn't fit the mold. He didn't fit any mold.

Getting away from this place was his goal, but right now getting away from Zipper seemed most important. He went outside and stood under the rickety porch that they called a portal. The idea of a fresh start in California had taken hold, the chance of a future, anything would be better than this.

The sun rose higher, and Jack's sliver of shade disappeared. This place didn't amount to much more than rocks, dust, and sagebrush. He squinted at the cultivated plot, a sorry attempt to entice produce out of the sand.

"Those beans won't get picked by staring at them." Zipper had followed.

"I don't plan to stick around long enough to eat beans. In fact, the next time that . . . that vehicle goes to Taos, I'm out of here."

"That vehicle isn't a taxi. But I guess we could work something out."

"If I had any money, I wouldn't be in here in the first place."

"And yet, here you are. Everyone works while they're here."

"Gardening isn't my forte."

"If you eat, you help grow stuff. It's called a commune for a reason."

"What part do you play in this utopian scheme?"

"I throw the ball, you fetch."

JACK WALKED AROUND the farm to get some exercise and fresh air—fresh and free of Zipper. He kept an eye out for the dust clouds of police cars on the cosmic plain, for Ginger returning with a change of heart, for any sign of life.

What were they thinking? You could never grow decent food here. Fresh wholesome food for a trendy restaurant. His trendy restaurant. Signature dishes that he would create. Food he could pour his heart into, like Harpo. A laid-back, fun place filled with friends and laughter, an upmarket version of the Hog Pen. He'd never been to California, but the more he thought about it, the more he was sure that he could make it work there.

Alicia would love it. Mild weather year-round. Interesting and sophisticated people, at least in some places. A family-run business. Alicia would enjoy mingling with customers. She'd have a hundred ideas about the theme and decor. Maybe Edward or even Elizabeth would take over one day.

He caught sight of a sinuous motion as someone approached from the tool shed. Her flower-print skirt nearly touched the ground. He couldn't see any feet. She seemed to float toward him, fluid yellow strands of hair streaming behind her. Cinderella suspended on a cushion of air, as the high mesa winds propelled her toward the ballroom. Or in this case the chicken coop.

"Good morning, Mr. Crane."

"Just call me Jack."

"That's right, Jumpin' Jack."

"I'm afraid I forgot your last name."

"Meadow. Rosemary Meadow."

"That's nice. Quite appropriate here."

"Thanks. I started out as Rosemary Merkle but changed it when I joined a convent."

"You're a nun?" Jack snuck a quick look up and down her fantastic body. He didn't like Catholics much, and sex with a nun, even one with an ex- in front of her title, had creepy written all over it.

"I was."

"I didn't know nuns could quit."

"Sure. It's a convent, not a prison. Quite a few become disillusioned. Discover they're not allowed to change the world for the better, the way that they'd like to."

"What did you want to change?"

"The neighborhoods of the Bronx. Too many women abandoned and abused."

"Who had a problem with that?"

"Seriously? It's still a man's world, and especially a man's church. Half the people in the world, including me, are denied the chance of becoming a priest, the chance of becoming a positive influence. Then the war came along, and I drifted up here."

Floated up here was more like it. She might not be a preacher, but he thought she'd never pass up the chance to deliver a sermon. "I guess this farm offered more equality for women."

"For a while. Then human nature took over, macho men struggled for power, same old story."

Rosemary Meadow was the best-looking nun Jack had ever seen. He'd never seen an ex-nun, not that he knew of, didn't even know there was such a thing. He'd seen pictures of nuns, saw them in movies—black gowns and black hoods with high white collars. Did some of them look like Rosemary under all that?

"FOUL CALLED ON Central. Anderson will take two free shots."

Harwood listened to the game from out on the street—the championship at the end of summer basketball camp. The best players pitted against each other, for real tournament experience under the lights with an announcer, pom-pom girls, and seats filled with shouting parents. This would have been the first year that Tony was old enough to play in the tournament.

An outburst from the crowd carried out to him. Harwood muttered, "Go, Tony, go."

He didn't enter the gym, just walked up and down the sidewalk out front, unsure of why he was there. He paced and cursed as he bargained with the devil.

Then he realized what had drawn him there: What better place to devise a plan to even the score?

JACK HEADED TOWARD the lone Russian olive tree, where Cinnamon Stick sat in the shade with her two daughters. He hadn't talked one-on-one with Cinnamon yet, maybe she could help him get out of here. Her high cheekbones had a hint of freckles, which made her pretty in a tomboy way. Her upper lip was maybe one size too small for the rest of her face, her perfect shiny white teeth were constantly on display.

Tiger Lily and Pumpkin Patch were making posters, some kind of make-believe protest about preservatives and refined sugar in Kellogg's Sugar Pops. Tiger Lily smacked a mouth full of gum, a naturally sweetened brand he assumed.

"The girls seem to be getting into politics early," Jack said.

"It's their ten o'clock civics class."

"Oh, school."

"Homeschool. Don't want them brainwashed by a school system designed to produce lemmings."

"Aw, freethinkers."

"Nothing's free, not even lunch, unless you grow it yourself."

He might have thought she was being difficult, except that her voice stayed light and tuneful, more like she was sharing a joke than delivering a sermon. Taller than Jack, taller than Zipper, with long legs, high-top Keds, and a bounce in her step, she dribbled random thoughts and passed dubious wisdom with the ease of a Harlem Globetrotter. She seemed to fit in perfectly at White Rabbit Farm—no makeup, no jewelry, but loaded with quirky.

"Where you from?" she said.

"Lots of places. Moved around."

"Around where? You're from the South, aren't you?"

"No."

"You been to California?"

"Sure." He needed to lay a false trail.

"I could tell. I can always tell a West Coast dude by his vibe." She dug the toe of her shoe in the dirt as if looking for earthworms, then grinned. "You a surfer?"

"Nope," Jack said. He changed the subject. He still had to be wary of giving away too much information. "You married or divorced?"

"Fascist pigs running the government won't let me get a divorce."

"Why not? Have you consulted a lawyer?"

"No need to. Never got married."

"Oh."

At the end of each sentence, she would stick out her tongue an inch or so, cock it up to the right and flip up the tip; all the while, her eyes would track this movement. After observing this gesture ten or twelve times, Jack still wasn't sure if it was endearing or just plain weird.

"What are your plans when you leave here?" Jack said.

"Don't know."

"Are you and the girls going to catch a ride with Molly or Zipper, or take a bus?"

"Not enough room in Molly's pickup, if she ever gets the thing running. Don't have bus fare to get farther than Winslow. Might ride with Zipper if he heads west."

"I thought you and Zipper might be a couple."

"I wouldn't let that nut case diddle me for a plane ride to Paris."

THE SUN HAD risen, its workday just started. Jack felt the warm rays on his cot. Throughout the night his mind had kept churning, thinking about countries where he and Alicia might hide. Europe—too hard to get there. The Orient, they'd be conspicuous. Central or South America—lots of US citizens to mingle with, you could even drive there. But which country held any promise of making a living? A small restaurant in an out-of-the-way place. Cater to the unconventional tourist, nothing flashy, wouldn't want to draw much attention. Somewhere with a decent English-speaking school for Edward and Elizabeth. Costa Rica had excellent medical facilities. Brazil was huge, plenty of chances for Alicia to make friends. Did they have an extradition treaty?

According to the laws of chemistry,
LSD is a solution
Habeeb

Chapter
24

The old Wonder Bread truck looked like it had finished its rounds for good. Three tires were flat, one axle rested on cinderblocks, and spider-web cracks filled the windshield. The rounded corners and sloped front with bug-eyed headlights gave it a friendly, cartoonish look. Wonder Bread along with the iconic yellow, red, and blue circles were still faintly visible on the sun-bleached paint.

Jack watched from a distance, unsure that talking to Habeeb would be worth the hassle. He sure wasn't going to ride out of here in that truck. But what was Habeeb's plan? Maybe the guy had stashed away some money over the years. It's a long shot, but you never know.

"Contemplating morning tea with Habeeb?" Molly showed her little-girl grin.

Jack turned. Where had she come from? "Just wanted to talk."

"We call it the Wonder Wagon because we wonder what's going on in there. Go on over for a visit, he's a people person."

"Didn't want to disturb him."

"Nobody disturbs Habeeb. They just find him disturbing."

Jack refused to get sucked into matching wits with this sarcastic beanpole. He sure wasn't going to show a fear of Habeeb. What could the worn-out pothead do, shoot him?

The door was halfway open. A good sign. But as he got closer, he doubted that the rusty hinges could actually close. An oval logo to the left of the door declared, Good Housekeeping Seal of Approval. He didn't think that still applied.

"Who the hell's poking around out there?"

The skinny girl still watched from the edge of the field. Turning back now would be embarrassing. He cautiously climbed into the rusted truck.

A bluish gray cloud hung over a withered shape sprawled out on a wooden army bed. It had been jammed in sideways, and the dingy spring-less mattress looked like it had been through World War II. He wore a crumpled olive-drab shirt. A less faded V-shape on the shoulder showed that it had once been worn by a low-ranking soldier, two, maybe three stripes at most. Had

Habeeb fought in the war, or had he just picked it up at a surplus store?

In an attempt to stay out of the cloud, Jack sat on a wooden stool where the driver's seat should have been and rested one elbow on the bus-sized steering wheel. The flat steel instrument panel had two round gauges trimmed in chrome and two pull levers, one labeled Choke, the other Throttle. Very rudimentary compared to his Caddy. The small circular fan bolted to the center of the dashboard looked like standard factory equipment, early 1950s air-conditioning.

The small table in a corner overflowed with Bunsen burners, beakers, and assorted glass tubes. An acrid odor drifted from that direction. A declaration scribbled in Wild West calligraphy was nailed to one wall.

We preferred
our own way of Living.

We were no expense
to the government then.

ALL we wanted was peace
and to be Left aLone.
Crazy Horse
OgLaLa Sioux
1877

"You that new guy with the primo old lady?" A metal clip clenching the last of a stubby roach poked out of the cloud.

"She left. And she was less primo that you'd think."

"Bummer."

"That kind of sums it up." Jack gasped for air as the roll-your-own reached the end of its life. Everything in here seemed to be reaching the end of its life—the beat-up footlocker, the frayed Jefferson Airplane poster taped to the wall, the wind-up alarm clock with a bent minute hand.

"Be careful, man." Habeeb's eyes swayed in their sockets as though they followed an imaginary fly. "The government's watching."

"I'll keep an eye out for them. When did you get here?"

"Summer of '62. Coasted here in this wagon when the war heated up."

"Why? It's hard to find your way out here."

"Absofuckinglutely. But it's a hell of a lot harder to find your way back."

"Why not pick a place where you could actually grow something?"

"No way, Jose. Nobody picked anything. This place evolved." Habeeb marked the cadence of his sentences with his right hand. "Here's the skinny. Me and a dude from Minnesota, some cheese weasel from a farm in Iowa, and two awesome chicks, we just started farming."

"Could five people be self-sufficient?"

"The universe provided. Lots of cool dudes found us. And freaky-deaky chicks can smell a spliff forty miles away."

"Yeah, nice party, but how did you hold it together? Who made the decisions?"

"Consensus of the meeting, man. Everybody played a part. Everybody shared. It was perfect. No electricity, no running water, no government fucking things up."

And no future. "What part did you play?"

"Chemist, physicist, botanist, hydrologist, agronomist, and advisor on Canadian immigration."

Ah. He had this guy figured out. Habeeb knew how to get Aunt Polly's fence painted while he concocted exotic hallucinogens. A desert-rat version of Dr. Timothy Leary.

Jack noticed a thick hand-scribbled notebook on the bunk. "Are you writing a memoir or notes on your consultations?"

"A doctrine. To combat Hoover."

"J Edgar's been dead for seven years, you know."

"Yeah, but that closet queen's diabolical plots live on."

"What plots?"

"The government's watching, man." Habeeb scanned the room, sat up and leaned toward Jack. "Polio vaccination. The right-wing fanatics running this country have put a sterilizing agent in the vaccine that's handed out in what they term 'undesirable' neighborhoods. The poor, black, Muslim, Catholic, Jew, and most of all liberal-minded progressives don't even know what'll hit them. Twenty years from now, they'll start to wonder why their women don't get knocked up. The totalitarian regime has a plan to populate America with blond-haired babies."

Okay, there was nothing for him here. "See you later, Habeeb." Jack headed for the door.

"Do me a solid. Tell that foxy mama you rode in here with to stop by sometime."

"I told you she left. Gone."

"Too bad man, she had me stoked. Now the only thing I got to look forward to is flashbacks."

MOLLY SWUNG THE hoe into debris backed up behind a rock that had rolled into the ditch. She spotted that new dude wandering around aimlessly on the edge of the bean field and waved him over. "Give me a hand. Need to get this rock up out of here."

"Why in the world do you want that rock?"

"I don't want the rock. I'm trying to clear the acequia."

"The what?"

"Acequia. Ditch, to you. When the sluice gate is opened, a bit of water from the Rio Hondo is diverted to our bean field."

"Why bother to water, you're leaving soon?"

"Do you have something better to do today?"

"Wouldn't it be better to think about how you'll eat next month?"

He was right, she was wasting her time. But damn if she'd admit it. "I know your type—jam tomorrow and jam yesterday—but never jam today."

She glanced over at his sweat-soaked shirt. The shovel clanked against a rock as he cleared the ditch, a wren chirped in the olive tree; it all sounded good. He didn't seem to mind working hard, for all he tried to avoid it. She wondered what his real story was. Not many nice guys drifted in here, and none ever stayed.

"Tell me more about yourself," Jack said. "Where did you come from? What's it like there?"

"The birth canal was a bit tight—they never relax, the British." Molly smiled, until she saw how much he was blushing. "Mum wasn't around that much, not as much as I wanted her to be, or needed her to be. She moved back to England when I was eight. Her family owned businesses there—chemist shops she called them. Dad raised me as best he could, but for the most part that meant boarding schools and summer camp."

"That's why you're so smart about so many things."

"Don't know about smart, just exposed to a pompous education at Wellesley."

Jack seemed interested in her life. Maybe this guy really cared. They drifted toward the shade of the scraggly olive tree and settled on a shaky wooden bench. It teetered and complained, but they were comfortable. Jack listened intently while Molly opened up and told him of her childhood that had been privileged, yet lonely. "Dad's a well-known surgeon. The problem is, he spent all his time and energy ensuring that he stayed prominent. Never had any time left for me."

"You said you went to Wellesley. What was your major?"

"Articulate Conversation with a minor in Spousal Choice. My father expected me to keep up the family tradition by marrying well."

"So why didn't you marry a doctor from New Haven after graduation?"

"Never did graduate. Protested the war pretty heavy in my last year. Finally dropped out in the spring semester."

"Why not hang in there for a few months and get a diploma?"

"In Art Appreciation? Ending the war seemed more important. Maybe I just didn't want to deal with getting a job, having a professional career, feeding the greedy corporate machine. Or far worse, being a subservient wife."

"Why the momentous change in your last year of college?"

"The summer started out laid-back—sandals and

candles, some pot. Then I joined the SDS, Students for a Democratic Society. Fighting the war gave me something to believe in for the first time in my life, something that was wholly mine. In August, I went to the Democratic Convention in Chicago. Things turned ugly, pigs in the street. That set the stage for Eddy Ardell, an Arlo Guthrie sort of guy, smooth voice, and smooth stories. He followed me back to Wellesley and I spent most of my time listening to him rather than the professors. I was psyched by his visions of a commune in New Mexico."

She gestured to the remains of the commune. "I've spent nine years here, almost a third of my life. Happy years, most of the time. Eight of them coupled with Eddy Ardell."

Jack looked directly at her, never broke eye contact. "And?"

"A year ago, it all blew up. A student from the University in Albuquerque showed up. Bright eyed and perky, on a working spring break, doing research for her master's thesis, she said. 'Did the counterculture of the 1960s contribute significantly to today's social structure?' And her conclusion—it was pretty persuasive—was that the world didn't give a shit about us."

Jack looked sincere. It had been a long time since she'd seen sincerity in a man.

"But if you were happy here, who cares what the world thinks?" he said.

"I found out that free love isn't free," Molly said. "In the end, someone gets hurt. That someone was me. On April 7 of last year, spring break used up, Rebecca Ainsley vanished along with Eddy and all of my dreams." She stopped to catch her breath. More than a year had passed, and she'd never let it all hang out like that before, not even with Rosemary.

"It's Wednesday." Molly was ready to change the subject. "What you need is a good hot steaming bath."

"Where have you been hiding the Jacuzzi?"

"You're about to find out."

JACK FELL IN line as the entire tribe, except for Habeeb, hiked two miles along the Rio Hondo and then followed the high cliffs above the Rio Grande. They were hot and tired by the time they climbed down six hundred feet to a rock-lined pool of steaming water next to the river. When everyone started to take their clothes off, he tried to decide where to sit. Was the hippie convention man, woman, man, etc.? Or did they follow that southern tradition—men on one side talking football, women on the other chattering about whatever women chattered about. Zipper didn't follow football, and Jack realized that he had no idea who was playing this coming season. What did you talk about when everyone was naked? Surely, the children would be sequestered next to their mother.

Molly and Cinnamon had already jumped in. Jack lagged behind in getting undressed. He looked down at the clear water, only two-foot deep, three-foot max, in the middle. He felt too self-conscious to become aroused. But what if that changed? Seeing more of Molly had crossed his mind a time or two. And Cinnamon's legs were a turn on. Rosemary was everything Zipper had claimed, although he felt Molly's scornful look when his glance lingered a fraction too long in that direction.

And what about him? Would everyone laugh? He kept his eyes down and jumped in fast.

Jack tried to ignore it, but a teasing voice from the past whispered in his ear. *Don't forget to wash behind your ears, Jeremy.*

Molly giggled. "It tickles when the bubbles from the spring go up your butt."

"Careful, what goes in, must come out," Cinnamon said.

Molly slid over a few inches.

"You look a little nervous." Cinnamon looked at Jack. "Never skinny-dipped before?"

"Not with young children. There might be laws against it. At a minimum, I think God would be concerned."

"God only had one kid to worry about and look how that turned out."

Tiger Lily and Pumpkin Patch splashed and laughed and babbled. Beautiful canyon walls, the Rio Grande raging five feet away, a herd of mountain sheep grazing along the other side of the river; it was impossible not to be happy.

Jack felt his feet pulled out from under him. He splashed while he slid to the middle of the pool. When Molly surfaced and started to swim away, he slapped her bare backside. She squealed and threw him a smile over her shoulder.

The hot water felt good, even better than the spa tub at the clubhouse back in Kansas City. Of course, maybe he'd inhaled a little hashish from Zipper's pipe.

Jack squinted while watching Molly dip a galvanized army canteen into the hot pool. "What are you going to do with that water?"

"I'm lugging it back for Habeeb. It's loaded with lithium, smooths out his mood swings."

He was already looking forward to next Wednesday when he'd make a point of sitting next to Molly.

.

Chapter
25

Every cop behind a desk with a phone against his ear, every cop huddled in the tight circle reliving Saturday's game, every cop waiting for coffee to brew in the break room, every damn one of them turned toward Harwood as he raced through the gauntlet. Head up, shoulders back, his stride quick and even.

He wasn't Harwood anymore. He was poor Al. Poor Al, his son idolized him. Poor Al, he went to every game. And he would be poor Al until Pipkins fried—Harwood refused to let the sympathy drag on forever.

He grabbed the phone, slumped down, and dialed the desk sergeant all in one motion. "This is Harwood."

"No, Al, nothing came in overnight on that APB for the Marble Mine woman."

Every police precinct in the whole country probably had caseloads as heavy as Little Rock. Police overwhelmed with petty bullshit—paperwork, court appearances, drug dealers putting bullets in each other, shyster lawyers canceling it all out. But a good-looking bitch like that couldn't go unnoticed for long. Old habits would resurface. She'll pull some sort of scam, pilfer some money, turn a few tricks, something. And then he'd have her. And she would lead him to Pipkins.

"Hey, Al." Detective McArdle stuck his head in the door. "Can I do anything for you?"

"Yeah, coffee . . . and a donut, cookie, whatever you can scrounge up."

He needed to remember to stop at the store, get some milk, cereal...TV dinners. He hadn't realized he would miss having breakfast with Judy. As soon as this was behind him, he'd get back on track with her. Take her on a real vacation, the honeymoon they'd never had. They could slurp up syrupy rum drinks in the sun on a beach in the Florida Keys.

He checked the clock on the wall, eight forty-five already. At least most of the detectives had left, now a person could think. He needed to talk to a white guy with three broken ribs and a concussion over at St. Vincent's, then bang on some doors around West 11th and Harrison. Somebody went looking for excitement last night and he found it.

That could wait another half hour.

His thoughts returned to Pipkins. Either he had a ton of cash stored away or someone was protecting him. Not the father—he was so pissed off he'd probably shoot him on sight. Grandparents were dead. Everybody at the bank and those stuck-up assholes at the country club stuttered like a pimp with a pistol pointed at his dick. None of them had the balls to help Pipkins. That left the wife, but she hadn't seemed prone to help him on the one phone call he'd intercepted. And so far, she seemed clean. He'd keep checking on her.

Or maybe he needed to go back farther. Pipkins was a college boy, Princeton. Rich kid like that might have some old frat buddies. Varsity squad football, couple of people said. If he was good, a coach might remember who he hung out with, worth a shot. He picked up the phone and dialed directory service, then tapped a monotonous beat on the desktop while some clown found a number for the Princeton athletic department.

One screw up—leaving Danny Coyle alone in that parking garage. And now Tony was gone.

Pipkins would make his mistake, they always did.

JACK CONSTANTLY REMINDED his paranoid shadow that he was literally living in the back of beyond. It was a godforsaken place to farm but a great place to hide. No sudden state police roadblocks. No cop and his family would stop by for a picture. If he didn't do something stupid like call Alicia, no one could find him here.

On some days, that temptation didn't even enter his mind. Alicia had not been overwhelmed by his plans when he called from Branson. On other days, the temptation to call her was overwhelming. Fortunately, there wasn't a phone within twenty miles.

He hiked along the trail to the edge of the mesa, telling himself that he sought thoughtful solitude, knowing that was a lie. Molly sat cross-legged on the brink of a chasm, doing her evening meditation. Six hundred feet below, the Rio Grande River kept digging its gorge through volcanic rock. Sunset approached, not much moonlight, safe seemed an abstract concept. He silently sat down beside her. She glanced over her shoulder, threw him a coy smile that said, *Couldn't stay away, could you?* Then she went back to navel gazing.

Jack crossed his legs as best he could and joined her. Within two minutes he started to fidget. The amazing view didn't calm him. The rapids that swirled at the bottom of the canyon brought tension. The sheer drop energized his spirit. His brain was racing.

"You're supposed to chill out," she said. "Transport your mind to a quiet place. Think of nothing."

"I try. But my brain is in high gear."

"What crucial state of affairs demands your immediate attention?"

"For one thing, the future."

"The future or the past don't count for much. It's today that matters."

Jack had lived his whole life for the future. And now his past was a disaster. And the present, well, he just didn't know what to think about the present. "You have to think about the future sometimes. Without a future there won't be any more todays. There must be something you want in your tomorrows."

"A family is my wish for tomorrow." Molly cocked her head to the right and looked straight at Jack for an instant, a truly short instant, such a brief time that he didn't know what had happened. "White Rabbit Farm was my family, or the closest thing to it that I've ever known. At one time, there were fifty people here, all helping each other, sharing. But, just like real families, they changed, grew up, and moved on."

"There were a bunch of communes near here in the '60s. That life seemed to work for you. Why'd they fold?"

"Lots of reasons. White Rabbit got off to a good start with hardworking, disciplined founders. Then it attracted spiritual spongers, too bent, or stoned to work a farm. Morning Star East was a laid-back commune and didn't have any bosses, which was good, but they lacked direction and drifted. The acidhead militants at Reality Construction Company were too paranoid about fascists taking over America to do anything practical like plant or irrigate. The Hog Farm got too much attention from the antics of colorful lightweights and suffered from lazy heads drifting in and out. The Lama Foundation managed to survive their religious wars— aided by their spiritual teacher, Ram Dass, and his blend of Sufi beliefs, Zen Buddhism, and Karma yoga—along with a strict no drug policy.

"Then the FBI started checking up on all and sundry. We suspected one drifter of being a narc. He got us fighting amongst ourselves."

So Habeeb was right? The FBI was watching them? "Why would the feds care?"

"One rumor had it that they thought one of the communes was hiding Patty Hearst. Maybe they were afraid we'd invade the nuclear lab—Los Alamos is only seventy-five miles away."

He hadn't known that. "Invade?"

"Habeeb gets pretty mean when he's pissed off. And he's got some military training."

"So, for the most part, it seems that communes were a failure," Jack said. "They ran aground on human nature."

"They changed a lot of lives in a turbulent time. Communal living gave some people the strength to go back and face the not-so-real world. I wouldn't call that failure."

"I'm not sure I'd call it success."

"In the end, the world took notice and realized the war was wrong, that there is an alternative."

"I guess the counterculture did bring about the end of the draft and voting rights for eighteen-year-olds."

"I don't know. I think a lot about this. For the most part, the communes just went out of style as pop culture moved on to other things. As the children at White Rabbit got older, some families found it difficult—no privacy, and the Chicanos didn't like our kids in their schools. Maybe communes were impractical over the long run, or perhaps they just outgrew their usefulness."

"Everything does change."

"How about your family? When's the last time you saw your parents?"

She sounded so sincerely interested; he hated lying to her. But he couldn't drag her into his life as it was now. "Long time ago. I was young."

"Do you know where they are?"

"Not a clue."

"Well, have you ever looked for them?"

"No."

"Why not?"

"Afraid I might find them."

"Hey, nobody's all bad. You must remember something good. Some anecdote or bit of wisdom they passed on to you."

Jack shrugged and decided some truth was in order. "Well my father once told me a man couldn't make it through life without lying."

"You mean he told you to lie?"

"He told me to pick my lies carefully. And more important, be careful who I lied to."

"Is that what you really are, Jack? A liar, slinging bullshit to every chick that looks your way?"

"No." More honesty. "Mostly I just lie to myself."

A thin white paper appeared from somewhere. Molly held it down with two fingers and spread out brown leaves and broken stem fragments, then deftly rolled the paper into a neat tube. The movement of her fingers was sensual, forbidden, and naughty—he felt the tingling sensation of a twelve-year-old boy gazing at Playboy. She turned licking and twisting into an art form. A flick of her nimble fingers made a yellow flame flash on the end of a matchstick, a startling climax to Molly's performance.

She drew in a deep puff, then without warning pressed her moist, open lips firmly against his mouth. As he gasped, she exhaled her hot breath into his body. His entire body—passion, fear, affection, and repulsion—exploded within him. Not from cannabis—from this uninhibited, exciting, free-spirited, radical left wing, nymphet hippie.

Jack coughed, stiffened, instinctively looked over his shoulder.

"I'll keep an eye out, let you know if the cops get a whiff of this spliff." Molly giggled. "This your first time?"

"No, tried it once, at a party in college."

"I smoke now and again. Did coke a couple of times, but never took a serious trip."

They passed the joint back and forth, and he got comfortable with her company. Didn't feel an obligation for idle chatter.

Minutes later, some sort of critter scurried along the rock ledge. The silence was broken. Molly bent over a prickly-pear cactus and smelled its pale-yellow flower before it closed for the night.

"So, what now?" Jack asked, realizing that he now saw the cactus flower in a new light. "For you?"

"Maybe a family, something more secure than this. I'll find a way."

"So, you do think about the future. Did you ever think about having kids?"

"What do you mean did? I still do."

"What stopped you? I mean what is stopping you?"

"Finding a good guy to have them with."

"A pretty girl like you never found the right guy?"

Molly paused for a moment, looked off toward Lucero Peak. "Well, up to now, I never really took the time to look."

Up to now? He searched for a comeback and couldn't find one.

"How about you? You're older than I am. And not bad looking. Aren't there any little Jacks, out there somewhere, running around?"

He clamped down, made sure his feelings didn't show in his face. "I had a relationship once. No kids."

"I bet you wanted kids." She touched the back of his hand, gently. "Some guys just shoot blanks."

"Not me."

"And."

"And . . . nothing. Maybe it was her. Maybe it was karma," Jack said.

"I'm sure you could spawn an offspring or two. Maybe you never met the right girl."

Jack wasn't sure if he was irritated, embarrassed, or turned on by her playfulness. Was she teasing or trying to weasel information out of him, or . . . was she a scatterbrain just like the rest of them?

The setting sun hid behind the Sangre de Cristo mountains, but like a young child playing hide-and-seek behind a scrawny tree, its presence was obvious. Brilliant orange tints lit the sky. The mountains looked like black jagged teeth. The clouds were on fire.

"I told you how I wound up here. How about you Jack, what's the real story?"

He had a story prepared, but he couldn't bring himself to lie any more. He was tired of it. "Somewhere along the way I took a wrong turn."

"I heard my mum say once that sometimes taking a wrong turn gets you to the right place."

"Your mother said that to you?"

"Not to me. She talked a lot, but seldom to me." Molly's mood seemed to change. "What about you, Jumpin' Jack Crane? Where are you jumpin' to next?" There was a lighthearted inquiry in her voice, but a serious question in her eye.

"Somewhere new, somewhere far from the past."

"Lot of people start traveling, looking for a clean break with the past. But there's no such thing. Any break you might find is jagged and torn. Like the page in a book that you'd like to forget. You can tear it out and destroy it, still the ragged edge along the spine remains. Life's lessons—learned, then forgotten—or simply ignored and repeated, over and over again."

He hadn't seen that coming. He'd originally classed her with those bimbo secretaries at the bank, easy to look at, hard to talk to. Not that he'd ever asked a secretary for an opinion.

But he realized that Molly was right. You can't completely separate yourself from the past. You are your past, a culmination of all your experiences, that's who you are.

So who was he now?

Chapter
26

Molly stirred a big black pot with a wooden spoon and daydreamed of what it'd be like to be a real housewife, with a husband, with children, like in the movies. She'd never lived in a real home, with a real family, just her and her father and a sequence of bitchy housekeepers rattling around in a museum-like house. She clearly remembered a morning when she was seven and woke up to find no money under the pillow again. When the kids at school saw a tooth gone, they'd said, "How much did you get?" She couldn't tell them that her father forgot; that he didn't think it was important enough to remember. She knew she was a bad liar, but she needed some sort of story. "It fell out this morning," that's what she'd said.

The cook house door slammed; Molly jumped back to reality. If that damn Zipper messed up this clean floor . . .

"Smells funny." Jack made a face as he walked in the cook house. "What are you cooking?"

"A special treat." Molly kept on stirring and smiled.

She had to admit, the greenish sludge in the pot didn't look particularly special.

"How do you eat that stuff?" Jack asked.

"On a slice of fresh hot bread, as soon as I pull that out the horno."

"What are you talking about? Doesn't sound like anything Mom cooked up."

"It definitely isn't. The horno is that beehive-shaped mud oven outside. I'm baking bread in there just like they do at the pueblo."

"Making bread in a wood-fired oven I follow, but what do you do with the smelly mess in the pot?"

"It's pot butter. You smear it on the bread."

"Pot butter?"

"It's my own special recipe. I grind up the seeds and mix it with stuff."

"Ah. Marijuana seeds?"

"After one slice, you won't know or care what you're eating."

"Don't you ever bake cookies?" Jack spread his arms out. "Like with chocolate chips."

"You're tracking dirt on my clean floor." Molly swooshed him toward the door with a broom.

"The wicked witch comes out." Jack ran for the door.

"Don't make me send for the flying monkeys."

She laughed and closed the door. With that funny . . . rogue, dork, whatever he was, out of the cook house, she drifted back to thinking about how a lonely childhood had led to her bonding with peers in high school, a home away from home. As school years had progressed, members came and went. Eventually Molly was one of those who went, cast headlong into the turbulent '6os. She'd enjoyed college, but with all the distractions, her academic performance was nominal at best. She never followed militant bad asses like Abbie Hoffman and Jerry Rubin, yet she never felt ready for a picket fence, two kids, a dog, and a bowl full of goldfish. Eventually she found refuge and subterfuge, tranquility and transgression, friendship and hardship, here at White Rabbit Farm. For the past few years, it had gotten her by. Then the meager stipend from dear Aunt Molly ceased, and commune life disintegrated into history. Time to book out.

Now along comes this dude, the first considerate man she'd seen in months. A real gentleman, easy to talk with, a man who doesn't complain too much about her shortcomings. A complex sparring partner; complicated enough to maintain her interest. A solid man who knew how to care for a woman. He clearly had a past he didn't want to talk about, but that wasn't a problem. Her own history had a chapter or two she wasn't going to reveal any time soon.

Problem was, he sounded like a right-wing doofus who didn't know jack squat about the genuine world. He could turn out to be a spaz, hell-bent on changing her.

Jack Crane! Her mother's voice echoed throughout the cook house. *Jumpin' Jack, a lightweight. Definitely not a dream for anyone's future. Young lady, beware of that poster boy for heartache and pain.*

NEXT AFTERNOON, JACK showed up in the kitchen a half hour before Molly usually started cooking dinner. He lined up an industrial size can of baked beans and spices that he had talked Zipper into buying at the co-op in Taos. He had a surprise for Molly—a genuine Harpo's bean batch. He'd prepared his speech; he didn't want to offend her cooking, but . . . The moment the door opened, he started in. "Your dinners are good, the only thing they need is a little zing."

"Sorry, didn't plant any zing this season."

"Not to worry. I'll show you how to make up a bean batch, like Harpo showed me."

"Okay Groucho, I'm all ears."

All ears? She was usually all mouth. But he kept that thought to himself and kept struggling with the bean can—the opener was only slightly better than Harpo's gadget.

"You're not going to feed us that canned garbage, are you?" Molly said.

"I thought you were all ears. Zipper may not have procured the finest beans on this planet, but that doesn't matter. Sprinkle a little kindness in the pot and we'll put a lot of love on the table."

He noticed that she watched intently as he stirred the pot. It surprised him to feel so good while teaching someone. At least when that someone was Molly, and he was showing off, just a little.

When it started to bubble, she peered into the pot, breathed in, and smiled. "Where'd you learn to cook like this?"

"From the kindest black gentleman east of the Rio Grande." His smile was almost as big as Molly's. "Man was like a father to me."

God Bless America, that does have me puzzled
Molly Hollingsworth

Chapter

27

"You clean up real pretty." Jack tried to sound clever. He had washed his blue jeans, shaved extra close, and combed his hair.

"Thanks." Molly slipped a rawhide necklace with colorful clay beads over his head.

She seemed unusually self-conscious after spending all morning dressing up for the FIESTAS DE TAOS. She wore bib overalls, somewhat well fitted—they didn't look exactly like something that a farmer would wear, especially since she wasn't wearing a shirt. A purple aster highlighted her shiny brown hair. Jack noticed that her bare tan shoulders were unblemished. A silver necklace inset with turquoise drew his attention to the bib of her overalls. The tops of round breasts were barely visible, not too big, no hint of a bra, incredibly enticing.

He realized he was staring. "That silver necklace is very attractive."

"Got it at Santa Domingo Pueblo. Turquoise brings peace and serenity."

"Good . . ." He tried to elaborate on his compliment. He searched for the right words. The moment passed.

Everyone had spruced up and put on a smile. Taos's largest annual event had traditional Mexican mariachi music and eclectic rock bands, sack races, food vendors, artists, and craft booths. The whole commune looked forward to a big day at Kit Carson Park. Except for Habeeb, who had elected to study the wisdom of the Greek philosophers and experiment with pharmaceuticals in the comfort of his bread truck.

Zipper's VW Microbus—un-affectionately referred to as the Randy Rabbit for some reason that everyone refused to explain—was the only operating vehicle at White Rabbit Farm. The Studebaker pickup hadn't been running for years, and nobody had ever seen Habeeb's Wonder Wagon move. With a grinding squeal worse than fingernails on a chalkboard, the Randy Rabbit cranked up on the third try. In a previous reincarnation, it may have been traditional pale-yellow family transportation. Now it looked like a true hippie van with dents, daisies, and hand-painted turquoise letters declaring Nirvana Now—Friendship Forever.

PORTABLE CANVAS STALLS lined the winding sidewalks in shady Kit Carson Park. Pueblo Indians sold fry bread from small folding tables, and yet-to-be discovered Anglo artists displayed paintings of Pueblo Indians selling fry bread. Jack watched a Chicano vendor working the crowd as he sold cheap jewelry and trinkets. He seemed gracious and welcoming. If a roaming jewelry store had ever shown up in Kansas City, passersby would look up and down, then whisper among themselves.

A dozen Chicano niños and Indian kids from the pueblo played tag on simple playground equipment—a seesaw, swings, a push merry-go-round. They waved Tiger Lily and Pumpkin Patch over to join in the chaotic fun. Jack realized that at six years old, he had never asked his father to go to the park and play. He already knew the answer—a bank did not run itself. How about Edward and Elizabeth—had they bothered to ask?

When the sun faded and the high-desert temperature dropped, they decided to explore all three blocks of downtown Taos.

As they were leaving the park, Jack noticed a vendor with a Polaroid Land camera around his neck, the kind of camera that spit out a small square photo in about a minute. He had stayed later than the rest, still hoping to sell a photograph even though the likely prospects had dwindled to a few hangers-on who were drunk, stoned, or looking for romance.

Jack reached in his pocket, three bucks and a couple of nickels. He felt a knock on his hip and saw a warm smile, Molly handed him two crumpled dollars.

"We'd like a picture of the two of us together," he said. "Got five bucks and two nickels, is that enough?"

Everyone's smile got even bigger. Molly and Jack

walked away slowly with their hips touching. They stopped at the edge of the park, still close together, and looked at the photo, the one thing in the world that they owned together.

T HE OUTRAGEOUS GROUP got attention as they meandered from Kit Carson Park toward the Taos Plaza. Anglo tourists snickered, Chicanos mumbled in Spanish, one gallery owner scowled in his doorway. On the far side of Bent Street, a photography enthusiast snapped away with a foot-long telephoto lens.

After five weeks on the mesa, the hodgepodge of old adobes and cinderblock buildings that was Taos felt like Manhattan. But it didn't take long to appreciate the simplistic charm. As usual Zipper led the way. Molly and Jack straggled behind.

America—Love it or Leave it. Molly squinted at the chrome bumper of a tan four-door Fleetwood. "Saw that damn sticker too many times in New England."

"Bumper stickers are a bit crass," Jack said, the only thing he could think of to say, "and hard to remove."

"Especially from the big, expensive cars that usually wear that one."

"Maybe people who drive Cadillacs are more patriotic?"

"Maybe the American Dream came true for them and they don't want anything to change."

Jack trailed two steps behind as they crossed a side street, drew a deep breath, and caught up. "I know you're not a huge fan, but capitalism works, on the whole."

"Like sex, booze, pot, money, and rough stuff, most everything is good . . . in moderation."

"Rough stuff?"

"You know. Sticks and stones may break my bones, but whips and chains excite me." She quickly turned away, cocked her head up and looked straight into his eyes with a coy girlish grin.

Damn it, she was cute. And knew how to tease. An angel and Satan topped with a brown bandanna.

They kept marching on the main road that ran the entire length of Taos, a long flat road surrounded by mountains. Jack felt like he had lost that round, but his ego forced him to stay in the fight. Pointing toward a spotless red pickup that looked as though it had never done a days work in its life, he boasted, "Hard to take issue with that bumper sticker." *God Bless America.*

"Actually, it does have me puzzled."

"Thought you'd have an opinion of some sort."

"If God decides to bless America, does she take a neutral position on the other countries?"

"She?" Jack said, louder than intended.

"Or maybe she makes a naughty-and-nice list, like Santa Claus. I wonder where she comes in on Canada and Mexico—they're kind of close to us. After backing the Vietcong, I'm sure China never gets blessed. And Godless Russia must be at the bottom."

God bless America, three patriotic words, and she rattles off a three-minute dissertation peppered with Marxist ideology. Wouldn't be surprised if she was a Darwinian disciple, with agnostic views on creation. He sped up and rejoined the group.

"Wouldn't it be fine to go there one night?" Cinnamon nodded toward Doc McPheeters Hotel and Restaurant.

"I tried to walk in there once," Zipper said. "They said I was too unkempt."

"Unkempt!" Cinnamon said. "How kempt do you need to be? What the hell's that mean?"

"It means you don't get in," Rosemary replied.

The Plaza looked idyllic. A grass-covered block with tall trees and a bandstand. It was bordered by a small hotel and storefronts sheltered from the sun by wooden portals. All brown with splotches of bright colors on the doors and window frames.

"I bet she blesses Denmark sometimes," Molly said unexpectedly. "It's a cute little country. And they hardly ever hurt anybody."

Let it go. Anyway, God hadn't been on his side lately. Not that he ever had been—most of what he'd heard growing up involved smiting and fire and brimstone. But he knew one thing for sure—God wasn't a girl.

Chapter

28

Molly slammed the eggs against the edge of the griddle. One by one. With more force than needed to crack their tender shells. Fragments of shell spewed onto the sizzling yolks. She didn't care.

Damn Jack!

Last night everything seemed perfect. On the ride back they'd held hands with her head on his shoulder. Then all of a sudden, he changed. Without a word he hopped out of the Randy Rabbit and trotted off to his room.

If he just didn't care, why pay her so much attention? Decide to work in the garden when he saw her hoeing, always jump in on the nearest row. And help in the cook house? His fascination with restaurants couldn't be the reason he wanted to help wash dishes every night. He was always struggling to come up with clever comments.

So why in the hell didn't he ever follow through? If he was trying to forget a woman, what better way than to get involved with another? Most likely, he was plotting and scheming to get some lost love back. Chilling out, until she tired of some new knight in gradually tarnishing armor, then he moves back in.

One thing is sure, he's one conflicted bastard. Ah, so what's new? The world is full of them.

Molly turned as Rosemary walked in. "You and your Rolling Stone hero were really cute last night."

"What hero?"

"The one and only Jumpin' Jack."

"He's not exactly the one and only."

"He was the one and only thing on your mind last night."

"It was just a kiss and a cuddle."

"The lady doth protest too much, methinks."

"You're drifting from cryptic to melodramatic. Pick that up in the convent, Sister Rosemary?"

"Don't be ridiculous. I learned it on the streets of the Bronx, like the best of them."

"He's just here to forget," Molly said. "We're all here to forget. Unjust wars . . . unjust governments, unjust religions, unjust lovers."

"We're all about to remember something, too. Two weeks, max. Then back to the real world."

Molly shook her head. "I'm not ready for the real world."

"How do you know you'll get hurt this time? Eddy was an asshole. This guy's a lot different."

"That's true, he puts on a show." Molly pulled a face. "But underneath he's sincere and serious."

"Sincere and serious, sounds kind of worthwhile. Not that I have much experience."

"Depends on who you're serious and sincere about."

"He looks awful serious about you."

"He's running away from something. Or toward something. And I don't think he knows which."

"Why not both? He is a man. Has he given you the lowdown on his past?"

"He won't even tell me where he's from. From his attitude, I'd say it wasn't one of the coasts. No southern accent, so he's probably from the middle of the country. Someplace that hasn't figured out that the war wasn't about freedom in Asian rice paddies. Someplace where the flag still flies on every front porch, and preachers still convince people that God hates commies."

"Wow, you're such a romantic. How can he resist you?"

JUST BEFORE DARK, Jack leaned against the bunkhouse wall and took a deep breath of fresh evening air, while daydreaming of Molly out in the bean patch. Her breasts firm and pointed, nipples showing under a sweat-covered T-shirt. He fantasized about her lying on his cot, naked, her skin warm, smooth. He felt Alicia's hard nipples.

Alicia? Had they become interchangeable partners? Part of his harem? The gray tie on Wednesdays, the blue one on Thursday?

His thoughts drifted back to Molly, straight shiny hair framing her natural beauty, the brown bandana across her forehead, quizzical brown eyes, round firm backside, the bounce in her step, the way—

He raced toward the cook house. Molly stood at the

sink. In a thin T-shirt and long skirt. Her back to him. She hummed. The plates clinked in the sink.

"You sound happy," he said.

She tossed him a smile over her shoulder.

He placed his hands on her shoulders.

"Oh, so you've decided to notice me again?" she said, though without much edge.

He slid his hands down her arms, felt her soapy hands, touched her palms with his fingers. "I've always noticed. I've just been too stupid to know it."

Her soapy hands fell still. Had she cringed or did her heart skip a beat?

"You going to finish washing up?" she said.

"Ah . . ."

She slipped from his arms and dashed to the doorway. He slid toward the door on a trail of soapsuds. He looked in all directions, but she'd disappeared in the dusk. He searched around every corner. Glanced in every window. Passion had grabbed him, and now he felt empty. He opened the plank-board door to his room.

Molly looked up, buck naked, with the grin of a schoolgirl who was harboring a secret. "Gee whiz, you've done a fantastic job with the decoration." She slowly passed her brown eyes across the barren room and let them fall on Jack. "I'm especially fond of the way the olive-drab canvas on the cot complements the reddish-clay mud walls."

His mouth hung open. No words came out.

"But no pin-up girls spicing up your bachelor pad?"

They giggled like teenagers in a car after the movie. Jack locked eyes with her and refused to let go. He sat on the edge of the cot, took her hand, and waited for his pulse to slow, just as hers rose.

Their heartbeats synchronized, met in the middle.

He inched his index finger along the outside of her hand, traced its outline, up to the tip of her littlest finger, over the top of her nail, and into the valley, and slowly up the next finger. Letting her sense his feelings, the up-and-down motion, until reaching the side of her thumb, then gliding across her soft palm, a tingling sensation.

"Why now?" She had a tear in her eye. "What changed?"

"Not sure. One minute I saw the sun going down. The next I saw you."

"Just got needy?"

"Well . . ."

"Needed someone?" Molly's eyes began to wander. Searching the room.

His words finally came. "Needing you."

He placed his hands on her cheeks, stared at the moist droplets that were falling from her eyes. They lay next to each other, soaking in the emotion. He was overwhelmed by the subtle smile on her face. At this moment he felt close, a soothing wave.

"It feels soft." He gently brushed her short brown hair. "Each strand is so fine."

"Even when I was a teenager, my mum said my hair felt like a baby girl's."

He ran his fingers along the inside of her outstretched arm, inhaling the complex essence, knowing all of her. Ecstasy. Fingers exploring down ribs, marking dainty bones, one by one, barely a movement, tense anticipation.

Make it last. Do it now. Stay with me forever.

Lips brushed together. Mouths opened. Tongues touched.

293

"You kept it." Molly stared up at a small photo taped to the wall.

"Kept what?"

"Our picture. The Polaroid from the Taos fiesta."

She threw herself into his chest, and they tumbled against the cot, clung tight together as sweat gathered and melded their bodies. His clothes fell on the floor, no words passed between them. Clumsy lovers at first, unsure of what they wanted that night, unsure what they wanted from each other. Drifters passing in the night or perpetual partners?

Passion took over.

"Fuck me hard!" flew from her lips.

I've made a decision flashed through his mind.

A RAY OF SUN shot through the window. Jack felt the sting on his back from eight jagged serrations. She'd clawed him; last night he hadn't noticed.

Could she get pregnant? Did she have pills? How many men had been in her bed? Did she have gonorrhea? Or herpes?

A trap? Was she trying to get pregnant? Have the family she wanted? How do these hippie minds work?

Could Alicia forgive him?

Did it matter?

He coasted back into the warmth of her body. Held her tight. All the marauding black knights melted away.

JACK PUSHED THE curtain aside. Molly had slipped out of his cot and started earlier than usual, pulling a weed here and there, checking the leaves on her bean plants, looking for signs of a hungry rabbit. Why? According to Zipper, they had to get out of there soon.

At least the mesa would have some fat rabbits instead of those scrawny things that coyotes munched on for dinner.

He watched Molly bounce through the bean patch, a whirling dervish in a colorful skirt. She looked different, even livelier. Was that possible? She softly conversed with a brilliant blue sky, "God's in his heaven—All's right with the world." And she quotes Robert Browning accurately, that guy knew God's gender.

Was last night just a diversion? Were they just horny, or . . .

When he was back with Alicia, this would all seem a dream. Or a nightmare.

Don't flirt, don't mislead her, don't muddy the water. For once in your life do the right thing.

Molly bounced from furrow to furrow with the exuberant energy of a kid at Christmas. She wasn't gorgeous, not in a sexy way—although in the bean patch, laughing and hopping . . .

He opened the door, snatched up the hoe, and stomped into the field. How did he get sucked into this back to nature, ban-the-bomb ethos?

"Somebody woke up a little grouchy this morning," Molly said playfully. "Don't you enjoy this life, living off the land?"

"While I'm doing it, yes. Then I think, how can you ever get ahead, save up some money?"

"Money for what? Big cars, big houses, big headaches?"

"Big medical bills, big education for the kids, something for a rainy day?"

"If it's going to rain, it will rain." Molly shrugged. "You can't buy sunshine."

"You've got a point there. Sometimes I feel like I'm about to fall off the conveyor belt."

"Fall off the conveyor belt?"

"Life is a factory. On the day we climb out of the womb, we're set on a conveyor belt that moves us along. At the end—we fall off."

"And you're okay with that?"

"When God made man, he didn't ask my opinion."

"Maybe it happened the other way around? Maybe man made God?"

Now she was trying to pull the rug out from under God. Atheist notions, that was taking it too far. He gave her the benefit of the doubt and put her down as agnostic.

"Hurry up. Some of these beans are ready to pick." She handed him a wicker basket. "Give me a hand while you're still on the belt."

"How many beans are you going to store? This commune won't be here next month, and you can't stay out here by yourself. What'll you do?"

"Re-engage." Her smile disappeared. "Get back in the conflict."

"And you don't think that's some kind of a treadmill?"

"A necessity as long as the government considers people a renewable resource."

"What the hell does that mean?"

"Young guys are just cannon fodder. They get blown up; you just grow some more."

"Isn't it time to relax a little? The war's over."

"Sure, but men never learn. It won't be long before the next one."

"Some wars are unavoidable. We've got to stop

communist expansion somewhere. Better over there than here."

"Yeah, I'm sure the commies will be swarming in to claim the agricultural opportunities on this mesa." Her knuckles turned white as she gripped the hoe tighter. Jack stepped back in case she decided to swing. "The rich soil, the vast mineral wealth. Coronado's lost city of gold."

"Not out here. In America. The real America."

"Oh . . . You buy into Eisenhower's bullshit Domino Theory."

"I don't buy into anything. I keep an open mind and stay neutral."

"People who stay neutral allow oppressive rulers to succeed."

"Oppressive? Do you mean the police enforcing laws against marijuana? Or preventing defacing of the American flag? I think oppression's a lot worse in Russia."

"I mean the industrial military complex. And the whole damn Republican Party."

"Remember, Vietnam was a Democrat war. The press humiliated Kennedy because he looked weak when he met Khrushchev soon after the inauguration in 1961. So, he picked a fight with North Vietnam to show that he could be tough on communists. He thought a handful of military advisers would wrap that up in a few weeks."

"Then the missile crisis scared the shit out of him, and he started to think about peaceful solutions."

"Sure don't recall any peaceful solutions."

"You're right there. He never had the chance, got a bullet in the head. Most likely a CIA hit, co-opted by the mafia or aristocratic Cuban exiles."

Oh, no, was she also a Kennedy conspiracy wacko?

That was a pointless argument. Obviously, the Russians backed that assassination. "It didn't matter who was president. We had no choice. We had to stop them."

"If I remember correctly, we didn't stop anybody. We lost."

"The South Vietnamese lost."

"Yeah, they lost thousands of innocent women and children when our sticky napalm infernos stuck to their skin."

"The Vietcong's fault. They hid in the villages and mingled with peasants."

"All of the Vietnamese were just peasants. We burned and butchered thousands without justification."

"Collateral damage. The end result, that's what counts."

"Sounds a bit like Karl Marx." She gave him the hairy eyeball. "The end justifies the means?"

"You're twisting things . . . The slaughtering of cattle is horrible, but everyone likes a juicy steak."

"I don't. Some of my best friends are cows."

He didn't know where to go from there. The war couldn't have been for nothing—veterans' sacrifices, the scars they returned with, the nightmares they suffered. The smartest minds in the country had supported the conflict. How could a ragtag bunch of beatniks waylay the most powerful army in history? It was because the foundations of the American way of life—Christian religion and family values—were breaking down. History would show that all of those lost American lives weren't a mistake. If we'd just had the guts to stick with it another year, use the full force of heavy bombers on Hanoi, we would've won.

But he didn't say any of this. It was time to stop

playing farmer in this peace-loving desert and rejoin the real world. But at this point, was it possible to rejoin Alicia?

E VERY DAY OF the last week, Zipper had gone into town by himself. No one mentioned it, but Jack and the women were worried that one day he might not return. Perhaps he considered them a liability, but all they wanted was a ride to somewhere. Surely, Zipper knew that.

Jack ran his right index finger along the small groove on his ring finger, a now barely detectable indentation left by a ring that waited at Old Roy's Pawnshop.

The only reasons he stayed: no money, no transportation, no place to go. Hanging around this last hippie holdout had one advantage; it put time between him and that . . . tragic cave death. Time for the newspapers to move on to the next scandalous indiscretion—a politician cavorting with call girls or a movie star's fascination with cocaine.

He headed out alone toward the large rock at the edge of the compound, his favorite rock, the one with a view of the Sangre de Cristo Mountains.

He had started to feel that White Rabbit Farm with the cute hippie who cooked pot butter might actually be idyllic. Then it all fell apart. She was flighty and erratic, with unrealistic dreams of a world where everyone got along. And far too young. She wanted to start a family. He was past going through that again.

One thing churned in his gut. He'd talked to Molly for hours, made love to her, argued with her, he wasn't able to put her aside.

"It doesn't seem to be working out for you here." Molly suddenly showed up again, looking serious. "Have you thought about going back to whatever it is that's important to you?"

"I have. I can't."

"Life's not a one-way road. You can always go back."

"Sometimes the road narrows. And U-turns aren't an option."

Chapter

29

The sun hovered forever, as if trying to decide to take the plunge, the precipitous drop below Lucero Peak's serrated edge, marking the end of the day. Jack sat on the brink of the precipice, his feet dangling high above the river, trying to make a decision.

He kicked a rock with his foot. It fell and fell and still had a long way to fall when it disappeared from sight. A body was heavier; would it make the trip faster?

Jack's thoughts flashed to high school physics. No. Galileo said no.

He hoped he'd make it all the way to the bottom without bouncing off granite rocks. Or worse, get snagged by a juniper tree halfway down, hung up there, waiting for cougars.

Alicia. She should know what happened to him. A message of some sort, a note.

No, the world would read it and share in his last thoughts.

A phone call, one last sound of her voice, a sign from him that this nightmare was finished, she could move on, start a new life, for her and for the children, a new life with . . .

It wouldn't matter now if the police traced the call. Could they listen in? To his private message? But he had no personal thoughts left. To the world he wasn't a person, just a deranged murderer, something to gossip about, a violent aberration. He'd do them a favor, but do it in silence, and not add to their self-righteous thirst for revenge.

Would this void his life insurance policy? Hell, it doesn't matter. She'll be left with plenty of money.

What he wouldn't give for one last tea party with Elizabeth. At five years old her imagination had run wild. The Mad Hatter often joined them, gobbling up chocolate-covered cookies and slurping his tea. And the Saturday morning round of golf with Edward had been the highlight of every week. Edward routinely outputted him, especially when the greens ran fast.

A hot barbecue sandwich, slow-roasted pulled pork, he could smell it. Harpo had ignited his passion for cooking and taught him things his father could not comprehend.

Even Ginger would be missed. What a dull world without flamboyant, deceptive beauty.

Then there was the girl who grew beans, the girl who never ate meat. Was she destined to meander on the fringe of society, frustrated because she couldn't sway the world with her naïve belief in social justice? Their hours together went fast, too fast. He had more to tell her, but to what end? Why add to her anger? And his?

Would it be fair to have Molly searching the mesa for days trying to find him? Would she bother? Or would she flutter on to the next soul mate who wandered her way? Would he disappear and become part of this landscape? Or wash down and be discovered as bits and pieces in pueblos and chili farms?

Jack made up his mind. He'd sparrow down. Ride the air current. One last adventure.

"So, Jumpin' Jack. You finally going to live up to your name?"

There she was again, his bright-eyed, giggling shadow. She casually plopped down beside him with no more than a glance at the sheer drop.

"Ah . . . just trying to sort out the good guys and the bad guys."

"How about you, Jack? Which are you?"

"Kind of in between, I guess."

"There's no in between. That's the facade you see in the mirror. The one people make up so they can live with themselves."

"I guess you think I'm a bad guy."

"My guess is—people change. During one of her theatrical moments, I remember my mother saying, 'What happens to you doesn't matter as much as what happens inside you.'" Molly pulled out a stubby joint, flicked a match, inhaled deep.

They stared down to the Rio Grande.

Molly broke the silence. "To die would be really exciting."

"What makes you so sure?"

"Peter Pan thought so. Who am I to argue with him?"

Jack had tired of adventure. He had bartered his secure life for an awfully big adventure, and now he was done.

The setting sun balanced on the edge of the earth.

Jack and Molly sat silently, hands touching slightly, catching their balance.

"I guess you think there's a heaven?" she said.

"Of course."

"That's what I figured. You look like you're in a hurry to get there."

"Everybody wants to go to heaven."

"That's what people say, but for some plastic reason they don't want to die in order to get there."

"Maybe I'm the exception."

Molly laughed. To his surprise, Jack laughed too. It was hard to be serious for long with this woman. Maybe she was right when she'd told him that life was too short to take seriously.

Working on a goal would give his life a purpose. Moving on would snap him out of this bout of depression. He had gotten too attached to Molly, a diversion from his key goal, getting his family back together. But Molly was clever, hard-working. Maybe they could help each other get their lives on track.

Before they could leave, that idiot Habeeb would need medical attention; he'd die if they left him behind. Zipper wanted to dump him outside the hospital entrance. Molly complained that they'd trace him back to White Rabbit, and the sheriff would show up. Rosemary knew a free clinic for migrants that didn't ask questions.

After Habeeb was cared for, everyone would scatter. Zipper wouldn't be crazy about him hitching a ride, and the tires on the Randy Rabbit might not make it out of New Mexico. Their motley group stranded along the road would draw the attention of the highway patrol.

He needed to keep it together for just a few more days. This place had a way of driving people crazy. And there he was, feet dangling over the edge, alongside a vegetarian anarchist.

There must be a way out of this mess. Experience had taught him that quick thinking and stealth precision could solve any problem—just like a bank deal, except this time his life was the collateral. And his quick thinking had kept him alive and free . . . so far.

THAT MORNING FELT different. Everyone stared at the door as Harwood rushed in. No subtle turn of the head as he passed, they openly followed his charge through the squad room. Something was up.

The phone in his office blared while he marched down the hallway. He scooped it up without sitting down. "Harwood."

"Got a hit during the night. LAPD picked up a bookkeeper at the Aldington, a ritzy downtown hotel, had her fingers in the till, embezzlement, and possible tax fraud. After some persuasion, they traced her back to New York, then it turns out she's the infamous Ginger Feliciano, and—"

"What's LAPD's number?"

J ACK THOUGHT HE would need to talk Molly into it. He thought wrong. All he said was, "Do you think that old truck can be fixed?"

"Yeah."

"Let's check it out tomorrow."

"Since we blew all our bread on a Polaroid photo, maybe we'll have better luck tonight."

Minutes later, he found himself lugging a toolbox down the so-called road. "Who actually owns this truck?"

"When asshole Eddy buzzed off, he left two things behind, that Studebaker and me. He'd probably have taken the pickup if he hadn't been too lazy to swap out the generator."

"It's just a generator? If everyone knew what it needed, why didn't somebody fix it?"

"Zipper liked having the only transportation, it gave him control. I wasn't in a hurry to leave, but it's time to put my backup plan into action."

The mystery and excitement of the covert operation got his adrenaline flowing, but he struggled to keep up with energetic Molly, the tools were heavy, and in tight Levi's, her backside was a major distraction. Fortunately, a full moon kept them on the rough dirt track, most of the time.

At Arroyo Hondo they headed north, and a mile

later veered onto a dirt road that looked like it might actually go somewhere. At the top of a rise, the outline of sleepy San Cristobal village glowed in the distance. A small shack fifty yards up the road had a collection of junkers scattered around it. The place looked abandoned apart from the Ford pickup parked near the door. They approached quietly in case of a light sleeper or guard dog inside. If a yard dog had been prowling, it would've already shredded their pants.

After meandering around rusted fenders and stumbling on discarded wheel rims, they locked in on a possible target—a bullet-nosed Studebaker sedan. Jack could name the make and model of every car made since 1960, but he was unsure what was under the hood of 50s era vehicles.

"That doesn't look anything like my truck," Molly whispered.

"Studebaker most likely used the same generator in their cars and trucks."

It took a while to pry the hood open without creating a disturbance. The moonlight didn't penetrate into the engine compartment, so they risked the flashlight.

"Do all cars have a similar generator?" she said.

"Modern ones don't even have one. They have an alternator."

"I've heard of those."

"These old generators put out six volts of DC current. Alternators supply twelve volts of AC, more cranking power to start the engine."

He wiggled one of the rusted fan blades back and forth until it broke off and gave him more room, then he ripped out the cracked rubber fan belt. Twenty minutes later they were lugging a fifteen-pound device back to White Rabbit Farm in hopes that Studebaker had cut down on production costs by standardizing components.

Chapter
30

Every person at White Rabbit Farm crammed into the old Wonder Bread truck that Habeeb called home—everyone except Zipper and Cinnamon's girls. Zipper was in town, doing whatever it was Zipper did in town. Today, washing and storing green beans would shield Tiger Lily and Pumpkin Patch from life's reality.

Sweat poured from Habeeb's body. Huge pupils filled hollow eye sockets. Tremors shook the bunk. "They're coming, man."

"Somebody do something!" Cinnamon shouted.

"Jack got the truck running this morning," Molly said. "We can go to town for help."

Everyone looked at everyone. Help from whom?

"They're coming. They're coming. Close the goddamn door."

"Think—think of something." Cinnamon stared straight at Jack.

Jack stared at the wall. He certainly didn't want cops out here checking on potheads.

Rosemary Meadow had finished half a semester of nurse's training before joining a convent. That was credentials enough to put her in charge. She broke the uncomfortable silence. "Pulse, sixty and weak."

Jack tried to comprehend what was happening as all three women started to jabber at once.

"Sixty? If he dropped acid his heart would be racing."

"He might've mixed stuff."

"If he'd freaked out on a bad trip, he could've turned self-destructive."

"What happened?" Jack said.

"That's what we're trying to work out," Rosemary said. "Maybe overdosed or got hold of some bad stuff."

"What kind of stuff?"

"I think he figured out a way to make his own acid from a fungus that grows on rye."

"Could he do that?"

Rosemary pointed at Habeeb. "Apparently not very well."

"What does LSD actually do?" This whole drug culture puzzled Jack.

"Gives you a serious disconnection from reality."

"Why in the hell did he take it?"

"Maybe he wanted a serious disconnection from reality."

"LSD isn't addictive like some other drugs," Rosemary explained. "But you build up a tolerance, so you need to take bigger doses to get high. The problem is, every trip is unpredictable, you don't know which way they'll go."

"Shit, who knows?" Molly said. "He popped peyote buttons, mushrooms, and got PCP from somewhere."

"PCP!" Cinnamon shouted. "That'll pull down your heart rate if you take too much."

"It's got to be more than that," Rosemary said. "Something's eating his guts."

"He's been acting stranger than usual since Zipper decided to shut this place down. I've seen him have flashbacks and panic attacks."

"Absolutely paranoid. Leaving here is more than he can handle, nowhere to go, end of the line."

Habeeb's face turned ashen. His wide eyes went blank.

Jack had to steer them away from involving the authorities. "He doesn't look like he would last long riding into town in the back of the pickup."

"No, we shouldn't try," Rosemary said.

"Maybe when Zipper gets back," Cinnamon said.

"Maybe."

Jack started to sweat more than Habeeb. If they didn't get real medical attention, would he be involved in another death? If they did manage to get to Taos, how many cops would start nosing around?

"Get on the other side, Jack. Help get his head up." Rosemary was struggling to control his thrashing body. "Now tip him this way. He's choking on his own vomit."

"That's what did Jimi Hendrix in!" Cinnamon was going over the edge.

The convulsions kept shaking Habeeb's body. A deep sound from somewhere inside him dominated the room. Sweat flowed from every pore. His stomach rose and fell like violent waves attacking the shore. Greenish-yellow bile spewed from gaps between tightly clenched teeth.

Silent pleas and mournful eyes were the only comfort offered.

Then . . . no movement—no sound.

"He's gone," someone said.

His struggle was over. His body lay still. Habeeb had done hard drugs. Where did he get them? Where did his money come from? Where did he come from? Who was Habeeb? Or who had he been? Draft Evader—Peacenik—Pothead—Scholar—Anarchist—Chemist—Pacifist—Lazy Son of a Bitch.

Long minutes passed.

"What do we do now?" Molly asked quietly. "Zipper will probably stay in town all day."

"Should we call the police, an ambulance . . . I mean, co—coroner?" Cinnamon said, sobbing.

"That would require a telephone," Molly said.

"Cops, they'd be climbing all over this place." Jack swung his arm across the room.

"Need to catch our breath," Rosemary said. "Reestablish our bearings."

"Right," Jack added. "Let's meet in the cook house, say, thirty minutes."

Jack had never felt that anyone actually liked Habeeb. But they'd all respected his knowledge and principles. Too bad he never applied them in a meaningful way. Maybe he was ahead of his time. Or way behind the times. But he was never on time. And now his time had run out.

SALLY HARWOOD SAT on the front steps, a backpack on her knees and a new sleeping bag rolled up beside her. She couldn't sit still, she had gotten up early and dressed fast, all excited about her first real campout. Fishing all weekend with Dad, and camping, and cooking hot dogs. And marshmallows, too.

She would have fun with her father. Just like Tony did.

JUMPIN' JACK LEAPT toward the bread truck, hoping to arrive unseen. He flung the door open and ran toward Habeeb, trying not to look at him—he hadn't gone there to pay his respects. His hand dove into the jean pockets; they were stiff and tight, stuck to his flesh. Jack couldn't help but wonder when Habeeb had last changed those pants.

He wasn't going to think about that now.

The front pockets were downright empty. One rear pocket contained what may have once been a handkerchief, but now resembled an oily dipstick rag. In the other, a billfold, missing some stitches, held together in one place by a piece of duct tape. It didn't take long to search that grimy piece of leather—a five and two singles. No driver's license, no pictures of loved ones.

No goddamn Social Security card.

It had hit him while he was trying to work out what to do with the body—Habeeb must have had a Social Security number. It would solve Jack's biggest problem— how to live a life without hiding, a life with a normal job, maybe even a career. How to actually have a new identity.

He scanned the room for a hiding place and spotted a three-foot high stack of books in one corner. *Galois Theory, Yang-Baxter Equation with regard to Statistical Mechanics, Proof of Fermat's Last Theorem.*

Molly popped her head in the door. "I checked the

Studebaker in case we need it to transport the body. You did a good job hooking up the generator, fired up on the first try. We ready to head for the cook house?"

"Ah . . . was Habeeb some sort of physicist or mathematician?"

"Don't know what he was. Someone said he had worked at the nuclear lab over in Los Alamos. Most of us thought he was a Vietnam vet. Though he often mumbled about working on a solution to the square root of negative one."

"That's an imaginary number."

"Habeeb imagined quite a number of things."

MINUTES LATER, EVERYONE gathered in the cook house.

"We should have a service or something." Cinnamon's enthusiasm rose and burst like last night's champagne, flat and unwanted. "At least someone should say some kind words."

"We all respected him," Molly said, "but it would be hard to express it in kind words."

"There's some goodness in everyone." Rosemary raised a finger to make sure everyone was paying attention. "Habeeb kept this place running by sharing his knowledge of science."

"True enough," Molly said. "He could make internal combustion, hydraulics, and physics sound exciting."

"Rosemary, you were a nun. You know what to say."

"For two hundred and thirty-seven days, in a teen counseling center." For once Rosemary looked embarrassed. "I've never even been to a funeral."

Molly stood up slowly, looking at no one at all. Her

lips parted slightly, unsteady at first, then gaining cool, her voice crystal clear, in perfect tune. "Some pills make things hazy—other pills make you lazy."

Molly's watery eyes looked straight ahead. Although he was sitting to one side, Jack felt those eyes looking directly at him, like the Mona Lisa. Was he feeling what she called telepathic communication? How odd to connect at a moment like this.

"But the ones you been poppin—just made you crazy." Still on key, Molly finished.

"I hope Habeeb is happy," Cinnamon said. "Chasing rabbits with Grace."

"Amen." Rosemary bowed her head.

"Awomen." Cinnamon clenched her fist.

For the first time ever, Jack thought Cinnamon looked gloomy. "Were he and Grace together long?"

"Grace is Grace Slick, and he never even met her. He went to a Jefferson Airplane concert in Albuquerque—1972, I think—been in love with her ever since. Used to listen to White Rabbit all the time." Cinnamon's bond with Habeeb had been deeper than he'd realized. "He was a founding member of the commune, insisted on naming it White Rabbit Farm."

"Weird."

"More like sad. Habeeb once told me that his only regret in life was not making love to Grace Slick."

Silence fell over the room. He'd been detested for the past months as drug addiction had taken over his life. But they missed him now. He had seldom left the commune, just a weekly foray, ostensibly to procure personal items. Never stayed in town during the evening. Never went to the river for a bath, a frequent topic of complaint.

A long silence ensued.

Rosemary finally broke it. "We're no longer self-sufficient, we can't survive out here any longer. If the cops get involved, we'll be forced to stay while they investigate."

"Time to bug out," Cinnamon said. "No telling what kind of trouble they'd cause."

Jack jumped up. "Let's just get rid of the body, wipe the slate clean."

"We can't just throw him out!" Cinnamon said. "He was one of us."

"Jack's right," Molly said. "Anything else will cause months of disruption."

"I don't want any part of it." Cinnamon ran from the room.

That left Rosemary, Molly, and Jack to tend to the details. Details Jack desperately needed to take care of on his own, and quickly, before Zipper returned.

"I'll help Jack clean up the wagon." Molly headed for the door. "I'm sure Zipper will have an innovative idea about what to do with the body."

"Let me take care of it!" Jack caught hold of himself and backed off. If he pushed too hard, it would arouse suspicion. He needed time alone in the Wonder Wagon, time to find a Social Security card, or at least a number, and with luck a driver's license too. "You've had way too much stress for one day."

THE DEPARTMENT SPRANG for a plane ticket without squawking. Since Tony's death, they hadn't bitched about the Pipkins case once.

The plane made Harwood feel claustrophobic, and he'd made the mistake of answering the woman from

Prattsville when she asked what he did for a living. Every ten minutes she had a new question that he quickly evaded; he was good at it, for years he had dealt with people who evaded questions for a living.

"Would you like something to drink, sir?" The stewardess bent over and placed a napkin on the tray.

"God, yes. Bourbon."

"What brand would you prefer?" She held up two small bottles.

"One of each, with branch water."

The woman from Prattsville quit asking questions. The stories of her grandkids and the new preacher at the Ozark Bible Tabernacle ceased. Sitting next to a man with a glass of whiskey in each hand—that would be a topic of discussion at the Morning Glory Café.

Silence at last. Now he could plot a strategy. It would be after 6:00 p.m. when this flying tin can landed in Los Angeles. Lieutenant Conrad Dawkins of the LAPD had said he would come by the hotel tomorrow afternoon. He'd rather get started on the Feliciano woman first thing in the morning. At least they weren't making him wait until Monday—he had played the cop killer card.

He'd play any card necessary to get cooperation.

HOW COULD A guy live in a bread truck, not for days or months, but for years? The answer had left this earth with Habeeb. Jack had to work fast, had to think smart, smart like Habeeb.

Only two objects vaguely resembled furniture—an old Indian drum and a battered trunk. The drum didn't look like a tourist trinket—it seemed to be made from a hollowed-out two-foot log. The deerskin stretched over the ends had hardened and developed a rich brown patina. Jack imagined that it had knocked around one of the pueblos for decades. The ancient drum served as a bedside table. Its top hide had a five-inch gash but managed to support three personal necessities—a kerosene lamp with BSA hand-painted across the base. A poker-size card deck bound with a rubber band. And his constant companion, a chipped coffee cup without a handle, still proudly promoting the 37th Annual Steubenville Pancake Breakfast.

A small green canvas bag had been tossed in a corner. He tugged at the clogged zipper and peered inside. A toothbrush with a broken handle and smashed bristles. One tube of Colgate firmly rolled. Drug paraphernalia that made Jack shiver. A brushed-steel Zippo lighter. An empty cone-shaped bottle with a three-mast sailing ship and old English script that said Old Spice.

A handsome brown leather case leaned against a wall, a few inches wide and three feet long, secured by a sturdy brass clasp. It protected a two-piece hard-rock maple pool cue. The tip had a coat of blue dust. The thick handle section had artfully crafted inlaid letters, EJM. Probably something he picked up in a pawnshop.

No shelves, no drawers, no place to store things except an old military-surplus, piece-of-crap footlocker. Locker was right. Locked, with a heavy-duty padlock. He flipped the footlocker around, or at least tried to, heavy as hell. A close look at the hinges revealed rivets—that would take tools, no time for that. There must be a key.

Jack pulled up the edge of the mattress, no place to hide things, no box spring, just a wire grid attached with springs along the edges. He rapidly checked all the edges, searching for a key strapped to the wires or springs. Then he crawled under the bed, clawing his way through old socks and other things he didn't want to think about. Lot of junk, but no key. The guy owned nothing but books, a bed, a drum, and a footlocker. He grabbed the lantern and shook it, no rattle. Then he grabbed the drum, examined the edges, where deerskin met wood—still no key.

He sat on the stool that substituted for a driver's seat. Checked the ignition switch for a ring full of keys; no surprise there, this thing didn't have an engine. Glove box, ashtray, storage compartment—all too luxurious for a bread truck. He got on his knees to look under the rubber floor liner. Nothing. He pried back a hinged access plate in the center of the floor. Nothing there but the emergency brake mechanism, transmission, and mouse turds.

Still on his hands and knees, searching the floor, he looked up, and bright sun shone through the passenger's window—or whatever the far-side window is called in a single-seat bread truck. A sparkle from under the dashboard caught his eye, and he reached toward it.

Molly burst through the door. "Had trouble finding the mop bucket."

Jack hit his head on the steering wheel as he quickly jumped up. Those old wheels were huge and didn't give at all.

"I'll take care of it," Jack replied abruptly, with a steely-eyed stare. His compassion for Habeeb was gone.

"You'll need help. I'm not squeamish like Cinnamon."

"Get your truck and bring it around."

"Yes, sir, Mr. Ass McHole."

The moment the door clicked, he dove under the dash, yanked the key free, and leapt towards Habeeb's treasure chest. Everything the guy owned in one lousy box, years alone in a truck, waiting for a damsel to discover his distress. Tough luck.

At least a dozen barbell weights, gym shoes, and one small fishing tackle box. Why lock this junk up? No documents or letters, nothing from home. No framed picture of Mom when she was young. No trophies or diplomas. Did this guy really exist?

The tackle box had a built-in lock. No. Not more keys. He slid the lever on the latch to one side, it popped, and the lid noisily jumped up a fraction. Jam-packed with letters and papers.

A rumble got louder. Molly's truck. He slammed the tackle box lid. Lifted the floor access plate. Wedged the tackle box on top of the transmission. Then he closed the hinged plate.

THE SUN HAD heated the concrete steps until they felt like an oven. Sally Harwood sat on her backpack and leaned against the sleeping bag. How long would it take to get to the lake? Could they set up the tent and build a campfire before dark? Had Daddy disappeared just like Tony?

"I'm still trying to get him on the phone," Judy Harwood said through the screen door. "Let me know if he shows up."

HABEEB HAD STARTED to stiffen, yet Molly and Jack tried to handle him gently. Why? The truck bed had a smooth-worn surface that allowed Habeeb's body to slide into place. He looked more comfortable there than twisted around in his army bunk. Jack couldn't let anyone know the location of Habeeb's final resting place. He had to disappear completely, so that a new Habeeb could take his place.

"I'll take it from here, Molly. He'll slide out of the truck bed easily."

"Let's wait for Zipper. The ground out here is packed hard as a rock."

"No. I can do it myself."

"I know how to use a shovel!"

"I'll do it alone."

"What's wrong with you, Jack? I'll grab some water. Be right back."

Damn, she was stubborn.

The moment she was out of sight he ran to his room, grabbed the full army-surplus canteen he used when working in the bean field and a Snickers bar, jammed them in his backpack and hurried back to the truck. He wasn't about to leave that backpack with a photo of Alicia laying around at a time like this.

JACK HEARD THE shovel clank in the truck bed each time the Studebaker flew into the air and landed on all four wheels at the same time. He cringed as though feeling Habeeb's pain.

He hated treating Molly this way, hitting the gas when she was in the cook house. He would savor the day when he could treat people the way he wanted to. But that was a luxury he couldn't afford right now.

He had turned off on a dirt side road, then crossed a ditch and headed cross-country. The old truck raced across the mesa faster than it had traveled in years. He didn't go as far off the road as he wanted—on that vast, flat mesa, there were few points of reference. A city boy could get lost. If he didn't finish before dark, and clouds blocked the moon, he would blindly spend the night out there and then prompt a search party at daybreak.

He scouted for a depression near the truck. Why not start at the lowest point? Besides what little rainwater that came along might settle there and—hell, it didn't make any difference. He started digging. Like everything else at the commune, this worn-out shovel had been left behind by some long-forgotten flower child, purchased at a garage sale, or pilfered from somebody's porch. Gloves. Molly would have thought of gloves, why hadn't he?

The ground hadn't seen water in months, and it had never seen a shovel. It looked soft, but the shovel pinged and flew back. Ignoring the shockwaves that ran from his hands to his wrists and up through his arms, he gouged out a trench, two foot by six foot. Twenty frantic minutes later, he reached the halfway point, eighteen inches deep. His target of three feet deep was a half-ass goal, for a half-ass grave, for a burned-out hippie from a half-ass farm, on a half-ass mesa, dug by a banker with a half-ass life.

Then the shovel broke.

"Damn it."

He threw the handle into the air, amazed by how far it flew. The shovel handle had snapped at the weakest point, where the wood slid into the metal sleeve. He staggered to the truck, grabbed the backpack, sat in the sand, and caught his breath while scarfing down the Snickers bar in three bites.

Using only the metal portion, he scooped out a few more inches of dirt. That would have to do.

It felt harsh, a cruel last gesture. But needs must. He

tossed the surrounding mound of dirt onto Habeeb. On his feet, on his chest, finally . . . onto his face. Filling his mouth with coarse sand and fragments of cactus. Small clumps of dirt stuck to Habeeb's bulging eyeballs. Why hadn't he pulled down his tired eyelids?

Why hadn't he left the bone-dry mesa weeks ago? Just walked away?

Why hadn't he led a much different life? Instead of complacently accepting the one that had been dealt to him.

"Miss Fontaine, this is Sergeant Harwood from Little Rock." Lieutenant Conrad Dawkins waved toward Harwood. "He would like to ask you a few questions about a case he is working on."

"Don't know anybody in Little Rock." She didn't look at Harwood. "Never even been there."

The room had the dimensions and charm of a used-car salesman's office, without the clutter. Small, harshly lit, designed to intimidate. Lieutenant Dawkins sat at one end of the table with a stack of important-looking papers in front of him. Harwood sat at the other end, holding a pack of Lucky Strikes in one hand, periodically tapping the pack on the table, as if to compress the tobacco tightly against one end of each cigarette.

He hoped the suspect smoked. He always hoped the suspect smoked. It was a chance to unnerve them, a chance to become their friend. Right now, Harwood needed a smoke. But Dawkins didn't approve of the habit, so Harwood would wait. Felicia Fontaine, aka Ginger Feliciano, sat in the middle, facing a one-way glass window. Calm and relaxed on the surface, her eyes flittered toward the door only once.

"You may be unaware of your partner's involvement in two murders, Miss Feliciano." Harwood made sure that he didn't blink.

"Name's Fontaine. Felicia Fontaine. And I don't have partners, just lovers."

"You should tell your eyes that, because they don't agree."

"Miss Fontaine," Dawkins said, "we've linked you to an embezzlement scam at an amusement park in Missouri. Your prints match those provided by Sergeant Harwood. Prints taken from a wine glass in the office of Mr. Frederick Fosdick."

"I don't give a damn about your problems at Marble Mine," Harwood said. "I know you weren't involved with the murder. Just want to locate your lover, the guy you knew as Jasper Jones."

"That limp dick's no lover. Who the hell got killed at Marble Mine?"

"My son."

For the first time, she looked straight at him. Good.

"I'm sure you weren't involved," he said, "probably not even aware. He's a psychopathic serial killer. Help us find him."

"This man also killed a police officer," Dawkins said. "Your help will be appreciated and duly noted."

"I want more than appreciation. I want to walk out of here."

Harwood leaned in; his voice deepened. "Do you know where the guy is?"

"I believe I could be helpful. Very helpful."

"Where is he?"

Ginger didn't move, didn't smile, didn't speak.

"I can get the DA to go easy," Dawkins said. "Your cooperation will go a long way with the judge."

She sat back and folded her arms. "If I talk, I walk."

Chapter

31

J ack hadn't slept at all. Not one single minute. Just laid there thinking all night long. Was there an error in his plan? Had he left a clue? Had he dug the grave deep enough? Gone into the desert far enough? Tire tracks. He should have obliterated them where he'd turned off of the road. It never rained here; tread marks stayed around a long time. All of the tracks must be smoothed out within a hundred feet of the road.

The sun had just poked above the horizon; he could examine the contents of the tackle box he'd retrieved from the bread truck. He thought about Habeeb, the man's whole life in one lousy box. Then he realized that his whole life fit in a backpack. A ripped backpack, just like the men at the Bentonville mission. Soon he might find himself back in a place like that.

No, he'd never give up. He'd get his own restaurant,

then hire one or two guys who were down on their luck, teach them to cook, give them a hand, like Harpo did for him.

He propped a chair against the door and spread the contents of the box onto his cot. A student ID card from Ohio State. A picture of a girl, about seventeen, in a light-blue blouse, plaid skirt, and navy-blue tennis shoes.

And a frayed, but original Social Security card—Easley Jonathan McQuade.

It was what he had hoped for, and nobody here even knew his real name.

There was more. An Ohio driver's license, expired. According to the birth date, McQuade was barely one year older than Jack—poor guy, he had looked much older. Form DD-214, Department of Defense, U.S. Army, BCD, Bad Conduct Discharge, not surprising. A Silver Star medal, a military decoration for valor, what an odd combination. Three letters, all from a Teresa Miller of Steubenville, Ohio. An old billfold stamped with the initials EJM. There was probably enough here to get a replacement birth certificate.

Jack pushed everything aside, then sprawled out on his cot to read the letters in chronological order. The first one read like a teenage romance novel; each of the ten paragraphs ended with, "I miss you darling." They obviously had not had sex; she was waiting for marriage. The second letter talked about her grandmother's birthday party, a part-time job at the Dairy Queen, and only one I miss you just before closing. The third was a Dear John.

Jack stuck the Social Security card, driver's license, and student ID into the billfold, then walked over to his backpack. It wasn't hanging on the nail as usual, or on the floor, or under the bed.

On the sand, where he'd scarfed up the Snickers bar. Criminals always made one fatal mistake. One minor detail that put them in prison. Had he just made his?

He stuck the billfold in his pocket. Looked down at the DD-214—nothing to be proud of, but it could provide additional identification—folded it twice and stuffed it alongside the billfold. Gathering the letters and picture, along with a book of matches, he headed outside. Destroying those ties to Easley Jonathan McQuade's past would be simple. Destroying his ties to the past with that photo of Alicia and his driver's license in his backpack would be far more challenging.

HARWOOD GOT OFF on the eighth floor. It was early on Monday morning and he hoped he wouldn't be kept waiting. Offices lined both sides of the hall. What did all of these pencil pushers do? They could run the whole state of Arkansas out of the first three floors of this building.

The reception area of Room 847 had four people sitting at desks wearing the fat and placid look of civil servants. Five minutes later Dawkins walked in and ushered him directly to District Attorney Roy McMullen's office, a big corner setup with a view all the way to the ocean. Harwood wondered if the district attorney in Little Rock could manage a glimpse of the river from his office.

The introductions were short. McMullen had a busy schedule. Harwood knew he needed to make his case fast.

But McMullen took the initiative. "Lieutenant Dawkins tells me that we are holding a person that you believe has information regarding murders in Arkansas and Missouri."

"Right. She knows where the murderer is," Harwood said. "She's ready to cut a deal."

"What is your definition of a deal?"

"She tells us where he's hiding, and the embezzlement charges go away. This Feliciano broad had no involvement or knowledge of the murders. She's of little consequence."

"The Aldington Hotel doesn't think so."

"Her partner on the last job killed a cop and killed my son."

McMullen leaned forward. "This man actually murdered your son?"

"Right in front of me. I still see it every day. He knocked me down, my head hit a rock, I staggered, he ran to Tony, a fifteen-year-old boy in shock, forced him over a ledge to his—"

McMullen sat back again. "This office is very sympathetic toward victims of violent murderers, especially when police and their families are involved."

"Then cut a deal with the Feliciano woman."

"The Aldington family is prominent in this city. I can't simply tell them that someone who stole thousands is free to walk away."

Dawkins held up a hand. "What if there were something in it for them?"

"Besides getting the money back, they'll want her locked up for a few years," McMullen said.

"She probably spent most of the money already," Dawkins said. "Publicity may be worth a lot more than revenge to philanthropists like the Aldingtons."

"Publicity?"

"Aldington Hotel Assists with the Capture of Serial Killer."

"Can you make it play out that way?"

"The media is pliable when you feed them a headline."

JACK WALKED THE six miles to the burial site; he couldn't risk another trip in the pickup. While Molly prepared breakfast, he avoided her and dropped the truck keys in her room.

Coyotes had feasted the night before.

Grisly remains littered the sand. One arm gnawed clean to bone. A missing leg ripped free at the knee, probably carried off to a coyotes' den to nourish pups.

Oh, God. The backpack was torn apart, but at least the picture of Alicia and his driver's license were intact. Foolish ties to his past, Jeremy Pipkins's past. Was it time to sever that bond? He sat on the ground, contemplating the grotesque scene. At first, a glimpse was all he could bear, in shock, trembling, unable to walk away. The same old story, some die so that others could live. But here on this desolate mesa, both life and death were more vivid and surreal.

"I didn't kill him!" Jack screamed. "He killed himself! I didn't kill any of them! It was an accident! They were all accidents! I'm sorry! I'm so, so, sorry!"

And then he curled up on the mesa and began to weep.

He wept for the cop in the parking garage and his family. He wept for the young boy in the mine, and for his father, robbed forever of his son. He wept for what he'd done to Alicia, for what he'd done to his children.

He wept for the life he'd lost, that had been ripped away from him.

And he wept for the colossal waste that his life had been in the first place.

Eventually, the storm passed. When it did, he sat up, trembling and exhausted, but feeling . . . clean. He looked at the remains of Mr. Easley McQuade.

He had to grab the opportunity to become someone new. To truly become someone new. Easley McQuade. He would do well by the name, live up to it in a way the previous owner hadn't. He owed him that.He watched the circling ravens descend. Right in front of him. They tore soft fragments of tissue with sharp beaks. Intense sun glistened on shiny, bluish-black feathers as a raven picked at one hand, erasing the swirls and patterns of fingerprints. One last indignity for Easley McQuade.

Dust rose on the horizon. Jack froze—movement would give him away. Who would be out here? Damn, he hadn't obliterated the tire tracks near the road. Too much of a hurry to get here, he had meant to do it on the way back. Sweat oozed from his armpits. Pungent odor permeated the air. The spinning cloud of suffocating brown dirt closed in. The sound of tires on rocks was crisp and sharp.

Molly's rusted Studebaker emerged.

Molly jumped from the truck and caught her breath. "What the hell?"

"Just trust me, Molly, I have my reasons. I had no other choice."

"You look a bit wobbly, but I do trust you. Besides, I never did understand that digging a hole bit." Perspiration dripped from under her headband. "It's what my father called *being on the wrong side of the grass.*"

"As usual Molly, in a strange and wonderful way, you make perfect sense."

"This gets curiouser and curiouser. In the pueblos, burying people makes sense. And Native Americans don't bury dead people in boxes, they think of their spirits as being part of the earth, enabling nature, providing a means to survive. But Jesus freaks and Jews believe that God is above, that our spirit will float in the clouds. Why do Christians and Semites put dead people in the ground?"

"To avoid disease. Burial or cremation is the practical thing to do."

"Practical! Why don't they just take dead people, launch them up in a fucking balloon and get them started in the right direction?"

"For lack of a balloon and an abundance of coyotes and ravens, maybe this is the right thing." Jack thought he had a good reason for going insane. What was her excuse? Just living on Conejo Mesa might be reason enough.

"As right as it can be. You didn't murder Habeeb— Habeeb murdered Habeeb. Whatever your reason for doing this, I'm sure it's good. Maybe not obvious, but good. Under the surface, you're a good guy, Jack. I know that."

Jack held Molly's hand tight as they thought about Habeeb spread across Conejo Mesa, forever chasing rabbits. It wasn't a time to talk. It was a time to think. A time to feel. Jack imagined huge funeral festivals in Albuquerque, given that city's love of balloons. Molly— she sure could make your mind drift places you never expected.

She even believed in him. Just like . . . just like Alicia.

Down-to-earth, that had been Jack's life—rather it had been Jeremy's. From the day he was born, guided by rules, explicit rules, followed without question. When he was little, Mom had rule upon rule. At school, there were rules, there for a reason, he guessed. Of course, church had its rules, with the ultimate price. His father's banking world was constructed of rules. Banking and Father, he couldn't think of one without the other. Unambiguously melded together with rules.

He couldn't ever go back to that life; he knew that now. The question was, what did he still owe Alicia?

"If there is a God, she's up there working the strings." Molly glanced up toward the sky. "Playing us like puppets."

Jack looked at Molly. "If there is a God?"

"Sure. If not—we're just stupid enough to randomly dance about on our own."

Things were far simpler at the First Presbyterian Church in Kansas City—follow the Bible or suffer the consequence. Molly might ignore the rules, but she wasn't reckless. She had her own code of ethics. Treat everyone right. Everyone was pleased to be around her, even Zipper at times. Sunshine seemed to radiate from her.

If only Alicia . . .

Way back in college, she had kind of been that way. Bright-eyed dreamer, that's what he'd called her. Women's rights over reproduction, even went to some rallies. And acting class for a while, dreamed of Broadway. A year into marriage, time with his family, it all faded. Had he driven it out of her? Fallen in love with the carefree, then snuffed it all out?

333

He owed her at least a chance to get the carefree back. To blow the embers back into flame.

That was, if he wasn't just blowing ashes into his eyes.

"THIS IS YOUR lucky day," Harwood said, leaning forward.

Ginger returned the stare. "Is it your turn to play good cop?"

"We thought you might like to get out of this jail," Dawkins said. "The DA has made a very generous offer. Since your former partner—"

"Roommate."

"Since your former roommate is a worse criminal than you are. If you provide us with information that leads to the arrest of this Jasper Jones—you walk."

"Wait a minute. I can tell you where he is. If you don't arrest him, that's your problem."

"If he's where you say, we'll arrest him."

"Doesn't look like you done too well so far. What if you fuck up?"

"The deal is, he is where you say he is, you're off the hook!" Dawkins shouted.

"Also." Ginger showed no emotion. "His conviction isn't part of the deal."

"Yeah, now take the deal while it's on the table." Harwood scratched the palm of his hand. Sweat ran under his shirt, trickled down the side of his ribs. "This completely separates you from the murder raps."

"Okay—I had this friend from back East. We stayed in touch, kind of. She got mixed up with some hippie called Zipper in New Mexico—"

Harwood's bony jaw jutted forward. "So—what about Jones?"

"My friend had left. I dumped that asshole off there."

"Where's there?"

"White Rabbit Farm. Ten miles north of Taos. Near an egg sign."

Dawkins printed the name, even though they had it all on the recorder. Feliciano and Dawkins stared at each other.

Harwood ran out of the room.

M OLLY BOUNCED OUT of the truck. "What's happening?"

"Zipper insists on getting out now," Rosemary said.

Zipper was kneeling on top of the Randy Rabbit, tying cardboard boxes to the railings. Cinnamon and the girls scurried along single file with handfuls of personal belongings.

"If we're leaving, today is the best time," Cinnamon said. "It's a full moon in Leo tomorrow. That will complicate your day more than you can imagine."

"Are you going to follow us?" Tiger Lily shouted.

"Will you live with us?" Pumpkin Patch asked.

"Jack and I aren't sure," Molly said. "We need to talk it over."

"We're leaving now! I ain't saying where." Zipper pointed at Jack and Molly. "I don't want to know where you're going—you're both crazy."

Molly glared. "Whatever you say, brother."

"I never heard of Habeeb." Zipper kept lashing down the boxes. "If you have any sanity left, neither have you."

Everyone hugged and whispered optimistic words

of encouragement while Zipper made a final check of the compound. One last hurrah for the experiment in communal living.

M OLLY AND JACK retreated to Molly's room. Decisions didn't come easy for either of them, this one would be especially hard.

"I need to get to Kansas City, but don't tell the others," Jack said. "If you can drop me on I-40, I'll hitchhike from there."

"Nonsense, it's time I made amends with my father. I'll drop you off in Kansas City on the way."

"That would be a tremendous help."

"I'll pack my clothes, then pop over to the cook house to collect a few bits and pieces and pack up some food."

Jack scrambled to his room and gathered his meager possessions into a paper bag, as he didn't even own a backpack anymore. He had left Molly with a warning not to leave anything behind that would identify her. He gave his room one last wipe down, cautiously rubbed the few metal and glass objects; most of the wood wasn't painted, not fresh and glossy, he didn't think it would leave prints. Then he headed to the cook house for a similar procedure.

Minutes later, he saw her out in the field, bent over her beans with a gunnysack. "What the heck are you doing?" he yelled as he ran out to her. "Come on, we've got to go."

"I'm not leaving good beans. Especially since that's all we've got to eat—Zipper cleaned out the kitchen."

"How many beans can we eat? You've got half a sack full." He grabbed her up and threw her over his shoulder. She screamed and kicked, but she was laughing underneath. He felt the sting on his back from the gashes of her last attack. Not an unpleasant feeling. He plopped her into the passenger seat of the truck.

"My hero." She kissed him full on the mouth.

Love doesn't always last forever
Molly Hollingsworth

Chapter
32

Harwood could see for fifty miles in every direction. But he couldn't see anything worth a pot to piss in. Blowing dust, half-dead sage, and more blowing dust. He could only think of one reason to be out here, to get away from something, to stay away from something, most likely the police.

It had taken the better part of the day to gather support from the Taos Sheriff's office. Cop killer had been the only thing that got their attention. Local law enforcement didn't seem interested in rousting this alleged farm. Harwood knew that this part of the country—if you actually counted this as part of the country—had a reputation for letting people live any way they wanted to live. That's why draft dodgers and potheads—so-called hippies—overran these high mountain mesas back in the '60s. But this was the end of the '70s, the rule of law and common sense had returned. According to Diego Baca, the Taos County Sheriff, White Rabbit Farm was the last of the communes, the last holdout. And it would fold on the first of next month; the actual owner of the land had moved on and the bank had filed a foreclosure notice.

He'd have come out here on his own if there'd been the slightest chance of finding the place. And Harwood knew that if he poked around in the countryside asking questions, word would travel faster than he could, and everyone would scatter. Besides, folks out here had guns, maybe even peace-loving hippies. Impossible to hide from a rifle with a scope in this open country.

Finally, he was bouncing along, riding shotgun in a posse of five jacked-up four-wheel-drive trucks—possibly every law enforcement vehicle in Taos County. Pipkins's cohorts would probably spot them from miles away; plenty of time for him to climb into a rat hole.

They topped a hill and took a hard right. A half-melted mud wall lined one side of the road. Harwood felt like an intruder, an unwelcome alien witnessing the decay of a once-great society. They turned onto an even rougher dirt track at the egg sign that the Feliciano woman had mentioned. Even the sheriff, with a .45 automatic strapped to his hip and a 12-gauge pump latched between the front seats, looked uneasy. He couldn't be scared; there was a heavily armed brigade behind them. Could he be protecting the longhaired dopers that purportedly ran this self-styled farm? Was he sympathetic, an antiwar activist? Maybe he just didn't give a shit, had better things to do, afraid he might be late for supper. Or all of the above. These people had obviously been allowed to do whatever they wanted for many years.

The compound sat halfway up a hillside, in the middle of a hundred-acre plot. The half-dozen buildings were more substantial than Harwood had pictured; one circular structure looked to be two stories high. Even though it was desolate, there were some colorful trappings, hand-painted doors, and pots with flowers. Somebody cared about this place.

Diego Baca stood at the edge of the road and ordered his deputies to park outside of the cluster of buildings so that any tire tracks in the compound would remain intact. Two sets of prints were readily distinguishable. Narrow tracks from a heavily loaded vehicle were quickly attributed to the VW Microbus that had been seen around town. The other set was an unusual pattern. Probably mismatched tires. None seemed to be a current tread design, one was possibly a snow tire.

They fanned out to check the buildings. Harwood and the sheriff headed for the small lean-to attached to the large circular structure. It had the most footprints outside the door.

"Looks like they did the cooking in here." Harwood poked around several pots and pans.

"Compact and cozy." Diego Baca seemed indifferent.

"Yeah, and neat. Everything in place."

"Looks like a woman took charge in here."

"But one thing's amiss. A greasy frying pan and two plates in the sink. Somebody that is fussy about the kitchen wouldn't take off and leave dishes in the sink."

"Guess they left in a hurry."

"Why no plan? Why leave yesterday?"

"We're talking about hippies. Maybe their horoscope said, 'Good day for a move.'"

"The whole bunch wouldn't impulsively get up and go."

"Well, it looks like a mass exodus."

Harwood shook his head. "There are only two plates in the sink. I think they left in two waves. The loaded-down hippie van and the strange unidentified vehicle."

Harwood opened the thick door to the main room. His eyes widened, partially due to the dimness, partially due to surprise. He didn't bother to comment.

The tool shed and outhouse didn't give up any clues. On a bench under a tree, Harwood picked up a stuffed doll. "They had kids here?"

"Like any other community, they liked to procreate."

"Just what the world needs, more hippies. This doesn't seem like a good environment for children."

"Best I could tell, it was better than most. Fresh air, living off the land, lots of friends, and no crime."

How much did the sheriff know about this place? And "no crime" must not count drug use, open nudity, and draft violations. The media had documented it for years.

Harwood walked down the cultivated row. Surprisingly, green beans grew here. The stems showed evidence of freshly severed pods. Mid-row, the harvest had ceased; beans still dangled on the vine. Why suddenly stop? What had gone on here?

"These people actually tried to farm here?" Harwood found it hard to believe.

"Didn't just try." The sheriff sounded indignant, for some reason. "They seldom bought food in town. Just a few things they got with food stamps. At its peak, this place sold fresh milk and eggs to the restaurants in town."

"We need to question everyone these degenerates knew. Anyone who might know where these hippies are headed."

"About the only folks that came out here and associated with them were elders from Taos Pueblo. Some sort of spiritual bond."

"Let's head there now. Press them for information before they've got time to concoct a bullshit story."

"Things don't happen fast at the Pueblo. We'll need to leave a message for the war chief and wait to hear if he wants to meet."

"War chief?"

"That's what they call him."

"Just show up on his doorstep, catch him off guard."

"You get in his face and the tribal police will be questioning you."

"It's your county, isn't it?"

"It may be my county, but the reservation is a sovereign nation. Got no jurisdiction there. We need help, we ask for it, and we make sure we ask polite."

The pueblo connection was a long shot, not worth the trouble. Everyone out here would stonewall him.

Pipkins was on the move. Vulnerable. Off balance. Obviously left in a hurry. But he had a knack for finding refuge. It would take speed and agility to bring him down. Fast, decisive action. And he knew Pipkins's one weak spot.

Know your prey, Harwood's grandfather had said.

He couldn't find a single sign of Pipkins having been there. There weren't many signs of any human existence. Had they been able to haul away all their stuff? Or did they just not have much? This place didn't have many places to store things.

Still, the Feliciano woman's story seemed credible. She knew the name of this obscure place and its approximate location. She knew about the egg sign. She could be protecting him, but she didn't come off as the type that protected anyone except herself. Although if she had dumped him here, he might not have stayed more than a day.

Harwood made a sweep of the simple bunkhouse rooms that the deputies had already checked. They were all the same—dark, spartan, bare adobe walls with specks of straw poking out, painted wood doors. Nothing had been left behind, not even a pillow. His glare returned to the wall. A three-inch-square photo held with tape. A snapshot of a man and a woman. Looked like a Polaroid. He yanked it off and held it to the light in the doorway.

Damn.

Pipkins had gotten thinner, almost an athletic build. And he looked happy, although that wouldn't last long. And now Harwood knew what the current accomplice looked like. The second dirty dish.

If they were really tight, would the photo have been left behind? Was it overlooked in the hurry to leave? Or had their codependency played out and they parted ways?

What was it with this guy? Why were women attracted to him? Could be the bad-boy syndrome, bored with the nice boys that Mama approved of.

One of the deputies stuck his head through the doorway. "We've found evidence of a scuffle over in that rusted Wonder Bread truck."

Harwood thought scuffle was an understatement.

Although he found it hard to tell if most of this disarray was someone tossing the place or just an alternative lifestyle. There wasn't a single thing in that truck that conformed to mainstream habitation. The charred glass test tubes and antigovernment statement taped to the wall immediately got his attention. Then he spotted dried blood on the mattress. "Looks like he's murdered again."

"Someone may have cut a finger."

"Someone may have been shot, stabbed, or by the look of this place, cut to pieces."

"This isn't just blood." Diego Baca picked up one of the few glass test tubes that wasn't broken and poked at the dried mess. "It's mixed with vomit or bile. Looks like something that spewed out of a stomach."

"That's consistent with arsenic poisoning. The bastard is a serial killer. Continually changes his MO."

"Forensic will have to figure that out."

"Can your forensic team figure out how to get here?"

"We'll have to rely on the state lab in Santa Flush for this."

"Santa Flush?"

"That's what the hippies called our state capital, it's more commonly referred to as Santa Fe. Could be a few days before they can spring somebody free."

"A few days!"

"We don't actually have evidence that a crime was committed."

And he thought Kansas City PD was screwed up.

Kansas City . . .

If a guy has no money—and Pipkins obviously didn't by the way he was living out here—where's he going to go? Forced out of his hideaway at the end of the earth. What's his best option? Possibly his only option?

"Let's get out of here." Harwood headed for the truck. "I need to get to the airport."

B ACKTRACKING ACROSS THE middle of Kansas was the only route that made sense. Jack didn't want to stress the old pickup on an interstate highway. Fifty was the best the Studebaker could do, couldn't chance getting pulled over for going too slow, and the antique truck wouldn't be such an attraction on country roads. What would really slow them down was stopping every hour to let the engine cool off. The first portion would follow the route he and Ginger had taken, then they would veer northeast toward Kansas City.

The empty feeling he had when they drove away from White Rabbit Farm stayed with him. He'd thought he'd feel relief at escaping the barren landscape. Gain a sense of adventure on the open road. A sense of warmth at the prospect of reuniting with his family. All that was eluding him.

Instead, he felt loss. The loss of feeling close to the soil. Poor as it was, it was real and pure and independent, he needed it more than it needed him. He felt a loss of the sun and the sky and the moon. He missed the screech and yip of the coyotes, the irascible ravens, the sage that insisted on growing in barren sand, the frigid wind from the snowy peaks of the Sangre de Cristo Mountains, the soothing heat of Manby Springs. The farther away he got, the more he felt boxed in. By trees, then billboards, then buildings, then civilization.

He knew the biggest loss hadn't happened yet, but it was only hours away. It perched on the seat next to him and chattered away. He listened and listened. Maybe drove a little slower than necessary. He didn't want this to end.

But he had a commitment. A commitment that he knew he would keep. To Alicia. To Edward and Elizabeth.

They made their seventh stop on the far side of Dodge City. 367 miles. The temperature gauge was close to the limit, and the engine was ready for its seventh quart of oil and another three-hour cool-down. Fifty miles per hour, fifty miles to a quart—the truck was consistent. Jack hated to see Molly do it, but the only way they had of getting gas and oil money was panhandling at truck stops. Jack had tried it with absolutely no success—folks around Dodge had no sympathy for commercial-bank loan officers down on their luck. Molly, with her big sad eyes, did a bit better.

Jack couldn't make it all the way to Kansas City without some protein and sugar, but shoplifting would be dangerous—the Studebaker wasn't much of a getaway vehicle. So, at one stop, he grabbed a Slim Jim and a package of Twinkies, then when the clerk was busy, Jack slipped into the men's room. The possible embarrassment of being yelled at for carelessly taking a potential purchase into the restroom would be better than a call to the police. He devoured them in the stall, shredded the evidence, and flushed it down the toilet. He made a mental note of that place. One day he'd make this trip in reverse and leave an envelope with a ten-dollar bill for the manager.

He told Molly how to do it, said he'd pay them back one day. She said the sack of beans would get her to Kansas City.

They spent the second day in the pickup leaning against each other as they took turns driving, constantly touching each other, holding hands, her head on his thigh as she curled in the seat, his hand on her neck or rubbing her shoulder. Not saying much, not wanting to discuss the inevitable separation, another friendship lost, another uncertain future.

He came to realize that he liked this new life—the adventure, the conflicting views that Molly flung at him, the challenge of starting all over. He certainly wouldn't trade it for forty years in a suit and tie, followed by a few years on the golf course, then a shady plot under a thousand pounds of granite engraved with a sentimental three-word testimonial.

Miles of road, endless hours to think. He'd go by E. Jonathan McQuade, Johnny to his friends. The words Molly McQuade nearly slipped from his lips. He pushed the thought back, way back, back to the frivolous playground of White Rabbit Farm. He forced his mind to think of his responsibilities.

To Alicia. To his children. To the possibility of their new life together.

"You'd really like her," he said. "Beautiful and loyal, she's always believed in me. We've had to put our love on hold for a year. It's time, the waiting is over."

"Love doesn't always last forever. It's not like hate and revenge."

As they drove into Kansas City on Shawnee Mission Parkway, Jack watched increasingly familiar landmarks roll by—Brush Creek, the golf course clubhouse, and finally, Mission Woods Road. In minutes, he would see Alicia, though he had learned everything came at a price. As Alicia walked into the spotlight, Molly would fade, a loss he had so far refused to acknowledge.

Get it right this time. Don't screw up again.

Molly stopped his thoughts cold: "Maybe I won't go back to New Haven . . . Maybe Florida. Or Oregon, there's a big peace movement there."

"I thought you were going to see your father?"

"I don't know if I'm ready to deal with his sanitized reality."

"You're headed in the wrong direction. Oregon is back out west."

"The road isn't that narrow. I can whip a one-eighty."

The Studebaker climbed up the long driveway and stopped in front of the expansive porch. Molly held out her hand. "Goodbye, Jack. Or Jonathan. Whoever you are now."

"No, wait. You need cash for gas, oil, and food. I'm sure Alicia has enough on hand to get you where you're going. And you must meet Alicia. I'll go in first, give her the news, then introduce you as the person who saved my life."

"Then she shoots me."

"Of course not—please wait."

"ALL YOU'VE GOT is a diaper-brown Chevette? I'm a police officer, I need a real car, an Impala, or at least a Malibu."

"Sorry, sir," the rental agent said. "Every full-size car in Kansas City is booked. There's a petroleum convention in town. Everybody trying to impress everybody."

"I can't apprehend a felon in a three-door hatchback. I want to intimidate, not amuse."

"Don't you have a police car?"

"From out of town. Don't have time to wait for local

assistance." Harwood flashed his badge. "Give me that goddamn Olds 88 gas hog parked out there."

"That's reserved."

"Un-reserve it."

The out-of-patience Hertz employee reached for the phone.

Harwood rubbed the palm of his hand. He needed to get a grip on himself. The rage was no longer staying inside. What did it matter what he drove? Revenge had replaced good judgment. Revenge for Tony. The clock was ticking. He needed to act while Pipkins was still off balance. Before he found refuge.

"Give me the Chevette."

E. JONATHAN MCQUADE waited nervously on the doorstep. He hoped Alicia would answer and not one of the children; he wanted to explain his plan to her first.

But it was an attractive woman with long brown hair who answered the door.

"Hello, I'd like to speak with Mrs. Pipkins."

"Please come in."

He quickly scanned the living room. Nothing looked familiar—new colors, new furniture, new . . . "You're doing an excellent job keeping things up here."

"I'm not the help," the woman replied. "I'll get Alicia, she's in the bathroom."

She seemed to know who he was. Almost expecting him to show up on the doorstep.

A bit unsteady, Jack settled into a petite, floral-patterned chair. Certainly not furniture he would have selected, nor Alicia. Who was this woman? Was she just going to burst into Alicia's bathroom? The large painting that dominated one wall was ultramodern and garish, the furniture mismatched and not proportionate to the room. The interior decorator certainly had an outlandish sense of style, not at all in keeping with the culture of Mission Hills.

Who was he to judge? He'd been living in an adobe bunkhouse in the middle of a bean field.

The familiar pitter-patter of Alicia's feet jarred him into the present. She swept into the living room, the woman who'd answered the door beside her.

"Alicia," he said. "At last."

"At last what?"

"I found a way—we can start over—a new life."

"Oh, Jeremy. Thank you but . . ." She took the charming brunette by the hand, just as if they were . . .

Holy Jesus. Was this the woman from the party?

Alicia was smiling now, a sheepish smile. "You see, I have a new life."

M OLLY FIDDLED WITH the gearshift as she waited in the truck. She'd have taken off right away, but she dreaded begging for money around the gas pumps, especially without Jack for backup. But this was crazy. She didn't want to see the woman who was stealing Jack. Was about to take the only man she had ever really loved. Her chance to have her own family.

It had been ten minutes or more. They were probably passionately kissing by now. She turned the key, the Studebaker rumbled, coughed a couple of times, and most of the cylinders came to life. She slammed it in gear, wiped a tear from her cheek, hit the gas.

She spotted him in the faded rearview mirror, running

full speed toward her. Before she came to a full stop, the door swung open. Jumpin' Jack jumped in.

"Turn right at the stop sign," he gasped. "Then head for Shawnee Mission Parkway."

"Eastbound or west?"

"Sure, okay."

"My thoughts, exactly."

"I've got to say this quick, because we need to move, the police have been watching the house."

"The police, huh?"

"It's a long story, and I'll tell you later, everything, I promise. But I was here mostly out of a sense of obligation, and now I know my obligations . . . I don't have to worry about them anymore. Believe me. From now on, I'm all yours, and that's the way I've always wanted it to be."

She took her hands off the wheel and planted a huge kiss on his cheek. Which was a mistake since the Studebaker headed for the ditch as soon as it was on its own.

She grabbed the wheel and wrestled the truck back on track.

As they drove away, a brown Chevy hatchback sped past them and turned up the drive toward Alicia's house. The stern-looking driver with the pointed chin was definitely on a mission.

E. Jonathan McQuade placed his hand firmly on Molly's.

She gave him a big smile, the one that barely fit on her face, a smile that said everything he wanted to hear.

The Studebaker sputtered, and a blue cloud of smoke from its tail pipe covered the past.

Epilogue

The governor of Arkansas stayed in office and did pretty well for himself in a long political career, though he kept appreciating the ladies more than he should.

Harwood never mentioned finding a photo of Pipkins and the hippie girl at White Rabbit Farm, the DA claimed Ginger had given false information. She did three years of a ten-year sentence at the Central California Women's Facility in Chowchilla, California. She got out early for bad behavior with the warden.

Marble Mine Village is bigger and better than ever. Private equity funded six new thrill rides including the sixty-eight miles-per-hour, triple-inversion Wilderness Whiplash. After Mr. Fosdick sold out; he and his new wife spend most of the time looking down on Boca from their twenty-sixth-floor penthouse.

Harpo's place is still on Arrow Point Road. The new owner calls it the Holy Smoke Rib Shack. It has gained a reputation as a cheap place to feed the kids after a full day at Marble Mine Village. Harpo rested peacefully next to Hattie on the hilltop behind the Hog Pen, until a developer bulldozed the land when no one was looking. The Shepherd of the Hills Condominium Complex is seven stories high.

Susie and Anita continue to optimistically search the bars around Branson for cowboy heroes.

The communes outside of Taos suffered the fate of all mankind—human nature took over. A retired dentist from Dubuque now owns White Rabbit Farm. He fixed it up and rents out a couple of rooms as a bed-and-breakfast. Sometimes a twenty-something will come by and say, "I was born in that room, my mom was a hippie." Zipper drifted back years ago and lives there gratis. If you catch him in a good mood, he'll tell you how it really was back in the day.

Cinnamon Stick and the girls have a condo in San Diego. They support each other while men drift in and out of their lives. Cinnamon has some health problems, but the girls take loving care of her. Tiger Lily waits tables and volunteers at Saint Benedict's Home for Women. Pumpkin Patch works for a nonprofit that provides health services to migrant farmworkers.

Rosemary Meadow settled in an obscure commune outside of Salida, Colorado. They work the land and live in peace, oblivious to a world filled with turmoil.

Al Harwood keeps in touch with Judy, even though she's now married to an insurance broker. Sally lives in Dallas, and he sees her at Christmas. He keeps an eye on the bulletins and from time to time checks with Pipkins's wife and the folks around Marble Mine Village. He knows criminals usually wander back to their past and believes it's only a matter of time.

Alicia and Janie did fine—a new, modern family. Edward studied music at Julliard and owns a gallery in the Village. Elizabeth sits in her grandfather's old seat at the head of the conference-room table. The bank now has a Human Resources Department and a generous maternity-leave policy.

Johnny McQuade and Molly? Well, that's a whole nother story.

BOOK CLUB DISCUSSION QUESTIONS

1. Can a man such as Jeremy Pipkins, who is out of control in a midlife crisis be saved from himself? Is it worth the trouble? Could Alicia have done something different?

2. Did the state attorney general just do what it takes to get elected? Or did he take it too far? Over the centuries dirty tricks have played a role in gaining power, is that more prevalent today on both sides of the fence? Should indiscretion in a politician's personal affairs influence our decisions in the voting booth? Think Kennedy, Clinton, Trump.

3. Was Jeremy's father really the root of all the conflict? Or was Jeremy too self-centered and fearful that life was slipping away?

4. Have big box stores like Walmart changed the American landscape for the better? Do "Everyday Low Prices" help lower-income people get by or do they encourage excessive consumption? Is putting inefficient small-time merchants out of business good because it makes our economy more efficient or does it destroy the individual character of communities?

5. Are theme parks like Marble Mine Village that emphasize American heritage a good thing? Or do they overly glamourize and distort historical reality? How about Frontierland at Disney World? Are these parks

a good family experience, or is braving the crowds not worth the hassle? Is spending a fortune on overinflated extravaganzas a bad example for the children?

6. Should Jeremy have followed his desire for a different career and a different lifestyle, or should he have exercised more self-control and let his conscience guide him toward obligation to his family?

7. Should drug abusers like Habeeb be forced to change their ways? Will it do any good? Is the war on drugs a useless campaign slogan? Should drug use be a criminal offense or treated like it is in the Netherlands?

8. Did hippies like Molly, Rosemary and Cinnamon Stick with their antiwar, communal way of life, alter today's society? How about gay rights, improved social services, elimination of the draft, appreciation for naturally grown food, respect for our heritage and indigenous people? Or was it all a waste of time and human nature has caused us to live the same way we have since Adam hooked-up with Eve?

9. Are there any active communes like White Rabbit Farm left in the U.S.? How about other countries? Can they work for long periods or do power struggles and people's changing needs cause them to fail? Can they exist near traditional communities with opposed value systems, such as the struggle that took place in Taos? Is farming on a small scale viable today?

10. Is "God Bless America" a patriotic declaration as Jack believes? Or is it arrogant of Americans to think that if God exists, she favors the USA? Are slogans such as, "America, Love it or Leave it" reasonable demands or are they propagated by people who like the way the pie is divided and they do not want anything to change?

11. Did the ending work out best for everyone involved? Well, perhaps not everyone. What would have been a better resolution?

Made in the USA
Middletown, DE
08 February 2021

33326677R00217